SECRETS O

REGENCY RO… …ON

JOYCE ALEC

Secrets of London

First printing, 2018

Publisher
Love Light Faith, LLC
400 NW 7th Avenue, Unit 825
Fort Lauderdale, FL 33311

A DUKE'S PROMISE

SECRETS OF LONDON

First printing, 2018

Publisher
Love Light Faith, LLC
400 NW 7th Avenue, Unit 825
Fort Lauderdale, FL 33311

1

London 1814

"I am afraid it is a very serious illness, my lord."

Matthew Arthur, the Duke of Harrogate, ran one hand through his carefully styled chestnut-colored hair, sighing heavily.

"I am sorry, your grace," the doctor continued with a shake of his head. "It appears the duchess has contracted an illness after the birth of your daughter."

A heavy weight settled in Matthew's stomach. He barely knew the duchess, and now it appeared that she was to be gone from this world in a very short time.

"I should send for her parents," he muttered to himself, passing one hand over his eyes before blinking at the doctor in an attempt to order his thoughts. "They should be here, should they not?"

It was a question meant to ascertain just how ill the duchess was, and with only a momentary hesitation, the doctor nodded slowly.

"Yes, your grace, I think that would be wise," he said softly. "I am sorry I cannot do more."

Matthew nodded mutely.

"You have a wet nurse for the child?"

That brought Matthew's head up sharply. He had almost forgotten his newborn daughter, the one who was now being held tightly in the nurse's arms in the corner of the room.

"I do," he replied, swallowing the sudden lump in his throat, as he thought of his daughter growing up without a mother. "She has taken good care of my daughter thus far."

"I do not mean to question you, of course," the doctor murmured, glancing behind him. "But so often these things can be forgotten in the wake of tragedy."

A sudden terror clutched at Matthew's throat, making him lunge for the doctor's shoulder as he turned away.

"She is not ill?"

Lifting his grey, bushy brows, the doctor looked back at Matthew inquiringly.

"My daughter, I mean."

"Oh," the doctor replied with a sad smile. "No, she is not ill. She is as hale and hearty as I have ever seen a babe, and one of the female persuasion at that! Ensure she has a good nurse, plenty of milk, and she will remain just as vigorous, I am sure of it. Send for me again if you require me, your grace. I am at your disposal."

"Thank you, doctor," Matthew murmured, as the man turned away again and headed for the door. "I will ensure that you are paid for your work here."

There was no reply, and as Matthew turned his gaze back to the small, frail figure in the corner of the room, he felt his breath escape him in a long, painful sigh.

This was his wife, the Lady Elizabeth Donnington, who had been placed on his arm only a few days before their wedding was due to take place. He had never laid eyes on her until that day, and it had been a disappointment to realize that there would never be any kind of love between them. Not that he expected that, of course, for a gentleman such as he was, had to marry responsibly and that meant a marriage of convenience and practicality. Lady Elizabeth Donnington had been his chosen bride. She was not chosen by him, of course, but by his father when he had been in infancy. Mathew's father was quite happy to see Matthew wed, and relieved to know that Matthew's wife was with child. Apparently awash with relief, the duke had taken to his bed and succumbed to his weak heart. That had only been a few months ago, and now, it seemed, Matthew was to stare death in the face all over again.

Walking toward the bed, Matthew looked down at the pale figure lying there, his heart sore for her. It was not as though he had ever loved her, nor had she ever loved him, and since the very day of their marriage, they had lived very separate lives. It had brought about a degree of loneliness, which he had never quite been able to remove from himself, and now that loneliness was to deepen only further.

A slight murmur came from the corner of the room, and glancing over at the nurse, Matthew saw her throw him a slightly terrified look before shushing the baby quietly.

"Do not worry," he murmured, not wanting the wet nurse to think him cruel. "She is a baby, I suppose." He held his arm out to her, his heart thundering with a sudden, furious tension. "Bring her to me."

He had not held his daughter yet, since his wife's condition had worsened with almost every passing hour these last three days. Now, however, he wanted to hold his child in his arms, to look into her tiny face and see if there was anything of himself there.

Not quite sure how he was meant to hold her, he glanced at

the wet nurse, who gave him a small smile, clearly less afraid of him now.

"There, your grace," she said quietly, lifting the baby from the crook of her arm. "Just like that. Put her head in your elbow and hold her close to your body with this arm." She smiled again as Matthew took the tiny baby from her, doing exactly as she said and felt as though he might break his child were he to hold her too closely.

"Perfect," the nurse whispered, tugging the blanket a little more snugly around the child's neck before stepping away to sit back amongst the shadows.

Drawing in a long breath, Matthew looked down at the baby in his arms. She was sound asleep, her cheeks pink and tiny, rosebud mouth half open. She was the most delicate, most beautiful thing he had ever seen, and deep within him, Matthew felt his heartbreak open with a love he had never experienced before.

How he could love someone he had only just met, only just seen, was quite beyond him, and yet, from a well of love springing into life within him, Matthew knew that he would never let this child go. He would do everything he could for her, showing her the love and affection a father ought to show to his daughter. A love he had not experienced from his own father.

"If you will forgive me, your grace," the wet nurse said quietly. "Do you have a name for the child? I was not told."

Blinking, Matthew lifted his head and looked at the nurse, who was sitting with a patient expression on her face. Had he truly never given his daughter a name?

"Of course," he mumbled, his gaze dragged back down to the child in his arms. "She should be called after her mother." But even as he said those words, Matthew felt his eyebrows draw down into a dark frown. Yes, the girl should be called after her mother, but there was something in him that did not want to remember the pain of his arranged wedding, and the loneliness that had grown between them. "She will be Sarah Elizabeth," he said, firmly, taking his mother's name and setting it before his wife's name. "Sarah Elizabeth. Yes, that will do."

"A lovely name, to be sure," the wet nurse murmured, coming over to him and holding out her hands as Sarah Elizabeth began to fuss. "I should feed her now and put her to sleep."

It was as though he were the servant and she the master, for Matthew found himself doing exactly as the wet nurse said. Handing over the child, he paused for a moment, as her tiny hand wrapped around one of his fingers, making him catch his breath.

She was utterly perfect. The only good thing to come out of what had been a difficult and lonely marriage between two people who did not care for one another very much at all.

And then his wife drew in a long, sharp breath and let out a soft moan – before falling completely silent.

The wet nurse hurried away, the servants by his wife's bed gasped, and Matthew hurried to her side.

Taking her cold hand in his, Matthew tried desperately to find a pulse, but there was nothing there. A sheen of sweat was on her brow, and as he wiped it away, he felt the coolness of her skin beneath. Her eyes were closed, purple veins showing through her almost translucent skin.

"My wife is gone," Matthew said quietly, reaching for the blankets and pulling them up around her shoulders, as though to warm her. "Send for the coroner."

The servants left the room at once, the wet nurse with them. Matthew was left alone with his wife, the blackness tugging at his heart and mind all over again. He was alone. His mother had gone some years before his father, and now his wife had left him alone in this world. With only a brother to speak of – a brother who was something of an adventurer and currently traveling the world – Matthew felt more isolated than he had ever done before.

"I am sorry, your grace," the butler murmured, as he came into the room to stand next to Matthew. "She was so young. It was not her time."

"It appears it was, Jenkins," Matthew replied heavily. "Have you maids to dress the body?" The words were torn from his lips, his heart so heavy with a sudden grief that he felt as though he could barely stand.

The butler nodded. "The maids are ready, your grace. Just whenever you wish it."

"Now is as good a time as any," Matthew muttered, taking one last look at his wife. "I shall be in my study."

"Very good, your grace," came the quiet reply, and on legs that felt like blocks of wood, Matthew walked from the room and made his way to the solitude of his study.

Once there, he poured himself a stiff drink and sat down by the fire, his eyes looking deeply into the flames. His mind thought of nothing, his expression blank and eyes distant. It was not as though there had been any love between himself and his wife, but yet there came a sadness with her passing. It was as if he had hoped for them both to find a way together, as though sometime in the future they might grow closer. He had perhaps thought that the baby would be the reason for such a change, that the child could draw them closer. That, somewhere in the distant future, there might be a true friendship and even an affection between them.

All that was gone now. His hopes shattered. His dreams in pieces at his feet.

"I shall be both mother and father to you, Sarah Elizabeth," he said softly, half to himself, as he continued to watch the flickering flames of the fire. "No matter what we will face, we will face it together. I will never leave you. I will always be by your side."

Lifting his glass to the flames in memory of his wife, Matthew drank deeply, but the liquor took none of his pain away.

2

Five Years Later

"There is nothing for it, I am afraid. You are going to have to find yourself a situation."

Miss Sophia Weston stared at her brother in shock, her whole being crumbling beneath his scornful gaze.

"A governess or the like," he continued airily. "Something in that regard. I am quite sure there will be plenty of men looking out for such a thing."

"In fact, I have managed to procure you a few advertisements," Sophia's sister-in-law crooned, holding out a sheaf of papers. "And one from a duke as well! My dear friend, Lady Margaret, had a letter from him and thought you might be inclined to reply to him. I am quite sure you will be able to find something suitable."

Sophia did not take the papers from the new Viscountess Brookridge, keeping her gaze trained on her brother, who was looking away from her with all the careless disregard she had grown used to.

"Why are you doing this, Peter?"

Her brother drew himself up, as though he expected her to

refer to him now as 'my lord' instead of the usual Christian name she had used for two decades. "You, Sophia, cannot live on my charity any longer. It is time that you found your own path in life."

"But you promised Papa that you would take care of me!" Sophia exclaimed, her vision blurring with tears, as she thought of her dear father, who had passed only a little over a year ago. "You stood by his deathbed and vowed that–"

"And this is how I have chosen to take care of you, Sophia," he grated, interrupting her. "When I made that promise, I did not mean that I would allow you to live here, using my possessions and eating up my wealth." He gave a harsh laugh, just as the viscountess smiled in agreement. "You are somewhat plain, and I have no intention of allowing you a Season—for that would simply be even more of my funds lost for no good cause, so I think a governess would be best."

"Or a teacher, should you care to write back to one of the many schools that are keen for new blood," the viscountess said, setting the papers down on the table to her left. "You will not, I am sure, refuse to thank me for all my hard work in finding these positions for your scrutiny." One arched eyebrow rose, as she fixed Sophia with a stern gaze, as though reminding her that she was less than nothing in her eyes.

A deep, unsettling fury began to rush through Sophia's very core, sending molten heat into her veins.

"I will not thank you for throwing me from my own home," she breathed, her eyes narrowing as she looked back at the lady she had once hoped to call a friend. "This is your doing, is it not? You are the one who has persuaded my brother to push me aside, to send me away from the only home I have ever known. And to think, all of this so that he can spend more money on you!"

She did not know where the torrent had sprung from, but

the anger made her say things she had kept within her for so long. The fury at being so discarded, being so easily cast aside by the brother who had promised to care for her, burned hot and furious.

"You, *dear* brother, have treated me with more disdain than I ever thought possible. You made a promise to our father, which you are now reneging on. Taking away any hope of a future from me by sending me away was *not* what our father intended for me, and you know it! How can you be so unfeeling?"

Drawing in a sharp breath and aware of just how hot her cheeks were, Sophia waited impatiently for her brother to speak, ignoring her sister-in-law entirely. Peter shifted a little uncomfortably, one hand tugging at his cravat, as he cleared his throat.

"I suggest you look through those advertisements, Sophia. They may be your best chance at a successful post, as Evette has done her best to vet each of them carefully. I would have expected you to be a little more grateful that she showed you such kindness, but then again, you have become rather churlish of late." He sniffed disdainfully, although his eyes did not quite meet her gaze. Linking arms with his wife, he lifted his nose in the air. "Come, my dear. Let us leave my spoilt little sister to consider her future."

As he walked away, Sophia felt herself begin to crumble from within, tears clogging her throat. Blinking furiously to keep them at bay, she silently urged her brother and his wife out of the room so that she might finally collapse with grief and pain without their knowledge.

"Oh, and Sophia," came her brother's voice, just as they reached the door. "I expect you gone within the month. So, do get on to writing those letters just as soon as you can."

A quiet chuckle came from the viscountess, as he led them both out of the drawing room. Sophia, her lungs gasping for air as she forced herself to take short, slow breaths, clenched her hands tightly together in an effort to stop herself from trembling.

As the door closed behind her brother, Sophia sank down into a chair, the sheaf of papers just to her left. Tears began to pour from her eyes, her soul sinking into despair. Her brother had once been the kindest, gentlest man imaginable, and she had hoped that their relationship would always be one of care and consideration, given just how close they had been. However, her brother's marriage appeared to have changed all that. Now, she was little more than an afterthought.

Wiping her eyes, Sophia hung her head and stared at the floor, her mind scrambling for an idea of what she might to do counter this plan for her life. After all, she was the daughter of a fine family and had a significant dowry tucked away for her, but now, it seemed, she was to be sent away because of the proclivities of her brother's new wife. There appeared to be no way out. How foolish she had been to ever hope that she and Evette could become friends. Evette had hated her presence in her new home ever since the day they had returned from their honeymoon, even though Sophia had her own bedchamber and drawing room. It was not as though they were even much in each other's company, but it was now evident that the little time they spent together was too much for her sister-in-law. She had clearly been collecting advertisements for a few weeks, given the number of papers on the table.

"Oh, Papa," Sophia whispered, pain rifling through her, as she thought of her dear, loving father, who had never had a cruel word to say to anyone. "How much I miss you."

With a deep, heart-wrenching sigh, Sophia picked up the papers and stared at them blindly. So, this was to be her future. She was to be sent away, entirely without love or loyalty from her family, to start life as a governess. She had never taught a child before; she had never even been involved with children, and yet, this was what she was expected to do. There was no doubt in Sophia's mind that her brother meant every word he said. Were she not to find a position, then she would be left on the doorstep of the manor house with all her earthly possessions in a few bags at her feet. The cruelty within him had grown steadily, ever since he had taken a wife.

Closing her eyes, Sophia forced herself to draw in a few steadying breaths, forcing the rest of her tears back. Were she to get through the next few weeks, she would have to find a determination within herself, a strength of character that she had not often had to call upon before this day. She would separate herself from her brother as much as possible, take meals in her room, and concentrate on what she would need to take up the role of governess or teacher, whichever came her way first. Her fine gowns would have to go, although Sophia knew she could not bear to part with them all. New, dowdy, plain gowns would be bought and worn, dark colors surrounding her, as was expected of a governess. No longer would she have the beauty and light and color she was used to. Peter had taken all that away.

Leafing through the papers with shaking fingers, Sophia read each one in turn, trying not to feel the pain that deepened with every word she took in. There were posts for teachers, posts for governesses, and even one for a matron, which she disregarded at once.

None caught her interest; none tugged at her heart. There was not a situation that called out to her more than the others; they were all much the same. Besides which, Sophia knew she could not afford to be choosy. To be out of her brother's home in a month meant that she would have to write back to each of these advertisements at once, aside from the request for a matron. Five letters, each with the hope that she might receive at least one response.

Her heart filled with heaviness and feeling a weight settle on her shoulders, Sophia made her way from the drawing room and slowly climbed the staircase to her bedchamber. Closing the door behind her, she turned the key in the lock, feeling as though this was the only place she might have a little privacy from her brother and sister-in-law. They would not see her torment, as she scratched out each reply; they would not see the tears on her face, as she sealed up each one. They had already done more than enough damage.

By the end of the day, Sophia was completely spent. Her tears had long since dried, but her heart was still broken. Taking a dinner tray in her room, she ate quickly, eating only because she knew she needed to keep up her strength and not because she was particularly hungry.

Life was going to change for her now, and the only thing she could do was accept it. Her brother was not likely to change his mind, and it was more than obvious that her sister-in-law did not want her company in the house any longer. How much she had hoped for when her brother had first married – and how much had been dashed from her.

Rising a little unsteadily from her chair, Sophia made her way to her wardrobe and opened it up completely. Gowns of all colors and shades spilled out, reminding her of all the wonderful times she had with her family, or enjoying a pleasant evening with a few friends. Even though she had not yet had a Season, her father had always ensured that Sophia had occasion to enjoy a country ball or a musical recital or two. She would have enjoyed her Season two years previously, had it not been for her father's ill health, and then, of course, the year after that, her dear father had passed away. The gowns that had been bought and prepared for her Season now hung, unworn, in her wardrobe. They would never be worn, for a governess did not wear such things.

Pulling them out one after the other, Sophia flung them heedlessly onto the floor, her pain and sadness overwhelming her entirely. Tears ran down her face in rivulets, pain tearing her apart until she thought she might not be able to contain it. Unable to stand, Sophia sank down amongst the soft gowns, burying her head in her hands as she sat amongst them, sobs shaking her frame.

Her life as she knew it was over. Her brother and sister-in-law would no longer be a part of her life, for Sophia was sure that, once she found a new situation, they would not so much as think of her again. She had no fortune to speak of, only her dowry, which would never be given to any man given what now lay in her future.

Darkness billowed around her as the flames in the grate began to flicker. Shrouded in gloom, Sophia felt her heart sink all the lower, beginning to shatter within her. Everything was gone with the hopes for her future discarded.

From now on, she would be entirely alone.

3

"Sarah Elizabeth!"

Matthew tried hard not to smile as his precocious five-year-old daughter stopped what she was doing and looked up at him, a somewhat guilty expression on her face.

"What is it you think you are doing with that creature?"

His daughter stood up slowly, a small, black, furry kitten nestled in her arms.

"Papa, I found this."

"This?" Matthew repeated, arching one eyebrow and trying not to allow the swell of emotion he felt on seeing his daughter so tenderly patting the small creature to push the frown from his face.

"I found the kitten," she said slowly, her eyes downcast. "The cook was going to throw it outside."

A surge of compassion ran through him for the poor creature, seeing just how tiny it was. Most likely it was the runt of the litter, and the mother cat had simply left it behind. It happened all too often, unfortunately.

"It is too small for you to look after, Sarah," he said softly, coming toward his daughter and bending down to look her directly in the eye. "The cat obviously had her kittens somewhere warm, and she has left this one behind when the rest were big enough to be moved."

His daughter's eyes filled with tears. "But why?" she whispered, as the tiny creature let out a small squeak. "It is so beautiful. Why would its mother leave it all alone?"

Something tore in Matthew's heart as he looked at his daughter's big blue eyes, his throat aching. Was she only asking about the kitten, or was there more to her question? He had often wondered how his daughter was faring without a mother of her own, even though she had a wonderful nurse and a maid who doted on her almost as much as he did.

"It is just something cats do," he said with a shrug. "This kitten is very small, Sarah. The mother cat probably just had too many kittens to look after all on her own."

His daughter sniffed loudly. "Then, I want to look after it, Papa."

As much as he wanted to refuse her, Matthew found that he could not speak those words. She looked so forlorn, and the creature was so completely tiny, and Matthew knew it would not survive were he to return it to the cold.

"Very well," he said heavily. "But it will be entirely your responsibility, Sarah. It will need milk and scraps of food if it is to get any bigger. It will need a warm place to sleep and plenty of loving care." His smile dimpled, as he looked down at his daughter, seeing her tear-filled eyes now shining brightly. "Do you think you can do that?"

She nodded at once, her expression serious. "Yes, of course I can, Papa. I will take very good care of it." She set the animal down on a small scrap of blanket she had near her, only to throw her arms around his neck and hold him tightly. "Thank you, Papa," she said again, as the kitten let out another tiny squeak. "He will be a lovely cat; I know it."

Matthew chuckled and patted his daughter's cheek. "I am sure he will be. Although, I would make sure to check with nanny whether it is a boy or a girl before you name him."

His daughter's eyes opened wide for a moment, her mouth forming a perfect circle before, with a cry of, "Yes, at once, Papa!" she scooped up the forlorn kitten and hurried from the room back toward the nursery.

Matthew stood up slowly, his lips stretched wide into a smile as he took in his daughter, seeing her bouncing curls and flying dress ribbons as she practically ran down the hallway. She had all the impetuousness of youth, but he could not chide her for it. That was part of her character, and Matthew was sure that, in time, she would learn to think things through more carefully. However, he adored her soft heart, her compassion for creatures more helpless than she, her desire to help them in any way she could. The kitten was just another example of her sweetness, and whilst it was a tiny scrap of a thing at the moment, Matthew was sure that by the week's end the kitten would be well on its way to good health. His daughter would dote on it and feed it only the best food she could wrangle out of the cook, who, Matthew knew, would end up being more than willing to give her whatever she wished.

His smile faded as he turned toward the window in the drawing room, looking out across his wonderful, ornate gardens. His home had been a happy one these last few years, for the most part. That was not to say that there had not been times when he had been confused, lonely, and afraid about his child and how she would fare without a mother. But as the years had gone on, he had seen just how wonderful his daughter had been. She was not troubled by lack of a mother—although it did, at times, come to the forefront of their conversation. Sometimes, when she tilted her head to the side and regarded him, he was caught by a memory of Lady Elizabeth, seeing her in his daughter.

He had done all he could for her thus far, making sure to spend as much time as he could with Sarah Elizabeth, and that had gone a long way to soothing his lonely soul. It was not that he missed the love he had once shared with his wife, for they had never had any kind of affection to speak of, but rather it felt as though his heart had been longing for something that could never come to pass for him. That desire for love and companionship from the one he had called his wife had never been fulfilled whilst Lady Elizabeth had been alive. Now, five years a widower, he had no expectation for it ever coming to pass.

Dragging his thoughts away from the melancholy, Matthew sighed heavily to himself. He would have to, at some point, find another bride so that he might ensure to provide the heir for his family's line, but that held no hope of the love and affection he craved. He was a duke and that meant that the ladies of the *ton* would see him as nothing more than a title and fortune to which they could attach themselves. It would all just be the same as before.

Sighing heavily, Matthew shook his head to himself and walked from the room, knowing he had some correspondence to deal with in the study. He had time to think about London much later, for the Season was still a few months away. Springtime had only just arrived, and his estate was busy with all that needed to be done so that they might have a productive harvest. Of course, it was not as though Matthew himself was involved in the tilling of the ground or the planting of the seeds, but he did, at least, oversee it all and have timely reports from his steward. There was more than enough for him to do, more than enough to distract him from all thoughts of London, the *ton,* and the need to marry.

"Ah, your grace!"

Coming to the door of his study, Matthew was met by the butler, who was holding a few letters in his hand.

"Your correspondence, my lord. Some only arrived a few minutes ago with the post. Shall I set them on your desk?"

"No, I will take them," Matthew replied, holding each letter carefully. "Although can you send down for some fresh coffee and perhaps any of those orange cakes the cook had yesterday?"

The butler nodded, a ghost of a smile on his face. "But of course," he replied, inclining his head. "I believe the cook made a fresh batch this morning, knowing that you liked them so much."

Matthew chuckled and opened the door to his study as the butler hurried away. His staff had been with him for a good few years now, and he found their company to be something of a support to him. The butler knew him and his ways very well, and the cook often went out of her way to cook things she knew Matthew would like. They all doted on his daughter as much as he did, showing her so much care and consideration that it gladdened Matthew's heart.

Sitting down at his desk, Matthew spread out the seven letters, considering them each in turn. There was one from his friend, Lord Barton, back in London, who would most likely be encouraging Matthew to return to the city again very soon. He had been doing so for the last four years although Matthew had never taken him up on his offer. Setting that one aside to read at his leisure, Matthew looked hopefully at the others, wondering if he would recognize his brother's handwriting. Alas, there was none that looked anything like Arthur's hand. He had not seen Arthur in as many years, although he had stopped by for a month or so a year after the duchess had passed away. However, Matthew had been glad to see that regular letters began to come to the house from his brother. It was as though Arthur somehow knew that Matthew would be feeling somewhat tumultuously thrown about and had wanted to reassure him that he was not entirely alone.

Slitting open the first letter, Matthew realized that it was none other than a response to his notice for a governess. He had written to a few trusted friends and acquaintances, asking for their suggestions, and apparently, this was one of the responses. He quickly scanned the letter before picking up the next one and opening it, too.

Soon, five letters lay on his table, each one telling him just how appropriate a governess they would be for his daughter. They were all much the same, assuring him of their references and suitability, but none caught his interest. He knew that Sarah required a governess, but it was important to him that he chose that governess wisely. She would have to fit in with the family, would have to make sure to teach Sarah with all gentleness and wisdom, bringing her up to be a lady of quality. Whilst he could, of course, send a governess away if she did not suit, he would prefer not to have to do that. He knew that his daughter would be inclined to form something of an attachment with whichever lady he chose.

Sighing to himself, Matthew picked up the final letter and opened it carefully, noticing that it bore a wax seal, although it was one he did not recognize. Frowning slightly, he began to read the first few lines, his eyebrows reaching up so high they almost disappeared into his hairline.

The writing was shaky, the words sometimes almost indistinct so that he struggled to read it clearly. At the bottom, there was something like a tearstain that had marked the signature, as though the writer had been crying.

Somewhat confused as to what this might mean, Matthew read the letter again, taking it in slowly. From what he understood, the applicant was a lady of quality, the sister of a viscount. Why was she applying to be his daughter's governess? Had the family fallen on hard times and so she was required to do what she could to make a life for herself? On paper, she appeared to be the perfect lady, the answer to his concerns about whether he would find someone truly suitable for little Sarah, but he did not want to have a governess who was, it seemed, somewhat upset at having to become a governess instead of continuing with the life she had been born to.

Why had she not married? Was there something about her appearance or her manner that made her entirely unsuitable as a wife? Frowning, Matthew re-read the letter again, not quite sure either what to make of it or what to do.

Picking up his quill, he paused for a moment before scratching out a reply. He could not pass up on the chance of having such a lady for his daughter's governess, even if it was very strange for a viscount's sister to be looking for such a position. Sealing the letter with his wax seal, Matthew rang the bell and handed it to the butler to be posted at once. Sitting back in his seat, he piled up the rest of the application letters and set them to the side. He would see what Miss Sophia Weston had to say before he went in search of anyone else.

4

"It seems you have a letter, sister dear."

The voice from outside her bedchamber door was one filled with scorn as well as tinged with delight, which meant that it had to be the viscountess. Sophia closed her eyes for a moment, frustration rifling through her as she thought about what to say in response. She did not want to open the door to take the letter from her sister-in-law, knowing that the viscountess might simply push her way into the room whilst practically crowing with delight over the fact that Sophia had, most likely, found herself a position.

"If you just set it down, I will come to fetch it in a short while," she replied, not moving from her seat. "I am currently occupied."

There was a short silence from outside the door. Sophia held her breath whilst she waited for the viscountess to make her decision, knowing that more than anything, she wanted to barge into Sophia's private space. The place she had made all of her own these last few weeks.

"I really think you should read it just as soon as possible," came the reply. "Do you not want to find out who has written back to you?"

The truth was that Sophia *did* want to find out who had written to her so that she might know where her future was to lie, but the last thing she wanted was to face the viscountess in doing so.

"I can open it and read it for you, if you like."

Quick as a flash, Sophia hurried across the room, unlocked the door and snatched the letter from her sister-in-law's fingers. She only briefly registered the shock on the lady's face before slamming the door shut again, turning the key in the lock just as quickly as she could.

A sense of satisfaction rose within her as she heard the viscountess stomp her foot.

"Sophia, that was more than a little rude!" the lady cried, clearly upset now with being denied the prize of entering Sophia's chamber and finding out what the letter said. "Open this door at once."

Relieved to know that the only two keys for her door were now hanging by a hook on the wall by the door, Sophia ignored the viscountess's whining voice entirely and made her way back to the chair by the fire. There was a good fire in the grate today, with some coal in a bucket to one side, just in case she should feel cold. This was not the generosity of her brother, however, but rather the staff that had been with Sophia since long before her brother gained the title. The news that she was to be sent away had made its way below stairs, and the staff had rallied around her, in as much as they could do without being noticed. The second key to her door had mysteriously found its way from the housekeeper's ring of keys to her own room, just so that there was no way her brother could enter her room without her knowledge. In addition, the maids always brought in extra coal and wood for her fire, so that she would not be cold, and she had more food than she could ever eat sent to her rooms.

It was a gesture that had made her last few days here a little more bearable. She had barely left her rooms, save when a footman came to tell her that the viscount and viscountess had left the house for a time. Those had been the occasions where she had slipped from her room and scoured the house for her belongings. The one thing she had taken that had not been hers to take without asking her brother had been her mother's locket, the one that held a miniature of her mother and of her father. She did not think that Peter would notice it gone, and so she had taken it from her late father's room, sadly aware of the thin layer of dust that covered every surface. She had held the locket in her hand and squeezed it tightly, battling tears as she did so. Peter would never notice it gone; he would never care that she had taken it with her, whereas she needed it. It was a simple connection to her parents, to a life she was to leave behind. It was now buried in the bottom of one of her bags, wrapped in a soft linen cloth. It would go with her wherever she went.

Looking about her, Sophia took in the almost bare room, her heart crying out in pain. She now had practically everything she owned in her chamber, packed and ready to go with her the moment she was to leave her brother's house.

Turning the letter over in her hands, Sophia held her breath and closed her eyes for a moment, building up the courage to see what was held within. The viscountess's frustrated voice faded away, as she gave up trying to wheedle her way inside Sophia's rooms, leaving Sophia entirely alone.

Pulling her shawl around her shoulders, Sophia sat down on the floor by the fire, feeling the need to have as much warmth around her as she could. It was as if her blood was cold, sending shivers all through her, as she looked down at the letter in her hand.

The wax seal broke easily enough, and unfolding the letter, Sophia read the few short lines.

This was it. This was to be the turning point in her life. This was to be her new position, her new home, her new social standing. No longer treated as she ought, she would be somewhere in between the master of the house and the servants below stairs. Never allowed to mingle with either class, she would be, for the most part, entirely on her own.

Swallowing hard, Sophia brushed away a single tear that touched her eyelashes, not wanting to give into yet more weeping. She had done more than enough of that already.

Reading the letter again, she sighed to herself, as she saw that the Duke of Harrogate wanted her to move there just as soon as she could, which meant that she could make arrangements to leave and be gone within a day or so, well before her brother's demand for a month.

And yet, she did not want to go. To leave and step out into a new, unfamiliar world, sent terror to her very bones. To stay here with her vile sister-in-law and her—now unrecognizable—brother was entirely out of the question. In a way though, it seemed to be the better option than to start her life as a governess. It was not a life she had chosen for herself, but was instead, a life forced upon her. She had no idea how to work with children, how to teach them and educate them to a proper degree! What if the child did not like her? What if her lack of experience was much too obvious and she was sent away again? Where would she go? It was not as though her brother would welcome her back with open arms.

Dropping the letter from her fingers, Sophia drew her head down, resting it on her knees as she sat on the floor by the fire. Her breathing came quickly, as she fought the urge to cry, to give in to despair and hopelessness. Her life here was over. She had to face the fact that within a week, she would be the new governess to the Duke of Harrogate's daughter. She would have to let go of all she had here, all the hopes and expectations she had about her future. Acceptance was not going to come easily, but Sophia was determined to try and find some kind of inner strength that would allow her to go forward without this burden of sadness and pain resting on her shoulders.

Lifting her head, Sophia sniffed and gave herself a slight shake. There were things to be done. She would have to write to the duke and inform him that she intended to leave in two days' time, expecting to be with him within a week of departure. She had very little idea as to how far away the duke's home was, nor where she ought to stay to break up the journey, but somehow, she would find a way to get there. There was little hope in her using her brother's carriage, so Sophia supposed she would have to find a stage to take her to her destination. She had never done that kind of thing before, the very idea filling her with fright, but it would have to be done regardless of how she felt.

Perhaps the maids would be able to help her arrange something. The last thing Sophia wanted was to go to her brother and ask for his help, not after what he had done thus far. The sound of his voice telling her that she had to be gone from his house within the month echoed in her mind, seeming to bounce off the walls as she thought about the kind of man he had turned into. It was as though her brother had died alongside her father, his goodness and warmth gone from him. No, she could not go to him.

"Sophia?"

Jumping, Sophia heard her brother's angry voice from the other side of the door.

"Sophia, open this door at once! Explain your behavior toward my wife!"

Closing her eyes, Sophia got to her feet and made her way toward the door with very little intention of opening it. "Brother,

I am going to do no such thing," she said calmly. "This is my bedchamber and has been for many years. I will decide who is to come in and who is not."

There was a short silence before a sudden, heavy thump made her jump in fright.

"You are a spoilt, headstrong girl," her brother snarled, from behind the door. "Just as well you are to go from this place. I assume you have a position?"

"I do," Sophia replied calmly. She did not need to tell him where it was nor whom it was with, although she was quite sure the viscountess had taken a good, long look at the seal.

Her brother chuckled darkly. "Good. So, you will be gone very soon. A new life for you, Sophia, one where you will have to learn not to be so dependent on others, one where you will have to let go of your selfishness and pride."

Closing her eyes, Sophia leaned against the door, the pain of her brother's words piercing her heart.

"One of the grooms will take you to the village to catch the stage whenever you require it," her brother continued, thumping the door again so as to make sure she was listening. "The sooner, the better, Sophia. Do you hear me? The sooner, the better."

"I hear you, Peter," Sophia managed to say, refusing to allow him to hear any tears in her voice.

Something slid under the door, and Sophia glanced down in surprise to see some notes being shoved underneath.

"These are not for your fripperies, Sophia, but for the stage," Peter continued. "I just want to make sure you get to your destination without any difficulty. The last thing I need is to come and rescue you from some far away inn because you have no money left."

Torn between gratefulness and deep agony, Sophia picked up the notes and clutched them to her chest. At least she would not have to scour her room for any remaining pin money in order to pay for the stage.

"Thank you," she whispered, the words coming unwillingly from her mouth.

He did not say anything more, the silence growing between them. Then, after a moment or two, Sophia heard the sound of his footsteps, as he turned from her door and walked along the hallway, leaving her alone once more.

She did not think she would ever see him again.

5

"This be you, miss."

Jerked into wakefulness, Sophia stared at the man at the door, blinking furiously as she tried to remember what she was doing.

"You are here, miss," he said again, stepping aside and waiting for her to climb out of the stagecoach.

Her limbs felt like blocks of wood as she climbed out, seeing her bags being set down by the side of the road. Just ahead of her, up a long gravel drive, there was a huge manor house gleaming in the late afternoon sunshine. It was cold, with the February wind chilling her to the very bone.

"Is this the Duke of Harrogate's house?" she asked, as the last of her four bags were set down by her side.

The man grinned, his eyes dancing. "Yes, indeed. What are you going there for, miss, if you do not mind my asking? There ain't been anyone new in that place for a long time."

"I am the governess," Sophia whispered, already feeling like a fraud by simply letting those words pass her lips. "I mean, I am going to try to be."

Frowning, the man studied her for a moment. "There ain't

nothing to be afraid of, miss. The Duke of Harrogate is a good man, do you not know? A good master to his tenants, so I am told. You ain't got nothing to fear from him."

His words penetrated through Sophia's anxiety, bringing her a slight tinge of relief.

"Thank you," she murmured, looking down at her bags and then back up at the faraway manor house, not quite sure how she was to get her things to the house by herself. "That is good to know."

The man smiled again and patted her shoulder. "Well, all the luck to you." He doffed his cap, climbed back up into the driver's seat, and the stagecoach rolled away, leaving her standing alone on the road with her bags all about her.

Sophia did not know what to do. She was already overwhelmed by all that had happened, the days of traveling, her mind going over and over what she might find and what kind of man the Duke of Harrogate might be, only to now find herself deposited half a mile away from the manor house.

Gritting her teeth, Sophia drew in a long breath and lifted her chin.

"I have got to find some strength from somewhere," she told herself aloud, knowing that she could not simply stand there and wait for someone to come and find her. If she was to start her new life, then she had to somehow find the strength within herself to do the best she could, no matter the circumstances. She would not fail at this. She *could not* fail at this. Her life was here, and Sophia knew she needed to find some kind of determination within herself, a strength of character that had to build up a resilience that would see her through. There would be no one else to help her, no one else to tell her what to do or to even so much as listen to the sorrows in her heart. From now on, she was going to have to find a way to live her life alone.

Picking up two of her bags, Sophia strode forward on legs

that wobbled just a little, depositing them just within the driveway and making sure they remained mostly out of sight. Walking back to where her other two bags were, she picked them up. With determination, she began to make her way toward the house.

By the time she reached the house, sweat trickled down her back, her hair was plastered to her head underneath her bonnet. Every muscle within her was aching with the effort of carrying them. Deep within her, there came a small burning satisfaction that she had, in fact, managed to carry her bags thus far.

Looking up at the front door, Sophia paused for a moment, not certain where she ought to go. The front door was meant for those who came to call on the duke whereas, since she was no longer a lady of quality but rather a governess, she should go to the servants' entrance.

She was still contemplating what to do when the sound of footsteps caught her ears. Turning around, she saw a tall, well-dressed gentleman coming toward her, having evidently been walking in the gardens. He looked at her with contemplative eyes, his dark hair flopping down over his forehead just a little. There was a youthful air about him. Although, as he drew nearer, Sophia saw the weariness deep within his gaze, as though life had treated him a little cruelly, giving him burdens to carry that he had not anticipated.

Putting her bags down, she bent her head and kept her hands clasped in front of her, not quite sure what she should do. Should she speak first and introduce herself? Or wait until he asked her?

"And you are?"

The words were taut and brittle, his voice a little irritated. Glancing up at him, Sophia saw that his jaw was clenched, his eyes glinting with something like frustration.

"I am your new governess, your grace," she murmured, dropping her eyes to the gravel at her feet instead of keeping them on his face as she as used to. "Miss Sophia Weston, at your service."

There was a short pause. Sophia dared not look up at him, suddenly filled with worry that he might choose to turn her away there and then. She could not imagine what her appearance was like, resisting the urge to sweep back her errant blonde curls from her temples and tuck them back into her bonnet.

"I see," he murmured, after a few moments. "And are these all your things?"

Looking up at him, Sophia saw the frustration slowly leaving his face. Apparently, she was acceptable. "No, your grace," she replied softly. "I have left two of my other bags at the bottom of the drive." Her cheeks heated, as she looked away. "I could not quite manage to carry them all."

"Of course," he replied at once, calmly. "However, you could have left them all at the bottom of the driveway, Miss Weston. My footmen will go to fetch them for you and set them in your rooms." He gestured toward the house, as one of the footmen came scurrying toward them, picking up Sophia's bags as though he had heard the duke speak. The duke murmured something in the footman's ear, and without a word, he hurried back into the house to do the master's bidding.

"I do not think you need meet my daughter today," the duke continued, as Sophia fell into step alongside him. "It is already growing late, and she will be going to bed very soon." He turned his head to regard her, as they climbed the steps, and Sophia felt herself grow hot under his scrutiny. "I think, mayhap, a time to get to know you a little better would be best, Miss Weston. I do have a few questions for you, you see."

"Of course, your grace," Sophia replied automatically. "I will do whatever it is you wish of me."

A chuckle came from his lips, making her look over at him in surprise. She had not expected any kind of mirth from him. Was it because of what she had said or because of how she looked? Did he find her changed situation to be one of hilarity? Her cheeks burned, as she turned her face away, looking ahead of her into the house.

"Thank you, Miss Weston, that is very good of you," the duke murmured, as he walked into the house ahead of her. "I am not a hard man, as you will soon come to know, although I do expect my staff to work to the very best of their ability at all times. However, I will not allow you to simply agree with me at all times, Miss Weston. When it comes to my daughter's education, I will want you to speak to me about what you have been considering for her, what your thoughts are for her future, and what subjects you intend to focus on. Provided the situation works out, of course."

"Of course," Sophia echoed, her stomach swirling with a mixture of nerves and a feeling of being entirely unprepared for what was expected of her.

"I will not have you doing what I ask and what I say without allowing me into your own thoughts and opinions, Miss Weston," the duke continued, as they made their way to the bottom of the staircase that led up through the grand house. "I want you to be very clear on this issue," he finished, turning to face her. "This is vastly important to me, and I want to ensure that we are clear on this from the start."

Still feeling entirely overwhelmed, Sophia found herself nodding without being altogether sure of what she was agreeing to. The duke gave her a small smile, his blue eyes still lingering on her and giving Sophia the impression that she was being scrutinized by him. Did she live up to his expectations?

"So, rest and eat, and then I shall send for you," the duke said, as a maid hurried forward to stand by her side.

Seeing the maid walk ahead of her and realizing that she was expected to follow, Sophia curtsied quickly – although as gracefully as she could – and then began to make her way up the stairs, leaving the duke behind.

Her mind was so full that she barely took in the grandeur of the house. She hardly saw the ornate carpets, the beautiful tapestries, and marble busts that decorated the hallway. The maid hurried her along to the end of one long hallway, turning left and then right until Sophia found herself in a small alcove with one door on either side.

"This here is the nursery," the maid said quietly. "Lady Sarah will be getting changed for bed, so I will not show you in at the moment."

Sophia nodded, looking toward the other door. The maid opened it and ushered Sophia in, standing just outside the doorway.

"And this will be your room," the maid continued softly. "The master is very kind, miss. He thought you should have a bath in your room. Just pull the bell when you are ready and it will be emptied for you."

Sophia could hardly breathe, such was her shock. The room, whilst smaller than her own bedchamber at home, was beautifully decorated with the bed at one end of the room and a table, chair, and rocking chair by the fire at the other end. There was a screen where she might change, with a large wardrobe next to it, and best of all, there was a large tub filled with water that was already gently steaming, just waiting for her to step inside.

It was a kindness and a consideration she had not expected, especially given her now-lowly situation.

"Thank you," she whispered, as the maid smiled at her. "This is truly wonderful."

The maid's smile broadened. "The duke is a good master, Miss Weston. You will find him not to have a harsh word for anyone, unless they deserve it." She walked toward the door, her hand on the door handle. "I will bring you up some refreshments in an hour or so."

"Thank you," Sophia said again, her numb fingers trying to untie her bonnet ribbons. "This is more than I ever expected, truly."

The maid said nothing but shut the door gently, leaving Sophia to look around her new room with a slow-building happiness settling in her heart. Perhaps her life here would not be so bad after all.

6

Matthew settled back in his chair, his brandy in his hand. It had now been some hours since the new governess had arrived. His first impressions had not been particularly positive. She had been younger than he had expected, thinking her to be something of a spinster whereas, from the youthfulness of her face, she ought to be in London for the Season, although she was certainly no debutante. She had looked bone weary and utterly bedraggled, but there had been a slumping of her shoulders that told him she had not wanted to come to his home and take on the role of a governess. That did not bode well for their ongoing relationship, especially when he was handing her full care of his daughter.

He had been a little abrupt initially, of that he could admit. He had come from the stables and found one of his horses to be lame. Thankfully, it had appeared to be nothing more than a stone and a large thorn embedded into the hoof, but it had not been noticed by his stable hands until this morning when it was apparent that it had happened yesterday at some point. His mount would be back to full health soon, but he had been forced to give a few stern words to his stable hands, and they had been left with no doubt as to his anger and upset over what had occurred.

Then, he had made his way back to the house only to come across this disheveled-looking woman, and his irritation had made its way into the words he had spoken to her. Perhaps she had not had the best impression of him either, which might have accounted for the fearful way she had regarded him. Hopefully, the bath he had ordered for her had helped with her impression of him.

Sighing heavily, Matthew sat back and took a swig of his brandy, worrying that he had made the wrong decision. Miss Weston had looked afraid and vulnerable, and as much as he had not wanted to admit it to himself, his heart had swelled with sympathy for her. There was certainly more to her story, and that was why he had chosen to have a conversation with her this evening. He wanted to know what it was that had occurred to make her step down from her place in society to a much lesser one. That meant that there had to be some reason for her to be as she was, which might explain the deep sadness that had covered her as she'd talked with him. Mayhap she had tried and failed to find a husband, for she was not exactly a beautiful woman, although certainly not unattractive. Did her father not have enough funds for another Season? Had she become a financial burden, forced to take on a role as a governess until her father's situation improved? Question after question about the lady burrowed into his mind, unsettling him further.

This was not something he could afford to get wrong. Little Sarah would form an attachment with any governess he gave her, and he had to ensure that the lady was the right governess for her. He could not bear to tear a governess away from his young daughter once an attachment had been formed, knowing that his little girl was already so gentle-natured that such a thing could injure her greatly.

There came a quiet scratch at the door, the butler stepping inside at Matthew's call to enter.

"The governess," Matthew began, getting to his feet. "Tell her that I would like her to come to the study within the next half hour, whenever she is ready."

"Very good, your grace," the butler replied, inclining his head.

"In the library, I think," Matthew continued, thinking that the study might be a little too imposing for her. "And send a tray for her, and one for me. No tea or coffee for me, however." He lifted his glass of brandy and chuckled. "I have more than enough here."

The corner of the butler's mouth quirked, as he nodded. "At once, your grace."

"Thank you, Jenkins," Matthew replied, as the door closed behind the butler. It was one thing he had always been truly grateful for – a staff that was loyal to him. The butler had been with him for a good many years now and knew Matthew's ways very well. He just had to hope that the Miss Weston would manage to fit into his household without too much difficulty, *if* he decided to keep her on.

It was not more than ten minutes before Miss Weston knocked on the library door and stepped inside, her sapphire-colored eyes wide, as she took in the large room and the great many books held within it

"Miss Weston, thank you for coming so promptly," Matthew said, getting to his feet. "Please, come and sit here."

Miss Weston swallowed once, hesitated for a moment, and then made her way toward him, sitting down opposite him. There was a tenseness to her movements, as she sat down on the very edge of her seat, her fingers clasped tightly in her lap.

"You need not have any kind of fear of me, Miss Weston,"

Matthew said at once, wanting to put her at ease. "I am not about to throw you out on your ear."

"No, your grace, of course I did not think that," came the soft reply as her eyes darted all over the room. "I just thought... I mean, I am a little unused to..."

Realizing the reason for her discomfort, Matthew nodded slowly. "I understand. I can fetch a maid here, if you wish."

Her eyes flickered to his for a moment only to dart away again. "No, thank you, your grace. It is just going to take me a little time to become used to it, and I beg your forgiveness for that."

That had him wondering about her, taking her in properly for the first time. She did not have that bedraggled look about her any longer, looking a little more rested and less afraid. Her eyes were still a little widened, as though she were still taking everything in, still a little overcome with it all. Her high-collared, grey dress did not become her in the slightest, her fair hair tied back neatly into a bun with only a few wisps escaping to curl around her temples. Whilst neat, Matthew was sure Miss Weston was entirely unaccustomed to wearing such things.

"I am afraid I shall have to ask you some somewhat probing questions, dear lady," he said firmly. "I know that there will be some questions you will not wish to answer, and I will not press you on them, for you have your own right to privacy. However, I must ensure that you are a suitable lady for my daughter. I cannot trust her into another's care without being settled in my own mind as to whether or not that person is entirely right for her." He lifted his chin a little, making sure to keep his gaze steady. "My daughter is a gentle soul and one who will grow to love you with very little effort on your part."

"What a lovely child she must be," Miss Weston replied softly, her eyes growing gentle. "How old did you say she was?"

"She is five years of age, due to be six this year," Matthew answered, surprised to see her so unperturbed by his stern gaze. "Do you have much experience with children, Miss Weston?"

Her soft expression faded to one of anxiety. "No, your grace, I do not," she replied honestly, without even the slightest hint of guile. "I will be truthful with you and say that this is my first charge." Her gaze faltered, as the words slipped from her mouth, as if worried he might immediately ask her to leave.

Matthew nodded slowly. "I see."

"However, I myself have been brought up with all the refinements expected of a lady," she continued hurriedly. "I can teach them to your daughter, I am sure."

"You are a lady of quality," Matthew stated, questions beginning to burn in his mind. "That was precisely the reason I asked for you to come here, Miss Weston. I knew that a lady such as yourself would be able to teach my daughter all that she will need to know as the daughter of a duke."

Something like relief flashed across Miss Weston's face as she nodded, although Matthew could see the way her lips trembled. Feeling a trifle sorry for her, he indicated the tea tray to her left, suggesting she pour herself a cup whilst they talked.

His keen eyes did not miss the way her hands shook slightly as she did so, although he rose to pour himself another brandy so that she did not feel him watching her. He was tempted to give her the opportunity to prove herself as a good governess for Sarah, but still there was so much of a mystery about her that nagged at his mind, pressing him with doubts.

"You were not pleased, I think, to come here," he said, sitting back down and fixing his gaze on her once more. "You need not try to find an excuse, Miss Weston. I saw your face when you arrived and that told me more than you could ever say." He saw her flinch but kept his eyes on her, not allowing himself to be swayed by the sudden agony etched on her features.

Miss Weston pressed her lips together for a moment, her

eyes darting here and there before settling back on to his face. "Your grace, I am very glad to be here," she said, slowly. "It is not what I expected for my life, that is true, but you have been kind enough to invite me to take on the role of governess, and I will do all I can to teach Sarah everything I know."

The answer was a truthful one, Matthew would swear on it. There was no guile in her eyes, no looking away as she spoke.

"I will not press you as to why you have been made to take on this role when you are a lady of refinement," he replied, seeing the relief in her gaze. "However, should any difficulty arise for any reason, I wish you to come and speak to me freely about it. Your situation, as it is, is a temporary one here, until I decide whether or not to make it a more permanent arrangement."

She lifted her head, her eyes widening. "Does that mean that I will be allowed to meet your daughter tomorrow?"

"It does," he replied, his heart still filled with doubts and questions which he had to continually silence. "There shall be a month's trial, starting from tomorrow. At the end of the month, you shall give me a report on my daughter's progress. I will speak to her myself and to the nurse. If they are satisfied with you, and if I am pleased with her progress, then I will consider a more permanent arrangement for you. Does that satisfy you?"

Miss Weston's eyes were glassy as she nodded, her gratefulness evident. "Thank you, your grace," she murmured before lifting her teacup to her lips and sipping delicately. It gave her a moment to blink back her tears, meaning she was able to lift a smiling face toward him again.

"I look forward to meeting your daughter and beginning our lessons," she said, after a few moments of silence.

"Very good," Matthew replied, getting to his feet, just as she made to do so. "No, Miss Weston, there is no need for you to rise. You may remain in the library for as long as you wish. In fact, the books are at your disposal, for I think they would do you and my daughter a world of good. In addition, you are free to walk the grounds whenever you wish, although I would be grateful if you made sure Sarah is always warmly wrapped up."

She nodded. "Of course, your grace."

"In addition, you are to work with my daughter after breakfast and until the dinner gong sounds," he continued, laying out her terms. "Your pay shall come at the end of every month, and you have Saturday afternoons and Sundays free to do as you wish. There is a small village nearby, which has a few shops, and there are some lovely walks in the grounds themselves, as well as the woods beyond."

Miss Weston looked surprised.

"I like to spend time with my daughter, Miss Weston," he explained, aware that he was one of the few gentlemen who enjoyed spending time with their offspring. "You are to accompany us to church on Sunday morning, but thereafter the time is yours."

A slow smile began to spread across her face, making Matthew's heart suddenly skip a beat. It was the first time she had shown any kind of happiness in her expression. To his surprise, it completely transformed her features. Gone was the sadness that had lingered there for so long, her blue eyes sparkling with delight.

"You are very kind, your grace," she murmured, lowering her gaze respectfully. "Thank you for allowing me this opportunity to prove myself."

Clearing his throat, Matthew walked toward the door, a little confused as to the strange spark that had shot through his heart when Miss Weston had smiled at him.

"Tomorrow then, Miss Weston," he said, glancing back at her for one last moment before stepping through the door and out into the hallway.

7

"It is very nice to meet you."

Sophia tried her best to smile at the little girl who was staring up at her with big blue eyes, so like the duke's. There was no smile on her face, but no anger or upset either. Instead, there was simply a consideration of her, as though the child was assessing her in some way.

"Curtsy, Sarah," the duke murmured pressing his daughter's hand. "Can you show Miss Weston your very best curtsy?"

The girl frowned for a moment, before her face split into a wide smile, beaming up at her father. She did her very best – almost tumbling over in the process since she bent forward a little too much, only to laugh aloud as her father caught her.

Sophia was in love.

The child was beyond beautiful, her adoration for her father evident. The duke had been a little intimidating last evening, but today, in front of his daughter, he was much softer with a great deal of tenderness displayed. Sophia had been surprised to learn that she was to have so much time free from her duties as governess—for she had not expected the duke to care so much about his child. Now that she saw them together, she quite understood. They had such a strong bond that she did not think the duke would be able to go even a single day without seeing his daughter. It was a bond she had shared with her own father, albeit later in life when she had taken more of a role in the running of the house, but it had been wonderful nonetheless. A stab of pain shot through her heart as the duke lifted his face to hers, his smile for his daughter still lingering. Oh, how she missed her father!

"Miss Weston?"

Wiping the pained expression from her face, Sophia smiled brightly down at the child, not wanting to give a bad first impression. "I am sure we will get on splendidly, Lady Sarah. I can see that you have already learned to curtsy very well, and I am quite sure that come the end of the week, you will be able to do it perfectly."

To her consternation, the girl frowned. "My name is Sarah. Not Lady Sarah."

A little confused, Sophia looked up at the duke, who was laughing quietly.

"I do beg your pardon," she mumbled, her cheeks burning red, as she wondered if she had somehow misstepped. She had thought it was perfectly appropriate to refer to the duke's daughter by her correct title, but apparently, she had been wrong.

"Do forgive me, Miss Weston," the duke chuckled, shaking his head. "My daughter is unused to such formality, although I suppose it is best that she begins to get used to it."

"No," the child interrupted, folding her arms. "I do not like being called Lady Sarah. I am just Sarah."

"Very well," the duke grinned, shrugging slightly, as he turned his eyes back toward Sophia. "Miss Weston, I believe my daughter would like to be referred to without her title at the moment. I am sure that in the years to come, she will grow to understand the significance of it."

"I am sure she will," Sophia agreed softly, finding even the child's stubbornness to be something of a delight. "I would say that such determination is a good quality, your grace."

He nodded slowly, the smile fading from his features as he contemplated her. "I suppose it is," he said eventually. "Just so long as she does not become accustomed to always having her way, you understand."

"Yes, indeed, I quite understand," Sophia replied, looking down at the girl who was looking up them both with a slightly puzzled expression. "Might I take Sarah to the schoolroom now, your grace?"

"Of course."

The duke bent down to look into his daughter's face, instructing her to do everything that Sophia asked of her and telling her that he would be getting a report on her progress by the end of the week. This seemed to give little Sarah a determination to do as well as she could for her father, solemnly promising that she would do just that.

The duke smiled and rose to his feet, standing a little closer to Sophia than he had done before.

"Do come and find me this evening, once you have eaten," he said, his eyes still on his daughter. "I would like to know how everything has gone."

Her heart quickened as she looked up into his face, seeing his gaze slowly travel toward her. There was a moment of silence, a moment of something sparking between them. Then, it was gone.

He did not say another word, but turned on his heel and left the room, leaving her with her new charge staring up at her and a heart that was suddenly pounding with confusion.

The schoolroom had been dusted, tidied, and aired by the

maids, and Sophia had only had the briefest of visits to it before she had been called to meet Sarah. Walking into the room now, she felt a fresh new responsibility settling on her shoulders, seeing the little girl coming in behind her as they stepped inside.

"I have not been here before," Sarah said loudly, looking at the chalkboard and then at the map on the wall. "What is it we are meant to do?" She looked up inquiringly at Sophia, who immediately tried to think of the best explanation she could give.

"Well, Sarah, in this room, we are to start to fill your mind with all kinds of knowledge," she said slowly. "There is so much for you to learn that I hardly know where to begin!"

"I know my numbers and my letters," Sarah replied, with a slight air of indignance. "Is that the kind of thing you mean?"

"Yes, that is it precisely," Sophia answered, pulling out a slate and a piece of chalk. "Why do you not show me your numbers, Sarah? I would very much like to see them."

The girl looked up at her for a moment, her eyes traveling from Sophia's face to the slate and chalk she held out in her hand. Then, with a slow deliberateness, she took the slate and set it down in front of her.

Sophia let out a long, slow breath of relief, having been a little concerned that the girl might not do as she asked. She had no idea what she was supposed to do if that kind of thing occurred, wondering if she would have to go and speak to the duke and ask him for his help, only to worry that in doing so, she would then appear to be entirely incompetent.

"Here," Sarah said, interrupting her train of thought. "I did them."

Taking back the slate, Sophia looked down at the scrawl of numbers. Some were back to front, some upside down, and some entirely wrong. Sophia smiled at the little girl.

"You have done an excellent job," she said, wanting to

encourage her. "I think, however, that we will do the numbers one at a time, and we shall do them together. That way, we can make sure not to have any mistakes."

Sarah nodded, giving Sophia the smallest of smiles as she came to sit next to her, her own slate in hand. She smiled back at the girl, her heart filling with a happy relief that Sarah now seemed to be a little more amenable to having a governess.

The day passed quickly, and to her surprise, Sophia found herself more than able to fill the day with lots of different activities. After doing their numbers, she helped Sarah to write her full name, explaining to her the reason she had referred to her as 'Lady Sarah'. After lunch, they had wrapped up warmly and gone for a brief walk outside, even though it was windy and rather cold. The girl had bounced about like a jack-in-the-box and made Sophia laugh, finding a spark of happiness beginning to build a fire inside her.

When the dinner gong sounded, Sophia was surprised to find that she was already looking forward to having another day with the little girl tomorrow. After all of her worry and concern, she had found the little girl to be a happy and bright child, who smiled readily and laughed often. She was sure that tomorrow would go just as well, if not better, now that she had begun to get to know her.

"Good evening, Sarah," she said, rising to her feet and smiling down at the little girl. "It is time for me to go now. The nurse will be here with your dinner very soon."

Sarah nodded and got to her feet, setting the dolls she had been playing with aside. "Are you back again tomorrow?"

"Yes, of course I will be," Sophia replied, with a gentle smile. "I will see you again tomorrow morning after breakfast. I am sure we will have another wonderful day, Sarah. I will be sure to tell your father just how delightful you were today."

Sarah lifted her eyes to Sophia's, and to her surprise,

wrapped her arms around her waist. A little taken aback, Sophia did not know what to do initially, only to then press one hand to the little girl's head, her heart filling.

"Goodnight, Miss Weston," Sarah said, her voice muffled in Sophia's skirts. "Thank you for helping me with my letters."

Sophia swallowed the sudden lump in her throat, running one hand down Sarah's dark curls.

"You are more than welcome, Sarah," she replied, hoarsely. "I will see you again tomorrow."

8

Rubbing one hand over his eyes, Matthew groaned as he tried his best to fall asleep. Throwing himself over to the other side of his large, four-poster bed, he grasped the pillow and threw it over his head, hoping to drown out the many thoughts that were swirling through his mind.

It was to no avail. His eyes remained open, refusing to close, his body tense, as anxiety ran through his veins. And all because he had received a letter from his brother, which had forced him to do the one thing he hated.

Sitting up, Matthew yawned widely, as he swung his legs over the edge of the bed. This was useless. There was no point in trying to sleep, not when he knew it was futile. His mind was much too busy.

Perhaps he should go for a walk in the gardens, despite the late hour. The fresh air and quiet skies might bring peace to his thoughts, allowing him to return to his bed. Dressing quickly in shirt and trousers, he threw his greatcoat on, pulled on his boots, and headed for the door.

The night air was cold, so cold that it made Matthew catch his breath. Tugging his collar a little tighter, he hurried from the front door before he could change his mind and retreat back inside, shivering as he did so.

His footsteps left marks on the frozen grass, his breath like a cloud of smoke. He knew the way already, but the light of the moon aided his steps. Walking toward the rockery, the only place where green shrubs grew this time of year, Matthew let out a long sigh, his shoulders slumping heavily.

He had not seen his brother, Lord Arthur Arthur, for some years, although the letters had come frequently enough. He had been somewhat worried of late that there had been no correspondence from him, but now it seemed, his brother had returned to England and would be home within a fortnight. He had requested specifically to invite a few friends for a short visit, apparently desperate to reacquaint himself with society. So, unwilling to deny his brother this simple request, Matthew had dutifully written back to him, telling him that he had the freedom to invite ten guests to a small house party which would commence in two weeks' time.

He hated the idea already.

Arthur, of course, would enjoy every moment of it, for he was the kind of man who enjoyed frivolity and fun. Not that Matthew himself was incredibly dull or the like, but rather that he found himself often preferring a good book and quiet drink to loud, raucous laughter and dancing. That was why he had not returned to London these last five years, why he had not chosen to find himself another wife in place of Elizabeth. There had been no pressing need, and on top of which, he highly doubted that he would find a quiet, bookish lady from amongst the *ton*. There would always be the wallflowers, but Matthew would not be able to so much as talk to them, given that he would have his attention entirely caught up by various young ladies or their grasping mothers. Being a duke often brought its own difficulties with it, and this was one of them. Arthur, his brother, was apparently more than able to laugh and dance and converse with as many ladies as he liked without ever taking anything too seriously, but Matthew could not do the same. There was always a pressing need for him to be careful with what he said, thoughtful about who he danced with and how many times he had danced with them. He could never show anyone too much favor, give anyone too much time, or else the rumors and speculations about whom he might be interested in would begin to surface. All mothers wanted their daughters to be duchesses, but the problem was that he did not want a new duchess. Not yet, at least.

"Not until I absolutely have to," he muttered to himself in the darkness, his breath frosting.

Swiping ineffectually at some tall stalks of grass, Matthew made a mental note to remind the gardeners about ensuring they cut the grass soon. One of his gardeners was growing a little slow in his old age, but there was no intention on Matthew's part to remove him from his post, not until the time came where the man simply could not keep up. Whenever that occurred, Matthew had every intention of ensuring the man would have enough to live on for the rest of his days, as a thank you for the long service he had given Matthew's household. A respected master came from the fair and honest treatment of his staff, and this was one of the times when Matthew knew he could do some good.

Thinking of his staff led him to consider Miss Weston, his lips curving into something of a smile. She had been there for close to a fortnight now, and he had been delighted to discover that, not only did she teach his daughter, but that she had grown fond of her also. There was a blossoming relationship between Miss Weston and Sarah, and Matthew could not help but be pleased about it. His daughter needed an elegant, refined lady to help her turn into a beautiful young woman, ready to reach out into the world, and into society. By now, Matthew was quite sure that Miss Weston would be more than able to do so. The month's trial was not yet complete, but Matthew did not think he would have any cause to change his mind. She had done wonders with Sarah this far, having only been there for a short time, and he was more and more content with Miss Weston's presence in his home. Miss Weston herself appeared to be much more at ease, much more settled and happy to be in his estate. It was not often they met, but whenever they had done so, she had none of the fear and worry in her eyes that he had first seen when she had arrived. It felt as though Miss Weston was a part of his household now, and he had no intention of sending her away.

Shivering with the cold, Matthew turned back toward the house, wondering if perhaps a brandy might help him to sleep. He now felt even more wide awake than he had done before, a small niggle of worry continuing to nag at him. He did not want the house party, not when he was only just becoming used to the new situation in his life with the governess and Sarah. Arthur on his own would have been more than welcome, but to have a few more additional guests was not something he would particularly enjoy, especially as he would have to play host.

Sighing to himself, Matthew walked back toward the house, looking up at it for a moment and seeing a small light flickering in one of the windows. Narrowing his eyes, he saw it was the library, but given the hour, he would not expect anyone else to be awake. Had the maid forgotten to put out the fire? He had not been in the library himself that evening and so he had told the butler to ensure the fire in the grate was not attended to, not unless Miss Weston had intentions of finding herself a new book as she was inclined to do at times.

A little frustrated that he would have to go and see instead of returning to his bed and warm room, Matthew closed the door, bolted it, and then hurried up the stairs, glad for the strong moonlight shining through the windows. The library door was ajar, and as he pushed the door open, he saw that there was a figure sitting by the fire.

Frowning, he stepped in a little farther, only to see that it was Miss Weston, and she was sound asleep.

His heart clenched as he took her in, seeing the errant blonde curls framing her face, and the soft look about her eyes as she slept. Her lips were gently curved, as though she were having some kind of marvelous dream, her hand resting gently on a book that was still open. Evidently, she had been reading and the warmth of the fire and her own weariness had forced her eyes closed, pulling her into a deep sleep. Her stockinged feet caught his attention, seeing the slippers standing neatly to the side of the grate. Apparently, Miss Weston had been quite at ease, lost in a good book before drifting off to sleep.

And, strangely enough, it felt as though she belonged there, within his home.

There was no anger in him now, no irritation remaining deep within his heart. Instead, he found himself overcome with an altogether different sensation, one that caught him completely by surprise.

Fondness.

It was a feeling he did not welcome, having pushed aside all thoughts of affection or love for a great many years. He had believed it to be entirely foolish to hope for such things, particularly after his marriage to Elizabeth. Yet, here he was, some five years later, with a faint stirring in his heart as he looked at his sleeping governess.

His feet moved toward her of their own accord, his heart beginning to thump wildly as he looked down at her. Her skin was like alabaster, her cheeks a little pink from the warmth of the fire. How had he ever thought her plain? Here, now, at that very moment, he could think of her as nothing more than beautiful.

He did not mean to, but as if put there by its own force of will, Matthew found his fingers gently tracing her soft cheek. She did not move; she did not so much as stir at his touch, although a surge of heat raced up his arm and into his face. The sensations were growing stronger now as he continued to look into her face, pushing him toward something he was afraid to recognize.

Drawing in a sharp breath, Matthew turned on his heel and hurried away, frightened of whatever it was he was feeling. He did not want to think like this. He did not want to feel like this. He was perfectly content with his life as it was and had more than enough to think about with his brother and his many friends coming to stay. The last thing he needed was to have his heart twisted about by the governess, even though she was doing nothing to instigate that kind of emotion.

Closing the door quietly, Matthew made his way back toward his bedchamber, hearing no sound coming from the library. Apparently, Miss Weston still slept, unaware of his presence and of his touch. Relief rifled through him, his hand rubbing his forehead, as he stepped into his bedchamber and shut the door. That had been foolish indeed. He would have to make sure not to do anything so ridiculous again.

9

"No, no, Sarah," Sophia laughed, as the girl began to spin around the dance floor. "You are not listening to me."

"I am listening to the music," the little girl exclaimed, holding out her arms wide as she danced around. "Listen to it, Miss Weston!"

Sophia laughed again, unable to chide the girl. The pianist continued to play, regardless of what Sarah was doing, looking to Sophia for guidance, but she simply shrugged and let her express herself.

The last three weeks had been a wonderful, albeit very different to what Sophia had been used to. There were no servants to help her, although she did still have trays brought to her whenever she required them. She was expected to rise early and prepare her lessons for the day, to teach Sarah with care and consideration, before ensuring that everything was neat and tidy for the following day. Her gowns were black, grey, or a mixture of the two instead of the normal, bright colors she had been used to wearing, and there was no maid sent to dress her hair. Pulling it up into a bun every day had taken some getting used to, but by now she was more than proficient at doing so. While Sophia certainly found her life a great deal busier than before, and certainly difficult in terms of how she was seen by both the staff and the duke, she felt a growing happiness deep within her. That was all because of Sarah.

The little girl had been the happiness and the joy she had needed, sending light back into her soul with each day they spent together. There were times, of course, when the girl was disobedient or just downright unruly, but those times were few and far between. It often only took a few sharp words from Sophia to have her settle back down again.

Sarah, for whatever reason, had taken to Sophia almost at once, and she was an easy young lady to teach. She seemed to revel in learning as much as she could and was growing more and more proficient in reading with each day that passed. She knew her numbers and had begun to study arithmetic, although her greatest joy was to be out of doors, running and skipping and doing all the things a young girl ought to do at her age. It had been a joy for Sophia, too, to be allowed such freedoms as walking in the garden whenever she chose or finding a new book from the library.

Her brother, when she had been living at home, had severely curtailed Sophia's freedom the last few weeks she had lived there, even to the point of banning her from walking out of doors alone. So, to have that joy again brought Sophia a great deal of happiness. Most of all, however, Sophia was glad to have Sarah by her side each day. The gladness the little girl displayed on an almost daily basis on seeing Sophia at her door brought her such a happiness that, at times, Sophia did not quite know how to contain it all.

That did not mean, however, that Sophia did not miss the dreams and the hopes for her future that she had once had. They had been a part of her life for a long time, back when her father still lived. She had dreamed of going to London, of being courted and the like, before finding a suitable match for herself. Now, of course, that could never be. At some point, she was sure, the duke would remarry, and she might have to watch the family grow together whilst she remained on the sidelines, *if* she were permitted to stay.

However, Sophia knew she would simply have to accept that now. To linger on those dreams, to feel regret and sadness for the life she would never have, would only send bitterness into her soul. Instead, she would be grateful for what she *had* been given, for the duke's kindness in letting her stay on as governess even though this was her very first charge.

She laughed again, as she saw Sarah raise her hands up to the ceiling, her fingers wiggling back and forth as she spun around. She could see now why the duke had so much love for his daughter, for she was truly a remarkable young lady.

That thought made her pause. The duke himself was a man she had not quite managed to make out as yet. They spoke on a weekly basis, so that she might tell him how things were with his daughter, but he never gave very much away. He asked questions about Sarah and was always pleased to hear about her progress, but there was never any true conversation between them. Not that she should expect it, of course, but yet there was a small desire growing steadily in her heart, a desire to know the duke better.

It did not help that she was beginning to realize that he was truly a handsome gentleman, even though she had been a little afraid of him their first few conversations. When he smiled, she felt something glow within her, even more so when the smile was directed at her. The bright blue of his eyes was always warm whenever they conversed, usually fixed on her face instead of drifting elsewhere. He was a man who liked to give his full attention to whatever it was he was doing, and Sophia had never felt so aware of his consideration whenever his eyes lingered on her.

Were she still a lady of quality, not one who had been forced to remove herself from her position in her brother's home to a paid occupation, then she might have allowed herself to return some of his smiles, to allow the desire to develop her acquaintance with him to move forward. Knowing that she could do no such thing, Sophia had kept her distance and only spoken to him when he had asked a question of her. There had so often been a time when she had wanted to ask him about his home, ask him about his wife – Sarah's mother – who was very rarely spoken of, but she had kept her mouth closed and her lips silent. This was not her home and certainly not her place to ask such things. And so, her desires would be kept within her, kept secret and silent, as she continued her tutelage of Sarah, trying her best to remain glad for all she had been given instead of longing for more.

"Now, whatever is this?"

Turning on her heel, Sophia gasped as the duke walked into the ballroom, another gentleman just behind him. Waving a hand at the pianist, she curtsied quickly just as Sarah ran over to her father, throwing her arms about his waist.

"I do apologize, your grace," Sophia said hurriedly. "I was attempting to teach Sarah the first few steps of the waltz, but she was just enjoying the music too much, and so I thought to allow her to dance her own way for a time." Her cheeks burned with embarrassment, as the duke lifted one eyebrow and looked at her directly, aware that she had not been doing as was expected in his eyes.

"Oh, leave off, Mathew," the other gentleman interrupted, slapping the duke on the shoulder. "Your daughter was just having a bit of fun." He grinned at Sophia, who, not knowing who this man or what she was to do, curtsied again.

Bending down to Sarah, the gentleman smiled at her, his expression softening. "Well, well," he said softly. "Are you not just like your father, little Sarah? All the better, I say," he finished, patting her hand.

"Sarah," the duke interrupted, looking down at his daughter. "Do you remember Lord Arthur Arthur? He is your uncle."

"Uncle Arthur," the gentleman replied, rolling his eyes at the formality. "Uncle Arthur to you, dear child."

Sarah stepped away from her father and studied her uncle for a moment, before a smile of recognition came over her face, and she hugged him tightly. Sophia could not help but smile at the sight, finding it almost too intimate for her to be a part of.

"Should I leave you, your grace?" she murmured, as Lord Arthur and Sarah began to talk with one another. "I do apologize for the dancing, as well; it was only a few minutes of fun, I assure you."

Looking up at him, Sophia was surprised to find a curious gleam in his eye, as though a thought had suddenly struck him.

"No, you may carry on," he said abruptly. "Sarah, come here for a moment. Tell me, what dance was Miss Weston to be teaching you?"

"The waltz," Sarah replied, screwing up her face. "But I did not like it. I much prefer to do my own. I was being a butterfly, Papa."

Holding her breath, Sophia waited for the duke's reaction, only to let it out in a long breath, as he laughed, patting his daughter on the head. "Very good, my dear," he said, waving his hand at the pianist. "But I can assure you that you can be just as much a butterfly when you are waltzing as when you are dancing all on your own."

The music began to play again, and Sophia took a single step back from the duke and his daughter, thinking that he was about to lead Sarah onto the floor and show her some of the steps. However, much to her surprise, the duke turned to her and held out one hand.

"I think Miss Weston and I shall show you just what we mean, Sarah," he continued, his eyes still on his daughter, as he waited for Sophia to take his hand. "Your uncle may dance with you after you have watched us, if you wish."

Her throat constricted, as she stared at the duke, her heart quickening as her fingers hesitantly touched his. He grasped her hand firmly the moment she did so, as though not allowing her to escape, and they walked onto the dance floor.

Heat poured into her face as he let go of her hand and bowed, just as he might do had they met at a ball. Curtsying as best she could, Sophia trained her gaze to go over the duke's left shoulder, as he took her hand, jumping slightly when his other hand settled on her waist.

"I assume you know the steps, Miss Weston," he murmured, as he began to lead her across the floor. "No treading on my toes now."

Her eyes jumped to his, seeing the mirth there. Smiling a little hesitantly, she continued to allow him to lead, tension running through her limbs.

This was not right. A governess did not dance with a duke, not even when they were supposedly showing his daughter how it was to go. She could hear Sarah laughing and clapping as they continued to spin around the floor, her mind filling with thoughts and anxieties as the duke held her tightly.

"You must relax, Miss Weston," the duke murmured softly, "Look at me, please. You are wound like a spinning top; I can feel the tension in your hands."

"I do apologize, your grace," Sophia whispered, not able to drag her eyes toward his, as he had requested. "This is a little surprising for me."

He chuckled quietly. "That I can tell. You are a proficient

dancer, I am sure, but you still need to relax. Look at me, Miss Weston."

It was a command, not a request, and so, with her heart hammering in her chest, Sophia returned her gaze to his face.

His eyes were burning with a deep intensity, to the point that Sophia found herself entirely unable to look away. To her shock, he pulled her a little closer, a little too close given the impropriety of what they were already doing, and her breath hitched.

Something flickered over his face, sending a warm darkness into his eyes. Sophia clung to him, feeling entirely overwhelmed and feeling such a stirring of desire and affection within her that she was sure he would be able to tell were she to continue dancing with him much longer.

"Your grace," she whispered, through lips that were barely able to form words. "I–"

"Miss Weston," he interrupted, his words soft and for her ears only. "You are a wonderful dancer. Indeed, there is more to you than I ever expected. You have blossomed before my very eyes, as a beautiful rose might slowly reveal the beauty of its petals."

The compliment was as unexpected as the dance, her mouth going completely dry as he looked at her, a rush of heat crawling up her spine and into her face.

And then, the music came to a close. Sarah and her uncle were still busy dancing, although Sarah was getting none of the steps correct whatsoever, and much to Sophia's relief, neither of them seemed in the least bit interested in what had been going on between Sophia and the duke.

The duke slowly released her waist but kept her other hand in his. Sophia pressed her lips together as he lowered his head to her hand, his lips brushing the back of her hand as though she had truly been a lady at the ball, had truly been his dance partner for one of the two waltzes that would be played that evening.

Sparks shot into her vision, her skin prickling as he held her hand for just a moment too long. Nothing was said between them, but Sophia knew that she would never be able to see the duke in the same way again. She had been in his arms; she had felt the heat rushing through her veins, as she had danced with him and allowed her heart to fill with a rush of affection that could never be returned.

"Thank you, Miss Weston," he said, his voice a little hoarse as he stepped back. "I do hope my daughter was watching."

With one lingering look, he stepped away from her and walked back toward his daughter, who was still being spun around by her uncle. Sarah laughed aloud and ran toward Sophia, catching her hand and dragging her back toward the duke and Lord Arthur.

"My goodness, you are like a spinning top!" Lord Arthur declared, ruffling Sarah's dark curls. "I am sure you shall be just as good a dancer as Miss Weston one day."

"I am certain of it," the duke agreed, smiling down at his daughter. "Miss Weston is an excellent dancer and an even more excellent tutor, so I have no doubt that Sarah will turn out very well."

He did not look at her as he spoke those words, but the compliments brought Sophia a rush of pleasure.

"Thank you, your grace," she murmured, wondering when her heart would stop its furious thundering that had begun the moment the duke had asked her to dance. "I think it is time for our walk in the gardens, Sarah. Is that acceptable to you, your grace?"

"More than acceptable," the duke replied, lifting his eyes to hers. "Although dinner will be a little earlier than usual so that Sarah can join us."

Sophia nodded, setting her shoulders and drawing in a deep breath so that she might regain some sense of composure. "Of course. I will ensure Sarah is ready."

Lord Arthur cleared his throat, nudging his brother.

"Oh, of course, I quite forgot. Miss Weston, next week I am expecting a small party to join us at the house. My brother has recently returned from his travels and wishes to be reacquainted with a few friends."

Not quite sure how this affected her, Sophia nodded and glanced from one to the other. "I see."

"Sarah will be asked to join us at times during the day, and during your daily walks in the grounds, there may be others present," the duke continued, ignoring his daughter's squeals of excitement. "However, I will expect her education to continue for the most part, you understand."

"I quite understand," Sophia agreed, reaching forward and taking hold of Sarah's hand so as to quieten her. "Might I ask how long they will be staying for? Just so that I can prepare for some disruption to Sarah's lessons."

"No longer than ten days," the duke replied, with just a hint of displeasure in his voice, giving Sophia the impression that he was not exactly looking forward to his guests arriving. "You will have advance notice of when and where Sarah is to join us. Although, most days, I shall come to fetch her myself."

A hint of anxiety began to rattle through Sophia's chest as she wondered whether or not the duke expected her to join Sarah alongside the rest of the guests. She could not bear the thought of mixing with the *beau monde* again, not when she had been so removed from her status.

"Is everything quite all right, Miss Weston?"

Her eyes leapt back to his, and she nodded fervently, not wanting to explain her worries to him since that was not the done thing. "Yes, of course, your grace. Thank you."

He nodded, a slight frown settling between his brows, as she pressed Sarah's hand.

"Well then, good afternoon to you, Miss Weston. Sarah, enjoy your walk with Miss Weston. You are to join us for dinner. So, for heaven's sake, do not get yourself covered in mud or the like." His eyes twinkled, as he patted his daughter's cheek, making Sophia smile at the tenderness he displayed toward her.

"I will not, Papa," Sarah replied in a very serious voice. "I shall make sure to be perfectly clean."

"Of course, you will," Lord Arthur boomed, chuckling. "Enjoy yourself, little one. I will see you soon."

10

Try as she might, Sophia simply could not sleep. She had not so much as undressed, sitting by the dying embers of the fire with a book in her hand, although her eyes remained entirely unseeing as she looked at the lines within it.

The hour was late and still Sophia worried, her stomach turning over each time she thought about the house party that the duke was to host. She was terrified that he would ask her to join Sarah at some point and that she would have no choice but to step into the room filled with guests, aware of just how lowly her new position was. What was worse was that she was now concerned that one of the guests might recognize her, aware that she was Viscount Brookridge's sister, and that question after question would follow – along with a few mocking glances and scornful laughs.

Sighing to herself, Sophia tried to untie the knot of worry that had settled in her stomach but try as she might to calm her fractious mind, it would not leave her. Instead, it grew all the tighter, sending her heart fluttering, as she thought about what was to come.

"This is ridiculous," she said aloud, getting to her feet and walking to the mantlepiece to fetch a candle. "You just need to talk to the duke."

It was much easier said than done, however, for the thought of talking to the duke and telling him her worries and fears was not something she had ever done before. She had kept secret as much of her past and her family situation as she could, not wanting to tell him the shameful truth that she had been turned out from her own family's home.

Patting the locket that now sat around her neck, hidden entirely by the high collar of her dress, Sophia closed her eyes and let the wave of homesickness wash over her. It was not homesickness for her brother, but rather a longing for the life she'd once had with a happy, loving father and a gregarious, kind-natured brother. How much life had changed!

And yet, she had the blessing of Sarah in her life now. She was as loving and as sweet as could be, filling every day of Sophia's life with happiness. It took away the pain and agony that had been tearing at her heart, making her smile all the more ready and her heart all the more open to joy and delight. It was only the prospect of the houseguests that dimmed those a little.

"Well, come the morrow, I shall speak to him," Sophia determined aloud, opening the bedroom door, and with a candle in hand, slowly made her way along the dark hallways until she found the library door.

The library was one of her greatest delights in living under the duke's roof and she could not help but appreciate her good fortune in finding an employer so willing to allow her to read his books freely. The novel she had been attempting to read had not caught her interest, and so, thinking that another book might help her to rest her uneasy mind, Sophia stepped inside and closed the door.

"Miss Weston."

She shrieked in surprise, almost dropping her candle as she sagged back against the closed door, slapping on hand over her mouth in horror.

"I *do* apologize," the duke said, looking as horror-struck as she felt. "I did not mean to scare you."

"Oh, your grace," Sophia whispered, trying desperately to get her breath back. "I did not expect you to be here at so late an hour. I do apologize." Her free hand scrabbled at the door handle, desperate not to disturb him. "I shall return to my room at once."

"Wait."

The command hurried toward her, demanding that she let go of the door handle. She did so, her eyes closing tightly for a moment as she turned to face him. Only then did she see the fire burning brightly in the grate, the many candles lit around the room. Evidently, the duke had been unable to sleep also.

"I would not have you run away when you are obviously in need of a good book," the duke continued, as she turned back around. "Please, take as long as you wish."

Everything in her told her to leave, to hurry back toward her room, and to leave the duke in peace, but Sophia found her legs moving forward, her hand placing the candlestick down on a small table. Memories of how it had felt to be in his arms flooded her as she looked up into his eyes, aware that he wore no cravat, no jacket, and no waistcoat.

"I shall be very quick, your grace," she promised, hurrying to the other side of the room and as far away from him as possible. "I do not want to disturb you."

He chuckled and sat down in his seat, picking up his brandy glass. "You are not disturbing me, Miss Weston. In fact, I might be glad of your company for a time."

"My company?" Sophia repeated, finding herself a little at a loss as to what to do. It was not usual for a duke to spend time with his hired help, especially not when the doors were closed, and it was late at night. Embarrassment sent heat into her cheeks, and she fanned them with her hands, glad he could not see her.

"Indeed," the duke said quietly. "I cannot sleep because I have a great deal on my mind at present."

A sudden fear hit Sophia right between the eyes, her stomach tightening as though she had been punched. She slowly made her way into the light of the fire's glow, her eyes searching his face. "Do you mean, with Sarah?"

"Oh, no," he replied, with a wave of his hand. "You are doing a wonderful job, and you need have no concern in that regard. I assure you."

"Oh." The relief that flooded her must have shown on her face, for the duke laughed softly and shook his head.

"My goodness, Miss Weston, do I not let you know often enough that I find your education of my daughter to be more than acceptable? That is a failing on my part, and one that I must rectify."

Sophia, not quite sure what to say, simply cleared her throat and smiled, somewhat tremulously, in his direction. Her heart was beating quicker than before, aware of just how very alone they both were. Was this, perhaps, the time to talk to him about the worrying thoughts that were on her mind? He appeared more relaxed than she had ever seen him, and that gave her a little boost of encouragement.

"I think there is something on your mind also," the duke murmured, lifting the glass of brandy to his lips. "Do you wish to speak of it, Miss Weston? I am not much good with advice, but I would be glad to listen."

Her eyes lingered on the brandy glass, half wondering if it was the liquor that had made him so at ease, but deciding that she could not allow the opportunity to slip away, Sophia came to sit down opposite him.

His eyes flared as he watched her, sending a flurry of excitement into Sophia's belly. She tried her best not to feel anything but respect for her employer, but could not prevent the quickening of her heart or the warmth she felt in his presence.

"Your grace, you are quite right to suggest that I have something on my mind, for that is what has been keeping me awake this evening."

"Oh?" he queried, tipping his head to one side. "And what is it, Miss Weston?"

"It is about your guests, your grace," she explained, speaking quickly. "As you know, I come from a background of quality. For various reasons, I came to you as a governess – a position I am most grateful for."

He nodded, slowly, his eyes fixed on her own.

"I was just wondering if you would require me to join Sarah when she is to spend time with you and your guests," Sophia continued, lacing her fingers together. "I do not want to give the impression that I would not do as you ask, your grace, for I understand my position here very well, but it is that–"

"You are afraid that someone will recognize you," the duke interrupted quietly. "That would be embarrassing for you?"

Sophia nodded, the familiar ache returning to her throat as her mind turned to her brother. "I am afraid that my writing to you to seek the position of governess was not one of my own choosing," she said slowly, making sure to pick her words carefully. "I am very glad to have come here now, of course, but at the time, it was thrust upon me and came as a great surprise."

The duke's eyes grew curious, a slight frown between his brows. "You were given no choice in the matter?"

Pressing her lips together for a moment, Sophia thought about what to say. The duke appeared to be interested in what she had to say, more open to hearing her conversation than ever before, and despite her misgivings, Sophia felt herself grow desirous for him to know her better, even if he did not speak much about himself.

"My brother is Viscount Brookridge," she said softly. "My father died a few years ago, and so he took on the title."

"I see," he murmured, a slightly puzzled frown on his face. "I thought it might have been your father that had sent you to find such a position."

The ache in her throat became almost unbearable, as she drew in a long breath, steadying her frayed nerves. "No, your grace, it was my brother. You see, he married a little less than a year ago, and so, my position in his house became untenable."

A flare of anger crossed his expression, and he sat forward, his hands clasped firmly together. "Are you saying that there is no money for you? That your brother is almost destitute?"

"No, that is not what I mean at all," Sophia replied, realizing she was not explaining herself well at all. "My brother simply decided my future for me, so that I was not a financial burden to him any longer." Lifting her gaze from the floor to the duke's face, Sophia was surprised to discover that he appeared almost furious over what she had told him. "I do apologize if I have upset you, your grace," she finished shrinking back in her seat. "Perhaps I ought not to have opened my mouth."

"No," the duke murmured, leaning across and catching her hand in his. "I am glad you spoke to me, Miss Weston. I will confess to being very much surprised that your brother would send you here if there was enough money to continue to care for you." He lifted one eyebrow, and Sophia felt her embarrassment grow all the more.

"My brother did not allow me a Season," she whispered, lowering her gaze. "I will not go into his reasons."

There was a long pause. A pause where Sophia did not dare

lift her head, did not dare look into his eyes to see what expression there might be there. She did not want to see his pitying gaze, quite sure that this was what would be there.

Clearing his throat, the duke leaned forward in his seat. "Miss Weston, I quite understand your predicament. Of course, I will ensure that you have no need to encounter my guests when they are here."

Sighing with relief that she would not need to explain any more about her brother, and in particular that she would not have to greet any of the guests, Sophia lifted her gaze and smiled at him. As she did so, she felt his hand tighten on hers.

"I am sorry you have been so poorly treated by your own kin," the duke continued, his brows furrowing all the more. "That is shameful."

Shrugging slightly, Sophia's smile spread across her face. The way he had reacted to her story brought her a small amount of happiness, glad that he had believed her without question.

"I do not think it has turned out so badly," she replied honestly, allowing her fingers to intertwine with his despite the knowledge she should have pulled her hand away entirely. "I have met your daughter and find her to be such a delight that I have no cause to be upset or sad over my lack of family. I have had a happier time here these last few weeks than I have ever had at home with my brother. I can assure you that I do not find it a terrible situation, but rather one that has brought me a great deal of joy, and I thank you for that."

The duke did not reply for a while, simply looking into her eyes and keeping a hold of her hand. The silence grew thick, the atmosphere filling with a delicious tension that had anticipation rifling through Sophia although she had very little idea of what it was she expected.

"You are an extraordinary young woman," the duke whispered, eventually letting go of her hand and sitting back in his chair. "I believe myself to be quite blessed by your presence. Perhaps your brother has done us both a favor in being so unchivalrous, although I find myself rather angry with his uncouth behavior."

Sophia smiled and rose to her feet, feeling a burden roll from her shoulders. "Thank you, your grace. I do hope that whatever is on your mind will not keep you from sleep much longer."

He chuckled, only to look away into the fire with an almost sad expression on his face. Sophia wanted to ask him what was wrong; she wanted to find out what tore at his mind so, but instead, she held her tongue.

"Miss Weston," he said abruptly, as she began to move away toward the door. "Might you join me here tomorrow evening?"

"Tomorrow?" she repeated, a little confused. "Yes, of course, your grace."

His head twisted toward her, his eyes bright. "Good," he replied, with a smile on his face. "I find your company rather engaging and would like to continue our conversation."

Happiness burst through her, sending shivers up her spine as she saw the glint in his eyes. "I would be glad to, your grace," she murmured, bowing her head as she made her way toward the door. "Thank you and good evening."

"Good evening, Miss Weston," came the quiet reply.

11

The following day came and went, and as Matthew waited for his brother to choose to go to bed, he found himself growing all the more anticipatory for Miss Weston's arrival.

He had not seen her apart from a few passing meetings in the hallways, having been caught up with ensuring that everything was in order for the guests who would be arriving in three days' time. It was not something he was looking forward to in the least, although he had been enjoying his brother's company. Arthur had been full of tales about his adventures across the world, catching Sarah's attention completely over dinner, as he had regaled them both with story after story about where he had been.

Smiling to himself, Matthew got up and poured himself another whiskey, offering one to his brother, who accepted it without question

"That governess of yours," Arthur began, frowning. "There is something not quite right with her."

"Miss Weston, you mean?" Matthew replied, confused. "Whatever do you mean?"

Arthur shook his head. "She is much too proper to be a governess. The way she speaks, even the way she moves, tells me that she ought to be a refined, genteel lady. Instead, for whatever reason, she is here, teaching your little girl." He shrugged and took a mouthful of whiskey. "Not that this is a bad thing, of course. Sarah's a lovely little thing and is sure to turn out wonderfully with Miss Weston by her side."

Recalling how Miss Weston had spoken to him so candidly the previous evening, Matthew felt the same spurt of anger rush through him that he had felt when she had first told him of her past. "That is because she *is* a refined lady, Arthur," he explained, with a sigh. "I will not go into it, but I have discovered she was basically thrown from her brother's house for no good reason."

"Is that so?" his brother murmured thoughtfully. "What title does her brother hold then?"

"Viscount Brookridge, I believe," Matthew replied, with a shake of his head. "If I get a hold of him, I do not know what I will do. From what Miss Weston said, he turned her out simply so that he could keep more money for himself." He turned his gaze back to his brother, frowning as he saw him stare back at him, his eyes wide and cheeks pale. "For goodness sake, whatever is the matter?"

"Did you say, Viscount Brookridge?" he asked slowly, one hand now clasping the arm of the chair tightly. "Tell me you did not say Viscount Brookridge."

"Yes, I did," Matthew replied, understanding slowly beginning to dawn as horror filled him. "No, Arthur, it cannot be!"

"I do not know him particularly well," his brother pleaded, throwing back his whiskey in one gulp before shaking his head. "But I thought, since he has only recently gained his title, it might be nice to have him join us here."

His stomach roiled, as he thought of Viscount Brookridge

coming to stay in his home for a time, his hand tightening on his glass. "We must rescind the invitation."

"I do not think we can," his brother replied, heavily. "It takes a good few days of travel to come here, and by the time a letter reaches the house, they will have already left."

"I *cannot* have that particular gentleman here!" Matthew exclaimed, thumping the arm of his chair. "If what Miss Weston says is true – and I have no reason not to believe her – then to have him here will bring nothing but discord and upset. He is not the kind of man I wish to befriend, Arthur."

His brother stared at him for a moment, as though trying to find some solution but coming up with nothing. "I do not know what to do then," he muttered, eventually, passing one hand over his eyes. "I did not know, Matthew."

Aware that it was not his brother's fault, Matthew sank back into his chair, his heart painful. "I know you did not," he admitted quietly. "Nor did I until yesterday. Miss Weston has been very good at keeping her reasons for becoming a governess quiet."

"It is only ten days," his brother replied helpfully. "If Miss Weston is not to see the guests, and they do not see her, then there should be no reason for her to have any kind of contact with her brother and his wife."

Matthew shook his head. "I cannot keep this from her."

His brother frowned, tilting his head a little as he regarded him closely. "Do not tell me you have some kind of feelings for Miss Weston!"

The rebuttal did not spring to his lips as Matthew had expected. He opened his mouth to say something, anything, but it did not come to him. Staring at his brother, his heart began to quicken, urgency flooding him as he thought of something to say, only for Arthur to laugh out loud, slapping his thigh in the process.

"By Jove, Matthew! I never thought I would see the day."

Going hot all over, Matthew shook his head, trying to find something to explain all that was going on within his heart.

"Not that I think it is a bad thing, of course! I would have usually pushed you away from a governess, but since she was the daughter of a viscount, I can see no difficulty in you pursuing.... whatever it is that is between you." Arthur's mouth tipped up, his eyes glinting with mirth that Matthew could not quite understand.

"It is not like that," Matthew retorted, firmly. "There is nothing–"

"I did wonder, when I saw you waltzing with her," his brother interrupted, chuckling quietly. "My goodness, Matthew, I must say I am very pleased for you. After what happened with Elizabeth – God rest her soul – I think it is high time you found someone you actually held some affection for."

Swallowing hard, Matthew closed his eyes and frowned, trying to clear his muddled thoughts. His brother appeared so certain that Matthew felt something for Miss Weston—whilst he, himself, continued to grow more and more confused about what it was beginning to burn with him.

"You do not have to hide it from me any longer," Arthur continued, offhand. "It is a little surprising, but as I said, it is high time you had someone who cares for you in your life. I have seen the way Miss Weston looks at you, the blush on her cheeks when you speak to her. I am glad for you, truly."

"You are much too quick to assume things," Matthew retorted, opening his eyes and glaring at his brother. "I have no strong emotion for Miss Weston other than a desire to protect her from those who had mistreated her thus far. The rest is just muddled in with that particular feeling, I am sure."

His brother rolled his eyes, the grin remaining plastered across his face. "Is that so?" he murmured lazily. "Well, you can hide it from yourself for as long as you wish, but even from the uncomfortable way you look at me I can tell there is more going on than you wish to make known." He held up two hands, as though protesting his innocence. "Fear not, I shall not speak of it any longer."

"And nothing to Miss Weston," Matthew grated, suddenly afraid that she might walk into the library at any moment and find them both there discussing her. "As I said, Arthur, I am not altogether certain what is going on within my heart. It has all been rather confusing and has certainly come upon me rather quickly."

Arthur shrugged, getting up to pour himself another brandy. "Well, how long does it take for one to fall in love?" he asked, more softly than before. He raised his glass in a toast, his gleeful expression fading only to be replaced with a serious smile. "Do not shirk from this, Matthew. Do not run from it. I know how much you have despised the thought of returning to London's society, how much you dreaded going to meet the ladies of the *beau monde* in the hope of making one of them your bride. I know that you did not want to meet another like Elizabeth, that you have often dreamed about having more. It is not a foolish desire to seek affection between you and your bride, but being as practical as you are, you have sent that idea aside in the knowledge that it is not likely to happen." His smile broadened as he stretched his arms out wide. "And now, here is a lady right within your own home, one who has hoped for nothing but employment so that she might support herself. I can tell she has not tried to wangle her way into your feelings, that she has in no way attempted to find an association with you that might induce you into marrying her. Instead, she has put her time and effort into Sarah, just as she was expected to do. Does that not say a great deal about her character in itself?"

"Yes, it does," Matthew agreed, with a small sigh. "Except it is not her character that has ever come into question. It is the fact that I am unsure what to do about the unwanted feelings within my heart. I may only be wishing to protect her, angry that her brother has treated her so poorly. That does not mean that there is anything of substance there; nothing that will last the test of time."

Arthur nodded sagely, lowering his arms. "Then, mayhap, you need to have a few more conversations with her. Allow yourself to show something of your own struggles, your own life, with her, and see how she responds. Build a trust between you that can begin to grow into something more. That will let you know whether or not the feelings you have for Miss Weston can ever become something substantial."

Looking up at his brother, Matthew was struck by just how wise he appeared to be. It was as though he had experience with such things, as though he knew exactly what Matthew felt because he had felt the same himself.

"Something you want to tell me, Arthur?" he asked softly. "Someone you met on your travels, mayhap?"

His brother's smile grew a little mischievous, his eyes twinkling. "Perhaps, but that is not a story for tonight. Another time, I think, when your heart is a little more settled." He smiled at him, lifting his brandy glass again. "To your health, Matthew. Goodnight."

12

Sophia had made her way to and from the library on three separate occasions, but, each time, had retreated back to her own room having heard the duke and his brother talking.

Her stomach swirled with a delicious excitement, as she made her way back along the hallway, her slippered feet making no sound as she walked. The duke had wanted to speak to her again, and that in itself was something she could be glad about. It had been rather freeing to speak so openly with him last evening about her brother, although she had chosen not to express the depths of her feelings toward Peter in doing what he did. The duke had listened carefully and had appeared to be rather upset for her, which Sophia had found somewhat touching. Even though he did not know her particularly well, and even though she was the hired help, he was still angry enough about the whole situation—enough to allow it to show in his expression and his words.

And then he had asked her to come back and talk to him again this evening. She had not been able to refuse, aware that her pulse was beating somewhat erratically as he had held her hand in his. There was something growing between them, something that should be completely forbidden, and yet remained there, as undeniable as ever.

She should not be going back to speak to him again; she should not be so willing to be alone in his company, but the desire to do just that could not be ignored. She wanted to talk to him, to have him talk to her so that she might learn more about him, more about his life and his character, his hopes and desires, his struggles and dreams. It was, perhaps, foolish to hope for all of that to be shared since their association was still one of employer and servant for the most part, but the chance to simply talk to another living soul, to be able to speak with more freedom than she had been able to for a long time was so great.

There were no voices from within the library, and tentatively, Sophia knocked on the door, hearing the duke's low voice call out to her almost at once. With excitement rifling through her veins, she stepped inside and looked all about her, seeing the duke sitting by the fire, his head tipped a little to the side as she came in.

"Your grace," she murmured, coming nearer to him. "Do you still wish to converse this evening? I am more than happy to retire if you would prefer to be alone."

He smiled at her and warmth pooled in her core.

"No, indeed, I would be glad to speak to you," he replied, gesturing for her to come and sit down. "I have a few things I need to apprise you of as well."

She sat down carefully, folding her hands in her lap. "Oh?"

He waved a hand. "They will come later." His eyes lingered on her for a moment or two, his smile remaining fixed. "I was just thinking about our conversation last evening. I was sorry to hear of your brother's treatment of you. I can understand now why you appeared so upset when you first arrived."

She laughed, wincing just a little. "Yes, indeed. It was all a bit of a shock." Recalling how she had been dropped at the bottom of the driveway with her four bags, she shook her head ruefully. "The day I walked with my bags was only the beginning of all the changes I had come to expect. How glad I am that you have proven to be a kind and compassionate man, your grace. I have been truly blessed in coming here."

"That is very good of you to say," the duke murmured softly. "This home was once a place of deep sadness, and so I am relieved to know that you find it so appealing."

Sophia's breath caught, and she held it for a moment, waiting to see if the duke would say more whilst not wanting to pry. Sarah had never mentioned her mother, and aside from being aware that the duchess had passed away some years ago, Sophia was entirely in the dark about the lady.

"My wife passed away soon after bringing my daughter into this world," the duke murmured, his gaze now lingering on the flickering flames of the fire. "It was a long, hard labor, and a fever set in."

Her heart broke for him, wondering if his marriage had been a happy one and how much of a loss it had been for him to lose his bride.

"We were not long married," he continued, a faraway look in his eyes, as he glanced back at her. "It was a marriage of convenience." He shrugged, a sad smile on his face. "After all, it is what is expected of a duke."

"I am terribly sorry, your grace," Sophia whispered, a lump in her throat as she thought of him standing by his wife's bedside with baby Sarah in his arms. "That must have been a very difficult time for you."

He blinked and turned back to her, his eyes filled with sadness. "I did not care for her in the way I should have, Miss Weston, and I can assure you that she did not care for me in the least. Sarah was the only good thing that came from our marriage, aside from the connection created for both of our families." His eyes glazed over, his lips twisting, as he frowned heavily, his voice low and husky. "I swore I would never be in that kind of situation again."

Her hands tightened in her lap, as Sophia struggled to think of what to say. She knew precisely what it was she wanted to express, but as yet, she was not certain he would not think her rude if she spoke with such freedom as she might with a friend.

"My brother, of course, began to write to me a great deal more often when Elizabeth passed, but he has only visited once since then."

"I am sure you are very glad to have him back with you now," Sophia murmured softly. "He seems to be a very kind man."

The duke chuckled. "You saw him with Sarah, did you not? And that told you the kind of man he was?"

"Indeed," Sophia replied without any hesitation. "I always think how a gentleman or a lady treats either a child or a servant says a great deal about their character."

The duke nodded slowly, looking at her thoughtfully. "That is very astute, Miss Weston."

There was a short silence, as the duke looked back into the fire, clearly lost in thought. Sophia closed her eyes tightly, drawing in a long breath, as what she wanted to say, what she wanted to express, refused to let go of her mind.

"It sounds as though you were...somewhat lonely these last few years," Sophia ventured, her stomach tightening, as she finally gave voice to her thoughts, praying that he would not think she had overstepped in expressing such a thing. "I can well understand that, your grace. It lingers for a long time, does it not, even when there is company to be found?"

Slowly, he turned his whole body back toward her, his eyes pensive, as he regarded her carefully. She could almost see the way he was thinking about what she had said, her nerves stretched taut as she waited for him to respond.

"You have seen more in me than anyone else," he murmured, looking at her as though she were a gift sent from heaven. "Yes, that loneliness still lingers. My daughter gets all of my heart and soul, for she is the one that fills my life with joy. But yet, when it is late and there is no one else about, I have often felt wrapped in the arms of loneliness." A slow smile spread across his face, his gaze flickering across her features. "And yet I have found that feeling dissipating somewhat since your arrival."

Sophia shivered.

She could not look away from him, the only sound the crackling of the wood as it burned. She could feel a long, slow heat began to burn all through her, her breath quickening as he smiled slowly.

"You are good for me and for my daughter, I do believe," he said quietly. "I do not think I should ever want you to leave."

His words rang around her mind, capturing her heart. She could tell that he had surprised himself by what he had said, as though he had never meant to say it out loud. His eyes flared, and in a moment of embarrassment, he cleared his throat gruffly and turned his face away from her.

"I think I should retire now, your grace," Sophia said, aware that tension was now crackling between them. He had said too much; she had said too little; and whatever it was that she felt, or he felt, it was not to be said tonight.

"Thank you for coming to speak with me, Miss Weston," he murmured, as she rose from her chair. "I do hope I have not put you off coming to speak with me again another time."

A swell of relief ran through her, and she managed a quick smile, inclining her head as she remembered her place. She had forgotten that she was the governess for a few minutes, forgotten that she was Miss Weston, the hired help. She had thought herself back amongst the best of society, engaging in conversation with a gentleman of the *ton.*

"No, indeed not, your grace," she replied softly. "I will be glad to come and talk to you again, whenever you may wish it. I find your conversation to be very pleasant, and I have greatly enjoyed speaking to you."

He nodded, his lips quirking into a small smile. "As have I. Good evening, Miss Weston."

"Good evening, your grace," she whispered, leaving the room and closing the door softly behind her.

13

Unfortunately for Sophia, the fact that guests were soon to descend on the house sent the household into an uproar. She had no time to speak to the duke again, and—in fact—she barely saw him as she went about her duties. Her charge was in rather high spirits, far too excited about the ladies and lords who were to appear very soon, and so Sophia found herself giving all of her energy to the girl. Mathematics and writing took much longer than they ought, given that Sarah was so easily distracted, and to Sophia's frustration, she found herself growing irritated much more easily.

It was, therefore, something of a relief for the guests to finally show face. Sophia laughed, as Sarah danced about the room chattering wildly about the carriage she had spotted from the window.

"Go and sit down by the window and ensure you are well hidden," Sophia instructed, choosing to seat herself at the desk where she kept all of her notes as well as Sarah's own work. "You may describe the carriages to me if you wish, although I will warn you that there may be a great length of time between one carriage and the next!"

This, however, did not appear to put Sarah off in the least. A good two hours passed and only four carriages appeared, but there was enough business at the front of the house to keep the girl entertained.

Sophia listened with only half an ear, working through her notes of what Sarah had covered and what needed to be repeated or done in a little more detail. It was only when Sarah commented on a particular carriage that she frowned, giving the child her full attention for a moment, only for Sarah to squeal in delight as another carriage appeared just after.

Shaking her head wryly, Sophia continued with her own work, trying to ignore the ball of tension that sat in her stomach. She was feeling nervous about the guests inhabiting the house, even though it was for less than two weeks and she would, most certainly, keep herself away from them. In fact, she would not be in their company, and would therefore, most likely never meet any of them face-to-face.

However, just knowing that her peers were within the duke's house made her stomach clench. It was difficult knowing that she could easily mix amongst them, that her status as a viscount's daughter made it more than acceptable for her to do so, but that she simply could not. She had been demoted to a governess by her brother's choice, not by her own decision. To be in society now would be more shame than enjoyment.

And yet, she thought, glancing toward Sarah, there was a great deal of enjoyment in what she did. She was very fond of Sarah and had found her time in the duke's home to be a time of happiness. Mayhap, that was because the duke showed her more attention than should be expected. Regardless, Sophia found herself glad at her new position in life. It was better than living with her brother and sister-in-law, looked down on and discarded by them in all things and in all ways. Here she had company, purpose, and respect—more than her brother had shown her in a long time.

"There are so many beautiful ladies," Sarah sighed, pressing her face almost flat against the pane. "Look at them all, Miss Weston!"

Smiling to herself, Sophia made her way to the window just as the two horses and carriages were led away. A slight frown creased her brow, as she caught sight of the coat of arms on the side of the carriage, a stab of recognition hitting her. It was only the briefest of glances, and yet, she felt as though she ought to recognize it. The familiar feeling of worry settled over her again, growing almost queasy at the thought that an old acquaintance might be at the duke's house party.

Shaking her head, she threw her thoughts away and let herself get caught up in Sarah's excitement. Another carriage rolled up the driveway, and Sarah let out a gasp as a tall lady exited the carriage, her fine dress the object of Sarah's delight. Much to Sophia's relief, she did not recognize this particular lady, nor the gentleman who came out of the carriage afterward to stand by her side. What she did see was the duke greeting his new guests, her eyes fixing on him for a moment. He was as jovial as she had ever seen him, his delighted greetings reaching through the window to her ears. She could not hear any words in particular, but his effusions were obvious.

A small, wry smile tipped her mouth. She knew very well that the duke did not care for such company, and yet, here he was, playing the part of host with as much enthusiasm as he could muster. No one would doubt that he wanted them here, that he was looking forward to being with them in the house. Only she – as well as perhaps the duke's brother – knew the truth.

A sharp rap at the door caught her attention, and as she turned, she saw the footman step inside with a note in his hand.

"Thank you," Sophia murmured, taking it from him and wondering what it might be about. "Do I need to reply?"

The footman shrugged, a little more at ease with her than with the duke due to her station. "I was not instructed to wait, Miss Weston."

"Very well. Thank you," she murmured, as the footman closed the door. The note was not sealed, and unfolding it, Sophia looked down at the bottom of the page and saw the duke's signature. A flurry of excitement wrapped around her belly, and whilst giving herself a stern talking to, Sophia left Sarah where she sat and took herself back to her desk.

'Miss Weston,' the note began. *'There are some things I must speak to you about without delay. I had hoped to find a time to talk with you before the guests arrived, but I am afraid it is not to be so. Please come to my study this evening at precisely ten o'clock.'*

The note was not signed, ending rather abruptly Sophia's thought. Her excitement faded only to be replaced by a growing concern. Was something wrong?

WHEN THE NURSE came to sit with Sarah for dinner, Sophia was more than ready to spend some time on her own. Her head was filled with thoughts of the guests and the note the duke had sent, worrying about what it might mean.

Making her way from the nursery to her own room, she paused for a moment, looking down at the papers in her hand. She was due to give the duke a report on Sarah's progress, and whilst she knew he would be busy with all his guests, she did not want to delay her report.

"But you will be seeing him this evening," she murmured to herself, knowing that she did not need to go directly to his study at this very moment. Worrying, however, that the duke would wish to talk to her about Sarah's education, Sophia did not go into her room but rather looked down the empty corridor. The guests would be dining soon enough, for the duke kept country hours, so there was very little chance that she would meet anyone unexpectedly. Biting her lip, Sophia set her shoulders and began to walk swiftly down the corridor, knowing that none of the guests would be anywhere near her quarters. She would find a footman soon enough and would hand the papers to him to leave in the duke's study.

"Ah," she exclaimed, seeing a footman walking along the hallway toward her, having just reached the top of the staircase. "Might I ask you to set this in the duke's study?"

The footman frowned but took the papers from her.

"I would do it myself, but I do not want to meet any of the guests unexpectedly," she continued, aware that it was something of a poor excuse. "Thank you."

The footman, still looking somewhat unimpressed, turned his back on her and walked swiftly away from her, leaving Sophia to let out a long breath of relief before making her way back toward her own rooms.

"Sophia?"

The voice was high pitched and filled with astonishment, and with a slow sense of horror filling her, Sophia turned around.

Viscountess Brookridge, her sister-in-law, was staring at her with a slight smirk around her mouth.

"Good evening," Sophia said, crisply, aware of just how hard her heart was hammering. "You will have to excuse me. I am expected back."

"I hardly recognized you!" Lady Brookridge exclaimed, ignoring her completely. "I did not know that it was the duke who had taken you in!"

Sophia's hands grew clammy, as she held herself stiffly, desperate for this conversation to be over.

"It is good that I have found you, however," Lady Brookridge continued, with a slight sigh. "Your brother has come to regret what happened, Sophia. I think he wishes you to return home."

Suspicion lodged itself in Sophia's mind.

"You can come back with us, of course," Lady Brookridge continued, as though it was all settled. "We are here for the full ten days, and then we leave. Will you be ready by then?"

Sophia looked into her sister-in-law's cold, calm face and drew in a long breath, calming her frantically beating heart. "Lady Brookridge, I will not be returning with you and Peter. My place is here. I am employed here, and I am more than satisfied with my role."

Lady Brookridge laughed and waved a hand. "Nonsense, you'll be coming back with us. I am sure the duke will understand once he knows who you really are."

"He is already aware of my circumstances."

That seemed to take the wind from Lady Brookridge's sails. Her eyebrows furrowed, her hands clasping in front of her. For a moment or two, there was silence.

"If he is aware of who you are, then there can be no difficulty in explaining why you must return," Lady Brookridge said slowly. "We need you back at home, Sophia."

Seeing the lady touch her stomach gently, Sophia realized what she meant. Her eyes widened, her hands planting themselves on her hips.

"You want me to play nursemaid?"

Lady Brookridge looked astonished for a moment before laughing and waving one hand. "Well, you have already gained so much experience here that it would be most untoward not to consider you for what will be your own niece or nephew!" she exclaimed, as though Sophia was joining in with her mirth. "You will be a wonderful governess to our little one."

Filled with sudden, furious anger, Sophia stepped forward

and looked directly into the viscountess's eyes. She was not intimidated by her, nor was she about to give in to the viscountess's demands simply because of who she was.

"I will not be leaving the duke's home just because you decide that I am to be useful again," she said in a low voice. "I will *not* be returning; I will *not* be governess to your child and certainly will *not* be doing as you ask ever again. I am happy here and have every intention to remain. Now," she finished, lifting her chin a notch, "do excuse me, Lady Brookridge. I do not think that I will have either need or opportunity to see you again. I wish you a pleasant and safe journey home when the time comes."

Spinning on her heel, Sophia hurried along the hallway, her governess dress billowing out behind her. She was both angry and upset, feeling hot tears prick at her eyes. It had been a shock to see her sister-in-law here, but to be asked – to be *told* that she would supposedly be leaving this place to return home – was both infuriating and insulting.

Slamming the door of her bedchamber closed, Sophia slid down the length of the door before burying her head in her knees. Tears dampened her dress as her shoulders shook, sobs shaking her frame. Once again, she was being treated as nothing more than a possession, useful in various ways until her brother and sister-in-law decided that she was no longer of any kind of use. Then she would be sent away, married off, or some other option chosen by her brother.

"No," she whispered to herself, firmly. "I am going to stay here. They cannot force me to leave." Her head dropped, her shoulders slumping. "Can they?"

Her heart beat wildly, her eyes burning with fresh tears. The thought of leaving the duke, of leaving Sarah, put nothing but fear into her heart. A vision of the duke fluttered into her memory, the feelings of just how happy she had been to talk with him soothing her pained heart.

Should she tell him about what her sister-in-law had said? Would he want to know? Would he care? The answer was already in her heart, knowing that he would want to hear what had been said.

Her tears slowly abated, as the thought of speaking to the duke brought a sense of calmness to her injured heart. She did not have long to wait now.

14

Matthew wanted nothing more than to escape to the quietness of his study, and hopefully, to the company of Miss Weston. Yet, he was still forced to entertain his host of guests.

His brother, of course, was having a wonderful time. Matthew could see him down at the pianoforte, offering to turn the pages of the music for whichever young lady it was sitting down to play. He, himself, was enjoying drinking his port in one of the large comfortable chairs in the corner, managing to keep himself mostly separate from the large crowd of guests. Soon enough, he would be able to excuse himself, citing some business that needed to be seen to, although the minutes were ticking by with agonizing slowness.

"Your grace!"

Looking up, Matthew tried not to let a grimace settle on his face, as he saw Lady Brookridge approach him with her husband not far behind. Out of all of his guests, he could not find them in any way amiable. They were both rather full of themselves, loud and exuberant. They had both commented on practically everything they had seen, touched, or eaten since they had arrived, gushing over him and his home.

Matthew had not been impressed.

"Lady Brookridge," he murmured, getting out of his seat so as not to be rude. "How are you this evening?"

"Well," Lady Brookridge replied, with a gleam in her eye. "I was just telling my husband how surprised I was to discover that you have someone we know within your household."

A ripple of unease settled in his stomach. He had not had the opportunity to talk to Sophia about the presence of her family in his home. Now, it appeared that they had somehow met her already. What had been said? Was she quite all right? Had they upset her? Laughed at her? Mocked her?

"My wife tells me you have employed a new governess," Lord Brookridge chuckled, his eyes bright with too much liquor. "I do hope she is doing well."

They have no shame, Matthew thought to himself, his hands twisting together as he struggled to contain his anger. Most of the *ton* would be embarrassed to discover that their relation was in employment in another home, but it was clear that neither of them particularly cared.

"We had to send her away, of course," Lady Brookridge murmured, a little more quietly. "Circumstances had changed, and it was best for her to find employment."

"It was not as though she would have much success in London," Viscount Brookridge chuckled, rolling his eyes. "Such a plain thing, is she not? Best suited to a governess. Although, I do hope she has not let you down in that regard. Never too sure just how much she was able to take in, you know."

"Miss Weston is quite intelligent, and I am very pleased with her," Matthew grated, finding their company more and more intolerable the longer they spoke. "She has done a remarkable job with my daughter thus far."

Viscount Brookridge nodded slowly, shooting a glance toward his wife that had Matthew wondering what they were about. There was something more to this conversation than simple discussion, he realized, frowning heavily.

"We will have to take her back with us, you understand," Viscount Brookridge finished, clearing his throat briskly. "My wife is due to have our son or daughter in a few months' time, and we will require Sophia's help."

Matthew felt himself bristle with fury, their clear disregard for Sophia and her own wishes causing him a great deal of frustration.

"I am sure you will understand," Viscountess Brookridge continued calmly, as though it were all settled. "Ten days' time and we shall have to take her with us."

Clearing his throat, Matthew lifted his chin and pinned the viscountess with his gaze. He was not about to let Miss Weston go just because her sister-in-law decided that she wanted Sophia's help for her own child when the time came.

"Miss Weston is in my employ, and I have no intention of ending her employment here," he said firmly. "She is doing wonderfully with my daughter, and since I know she does not wish to leave, then I will be ensuring that she stays."

Viscount Brookridge frowned, his eyes glazing over. "I say, your grace, that is a little high-handed, do you not think?"

Matthew arched one eyebrow, as though reminding Lord Brookridge who he was speaking to, but the man did not so much as look away.

"*If* you will excuse me," Matthew said, aware that the conversation was not about to continue. "I think there are some matters of business that I need to see to." Leaving them standing together in the drawing room, Matthew caught his brother's eye and jerked his head. Arthur nodded and gave him a half smile, telling him silently that he understood exactly what Matthew was saying. He would continue as the host of the party until the guests chose to retire. Relieved that he could escape them, Matthew slipped out of the door and made his way along the corridor, breathing hard with anger.

He had known that he would not enjoy Viscount Brookridge and his wife's company but had never thought that they would ever find out that Sophia was within the household. It must simply have been a chance encounter, one that might have greatly upset her.

Clenching his fists, Matthew hurried to his study, looking up at the clock as he entered. She would be here within a few minutes.

Letting out a long breath, Matthew considered what life would be like without Miss Weston in his home. He was surprised at just how much pain stole through his heart at the thought, aware that it would greatly affect both himself and his daughter. Sarah would be devastated if Miss Weston were to leave, for it was more than obvious just how much she loved her governess. He had seen his daughter brighten the moment Miss Weston stepped into the room and had seen the happy smile on her face as she walked with Miss Weston in the gardens. There was so much love shared between them that he could not bear to think of it being ripped away from his daughter.

What would he feel about it all? Would he miss Miss Weston, were she to leave?

The answer was not something he needed to consider for more than a second or two. To have her gone from his life when they were only just beginning to get to know one another brought him nothing but sadness. He did not want to lose her.

"She cannot go," he whispered to himself, beginning to pace up and down the study floor. "I cannot be without her."

The feelings he had for Miss Weston suddenly flared to life, burning with a sudden, deep passion. They had been so small, so timid before, but now they burst through him with such an intensity that he fought to catch his breath.

His brother was right. He *had* been hating the prospect of returning to London for the Season, to find himself a suitable wife that would be no better and no worse than Elizabeth. He had resigned himself to the fact that his bride would neither love nor care for him, although he had hoped that there might be some kind of tolerable affection between them. The last thing he had wanted for himself and his daughter was a cold, distant woman so like his first wife.

And yet now, here in his home, he had a young, genteel young lady of good breeding, who loved his daughter with such gentle tenderness that it was obvious to everyone who saw them. He did not need to worry about Sarah when she was with Miss Weston, for he had no doubt that she was being both well taught and well cared for. Miss Weston was not someone who held her heart back from her charge; she did not keep herself from showing any kind of affection to Sarah. She was almost as devoted to his daughter as he was.

But marriage?

The thought pierced his mind, knowing that if he revealed his affections to her, then that would lead to one of two outcomes. Either he would have her as his bride, or she would leave his home and his heart forever. It was not as though he did not believe she had no thought of him in her own heart, for he had caught her shy glances and flare of light in her eyes when they had talked, when he had smiled at her, when he had told her that he could not think of his home without her in it. But to move to more than that was somewhat dangerous ground. He did not care about the scandal that might follow them should he marry her. After all, he was a duke and cared very little for what rumors might attach themselves to him. Besides which, it was not as though Miss Weston was in any way a poor, untitled spinster with no good family or fortune to speak of. She was the daughter of a viscount, which meant there could be no difficulty in the wedding. It might raise a few eyebrows, but that would not bother them here, not when they would live so far away from London.

"Good gracious," he murmured, sinking down into a chair as his legs grew suddenly weak. Was he truly thinking about marrying Miss Weston? Was he doing so in order to keep her in his household, or because he truly wanted to do so?

It was a question he could not easily answer, his emotions tied up in knots as he put his head in his hands, trying to sort out one lot of feelings from the other.

A quiet rap at the door signaled the arrival of the person he had been waiting for. Without calling out, he rose to his feet and went to open the door himself, turning the handle and pulling it back.

Miss Weston looked back at him, her eyes red-rimmed and face pale in the lamplight.

"Oh, Miss Weston," Matthew said heavily. "I am truly sorry for what has occurred. I meant to tell you. Please, do come in."

She nodded and stepped inside, her fingers knotting together in front of her. Feeling nothing but guilt over what he had neglected to do in warning her about the presence of Lord and Lady Brookridge, Matthew shut the door firmly and turned the key in the lock. He was not about to be disturbed.

15

"Miss Weston," the duke began, coming to sit down opposite Sophia. "As I have said, I am truly sorry for what has happened. I should have made it a matter of urgency to speak to you about their presence, but I did not think that you would have any chance to meet them."

Sophia saw the honesty in his eyes as she looked back at him, her hands growing painful as she tightened her fingers again and again.

"It is quite all right, your grace," she said slowly, her heart breaking into pieces within her. "You need not apologize."

"No, but I must," he said earnestly. "I should have shown you more consideration than that."

Sophia wanted to lean forward, to beg him to catch her as she cried in his arms, but she remained exactly as she was, her body tense. "I think it is best that I return with my brother and his wife when this house party is over." The words stuck to her throat, her whole body aching with agony as she said them aloud, knowing that she did not want to do anything of the sort, but that there was no other choice open to her.

The duke's mouth fell open as he gaped at her, his eyes wide.

"I-I am sorry," she stammered, not sure where to look as tears fell from her eyes. "I do not want to go, but I think I must." Closing her eyes, Sophia winced inwardly. She should not have said that. She was not to raise the slightest suspicion.

"No," the duke replied firmly, as she opened her eyes again. "No, Miss Weston. I will not discharge you from my employ."

Tears dripped onto her cheeks. "I am sorry," she whispered quietly. "I–"

"Do you not care for my daughter?"

His words were a lance to her soul, and she very nearly broke down. Drawing in a shuddering breath, Sophia tried her best to keep a control on her emotions, already filled with pain over the idea of leaving Sarah behind.

"I know you do," the duke continued, getting up out of his seat and looking down at her, as though he could not quite believe what she was saying. "I know you love my daughter almost as much as I do. Why then would you leave simply because your brother demands it? I had not thought he had such a hold on you."

"He does not," Sophia whispered, softly. "He–he has made some requests of me, and whilst my heart is breaking over the thought of leaving you – I mean, of leaving Sarah, I know that I must. It is the best thing for everyone." Her voice had lowered to a whisper, as she forced the words from her lips, her heart tearing with agony and causing her breathing to become ragged. Her head dropped, her gaze landing on the embroidered rug at her feet instead of up at the duke. She could feel his penetrating stare on her; she could see his shadow spreading out across the floor, but still, she remained silent. There was nothing for her to say, nothing for her to explain. She had to keep silent. They might be listening.

"Sophia."

His voice was nothing more than a whisper, catching her

ears and pressing itself to her heart. She began to sob then, hearing the tenderness in his voice, hearing the gentleness that urged her to tell him everything.

The duke dropped to his knees in front of her, taking her cold hands in his and looking up earnestly into her face.

"Sophia," he said again, a little more loudly this time. "I know you do not want to leave us. I know that something has happened that is forcing you to say these things when it goes against everything you want. I cannot allow you to go back to that house, where you will be mistreated and disrespected, robbed of your dignity, and forced to do whatever they ask for fear that they will throw you from the house if you do not. I know what you have told me and what you have left unsaid about your situation with your brother. I can see the pain written on your face. I have spoken to the viscount and to his wife and find them both to be exceedingly arrogant and practically heartless. Unless you give me a very good reason, Sophia, I will not allow you to leave with them." One eyebrow lifted, as a small smile played around his mouth. "Mayhap I shall keep you locked in the study until you agree to stay, or until they are forced to leave. Ten days is a long time, but I think I could manage to be in your company for that long."

His light manner forced a small smile to her lips, even though her heart was breaking all the more.

"I must go, your grace," she began, her throat working. "You do not understand."

Pressing her hands, he lifted one hand and let it trail down her cheek, forcing her to look into his eyes. Sparks shot through her, her mind whispering that she needed to trust him, that she needed to let him know all that was going on.

"They might be listening," she whispered, the words falling, almost unwillingly, from her lips.

The duke's gaze shot to the door and back again. "Then we

shall talk quietly," he said, getting up from his knees and pushing a chair toward her before sitting down in front of her. He did not hesitate but took her hands in his again; his eyes fixed on her own.

Sophia knew she was lost.

She could not keep this back from him, not when he could see through her so well. She had not been able to convince him that to return home with her brother and sister-in-law had been a decision of her own making, for he knew just how poorly treated she had been. Of course, he knew how happy she was presently, how much she loved Sarah, for had he not once told her that she appeared to have practically blossomed before his very eyes since the day she first arrived?

"I am afraid," she confessed quietly. "I am afraid of what they will do."

His eyes darkened. "You are talking about your brother and sister-in-law," he said slowly. "I am sorry you ever saw them."

"It was Lady Brookridge who saw me first," Sophia began, knowing that she would have to lay the full weight of her heart out before him. "It was purely by chance, you understand, but she demanded that I return home to care for their child when it is born." A twist of distaste clamped her gut. "I think they thought I would be more than delighted to do so, as though all I have been waiting for is the chance to return to their bosom."

The duke let out a small chuckle. "I can see that you found that idea less than appealing."

"I told her as much," Sophia replied, her brow creasing. "I think Lady Brookridge was a little taken aback. Perhaps she has forgotten just how much I dislike being in both her and my brother's company." She winced, realizing just how forceful those words sounded, but the duke did not seem to notice. "You can imagine my surprise when they appeared at my bedchamber door."

His eyes opened wide, and he stared at her, making her lips tip in a rueful smile.

"I will not blame any of the staff for directing them to my chamber," she continued quickly, not wanting anyone to be punished for doing something as innocuous as sending a viscount and viscountess where they wanted to go. "It was clear from the moment I opened my door that they were not about to leave my room without getting the answer they desired." Her eyes shut of their own accord, as she recalled that dreadful moment, the moment when it felt as though the ground had opened and swallowed her, holding her tightly until she agreed to do what her brother demanded. "Unless I return home, my brother will spread rumors about you and...and me, your grace," she whispered, feeling shame heap itself in abundance on her shoulders. "He has promised to make them so terrible that your daughter will never be able to hold her head up in society, not even when it comes time for her come out."

A sharp intake of breath caught her ears, and she opened her eyes slowly, feeling the duke squeeze her hands almost painfully.

"I am sorry," she finished, not knowing what else to say. "I think it is best that I go with them, your grace. I will not have any harm come to you or your daughter."

He did not say anything for a few minutes; his jaw clenched as his eyes darted around the room. It was clear that he was struggling to keep a hold of his temper, his breathing quick and fast.

"This is not something you need to apologize for, Sophia," he said slowly, his hands slowly relaxing over hers. "But the fact that you were willing to give up what you wanted in order to save the reputation of both myself and my daughter speaks volumes about your character."

"I love..." Sophia began, only to trail off, as she realized what she was about to say. "I mean, I love this place. I love Sarah. I cannot imagine any harm being brought to her. I would rather spend the rest of my years begin shifted from pillar to post at my brother's demand than see her future damaged in any way. I am sorry for all that has gone on. I have brought so much difficulty to your home." Embarrassment crept up her spine, making her face flush as she bent her head.

"No, Sophia," came the gentle reply, as two fingers lifted her chin, forcing her to look into his eyes. "No, my dear lady. You have not brought any difficulty here. That has all been the doing of your brother, and I will not allow you to take on any of the blame."

Her cheeks burned crimson. "You are very good, your grace."

His smile warmed her heart, telling her that she did not need to be afraid any longer. Sharing her burden had brought her both relief and happiness, knowing that the situation would, somehow, be resolved.

"I do not want you to leave."

Her answer sprang to her lips immediately. "I do not want to go."

She did not expect him to lean forward and catch her lips with his, her eyes fluttering closed, as the gentlest of kisses was placed upon her mouth. Her breath caught, her hands tightening on his, as he lingered there for a moment before settling back into his own chair.

"Sophia," he breathed, his eyes filled with some kind of deep emotion. "I am caught up by you. I cannot bear the thought of you leaving me, leaving Sarah. Each day, I look forward to seeing you, hoping for a time when we might talk together. I feel as though I am only just getting to know you for who you are and that there is so much more to discover." Tilting his head, he smiled at her softly, his heart open to her. "I confess this because I want you to know that I have an affection for you that is growing with every day that passes. I confess I have been confused as to whether I want to keep you here for Sarah's good or for my own, but now I realize the desire is one and the same. The love you show to Sarah is one reason for asking you to stay, but the other is so that I might show you that love in return." Pressing his lips together for a moment, he looked down at their joined hands whilst Sophia continued to stare at him, hardly daring to breathe. She struggled to take in what had just occurred, hardly believing that the duke had just kissed her.

"Will you let me handle this situation?" he asked softly. "I want to bring an end to it all, for good. I want to make sure that they will never have a need to come near to you again, my dear. I want us to be able to consider our future without fear, without worry about what they might do."

Our future?

Sophia could not get her breath; she could not form words. Her heart skipped wildly, filled to the brim with sheer happiness. She had gone from frustration and upset to overwhelming joy.

"My dear Sophia," the duke said quietly, a small smile lingering on his face. "Will you trust me with this?"

She nodded slowly, her mind still somewhat dazed. "I will, your grace."

A chuckle escaped him, his lips tipping into a broad smile. "My name is Matthew. I would be honored if you called me by my Christian name. After all, I did just kiss you."

"Matthew," she managed to repeat, her world suddenly bursting into life. "Thank you, Matthew. I do trust you, whatever you intend to do."

His smile grew tender. "Thank you, Sophia. I promise you that, by this time tomorrow, it will all be over."

16

The following morning, Matthew sent for his brother almost as soon as he was awake, telling the footman to insist that he come at once. He could not help but chuckle at the frustration on his brother's tired face as he stumbled into Matthew's study, clearly a little worse for wear.

"Good evening last night, was it?" Matthew asked, with a small chuckle. "You appear to have had a very good time."

"It is far too early," Arthur groaned, sitting down heavily in an overstuffed chair. "Whatever is the matter?"

Matthew waited for the butler and footmen to set down the trays on the table, seeing his brother reach for the coffee almost at once. Once the room was quiet, he turned to his brother who was now adding cream to his dark coffee, muttering under his breath.

"It is about Miss Weston and her *dear* brother," he began, seeing Arthur look up with a sudden frown. "All is not well."

Arthur's frown deepened. "Lord and Lady Brookridge were not particularly happy with you last evening, that is for sure," he said, sitting back in his chair. "Once you left, they huddled in a corner for a good half hour, talking together. I had very little idea as to what they were saying, but there were a lot of dark looks from them both. Whatever did you say?"

"They want to take Miss Weston back with them," Matthew said calmly. "I told them they could not."

That woke his brother up a little more. Arthur pushed himself up a little straighter in his seat and frowned at his brother. "What do you mean? I didn't think they knew she was here."

"By unfortunate coincidence, they managed to meet," Matthew replied, sipping his coffee. "Regardless, Miss Weston then came to speak to me to say she wished to leave. I soon discovered that her reasons for doing so were not because she truly desired to leave, but more that she was being forced to."

Arthur's eyes widened all the more.

"Lord Brookridge has said he will do all he can to disrupt my daughter's future by spreading the most vile and vulgar rumors about me," Matthew replied, aware of the hot rush of anger that spread through him still. "I do not take such things lightly, Arthur. This must be dealt with."

For a few minutes, Arthur simply stared at him, his mouth now ajar as he attempted to think of something to say in response. It had clearly come as quite a shock, especially since he had been previously acquainted with Viscount Brookridge before he had gained his title.

"I am sorry I ever invited them," he stammered eventually. "Truly, Matthew, I had no idea that Brookridge was this kind of man."

Matthew sighed and shook his head, feeling somewhat weary of the whole business. "Indeed, Miss Weston has said much the same. I believe the woman he married is more a serpent than anything else. Poisoned him slowly until he is no longer recognizable as the man he once was."

Arthur blustered for a moment or two, clearly now quite

awake. "Well, what are you going to do about it? The man cannot be allowed to take his sister back with him, not when he is clearly both cruel and vindictive, but neither can you let him say anything of the kind about you!"

"Calm yourself, brother," Matthew replied firmly. "That is precisely why I have woken you so early. I need you to go to the seamstress in town – the one a few miles away from here. It is a good distance away, which is why you must go with as much urgency as you can. Find the seamstress and ask her for the best gown she has in her shop. I do not care about price. In fact, I want you to buy a good number of gowns, although you need only bring a couple back with you. I had the maid come up with a few measurements earlier this morning, which should be contained in this note." He handed the scribbled note to his brother, who took it without a word. "Then return here as quickly but as carefully as you can. That gown is to go straight to Miss Weston. Once she has been prepared, Miss Weston will join us for dinner."

Arthur nodded slowly, aware that the rest of the household guests would not rise until the early afternoon, if not later. "You intend to introduce Miss Weston to the rest of the guests?"

"More than that," Matthew replied firmly. "I intend to ensure that her so-called family will be shown the error of their ways. They will be thoroughly shamed, and Miss Weston will never have reason to fear them ever again. I intend them to be as lowly as they have tried to make her, to the point that they dare not show their faces for the shame of it."

His voice had grown louder, more resounding as he finished his speech, his blood already beginning to boil as his thoughts settled on Viscount Brookridge.

"By Jove," Arthur muttered, getting up from his chair. "You have it all worked out, do you not?"

"I do," Matthew replied firmly. "I do not intend to let Miss Weston be treated this way."

His brother nodded but paused, his eyes lit with curiosity. "Does this mean that you are now willing to admit that there is something of an affection in your heart for Miss Weston?" he asked quietly. "I swear I shall be greatly delighted if that is the case."

Matthew paused for a moment, wondering whether or not to tell his brother all that he had planned but choosing at the last moment not to do so. "I care very deeply for Miss Weston," he admitted, "and she for me, I think."

Arthur grinned, thumping the top of the chair in delight. "Wonderful. I am very glad to hear it. There's something more to her than there ever was with Elizabeth, if you do not mind me saying so."

Not able to disagree, Matthew smiled and lifted his shoulder. "I have a real and true affection for her, which I never had for Elizabeth. Our match was one of consideration, practicality, and tradition. Nothing more. That is entirely absent with Miss Weston. I feel none of the coldness nor experience any of the distance I had with Elizabeth." Hoping he was not coming across as callous, Matthew let out a long sigh. "I hope I do not sound cruel, Arthur, but I barely knew my wife. She was a veritable stranger, who kept to her own rooms and who I took to my bed only the once. Of course, I mourned her, but there was no real pain there. When it comes to Sophia – to Miss Weston, I mean – just the thought of her leaving my home brought me such agony that I could not bear it!"

Arthur's smile spread, clearly delighted. "Well, may I say how glad I am to see you in love at last, brother. It is a wonderful state of being and one I very much hope to be in again, whenever the time comes."

"Thank you," Matthew replied, not sure what else to say. He

had said more than he had meant to but with the truth of his feelings came a sudden feeling of relief. He *did* love Miss Weston, even though it was only the very first fruits of such a feeling, and he was quite sure that, whether she loved him yet or not, such an emotion would soon be returned. It was just as he had said to his brother: he had never felt such emotions before, and it was opening up a bright new world to him.

"I'd better go if I am to return on time," Arthur said, making his way to the door. "Make sure not to start dinner without me!"

Matthew laughed, waving his hand to shoo his brother out of the door. "I do not think we can!" he called, sitting back down at his desk. "Now do be quick about it! It all depends on you."

17

Sophia was busy preparing for the first lesson of the day with Sarah when a knock at the door came. Looking up, expecting it to be the nurse or a footman, she was astonished to see none other than the duke step inside the schoolroom.

"Your grace," she exclaimed, blushing furiously, as he took her hand and pressed a kiss to the back of it. "I mean, Matthew..." She trailed off, the name still sounding unfamiliar to her lips whilst a rush of heat shot up her arm and pooled in her core. She looked into his blue eyes and saw them almost glimmer with something like excitement or anticipation. His promise to ensure that her difficult situation would come to an end by this evening had been like a candle held up in the midst of darkness, giving her hope when everything had seemed black. She could not help but give him both her trust and her heart. He had treated her with more respect, more consideration than her own brother, despite her lower place in his household.

"Sophia, how are you?" he asked softly, reaching for her hand and pressing it gently. "I have some news. Are you able to speak with me for a moment?"

"Of course," she breathed, finding herself growing more and more nervous as she looked up into his face. What was it he intended? How was he to resolve the situation?"

His expression grew solemn. "I regret to inform you, Sophia, that I can no longer keep you on as governess."

Sophia stared at him in shock, her face paling as he held her hands tightly.

"I cannot let the woman I love be a hired worker in my house," he continued, as she closed her eyes in relief. "Sophia, we have to consider the future."

Her legs were weak, making her sway slightly, as she tried to regain her composure. For a second, she had thought he intended to push her from his house, that she would have nowhere to go, but then the reassurance had returned to her heart. Of course, he would not do such a thing as that.

"Sophia," he said again, looking down into her eyes. "I believe myself to be falling in love with you. You have brought delight and happiness into my home and made my daughter an even brighter star than she already was. I cannot think of my home without you."

Confusion reigned. Shaking her head, Sophia frowned, her forehead creasing. "But I cannot remain here if I am not employed by you," she said slowly. "I will have to go back to–"

"No," he interrupted firmly. "You will never have to go back to your brother. Sophia, if you will accept, I intend to make you the Duchess of Harrogate."

She blinked, her legs refusing to hold her weight for a moment. The duke caught her tightly, her hands curling around the edge of his waistcoat as she held onto him tightly. The words he'd said resonated in her mind over and over, until she had no choice but to accept them.

The Duke of Harrogate wanted her as his bride. As his wife.

"I will have the banns called this Sunday, and we shall be

wed in a fortnight," he whispered in her ear, his arms holding her tightly. "What do you say, my love? Will you have me?"

It had all happened so quickly that, for a moment, Sophia was struck dumb. To become his wife would be the happiest moment of her life thus far, and she could not even think of refusing.

"Are you sure, Matthew?" she whispered, her throat aching with a sudden yet wonderful ache of happiness. "We have not been all that well acquainted."

"Something I fully intend to rectify in the next few weeks," he assured her, smiling. "Sophia, I did not love my first wife. She was, by all accounts, a genteel, proper lady, but that was all I knew of her. We did not spend time together; we did not so much as converse on a regular basis. When she found she was pregnant, we spent even less time together. I never had the urge to know her more, and she did not feel that for me either. It was all very convenient, very neat. That is not the case with you. I feel such a fire burning whenever I see you, and my desire is only to be with you. I want to spend hours talking with you, to have you in my company as my wife and not the governess. I know that my love will grow all the more, for I do not think I have ever felt such happiness in my life before."

Sophia closed her eyes to stop her tears from escaping, her lips curving into a beautiful smile. Her arms wrapped around his neck, a sigh of contentedness escaping her.

"Does this mean that you accept?" the duke asked softly, his lips whispering across her forehead. "You will have me?"

"I will," Sophia whispered, her lips finally meeting his for a brief, gentle kiss.

They stood there for a long time, wrapped in one another's arms and simply considering the life that now lay out before them. Sophia did not think she had ever been so happy, her very being seeming to come alive with sheer joy. She would be wife to a man she loved and mother to a girl she had come to care for so very deeply. Her brother and sister-in-law would have no grounds to come to her, to insist that she do whatever they say. She had nothing left to fear. The duke had taken care of it all.

"Now," he murmured, finally taking a step back. "I have already had your things moved. You are to have a proper bedchamber, as becomes your new station as my betrothed, and there is a bath being drawn for you. A maid will come to dress your hair, and Arthur is returning this very moment with a few new gowns for you. Although, you shall order yourself as many as you wish once the guests have left us. I think you more beautiful than anyone in your governess's dress, but I do not think it will be appropriate for dinner tonight, do you?"

Blushing furiously, Sophia laughed softly. "I do have some of my other gowns with me from home. Just a couple I could never bear to part with."

"That does not matter," he replied firmly. "You are to have a brand-new gown of the highest fashion so that I may present you this evening to the rest of my guests as my betrothed."

The thought had her worried for a moment, but he brushed it away with a gentle kiss to her forehead.

"Arthur will stay on with us until the wedding, so you need not worry about lack of propriety," he said gently. "Sarah will be delighted, I am sure. Although, now I realize I must find her a new governess!" He chuckled, as she opened her mouth to protest, patting her hand. "Come with me, my love. I will show you to your new rooms so that you might begin to get ready. Tonight is the night when all shall be revealed, when your brother and his devious wife will realize that their schemes will no longer be tolerated."

A flash of anger crossed his face, and Sophia felt a shiver creep up her spine.

He kissed her again, a little more firmly this time, and it was all Sophia could do not to melt into his arms. Within a few minutes, they had left the schoolroom behind, walking together to her new rooms within the main part of the house. She was no longer a governess. She was Miss Sophia Weston, the bride-to-be of the Duke of Harrogate. Sophia felt herself practically glow with happiness.

"Is this all right, miss?"

Sophia blinked at her reflection as the maid finished putting the last of a few incandescent pearls into her hair. It had been washed and dried and was now pulled up onto the top of her hair in an elaborate style, with a cascade of curls falling down onto her neck whilst still away from her face. A few gentle golden tendrils curled around her ears, reaching down to where a stunning diamond necklace lay. Sophia barely recognized herself.

"Thank you," she breathed, pressing one hand to her chest as she struggled to keep her composure. "You have done a marvelous job."

"And just in time too, miss," the maid replied, as a quiet knock sounded at the door. "I think you are quite ready."

Standing up carefully, her feet in soft slippers, Sophia made her way to the door and opened it, finding the duke standing there with his back to her. He turned around at once, his eyes widening and his mouth falling open as he took her in. Blushing furiously, Sophia saw him swallow hard, his mouth closing as he let out a long breath.

"My goodness," he muttered, shaking his head. "How am I meant to speak coherently with you by my side, Sophia? You take my breath away."

Looking down at the emerald gown that encased her frame,

Sophia spread her arms wide. "Your brother chose wonderfully, Matthew."

The duke chuckled and offered her his arm, which she took at once. "Do not think that Arthur had anything to do with it, my love. Most likely, the seamstress chose for him."

"I will be sure to send her my thanks," Sophia murmured, as they made their way down the staircase, one hand pressed lightly against her middle, as she fought to keep her nerves at bay.

As though he knew what she was feeling, the duke stopped at the bottom of the stairs, reaching for her free hand and taking both in his. "My dear, you have nothing to worry about. You will be the talk of the town, I am sure of it, whilst your brother will scuttle back to his manor house in disgrace. I cannot tell you how proud I am to have you on my arm. You have made me the happiest man in England."

Pressing his lips to her cheek for a moment, he smiled into her eyes, giving her the courage she needed. Lifting her chin a notch, she took his arm and began to walk forward toward the drawing room where the rest of the guests would be waiting to go through to dinner.

The door opened for them, and Sophia felt her stomach tighten as she walked inside. The small gathered crowd turned as one to look at them both, and Sophia felt her smile become fixed. She had no idea what any of them were thinking and did not dare ask.

"Ladies and gentlemen, may I present a somewhat late arrival to our party," the duke said, patting her hand. "This is Miss Sophia Weston. My betrothed."

A ripple of surprise ran around the room, but to Sophia's relief, no one appeared shocked or discomfited in any way by the announcement. In fact, most of the ladies there were smiling at her.

"Is your brother not here, Miss Weston?" she heard Arthur say, her eyes traveling across the room to find the duke's brother. He was leaning on the mantlepiece, a grin on his face. "Lord Brookridge, where are you? Are you not to offer congratulations to your sister?"

Sophia swallowed hard, as her brother and sister-in-law stepped forward, both with rather white faces and the viscountess with pursed lips. They did not look pleased in the slightest.

Before she could speak, the duke cleared his throat, capturing the room's attention once more.

"Unfortunately, I think I shall have to ask you both to leave my house this very night, Lord Brookridge."

An audible gasp came from the rest of the guests, as they looked from one to the next.

"It is my sad duty to inform you all that Lord and Lady Brookridge threatened to spread rumors all around London about myself, so much so that my daughter would not be able to enjoy her come out when the time came," the duke continued steadily, as the guests continued to look from one to the next. "I will not go into the specifics as to why you intended to do such a thing, but be assured that I will *not* allow it to stand."

"How dare you threaten a duke with such a thing, Brookridge!" Arthur exclaimed, coming away from the mantlepiece and striding toward them. "You ought to be run out of this place!"

The murmurs of the guests began to grow somewhat louder and angrier. Pointing fingers jabbed in the viscount's direction, who, to his own failing, did nothing to deny what had been said.

"You have failed in your scheme, Brookridge," the duke continued calmly. "Now, pack your things and get out. You and I will never cross paths again."

Sophia watched as her brother's face paled all the more, his eyes turning from Sophia to the duke and back again. He had no real courage in the face of the duke's anger, whilst the viscountess appeared to have nothing at all to say. It was as though she realized that her standing and her influence were now entirely ruined. There was no doubt that the news of what they had tried to do would spread all around London and Bath, meaning that she would not be able to show her face there for a good many years.

"Goodbye, Peter," she said softly, as her brother stumbled toward the door. He paused and looked back at her, his jaw working, but finding nothing to say, he quit the room.

A sense of relief washed all through Sophia the moment the door closed, and she felt herself slump inwardly. The room was abuzz with chatter, questions being thrown at both herself and the duke, none of which she could bring herself to answer.

"Now, now!" the duke called, bringing the room to quiet. "I know there is a great deal that must be asked and explained, but can I suggest we go through to eat? I would much rather explain it all over a good meal!"

There were a few chuckles, and after a moment or two, the guests began to file out of the room. Sophia felt her hand pressed, her cheek kissed, and whispers of congratulations filling her ears. Her happiness knew no bounds; her heart freed entirely of the shackles it had once been held in.

"My dear Sophia," the duke murmured, as the last of the guests quit the room. "You have shown so much courage and fortitude that I confess myself almost in awe of you." He turned to face her, smiling down gently. "You have a beauty in your character that draws me nearer to you every day. Sarah loves you and cannot wait for you to be a permanent part of her life." He swallowed, his fingers reaching up to gently lift her chin. "I love you so much, Sophia. I cannot wait to make you my wife."

Thinking that she had never experienced such joy before,

Sophia smiled back at him, her fingers twined with his. "And I cannot wait to be your bride," she whispered, seeing her bright and happy future in his eyes. "I love you, Matthew. With all of my heart."

THE END

AN EARL'S LOVE

SECRETS OF LONDON

An Earl's Love

First printing, 2018

Publisher
Love Light Faith, LLC
400 NW 7th Avenue, Unit 825
Fort Lauderdale, FL 33311

1

England 1815

Miss Sarah Weston hummed to herself, as she sat on the wooden bench in the corner of the garden. Spring had already made its way into the garden, and the sight of the new buds, as well as the snowdrops and bluebells, made Sarah's heart sing. It was a sight she was quite familiar with, having seen it every year for well over a decade, but still, it brought her a great deal of delight.

"Is that you, Sarah?"

Glancing up from where she sat, Sarah saw Mr. Stanton approach her. He was impeccably dressed, as always, with his greying hair a little wispy around his head. His small spectacles were balanced on his nose, surrounded by an overly large, bushy beard that was becoming more and more streaked with white. Sarah knew his dark brown eyes would be as sharp as ever, having not grown dim with age. Getting to her feet, she kept her hands in her lap and waited, wondering what her guardian wanted.

"Ah, Sarah," Mr. Stanton puffed, having apparently rushed

across the gardens towards her. "Mrs. Stanton requires your help. Something about tonight's table setting."

"Oh. Of course."

Sarah would not let her disappointment show, as she followed Mr. Stanton back into the house, knowing that she ought not to have let her hopes flare as they had done. There would be no come out for her, not this year—even though she was past due her time. Both Mr. and Mrs. Stanton had mentioned it on occasion, but it seemed nothing was to come of it. Not this year anyway. Perhaps next year.

But by then you will be older, said a small voice inside her. *Perhaps getting a little too old.*

Biting her lip, Sarah chased away her worrying thoughts with a will, knowing that she had to focus on whatever Mrs. Stanton wanted her help with. She had been well trained by Mrs. Stanton to know exactly what was expected of her on any given occasion. This evening, there was to be a dinner with a few guests from around the village, and Sarah was looking forward to it. It was always enjoyable to have a few extra people to talk with, since Mr. and Mrs. Stanton were, on the whole, a rather silent couple. It would make a change from her usual evenings sitting in front of the fire with a book, attempting to read by candlelight until she became too tired to do so.

"Here she is," her guardian commented, as Sarah walked into the house to see Mrs. Stanton all in a flap as she paced up and down the small dining room, her dark brown hair—with only the occasional grey—flying out from underneath her cap. "Have no fear, Mrs. Stanton. Our Sarah will aid you."

"Thank you," Mrs. Stanton exclaimed at once, catching Sarah's hand as her light green eyes darted from one table setting to the other. "Oh, Sarah, you simply must help me. We have too many gentlemen."

Closing her eyes for a moment, Sarah set her shoulders,

drew in a long breath, and tried her best to focus on the so-called problem at hand.

"Too many gentlemen, Mrs. Stanton?" she repeated, taking in the older woman's worried expression. "What do you mean?"

Mrs. Stanton continued to explain in great detail how she could not have the usual seating plan—with one lady seated next to one gentleman, going all the way around the table—due to the fact that Mrs. Churston, who was Mrs. Stanton's particular friend, had sent a note to say she could not attend since she had been overcome with a particularly nasty cold. That meant that Mrs. Stanton now had an extra gentleman, so who was she meant to sit together? Two gentlemen sitting next to one another was not what was expected, and so Mrs. Stanton had managed to get herself into something of a state over the matter.

Sarah sighed inwardly and began to discuss each of the guests, reassuring Mrs. Stanton that they would be able to find a gentleman who would be more than willing to sit wherever they were placed with whomever they were placed. She then made the suggestion that the extra gentleman be seated near the head of the table by Mr. Stanton, which would make it a little less obvious, and within half an hour, the matter had been settled—and Mrs. Stanton was more than a little relieved.

Sarah, who now had no opportunity to return to the garden, was then sent to her room to prepare for this evening's festivities, finding that Mrs. Stanton had ordered her a bath. A slight frown flickered across her brow, as she recalled the gentlemen guests who had been invited, wondering to herself whether or not Mrs. Stanton had any particular gentleman in mind for her. She hoped not, quite certain that she would not care for any of the men that were recommended to her by Mrs. Stanton.

It was not that Mrs. Stanton was not kind, for in the fifteen years Sarah had lived in this house, she had found both Mr. and Mrs. Stanton to be caring and considerate of her, especially since she was neither their daughter nor their niece. In fact, she was no relation at all, as far as she understood. Nothing had ever really been said about why she had been sent to this house at the tender age of four years old, and she had never been able to ask. There was a blanket of silence that fell on her guardians whenever she brought up the matter, which was more than a little frustrating. Over the years, she had asked numerous times about her heritage, her parents, and her family, but her guardians had not answered a single one of her questions. On one occasion, Mr. Stanton had lost his temper and told her not to ask another thing, that it was for her own good that she did not know who she truly was.

That had seemed such a strange sentiment at the time, and even now, Sarah did not know what to make of it. To be told that she was not to know a thing about who she really was or where she had come from was both frustrating and confusing, making her question almost daily why she was being treated in such a way. It was not as though she had done anything wrong, surely?

As she sank down into the bath, Sarah let out a long sigh as the hot water seeped into her skin. She was tired today, tired of having her hopes dashed so often. She was not going to have a come out, not even a small one. There would be no trips to London, no dancing, no gentlemen, nothing at all. What was to become of her? Was she to remain here, alone, for the rest of her days? What would happen once Mr. and Mrs. Stanton passed on? Whilst she knew that Mr. Stanton was a gentleman, she had no idea to whom the house would pass to, once he left this earth. It had not been discussed, like so many other things in her life. Closing her eyes, Sarah forced back the tears that came to her eyes, trying her best not to allow her thoughts to overwhelm her.

There was, of course, one easy answer as to why she did not know where she'd come from. Being only just four years of age when she'd first arrived, Sarah only had one or two very hazy memories as to where she had come from, with only the sound of laughter coming to her mind when she thought back. She hoped she had been happy, but the truth was that she believed herself to be nothing more than the illegitimate daughter of a wealthy and powerful man, a daughter who was not to be acknowledged nor thought of. She supposed that, if that were true, it would explain why she had never been allowed to question her parentage, and why there had never been any answers to the questions she had continued to ask regardless. It would also explain why she was not to have a come out and why, on top of that, she was never allowed to go to London even though it was only two days of travel by carriage.

She was unwanted. She was a secret to be kept hidden from the world. It was the only conclusion she'd come to, the only reason that she could think of as to why she had to live in such a quiet way. The village of Little Mybster was fairly remote and often very quiet, especially during the summertime when the Season began in London. Of course, there was enough company for a gentleman and his wife, even if they had to scour the nearby villages for guests for tonight's dinner, but it was beginning not to be enough for Sarah. She wanted more. She wanted to understand. She wanted to know *why*.

Sitting up, the water splashing dangerously close to the edge of the copper tub, Sarah frowned heavily. If she wanted to change things in her life, then she would have to be the one to do it. She was of age, was she not? She could easily set out by herself and....

And do what?

Lowering herself back down into the cooling water, Sarah squeezed her eyes shut as she grimaced. There was nothing for her to do. She had nowhere to start, nowhere to even consider. There was not someone else she could turn to for answers, no trail for her to follow. She had no funds of her own—not that she knew of, at least—and Mr. Stanton had never said anything about any money left for her by whomever had sent her to their home.

The familiar feeling of being trapped settled over Sarah again. It was as if she were in a prison, built by those she did not know, who were determined, for whatever reason, to keep her here. Mr. and Mrs. Stanton were kind, yes, but they were not her family. Did one not *need* family?

"I need to know where I come from," Sarah said aloud, her eyes burning with hot tears. "I *must* find out."

There came no easy answer, nothing to tell her what to do next in order to find answers. Instead, there just came the expected heavy silence that wrapped itself around her heart and shrouded it in darkness.

The water was cold now. Sarah saw, rather than felt, her skin prickling and rang the bell for the maid to come and wash her hair. She would do what was expected of her, just as she had done every other day of her life, in the hope that—one day soon—something might change.

It was the only hope she had.

2

Sarah laughed as Mr. Ferguson finished his story about his wayward horse, who had, it turned out, been entirely insistent on visiting another horse in a neighboring field, feeling a small stab of pain. She could understand the creature's loneliness, even though she was sitting amongst almost a roomful of guests. To have such a need to find another of your kind, another of your family, was a sentiment buried deep within her soul.

"And are you to have a come out this year, Miss Weston?" another gentleman asked, shooting a glance towards Mr. Stanton. "I would very much like to dance with you at the country ball next week, which I presume you are attending."

Before Sarah could speak, Mr. Stanton cleared his throat and caught everyone's attention.

"My dear Mr. Fredricks, I am delighted to inform you that Miss Weston is, in fact, out, and so she should be very pleased to dance with you next week, I am sure."

Sarah felt ice form around her heart, as Mr. Fredricks exclaimed in delight, asking Mr. Stanton when such an event had taken place. She could see Mrs. Stanton widening her eyes at her, telling her silently to smile, but Sarah found she could not. In fact, she could barely move.

"Oh, it was a very small affair," Mr. Stanton lied, his eyes bright with no hint of deception in his expression. "Very small. Quiet. Just as Miss Weston herself wanted it."

"I would not have liked a quiet come out at all, Miss Weston," exclaimed Mary Williams, a girl a little younger than Sarah. "I wanted a ball, did I not, Mama?"

"You did, my dear, and you got one," Mrs. Williams replied calmly. "However, not everyone has the same inclinations as you."

Sarah felt her throat squeeze around the lump that had formed in it, sending aching shivers up into her head. This was all a lie. There had been no come out, no formal arrangement where it might be made known that she was now ready to enter society, as little as it was around these parts. Why was Mr. Stanton lying? Why had he not organized something "small and quiet" as he had put it? She would have accepted that, of course. She would have been grateful for it, but now it appeared she was to have nothing at all.

"And so, you are to attend the dance next Friday then, Miss Weston?" Mr. Fredricks continued, sounding thrilled that he would be able to dance with her at last. "I must secure at least two dances from you."

"Thank you, Mr. Fredricks," Sarah managed to say, aware that most of the guests were now looking at her. "I would be very glad to dance with you."

Mr. Fredricks grinned and began to converse about what they might expect from Mr. Turnberry's dance, but Sarah did not listen. This was not what she had ever expected, to hear that she was now, apparently, out, without knowing so much herself.

Why had Mr. Stanton never spoken to her of it before now? Why had he not told her that he was going to say such a thing to the guests at the table? It had left her completely shaken, her mind trying to take in this new information about herself.

So, she was out. That meant that gentlemen that she might one day marry could court her. However, all the gentlemen around these parts had homes or country houses in this vicinity and were she to marry one of them that would mean resigning herself to staying in Little Mybster for the rest of her days.

Sarah knew she did not want that. She wanted to be free for a time, to have her own life set out in front of her in full view, so that she could make her own choices about what to do and where to go. There would not be any marriage in her future, not yet at least.

So long as that is not what Mr. Stanton is trying to do, came the thought as she set her fork down with a clatter. *What if he is trying to suggest that I marry someone here? What if he is trying his best to manipulate the situation so that this is precisely what happens?*

It would just be another way for her life to be ruled by Mr. Stanton and his wishes. The control of her life would pass from Mr. Stanton to her husband, whomever that was to be, and she would never have the opportunity to do as she wished. She might never be able to find out where she had truly come from, especially since most of the guests here believed her to be Mr. Stanton's niece, although she knew that was not the case. She could still recall the day that Mr. Stanton had sat her down and told her that, whilst she was not any relation of his, she was to play that part precisely. She would be his niece, she'd been told, to ensure her reputation was quite secure, and so she had accepted that without question.

Now, however, that association tied itself around her neck,

tightening whenever she thought about setting out on her own. With no name and no family, she could not get anywhere. As Mr. Stanton's niece, she had connections and a home to go to, but if she were to leave, she knew that association would cease. She could not call herself part of a man's family if she were not.

"Yes, I am quite sure that Miss Weston will play for us later," she heard Mrs. Stanton say loudly, drawing her back to the present. "I know, she plays marvelously well as you say, Mr. Sanders, and I am certain she has been practicing a new piece of late. Perhaps if you were to ask her, she might play it for you."

Sarah tried to smile as Mr. Sanders, a gentleman with a shock of blond hair and piercing blue eyes, looked over at her from across the table, a slightly calculating look in his eye.

"I shall make sure to speak to Miss Weston just as soon as dinner is complete," Mr. Sanders replied, turning back to Mrs. Stanton. "I would very much like to hear this new piece."

So that was it. This dinner was an opportunity for the gentlemen of Little Mybster to look at Sarah in a different way than they had done before. She was now available as a bride, she realized, her heart sinking into her toes. This was why there had been so many gentlemen asked to dinner, as well as the ladies to round out the numbers of course. They were here to admire Sarah, to hear her converse and laugh, to hear her play and perform for them all. She was to show them that she was, in fact, a perfect young lady, who was ready to take her place as a wife and then a mother.

A curl of anger spiked up through her, piercing her heart as it did so. She tasted nothing of the dessert that was placed in front of her, the sweetness turning to dust in her mouth. She did not hear any more conversation and certainly made no attempts to smile at anyone who looked her way. The truth had hurt her deeply. She was nothing more than a piece of Mr. Stanton's property, to be sold at the highest price. For goodness sake, she did not so much as know whether she had a dowry or not, for Mr. Stanton had never told her. Frustration raced through her, bringing with it a sharp increase in her pain. She would not do this. A lifetime of obeying what Mr. and Mrs. Stanton said and a lifetime of being grateful for their kindness to her had been replaced entirely with a mixture of frustration and anger.

Sarah was on her feet before she knew what she was doing. Drawing in a sharp breath, she saw Mrs. Stanton staring at her with wide eyes, a horror stuck expression on her face.

"I am so very sorry, but I suddenly feel quite ill," Sarah lied, turning her gaze to Mr. Stanton, who was looking back at her with those sharp eyes of his.

She did not flinch.

"A terrible headache," she said firmly, keeping her eyes fixed on her guardian. *If he can lie, then so can I,* she told herself, her fingers tightening together as she held them in her lap. "I have tried to manage as best I can, but I am afraid it is becoming much too painful."

"I did think you quiet this evening," Mrs. Malleby said, another one of the guests who was ages with Mrs. Stanton. "You poor thing. I often get headaches, and I find the best thing for them is a cool compress over the eyes and to lie in bed for a time."

Sarah grasped a hold of the suggestion at once. "You are most kind, Mrs. Malleby. I shall do just that." She put one hand to her forehead, rubbing it gently whilst wincing, hearing the murmurs of concern from the other guests. "Do excuse me. I am most dreadfully sorry."

"Not at all," Mr. Ferguson said, as she stepped away from the table. "I do hope you are recovered by Friday so that we may dance together."

Plastering a pained smile on her lips, Sarah bobbed a curtsy in his direction. "I am sure I will, Mr. Fredricks. Do excuse me, and please, again, accept my apologies."

Leaving the dining room, Sarah let out a long breath of relief, as she quickly made her way to her room. There was little doubt that she had upset Mr. Stanton, although she could not tell whether or not Mrs. Stanton had believed her nonsense about a headache or not. There would be a conversation in the morning, but Sarah was determined not to simply accept whatever rebuttals came her way. It was time to start making a change for herself. If she did not, then the rest of her life would pass her by without her ever receiving any answers, and she would continue to find herself controlled by those who were meant to care for her.

"A cool compress, please," she murmured to the passing maid. "There is no particular rush."

The maid nodded and left to fetch it at once, as Sarah made her way to the door of her bedchamber. The cool compress she had no intention of using, but it would be useful should Mr. Stanton question the staff as to Sarah's movements after she retired from the dining room early. It would give credence to her supposed headache, and since there were never any physical observations that accompanied a headache, Sarah knew that Mr. Stanton could not easily doubt her.

Pulling out her room key from her pocket, Sarah pushed into the lock and made to turn it, only for the key to stick. Frowning, she tried again but to no avail. Turning the door handle, she realized that it was not locked at all. Frowning, she looked all about her room, seeing nothing out of place. She had been quite sure that she had locked the door before going down to dinner, just as she always did. Her room was the one place she could call her own, where she could go and know that no one would disturb her unless she asked. Mrs. Stanton had a key, of course, but she did not often use it unless it was to have the maids go to prepare a bath or the like. So why was the door open now?

The maid returned just as Sarah was sitting down at the dressing table, removing her jewelry.

"I will just leave the compress by the basin, miss," the maid murmured, setting it down carefully. "Can I get you anything else?"

Sarah thought for a moment. "Tea, I think." The maid bobbed and made to leave, only for Sarah to speak again. "Did Mrs. Stanton ask for my room to be opened?"

The maid turned and shook her head, a slight frown between her brows. "No, miss. Your room was locked when I last checked it."

"You checked it?"

The maid nodded, a small dusting of pink on her cheeks. "I had some linens to put away, but the room was locked. I thought it best not to interrupt either yourself or Mrs. Stanton, and so I put them in the chest by the door." She opened the door a little wider and indicated the chest, where linens and things were often kept in preparation for being placed back in Sarah's room.

Sarah nodded slowly, her own brow furrowing. "I see. Thank you. There is nothing more."

Taking out her jewelry box, Sarah began to put her jewels away before getting up and wandering over to her bed. She would have to put on a bit of a performance for the maid, just so that the maid could tell Mr. Stanton that, yes, Sarah had laid down with the compress over her eyes after excusing herself from the dinner table. Besides which, Sarah was going to need the maid's help to get out of her dress.

Picking up the compress, Sarah walked back to her bed and tried to lie down carefully so as not to crush her gown. Placing the compress over her eyes, she lay back against the pillow, only for something hard to jab at her head. Frowning, she tried to adjust her position, only to feel the same thing.

"What on earth is the matter with these things?" she said aloud crossly, as she sat up and pulled one pillow away from the other.

Her eyes fell on a small box, wrapped in parcel paper, and tied with a small red ribbon.

Her breath caught.

Someone had been in her room.

3

Sarah froze, her stomach tight and tension rifling through her as she looked at the box. She had no idea what it contained, and for whatever reason, she did not yet want to touch it. The knowledge that someone had been in her room without her awareness made her sick to the stomach, as a few beads of sweat formed on her brow. Were they still here, waiting for her? Hiding in the dark shadowy corners of the room so that once she was alone, they might attack?

Slamming the pillow back over the box, Sarah got to her feet and began to search the room, picking up a candle so as to get as much light as possible. She would not give in to fear, determined to ensure that she was quite safe. The maid would return in a moment or two with her tea tray so should anything untoward happen, she would not be alone.

"Is anyone there?" she asked, peering around the corner of her screen where she often dressed. There was nothing there, her heart hammering wildly as she bent down to check under her bed. Half expecting someone to climb out from underneath it, Sarah let out a scream as the maid opened the door again, her tea tray in hand.

"I am so terribly sorry," the maid gasped, setting the tray down quickly on the table. "Are you all right, miss?"

Sarah drew in a long breath, one hand pressed against her middle. "I am quite all right, thank you. I just thought I lost one of my ear bobs, but it turns out I did not."

The maid nodded, as Sarah set the candle down. "Of course, miss. Is your headache still bad?"

"I intend to lie down once I am out of this dress," Sarah answered, as calmly as she could despite the frantic beating of her heart. "Might you help me?" Pulling the room key from her pocket, she set it aside on the dressing table so that she could lock the door once the maid had gone. Usually, she left it open so that they could bring her early cup of tea in at the usual time, but—tonight—Sarah wanted to keep it locked.

As the maid began to help her change into her night things, Sarah could not help but let her eyes rove around the room, as though she might somehow find clues as to where this stranger had been. She did not know what to think, terrified about what might be within the box. Would it be something that threatened her safety? Someone that knew where she had come from and was using this knowledge to ensure she remained exactly where she was? Had they somehow known that she was thinking to make her own path in life, somehow?

"You are being ridiculous," she muttered to herself, as the maid brought over her nightgown, eyeing Sarah carefully as though she were going mad in speaking to herself.

Not wanting to explain, Sarah dismissed the maid as quickly as she could, grasping the key and locking the door after her. Turning the handle to ensure that she was safe, Sarah turned around and looked back at her pillows.

Her hands began to tremble, as she lifted the pillow away to reveal the small parcel. Picking it up, she looked at it carefully, seeing the neat ribbon tying it all together. There was no indication as to who it might be from, for there was nothing written on the parcel anywhere.

There was nothing to do but open it to see what was within. Her breathing ragged, Sarah tugged at the ribbon which fell away easily, the paper still remaining in place once it was removed. Looking all about her for a moment, as though there might be someone watching her from within the room, Sarah unfolded the brown parcel paper, and setting it aside, she held the black box in her hand.

Swallowing hard, she got up to ensure that the drapes were completely closed, her heart now hammering wildly. Sitting back down, she lifted up the lid and heard herself gasp.

There, nestled within the depths of the box and surrounded by delicate lace, was a beautiful gold locket. It was decorated with seed pearls and had an amethyst at the center. It was, without a doubt, one of the most beautiful pieces of jewelry she had ever seen, and she was not even able to guess how much it was worth.

Setting the box down carefully on the bed, Sarah lifted the locket out of the box, feeling the weight of it in her hands. Running one finger over it, she found the delicate catch, and her nerves running wildly through her, she opened it carefully.

To her disappointment, it was entirely empty. There was no miniature within, no picture of someone she did not know, something that might have become something to her.

Sighing, Sarah closed it again, turning it over in her fingers. There was no inscription on the back, nothing to let her know who it was from. What was the point of sending her a piece of jewelry if there was nothing else with it? Why had someone come into her room and set this under her pillow if it was nothing more than a locket that she knew nothing of?

Rising to her feet, Sarah made to pick up the box so as to hide it somewhere on her dressing table, but to her surprise saw that there was a small, unfolded note hiding underneath all the lace which had held the locket so carefully.

Sinking back down onto the bed, Sarah set the locket aside and picked up the note, her fingers shaking slightly. This was more important than the locket, she was certain of it.

Unfolding it, her eyes glazed over for a moment as she saw the writing there. Drawing in a long breath, she fixed her gaze on it and began to read aloud.

"Ask Mr. Stanton about your fortune. Make your way to London. Find the owner of this locket. All will become clear."

She frowned, reading the note three times before setting it down next to the locket. Who had written her such a note, and why did they seem to know more about her than she did? What would Mr. Stanton know about her fortune? Did she have one?

A spiral of excitement coiled in her belly. If she did have a fortune, and if she was of age – as well as being out – then Mr. Stanton could do nothing if she wished to use her fortune for her own ends. He was her guardian, yes, but if she was of age, then it meant that she could do as she wished with her fortune. This was just what she had been hoping for. It gave her the chance to do as she pleased with her own life, although she did not intend to use her funds—if she truly did have some—to live in the lap of luxury. No, she would do what this note said. She would find the owner of the locket, and in doing so, she would find out more about who she really was.

A sudden thought struck her, making the smile on her lips fade. What if the person who had written the note did not have good intentions for her? What if they wanted her to go in search of the locket's owner for their own nefarious purposes, whatever that might be?

"If I am illegitimate," Sarah said aloud, giving voice to her thoughts, "then for me to appear with this locket will send such rumors around about my parent, whomever he might be, and bring shame and disfavor to his life." Perhaps someone wanted that to happen; perhaps they wanted her to reveal herself so that consequences could follow for her father or mother were they still alive.

Sighing, Sarah traced the delicate locket with one finger, her heart sinking a little lower than before. She was not sure what to do, having been caught up with a sudden flurry of excitement when she had first read the note.

A small, aching throb settled between her eyes, bringing a sharp pain to her head. Perhaps she was going to have this headache after all.

Lying back, Sarah held the box that contained the locket tightly in her hand as she set the cool compress over her forehead. Everything was muddled. She wanted desperately to do what the note writer had said; she wanted to go to Mr. Stanton at this very moment and demand that he tell her everything about her fortune, but instead, she lay exactly where she was and tried to think things through.

If she had a fortune, that meant that whoever had sent her to Mr. Stanton had been wealthy in his own right. Had Mr. Stanton received a generous sum in payment for his care for her? Was that why he had never complained about taking her in? Was he instructed never to talk to her about where she had come from?

Questions flooded every part of her being, each one being asked before spinning away without an answer. Suppose she did have a fortune, suppose she did go to London, what would she do next? The *ton* would be welcoming to her, she supposed, although she could not expect to mingle with those highest in society. However, she had no idea where to start when it came to finding the owner of this locket. Why London? Why there, the very place that Mr. Stanton had kept her from for so many years? Would she truly find answers there?

Her stomach began to churn, bringing a feeling of nausea

with it. The room grew chilled, and Sarah tugged the blankets over herself, setting the compress aside whilst keeping the box that contained the locket and note in her hand. Turning onto her side, she gently set them both back under her pillow, secure in the box she had found them in. Closing her eyes, Sarah tried to sleep, praying that the answer about what she should do would be there waiting for her in the morning.

4

Sarah had not slept well. The night had been filled with awakenings, her sleep clouded with dreams of unknown faces and grasping hands, of shouted words and terrifying screams. She had not been settled. And so, when the first lights of dawn crossed the sky, Sarah had chosen to rise, looking out at the cold morning sun with a feeling of dismay in her heart.

Everything was as muddled as it had been last night. She had not come up with any answers, had not made any kind of certain decisions. She was just as lost as before.

Gazing out at the grey sky, Sarah drew in a long breath and felt her bones shake. She was scared. Scared that the note writer might be telling the truth, that she *did* have a fortune that Mr. Stanton had hidden from her. The consequences of that were more than she dared to think of, knowing that she could not allow her questions to be batted away by him, as they had been so often before. Were she to speak to him about such a thing, then she would have to demand that he answer her, refusing to back down and go away in silence as he had no doubt expect.

She knew the note by heart, having read it so many times.

What was she to do with it? What she decided now would decide the course of her future, of that she was certain. If she ignored the note, ignored the locket, then her future would play out entirely as she had expected, with her husband chosen for her by her guardian. She would be wife and mother, respectful of her husband and obedient to his requests, just as she was to Mr. Stanton. If she chose to speak to Mr. Stanton about what she had discovered, then her life would take an altogether different direction, one that was clouded in confusion and uncertainty.

Find your courage.

Taking a deep breath, Sarah continued to look out at the gardens, her heart lifting. She would have to take precautions and would have to find herself a companion with which she could traverse the plains of society. However, anything was better than staying here and having her life planned for her. She would have to make sure that Mr. Stanton knew and understood that she was more than determined to do what she pleased with her life, knowing that he would be both astonished and horrified at her demands, but she would have to remain steadfast. There could be no shrinking back, no pretending that she was content to simply do as she was told any longer.

She would have to find her courage from somewhere, to do something she had never done before. It was time to take control.

~

THAT COURAGE SEEMED to disappear the moment she knocked on Mr. Stanton's study door. She had not gone to see him of her own volition but had, in fact, been summoned by a maid, telling her that Mr. Stanton wished to see her. Sarah did not need to ask why, aware that she was about to be heavily reprimanded for her sudden absence last evening. He would, no doubt, quiz her about her headache, his bushy brows furrowing as he made it clear that he did not entirely believe her.

"Mr. Stanton?"

He was sitting at his study table, his elbows on the desk in front of him and his fingers pressed gently together. His eyes took her in as she walked into the room, making Sarah's stomach churn with nerves. This was not how she'd wanted to feel – small, intimidated, and afraid. She had wanted to feel strong, brave, and determined, but just one look from Mr. Stanton's sharp eyes and she wanted to sit in the chair and accept his angry reprimand as she had done before.

"Sit, Sarah."

She made to do so, only to stop and look down at the chair, one hand grasping the top of it tightly.

"Sit down."

"No, thank you."

The words came out as a whisper, as her eyes shot towards him. "I think I would rather stand."

"And I would rather you sit."

There was an anger to his voice now, seeping into the lines on his face, but Sarah told herself not to move, her mind screaming at her to remain steady.

"Thank you, Mr. Stanton, but I will remain standing," she said, her voice a little louder as she remained holding onto the back of the chair with one hand, as though it would give her the strength she required. "What was it you wished to speak to me about?"

His eyes darted from her to the chair and back again as though he expected his silence to cajole her into doing what he had asked, but after a few minutes of Sarah's steadfastly refusing to be seated, he let out a long breath and sat back in his chair.

"You are becoming stubborn, Sarah, and that is not acceptable," he said, firmly. "Your excuse on leaving the table last evening was nothing short of ridiculous."

Ignoring her churning stomach, Sarah lifted one eyebrow. "I do not think that a headache is anything ridiculous, Mr. Stanton."

His lips thinned, his eyes darkening. "I know you had no such thing. The maid told me she found you scrabbling about on the floor for something – hardly the actions of someone who can barely keep their eyes open due to the pain."

Sarah kept her gaze on his despite the desire to look away and drop her head. She had to be bold if things were to change. "To be frank, Mr. Stanton, I did not want to stay at a gathering where I am to be presented as though I am some kind of prize to be won. I am more than aware that the gentlemen with us last evening were all there to hear that I am now out—so that they might begin to think of courting me."

"That is no reason to lie!" he exclaimed, now appearing quite furious. "You—"

"I believe I was not the only one who lied, Mr. Stanton," she interrupted, finding herself growing stronger with every word she spoke. "Did you not tell them all that we had enjoyed a quiet occasion for my come out? That is very strange indeed since I, myself, do not remember it."

Mr. Stanton glared at her, one hand thumping the table. "That is entirely different matter. You are to do as you are expected."

"I want full access to my fortune."

The words left her before she could stop them, and as soon as they had left her mouth, she saw Mr. Stanton's jaw go slack. His face grew pale, his eyes widening as the anger left him.

"I am of age, and therefore I should have already had full access and responsibility for it," she continued firmly, drawing herself up to her full height. "Why you have never spoken to me of it, I cannot understand." Something like satisfaction settled over her, as she saw how Mr. Stanton was staring at her. Apparently, every word she had said was true. Thus far, the note writer had proven to be correct. She *did* have a fortune, one that was being very carefully hidden by Mr. Stanton.

"How do you know about that?" Mr. Stanton asked, his voice hoarse. "You are not meant to know until..."

Sarah frowned as he trailed off, wondering what he was keeping from her. "Until when?" His eyes shot to hers, and Sarah saw the truth in his gaze. "Ah, I see. Until I am wed, is that it? I am to marry before I know that I am a wealthy woman so that any freedom I might have is then completely lost. Gone for good, unless my husband should die. Is that not so?"

Mr. Stanton looked away, passing one hand over his eyes, and Sarah knew she had hit on the truth. Anger settled in her stomach, a fiery ball that shot sheer fury into her veins.

"Why?" she said, walking over to his desk, as a new strength began to fill her. "What is it about me that is meant to be so secret?"

Mr. Stanton shook his head. "This is not to be discussed, Sarah."

"I intend to discuss it," she retorted, slamming her hand down flat on the table. "I will not have this kept from me any longer. I have spent years not knowing where I am from nor who my family is, and you have persistently refused to say a word of it to me. Well, I know more than you are aware of, Mr. Stanton. Tell me the truth."

He looked up at her, a slight anger sparking in his gaze. "You have no need to know."

"I have *every* need to know!" Sarah shouted, not caring that her voice was bouncing off the walls. "This is my life, and you cannot continue to order me about as you do. I will find out one way or the other. You can be sure of that, so you may as well tell me who sent me to you."

Much to her astonishment, he chuckled darkly. "And what if I do not know?"

Her anger died away at once, replaced with a sudden, overwhelming horror.

"You were sent here by a relative of mine, as a favor to a gentleman he knew. Funds are deposited in my account thrice yearly so that I might care for you. You were never to leave this place, not unless someone came for you. We were not to speak of your removal to us. Your fortune and dowry were to be in my care and only revealed to you when you married. Any income we receive stops the moment you leave this house. That is all that I know."

"Poppycock!" Sarah exclaimed, not believing his words for a moment. "You must know more."

Mr. Stanton's gaze lifted to hers, and Sarah recognized that there was nothing but honesty in his eyes. Honesty combined with a great weariness that told her he had been as confused as she.

"I know nothing more, Sarah," he said calmly. "I have done all I can for you and ensured that I lived up to my responsibilities, and yet you have found out about your fortune regardless. My solicitor is in the village today if you wish to see the paperwork that proves it."

Sarah did not answer the unspoken question, knowing that she did not need to tell him about the secret box under her pillow. "This relative of yours, who is he?"

Mr. Stanton shook his head. "It does not matter. He is dead."

The bottom fell out of her world, the only hope she had to discover where she had come from dying in an instant.

"Who was he?" she asked doggedly, her fingers digging into

the edge of the table as she clung on, desperate not to let the tears fall. "What was his name?"

Mr. Stanton shrugged, as though it did not matter if she knew. "Henry Percival, Earl of Thorndyke. He died, and the title and estate went to his son, James, who is now Lord Thorndyke. He is ages with you, I believe, if not a little older, and I can assure you, he knows nothing of the matter. In fact, I would go as far as to say that the man is entirely unaware of your existence."

Sarah swallowed the lump in her throat, her courage slowly fading away. "And was the earl my father?"

Mr. Stanton chuckled and shook his head, as though finding her question humorous. "Of course not. It was all very secretive for whatever reason, and I understand he was doing it in order to help a friend. I know nothing more; I assure you."

Sarah wanted to run back to her room and cry until there were no more tears left but with the last whisper of courage, she looked at Mr. Stanton directly in the eye.

"Send for your solicitor, Mr. Stanton," she said firmly, in a voice that only shook a little. "I want to know everything about my fortune and my dowry, including ensuring that I have complete control over it."

"And what will you do?" Mr. Stanton asked heavily. "Leave here? Go in search of someone who even I, as your guardian, do not know?"

Sarah lifted her chin and walked back towards the door. "I will do whatever I have to in order to find out the truth about myself. Please, send for your solicitor. That will be a good enough start for me."

5

Sarah did not leave her room for the next few hours, finding solace and comfort in her own company. She did not want to speak to Mr. Stanton nor to his wife, feeling as though she were even more lost than she had been before. She hoped that Mr. Stanton had done as she asked and sent for his solicitor, realizing that now that she knew about her fortune it was not as though he could deny her.

"Sarah?"

Closing her eyes, Sarah prayed that Mrs. Stanton would leave her be, but—to her irritation—the lady knocked again.

"Might I come in? Just to talk with you for a moment."

Seeing that she was not about to have any relief, Sarah walked to the door, unlocked it, and thrust it open. The anger that flared in her was demolished at once, as she took in the tears in Mrs. Stanton's eyes and the way she seemed to almost tremble in front of her.

"Mrs. Stanton, what is the matter?" she asked, a little less brusquely than she had intended. "If it is about dinner last evening, then I can only apologize. I did not have a headache, but instead grew annoyed with the idea that I was to be paraded in front of the eligible gentlemen who joined us."

Mrs. Stanton seemed to shrink all the more, her eyes darting around Sarah without ever actually looking into her face. "I did not mean any harm, Sarah."

Sarah felt herself deflate all the more. "I know you meant well," she admitted eventually. "But I would have preferred to know that Mr. Stanton intended to state that I was now out so that I could have prepared myself a little better. That untruth threw me quite off kilter."

Mrs. Stanton nodded slowly, her gaze traveling up to Sarah's face. "Mr. Stanton told me about what you said."

"About my fortune?" Sarah asked, seeing the flare of Mrs. Stanton's eyes. "Yes, I have come to learn about my fortune. I will have control of it very soon. By the end of today, I hope."

The lady nodded again, her eyes dropping to the floor. "And do you intend to leave us?"

It was not a question Sarah was truly prepared for. She did want to leave, yes, but only in order to find out the truth about who she was.

"I think I must," she said slowly, seeing the grief write itself across Mrs. Stanton's expression. "It is not as though I have not been happy here, but rather that the mystery surrounding my circumstances has never been solved and I do so wish to find out the truth." She tilted her head and regarded Mrs. Stanton carefully. "It is not something that *you* are able to help me with, is it?"

"Goodness, no," Mrs. Stanton said, looking as astonished as she sounded. "I knew nothing of the matter until the day before you arrived. You cannot imagine my joy, when I had come to learn that we could not have children of our own." Tears began to trickle down her cheeks, as she smiled up at Sarah, one hand reaching to touch Sarah's own. "But I suppose that every child must leave their nest."

Every last bit of anger and frustration blew away in an instant, as Sarah looked at Mrs. Stanton with fresh eyes. It was clear that Mrs. Stanton was devastated to learn that Sarah would be, most likely, making plans of her own. Evidently, the lady had believed that she would remain in Little Mybster for the rest of her days, married to a gentleman nearby. She had thought they would never be truly separated. Until that moment, Sarah had never truly understood just how deeply Mrs. Stanton cared for her. She had always been warm and friendly towards Sarah, but until this moment, she had never shown any kind of deep emotion towards her.

"I think of you as my own daughter in many ways," Mrs. Stanton continued, her voice now weak and shaking. "Wherever you go, you will write to me, will you not? I could not stand it if I did not know where you were."

Struck by just how much Mrs. Stanton cared for her, Sarah reached out and took Mrs. Stanton's soft hands in hers, smiling softly.

"Mrs. Stanton, you have been more than a guardian to me. You have been a parent. You have guided me, taught me, and helped me to grow. I do not have anger in my heart towards you although I will confess a lingering frustration with Mr. Stanton and his lack of willingness to discuss anything related to my life with me."

"Oh, but you do not understand," Mrs. Stanton responded, squeezing her hands. "He was told not to. Something about it being for your own safety. He may have appeared abrupt, my dear, but he was doing it for your own good."

Sarah hesitated before she spoke, fear clutching at her heart. Had he not told her anything for her own safety? What did that mean?

"Am I in danger?"

Mrs. Stanton shook her head, shrugging slightly. "We were not told, neither of us, and I confess I was just thrilled that I would have a child in our home."

"I understand," Sarah replied gently. "But I must find out the truth. I cannot remain here to be shunted from this house to that of my husband, whomever he was to be, without knowing my heritage." The words trembled on her lips, but she spoke them regardless. "Am I a bastard child, Mrs. Stanton? Is that why I was sent here?"

Mrs. Stanton did not flinch at the word but looked back at Sarah steadily. "I am not at all certain, my dear, but even it if transpires that this is the case, you have nothing to be ashamed of. Your character is good; you are sweet, kind, and amiable and have nothing to fear from those who might look down on you. Everything I know I have taught you so that you might be an elegant and articulate young lady for when the time came for your marriage."

Sarah smiled at Mrs. Stanton. "And I am grateful for that. However, I must go on my own way now. You are, of course, welcome to join me if you should wish it. I will need a companion."

She held her breath, and Mrs. Stanton considered the matter, before shaking her head.

"No, I think I had best remain here. Mr. Stanton will need me, and as much as I care for you, he must come first." She squeezed Sarah's hands again before letting them go, her eyes glazing over with tears again. "Promise me that you will write to me often, when it comes time for you to leave. I must know where you are and that you are well."

"Of course, I will," Sarah promised, suddenly feeling an ache in her own heart, as she thought about leaving the only home she had ever known. "I will write very often so that you need not concern yourself over me."

Mrs. Stanton smiled and made to turn away, only to stop herself. "You know that you will always have a home here with us, whatever the circumstances, Sarah. Should you wish to return, you only need to appear, and we will welcome you with open arms. You are as much our child as if I had birthed you myself."

"And you are the only mother I have ever known or will ever need," Sarah replied, feeling her own tears threatening. "Thank you. I will keep you informed of any changes to my plans."

Mrs. Stanton nodded and left the room, and Sarah was about to close the door when the maid appeared, telling her that Mr. Stanton and his solicitor were waiting for her in the study, just as soon as she could join them. Sarah spared herself only a few seconds to glance in the mirror and smooth her chestnut-colored hair before setting her shoulders and making her way back to the study, telling herself that she could not stop being brave now. Whilst Mrs. Stanton's conversation had brought her a sharp, unexpected grief at the thought of leaving, Sarah could not allow herself to show any kind of emotion now. She would have to be practical and sensible, showing both men that she had every intention of carrying on with what she had begun.

"Ah, Sarah," Mr. Stanton began, getting out of his chair as she came into the room. "This is Mr. Featherstone, my solicitor. He was in the village today from London, as I said to you before, so he was able to stop in at short notice."

"I had business with a few others in the village, so it is no trouble," Mr. Featherstone replied, heaving his great bulk out of the chair and inclining his head towards Sarah, who found herself staring at one of the largest men she had ever seen. The man was positively rotund, with a faint sheen of sweat appearing on his brow as he bowed. His thinning, fair hair was plastered to his head, his large nose rather red and his small, narrow eyes studying her intently. Sarah felt herself disliking him at once, but setting her personal feelings aside, she sat down with them both.

"It appears you have discovered something about your fortune," Mr. Featherstone began, tutting a little. "You are either a very nosy girl or someone informed you of the matter." He raised one eyebrow and looked Sarah up and down, sniffing disdainfully. "Might I ask which one it is?"

Sarah, feeling as though she was being reprimanded by this man she did not know, felt her cheeks turn scarlet as she fought to keep her anger under control. "I do not think that is any of your business, Mr. Featherstone," she replied caustically. "Please inform me about my fortune and dowry."

Mr. Featherstone did not appear to be in any way pleased by this response, but a look from Mr. Stanton prevented him from saying more.

"Very well," he said, somewhat stiffly. "You have an income of ten thousand pounds a year, Miss Weston, from the year you turned eighteen, which, I believe, was a little over a year ago."

"I am just now turned twenty," Sarah replied, trying to keep a hold of herself at the sudden wealth that was being poured into her lap. "And my dowry?"

Mr. Featherstone pulled some papers from his case and scrutinized them. "Twenty thousand pounds, Miss Weston. Oh, and there is a townhouse in London in your name, although I do not know whether or not it is furnished. There is no staff there yet, of course."

Reeling, Sarah clung to the arms of her chair and tried her best to breathe normally. This was more than a fortune; this was extravagance.

"You were not to know of this until you wed, which is what is most unfortunate," Mr. Featherstone continued, still sounding rather annoyed. "I believe it was felt that a young woman would not be able to manage such a great amount of money alone."

That caught Sarah's attention, bringing her back into the room with a sudden jolt. "I think you—and whoever suggested that—greatly underestimate me, sir," she replied firmly. "And I shall tell you what I intend to do with my fortune, if that is to put you at ease. I intend to give ten thousand pounds, from last year's income, to Mr. and Mrs. Stanton. Immediately."

There was a short, stunned silence. Sarah looked at Mr. Stanton, who was staring at her with wide eyes, his hands grasping the table in front of him.

"Mr. Stanton, I know you were given some income each year to care for me, but I would not have you struggle when that income ceases. I intend to ensure that yourself and Mrs. Stanton are able to live comfortably."

"I...." Mr. Stanton's voice grew hoarse, as he swallowed once, then twice, before shaking his head at her. "You are much too generous, Sarah. I did not expect this from you."

Sarah gave him a half smile. "And that is precisely why I want to give you this, Mr. Stanton. I will confess to being rather angry with you for the multitude of secrets that were kept from me, but I see now that this was not your doing."

Mr. Stanton looked up at her, his gaze steady. "I did what I had to for your own safety, Sarah," he said softly. "I am only sorry that I do not precisely know why or what is the cause of such danger."

Feeling a great deal more in control, Sarah smiled back at him before returning her gaze to the solicitor. Her smile faded from her lips as she kept her gaze firm, wanting to ensure that he knew she had no intention of changing her mind on anything she had discussed so far.

"And is there anything that *you* know, Mr. Featherstone?" she asked, narrowing her gaze a little. "I am sure that you need not hold anything back."

Mr. Featherstone shook his head, clearing his throat as he did so. "No, I know nothing, Miss Weston. I am, after all, your guardian's solicitor and nothing more. I do as I am instructed."

There was something about the way he could not look at her that made Sarah grow a little more suspicious of the rotund man, her fingers tightening in her lap as she kept her gaze fixed on him.

"There is nothing. I assure you," he said again, as if aware of her scrutiny. "What could I know that I would not share with Mr. Stanton?"

Choosing to drop the subject for a moment, Sarah sniffed delicately and turned her head. "Are there papers I need to sign?" she asked, somewhat sharply. "And I should like details of the townhouse in London as well, if you please."

"Why?" Mr. Stanton asked at once, as the solicitor began to shuffle papers about in his briefcase. "Is that where you intend to go?"

As the solicitor laid out papers on the table in front her, Sarah gave Mr. Stanton a slight shrug. "Yes, I think that I should stay there for a time. I know I will need both staff and a companion, but I intend to secure both of those things before I leave. I have already promised Mrs. Stanton that I will write to her regularly so that neither of you will have any cause for concern."

Mr. Stanton nodded slowly, his expression troubled. "I am always going to be concerned for you, my dear. I have not always made the best decisions, nor have I always shown you the care and consideration that you required, and for that, I am sorry."

For a moment, Sarah was struck dumb, not knowing what to say. Mr. Stanton had never spoken to her in such a way before.

"I think I speak for both myself and Mrs. Stanton when I say that we will miss you, Sarah. Our lives will not be as full as they once were."

Wishing that the solicitor was not present so that she might reach forward and take Mr. Stanton's hand for a moment, Sarah contented herself with a gentle smile. "Thank you. I know that I will miss you both very much, but I must go in search of Lord Thorndyke to see what he knows, if anything. I cannot have the rest of my life remain a mystery."

"I quite understand," Mr. Stanton replied, as Mr. Featherstone handed her a quill to sign various documents. "Just know that you will always be welcome here, no matter how long you stay away."

"Thank you," Sarah said gratefully, before turning to sign the papers that would open up the next part of her life.

IT WAS ONLY after Mr. Featherstone had left the house that Sarah felt herself able to tell Mr. Stanton the truth about the locket and the note she had found. It was not that she did not trust Mr. Featherstone, but rather that his attitude towards her had rifled her to the point that she did not want to say more than she had to.

"You were rather suspicious of Mr. Featherstone," Mr. Stanton commented, as Sarah began to tidy up her copies of the papers she had signed. "Might I ask why?"

Briefly, Sarah explained about the locket and the note, watching Mr. Stanton carefully. From the look on his face—the whiteness of his cheeks, the widening of his eyes—he had very little idea who had done this. Nor did he know who might have been watching Sarah so as to place the locket under her pillow.

"I cannot think that it would be one of the staff, for they have been here since before you arrived," he mumbled, looking away from her as his brows furrowed together in thought. "You must be careful, Sarah. The fact that someone has made this much effort to inform you of your fortune means that they have their own purposes behind it."

Sarah gave him a rueful smile. "And those purposes might be nefarious, yes. I had thought of that."

"It troubles me to know that someone has managed to make their way into my home without my knowledge," Mr. Stanton continued gravely. "If I were able to, I would insist that you remain here in safety."

Sarah laughed softly, seeing the wry expression on Mr. Stanton's face. "I know, but it is not something I am willing to do, Mr. Stanton. I will take every precaution; I assure you."

"Do," he said quietly. "It would be the death of me to know that you have been injured or the like, not to mention what it would do to Mrs. Stanton." He let out a long breath, sighing heavily. "This was not what I had intended for you, Sarah."

"I know," she replied quietly, "but I believe it is for the best. You will see. All will come aright in the end. I am sure of it."

6

One month later and Sarah found herself waving goodbye to Mr. Stanton and Mrs. Stanton, feeling as though her heart were about to break in half. She had not expected to feel so upset, but the tears on Mrs. Stanton's cheeks were enough to tear anyone's heart asunder. Their goodbye had been long and drawn out, and as the carriage left the grounds of the only home Sarah knew, she felt herself break into sobs.

"There, there," Mrs. Avis said soothingly, reaching forward to pat Sarah's hand. "You are being very brave so far, Miss Weston, and I am sure that you will do very well once we get to London."

Sarah drew in a sharp breath and tried to steady herself. "Thank you, Mrs. Avis," she said quietly. "It is just rather difficult leaving the home and the parents that have surrounded me for so long." Seeing Mrs. Avis's surprised look, Sarah gave her a small smile, as she dabbed at her cheeks with a handkerchief. "Mr. Stanton is not my father, and Mrs. Stanton not my mother, but they have become those things to me, although I did not recognize that until a few short weeks ago."

Mrs. Avis's eyes warmed with understanding. "I see. They seem heartily sorry to be losing you."

"They are," Sarah replied quietly. "And yet I know this is what I must do."

Mrs. Avis settled back in her seat and made no more comment, pulling out her knitting and beginning to continue with whatever it was she was creating. Sarah closed her eyes and let the sound of the knitting needles soothe her fractious mind, listening to nothing but their noise and letting all other thoughts drift away.

It was not until a few hours later that Sarah awoke, realizing with a start that she had fallen asleep within a few minutes of leaving the Stantons' home. Mrs. Avis was also asleep, her knitting now set aside carefully as her head rocked gently from side to side. Sarah had been glad of her company thus far, even if she had only been awake for a few minutes, but to know that someone was there with her when she awoke was a comfort indeed. Mrs. Avis had responded to Mr. Stanton's notice for a companion for his wife, but when she arrived for the interview, Mrs. Avis was told that a companion was needed for Sarah. Mrs. Avis had accepted this change with ease, and since Sarah found herself liking Mrs. Avis so very much, she had been offered the position within a few hours of arriving for the interview.

Mrs. Avis, who was an unmarried sister of some titled but thrifty lord, had a coil of grey hair pinned neatly to the back of her head, which matched the severity of her clothing. Regardless, Sarah found her to be an amicable and conversational lady, who she was sure would be more than an excellent companion. There had been a little too-ing and fro-ing as Mrs. Avis had returned home for her things, mentioning to Sarah about her quiet, nondescript cottage and somewhat feral cat, which had made Sarah smile. Mrs. Avis seemed as glad to have Sarah's company as she was to have hers, which boded well for their future together. Sarah was unsure as to how long she would require Mrs. Avis, but the lady seemed in no desperate hurry to return home, assuring Sarah that the cat had gone to a neighbor, who often took it in whenever Mrs. Avis went away.

Sighing to herself, Sarah looked out of the window into the growing darkness. It was to be two more days of traveling until they arrived in London, and they would stay in an inn nearby overnight, although she could not see any kind of village or town in the distance as yet. It felt so strange to be a woman traveling alone, a woman with wealth and fortune in her own right. She had been forced to purchase a great many things, including the carriage so that she might have means of transportation. Whilst Mr. Featherstone had offered his services, Sarah had chosen to deal with another solicitor entirely, one whom Mr. Stanton knew of in London. Her solicitor had taken matters in hand, working with her new steward, Mr. Fernley, who together had found her a new household staff and furniture for her home in London. Mr. Stanton, however, had insisted on vetting each member of her household staff himself, which Sarah had found both frustrating and kind. He was clearly still rather concerned for her welfare, and even though this lengthened the process, Sarah could not help but be grateful for Mr. Stanton's kindness.

Now that all was settled, Sarah knew she was certain to find her new home comfortable. A flurry of nerves settled in her stomach, as she continued to look out of the window, feeling as though she were a rabbit drawing purposefully closer to the hunter's snare. There was little point in worrying, she told herself firmly. She had made a plan and fully intended to stick to it.

Lord Thorndyke's manor house, Thorndyke Estate, was on her way to London. She had sent a letter, only to receive the response that Lord Thorndyke had gone to London for the start of the Season. That did not inconvenience her in the least, however, for she still fully intended to call on him in London in the hope that Lord James Thorndyke would see her.

Mr. Stanton had said clearly that Lord Thorndyke might not even know of her existence since it had been his father who had arranged everything with him regarding Sarah and her future. Even that was not about to dissuade Sarah from calling upon the man. Whether he knew anything about her or not, Sarah had to know the truth. She had no other place to start.

~

IT TOOK Sarah three days to reach London, given that one of the carriage wheels had broken during their travels, forcing her to remain at an inn for an extra night whilst it was fixed. She could not help but be even more anxious than usual that night, wondering if the carriage wheel was truly an accident or if there was something else, more sinister, chasing her.

Mrs. Avis had been somewhat unsure as to why Sarah had been acting in such a tense manner, and so—having not explained herself before—Sarah had chosen to tell Mrs. Avis everything. The lady had accepted everything calmly, showing no expression of surprise or even horror on hearing about the locket and note. Given that she had believed she would be accompanying a young lady of means around London in the hope of finding a husband, Mrs. Avis seemed to take the news that things were not as she had been told rather well. She had been able to reassure Sarah that carriage wheels sometimes do break or become damaged and that all this was entirely normal. She had been proven right, of course, for they had now reached London safely, and now Sarah found herself looking up at one of the grandest houses she had ever seen.

"Is this truly my home?" she whispered, as a footman helped

her down from the carriage as though she were some kind of titled lady. "I can hardly believe it."

The house had its own graveled drive with what appeared to be a small garden to one side.

"The gardens lead around the back, Miss Weston," the footman said, as though seeing her questioning gaze. "There is a small stable nearby for the horses and carriage."

"My goodness," Sarah whispered, hardly able to accept that this had been left to her by whomever her benefactor was. "This is extraordinary."

Mrs. Avis smiled at her, as she came to stand next to her. "Shall we go in, Miss Weston?"

Sarah nodded, but paused for a moment. "Sarah, please. I have rarely been referred to as 'Miss Weston' by those I live with, and I should like to consider us friends."

Mrs. Avis looked surprised but nodded, gesturing for Sarah to go on in ahead of her. Taking a deep breath, Sarah walked inside, seeing the butler holding the door open for her.

It was all so bewildering that Sarah did not quite know how to take it all in. The staff were well mannered and polite, just as she would have expected, but there appeared to be such a great number of them that Sarah was not quite sure what to do. Mr. Stanton had never employed a butler before, nor any footmen, so to have so many servants waiting on her was an altogether new experience. The butler introduced her to them all, one at a time, leaving Sarah feeling almost breathless with her sudden change in circumstances.

"Should you like a tour of the house, Miss Weston?" the butler asked, a tall, wiry man with a kind face. "It is large but beautifully airy with a well-stocked library and even a small ballroom."

"A ballroom?" Sarah repeated, astonished. "Good gracious."

"I will, of course, have your things taken to your room at

once," the butler continued, gesturing to a few footmen. "And I thought it best to keep country hours as regards the dinner hour."

Sarah realized that he was looking at her with a somewhat inquiring expression on his face, clearly waiting for her to speak.

"Yes, of course," she stammered, still very much unused to having her own household to run. "Thank you."

"There are also the menus for this week that the housekeeper would like to go over with you, but that is not of any particular urgency," the butler continued, his expression giving very little away. "Should lamb do for this evening?"

Swallowing hard, Sarah nodded and tried to smile, suddenly feeling quite out of place in her own home.

"Wonderful," the butler murmured, walking a few steps and opening one arm towards the rest of the house. "Should you like to start with the drawing room?"

Nodding, Sarah grasped Mrs. Avis's arm firmly, looping it through her own. She had suddenly felt very alone and did not altogether like that feeling nor the feeling that she required Mrs. Avis's company so that she would not feel so overwhelmed.

"Courage, Miss Weston," Mrs. Avis murmured, clearly aware of Sarah's astonishment. "You will become used to all this very soon, I am sure. Just do not give your staff any indication that you are feeling in such a way, else they might take advantage of that in some way."

Sarah, not knowing precisely what Mrs. Avis meant, simply nodded and followed the butler into the drawing room, lifting her chin just a little. This was her new life, the very first piece of the puzzle slotting into place. Whoever had sent her away had a great deal of wealth and was clearly part of the gentry. Did this mean that she was, perhaps, titled? Did she have a standing she was unaware of? Or was it that she was just meant to live comfortably for the rest of her days in the hope that she would never question her parentage?

"This is a beautiful house," Mrs. Avis murmured, pulling Sarah from her thoughts. "You are very blessed, Sarah, to be able to call this place your own."

Sarah looked around the room, taking it all in and finding her heart lifting with a tug of happiness. "Yes," she murmured quietly. "Yes, I believe I am."

7

Sarah gave herself three days before deciding to call upon Lord Thorndyke in person. This was now the third day that she had sent a note around in the early morning, as Mrs. Avis told her would be expected, but yet again, she did not receive any response.

"It is somewhat troubling that I have not yet heard from him," she murmured to herself, wandering to the drawing room window and looking through the lace curtains at the driveway beyond. She wondered what the London streets would be like at this time of day, wondering if they would be busy with the *beau monde* or if that was to come later, perhaps in the afternoon. One thing she had learned from Mrs. Avis was that it was important for those in the *ton* to be seen. This meant that each outing was carefully planned. Gentlemen would call on ladies that they had interest in, whereas those who were still without any kind of firm attachment might wander around Hyde Park in the hope of being seen before returning home to prepare for whatever evening's entertainment they had been invited to.

It all seemed rather pointless to Sarah, who did not care in the least for anything of the kind. All she wanted was to speak with Lord Thorndyke in the hope that he might give her some kind of clue as to where she had come from.

"You cannot go there without an introduction, however," Mrs. Avis continued, as Sarah came back to sit down opposite her. "I do not know the gentleman, and it is a little surprising for a lady to simply appear at a gentleman's door without having been introduced first."

"I do not have time for such things," Sarah replied impatiently. "Either the man knows something about his father's arrangements for me, or he does not. I shall have to find out which it is before thinking about my next steps."

Mrs. Avis did not look pleased with this idea, but Sarah disregarded her frustration at once. Mrs. Avis could not understand the deep, unsettling questions in Sarah's heart; she did not understand her urgency.

"You will come with me, will you not?" Sarah asked quietly. "I mean to go this very afternoon, even if he has not replied to me. I simply must know."

Mrs. Avis nodded without hesitation. "But of course. However, I insist that you wear one of your new gowns, Sarah, and allow the maid to fix your hair. If you are to go without an introduction, then you must make as charming an impression as you can."

Sarah, who was still getting used to having a maid not only help her change but do her hair in a variety of styles, groaned. "But it takes so long, Mrs. Avis."

"Then I suggest you go this very moment," Mrs. Avis replied with a warm smile. "I will be waiting for you, have no doubt."

~

IT WAS with shaking hands and swirling nerves that Sarah found herself knocking at the front door of Lord Thorndyke's townhouse. She had been so confident before, and yet now, standing here waiting for the butler to allow her in, she began to wonder if she had made some kind of terrible mistake. Perhaps Lord Thorndyke would think her unpardonably rude and would throw her from his house and demand she never return. Perhaps Mrs. Avis had been correct in suggesting they find a way to introduce her properly.

"Miss Weston, here to see Lord Thorndyke," she squeaked, handing the butler her card and swallowing her relief when he took it without question, silently thanking Mrs. Avis for insisting she find someone to make her some cards the very day they arrived.

"Lord Thorndyke is unable to see visitors at the moment, Miss Weston," the butler replied with an apologetic smile. "Might I suggest you return another time."

He made to shut the door, but caught by a sudden fear, Sarah put one foot in the doorway, ignoring Mrs. Avis's gasp.

"I *must* see him," she insisted, keeping her gaze as firm as her voice as she attempted to remain as brave as she could despite the nerves rolling in her stomach. "It is of great importance."

The butler frowned, his apologetic smile long gone. "This is highly irregular, Miss Weston. As I have said—"

"I will wait," Sarah said, firmly. "If you could just show me where to sit, then I shall happily wait for him to spare me a few minutes, for that is all I require."

The butler stared at her for a few minutes, his expression dark, but Sarah did not back down. She could not—not now. Especially when it seemed that Lord Thorndyke had no intention of responding to her letters.

"I have written to him the last three days and received no response," she said sharply. "I have come to London for the express reason of speaking with Lord Thorndyke and will not be refused again."

Still frowning, the butler let out a barely audible sigh and opened the door wider, allowing her inside.

"The drawing room is this way, Miss Weston," he murmured, with only a faint hint of disdain in his voice. "Although I may warn you that it could be some hours before he returns."

"Returns?"

Mrs. Avis shot her a look that told Sarah she should not be asking questions such as this, feeling her cheeks burn as the butler cleared his throat.

"Business, Miss Weston," the butler replied eventually, opening the door to a bright, airy drawing room. "Should you require a tea tray?"

Sarah nodded, sitting down carefully. "Thank you, that would be appreciated."

"I shall inform the master that you are here the moment he returns," the butler murmured quietly. "Do excuse me."

~

THREE HOURS PASSED, and Sarah felt herself growing more and more frustrated with the invisible Lord Thorndyke. He had not yet appeared, and Sarah felt as though he were deliberately avoiding her despite having never made his acquaintance.

"Do not be too hasty to judge him," Mrs. Avis murmured, as Sarah let out her frustration in a torrent of words. "Lord Thorndyke is clearly unaware of your presence in his home, and as such, he does not feel the need to hurry his business along. You have waited this long, my dear. Do not hasten away in frustration but be patient."

Crossing and uncrossing her ankles, Sarah sat back in her chair and let out a long breath, ignoring Mrs. Avis's sharp look at her lack of decorum. She did not care that she was not sitting correctly, not when it was just herself and Mrs. Avis within the room.

Suddenly, the sound of a loud, angry voice reached her ears, winding its way under the door towards her. Sitting up straight, Sarah readjusted her skirts, trying her best not to worry about Lord Thorndyke's reaction to her. It was clear that the man was unhappy, although whether or not that was to do with her presence, she was not at all certain.

"Remember to rise the moment he comes in," Mrs. Avis murmured, her face drawn with anxiety. "Goodness, he does not sound pleased in the least, Sarah."

Sarah did not have time to respond, for the door opened and in stormed a gentleman with nothing but fury on his face. Sarah rose at once and dropped into a curtsy, aware of just how angry the man was.

"Lord Thorndyke?" she asked, as he folded his arms and frowned at her.

The man was tall, broad shouldered. He had a youthful face and strong features, his brown hair matching the color of his eyes.

"Are you truly Miss Weston?" he asked, his voice loud and rasping. "Miss Sarah Weston?"

She nodded, her hands tightening, as she sat back down and placed them in her lap. Her legs were shaking, as her nerves assailed her, her heart hammering wildly at the fierce look in his eyes.

"This is Mrs. Avis, my companion," she said slowly. "I did not mean to upset you, Lord Thorndyke, but there are some question that I must ask you. I could not wait any longer, especially since my notes had not been returned."

He shook his head, passing one hand over his eyes as a quiet groan escaped him. "Miss Weston, did you never think that no response was, in itself, a response? I did not want you here. I never dreamed that you would call without introduction."

Heat seared her cheeks.

"But, then again, perhaps you do not know all that you ought for your station. You have not been living as the person you are, of course. I had forgotten that."

That made Sarah frown, her eyes darting to Mrs. Avis and back to Lord Thorndyke. It was as though he had been talking to himself, forgetting that she was there. "Whatever do you mean?"

"Had you stayed in your townhouse, then your presence in London might have remained quiet, but now, it seems, I must do what I promised. He will, of course, have had a man watching the house."

Frustration rose in Sarah's chest. "Who? Of what are you speaking, Lord Thorndyke? You are keeping me completely in the dark, and I do not find it in any way helpful. I have come here for answers and—"

"And you shall get them," he said gravely, "but not at this very moment. Come, Miss Weston. We must be off."

He rose to his feet and held out his hand, but Sarah remained exactly where she was, refusing to go near him.

"Now," he said, his tone brooking no argument. "It is imperative."

Sarah shook her head, sitting a little further back in her chair and folding her arms across her chest. She was suddenly filled with a deep dislike of this particular gentleman, who appeared to know a great more than she did and yet was choosing to order her about as though he had the right to do so.

"I will not be going anywhere with you, Lord Thorndyke," she said firmly. "Not until I have a reasonable explanation as to who you are and what you know of me."

Lord Thorndyke shook his head and reached for her, only

for Sarah to jerk backward in her chair, suddenly horrified at the realization that he intended to take her somewhere by force.

"Lord Thorndyke!" she exclaimed, as Mrs. Avis rose from her chair, hurrying to Sarah's side. "You will not touch me again!"

He growled, as Mrs. Avis elbowed her way past him, looping one arm through Sarah's as she rose to her feet.

"Mrs. Avis, I think it is best we go," she said firmly, ignoring the clamoring of her heart as it screamed in fright. "Lord Thorndyke, until you are willing to speak to me about what you know, I will go about my life just as I please. I have already had one man order my life for me, although he did it out of the goodness of his heart and because he was as much in the dark as I was. You, on the other hand, clearly know more about me and my heritage, and yet you appear to think you can order me about as you please despite not saying anything about your information to me." She stepped away from him, making her way towards the door. "I will not be treated so."

Lord Thorndyke's face grew angry, as she walked past him, his hands curled into fists. "Miss Weston, this is for your own safety."

"What is?" she challenged, turning towards him and arching one eyebrow. "What is it that I must do?"

He planted his feet and fixed his gaze on her, as though by sheer force of will he would have her obey. "You are to be my bride."

Sarah froze for a moment before a strangled laugh left her throat, her eyes wide with astonishment.

"That is one of the most ridiculous things I have ever heard. Good afternoon to you. I do hope that you will call upon me soon so that we might talk."

"You must," he insisted, hurrying over to her, as she opened the door. "It is too dangerous otherwise."

Sarah lifted her chin and glared at him, her foot wedged

painfully in the door as he leaned on it. "And yet I find myself disinclined to accept you without any knowledge as to why I should do so."

"I will tell you everything, but only after we are wed. You must be under my protection, and for what it is worth, we are already betrothed. My solicitors have the contract should you wish to see it, although I did hope that it would never come to this."

The thought of her fortune suddenly sprang to her mind. "I do hope that it is not that you wish to take possession of my wealth, Lord Thorndyke," she said slowly, seeing his face burn with a sudden fire. "You must be addled to think that I would simply agree to marry a man I have never met, just because he says so. Now, are you going to explain it all to me, or will you let me leave to return home?" Keeping her eyes on his, Sarah looked up at Lord Thorndyke steadily, her courage mounting with every second.

"I cannot talk about this now," he said quietly, as though trying to tell her something with the look in his eyes. "Please, stay, Miss Weston. Come to the church with me."

Sighing heavily, Sarah shook her head and wrenched the door open. "Good day, Lord Thorndyke. I do hope that we will have the opportunity to speak again soon." And, with that, she marched out of the drawing room and made her way to the front door with Mrs. Avis in tow, feeling stronger than she had ever done before.

8

"Are you not dancing this evening, Lord Thorndyke?"

James shrugged and threw back the rest of his brandy. "Not this evening, Higgs."

"That is most unlike you, especially at Almacks," Viscount Higgs replied, looking a trifle concerned. "You are not unwell, I hope?"

James shook his head. "No. Just caught up with my thoughts, Higgs."

His friend nodded sagely. "I see. Of course. One of the many responsibilities and duties of the title, is it not? To be caught up with thoughts?"

Unable to stop himself from smiling, James nodded. "Apparently so." Taking his friend's arm, he drew him back into the shadows, aware that he could tell him almost anything.

"Higgs, you are not to breathe a word of this, but the lady I told you about...she has appeared at my doorstep."

Lord Higgs sucked in a breath, letting it out slowly as his eyes widened.

"She did not immediately accept coming to the church with me, despite the contract and license," James continued with a slight shrug. "It was foolish of me to think that she would, but I could not tell her the reasons why she was required to do so."

"Why not?" Higgs asked, frowning. "She was in your home, was she not? What safer place could there be?"

James shook his head, his gut tightening. "She had a companion with her, a Mrs. Avis. I have no idea who she is, and until I do, I cannot talk openly with Miss Weston."

Higgs sighed heavily, shaking his head. "That is wise, I suppose, but it does make things a trifle difficult for you."

"Yes, it does," James replied heavily. "I had ignored her notes in the hope that I would have some time to collect my thoughts and make plans for the future, never thinking that she would be as improper as to simply appear at my house." To his surprise, James found himself chuckling as he remembered the mulish look on Miss Weston's face. "She is a stubborn creature; that is for certain."

"And a pretty one?"

James considered for a moment, recalling Miss Weston's dark brown tresses and the sparkle in her blue eyes. She had delicate features, and yet there was something that told him she had a hidden strength deep within. "Yes, she is that. I do not think I should mind having her on my arm once she is under my protection, of course."

"And are you certain you still need to marry her?" his friend said slowly. "Could you not simply find another way to ensure she is kept safe?"

It was a question that had dogged James's mind for some time, wondering if a promise made on his father's deathbed still held water. "I do not think I can go back on it now, not when I promised my father I would do as he asked. You can imagine my surprise on finding that I was not only betrothed, but that there was already a contract in place as regards the merging of our two families and the dowry that goes along with it. Apparently, Miss

Weston is to retain control of her fortune when we are wed, although the dowry comes to me." When he closed his eyes, James could still sometimes see his father's tired smile, as James promised to fulfill his betrothal should Miss Weston ever appear. He had promised to marry the lady, hoping that it would never come to that, but now it appeared fate had other ideas.

Lord Higgs rolled his eyes. "You are much too considerate, Thorndyke. Were I in your position, then I would marry whomever I wished and find some other way to ensure Miss Weston's safety – although safety from what, you have never really told me." A note of curiosity entered Lord Higgs's voice, but James shook his head.

"It is best that as few people as possible know what it is all about," he said slowly. "I am just relieved that Miss Weston will not be appearing at any kind of occasion. She should remain at home for most of the day, if I am any judge. She does not know anyone here and so–"

Lord Higgs suddenly grasped James's arm, cutting off the conversation completely. "My goodness. Who is that angel?"

Aware that Lord Higgs often lost his heart to a whole variety of eligible young ladies, James looked around to see to whom his friend was referring, only to see Miss Weston walking into Almacks with Mrs. Avis by her side. His stomach lurched as he took in her shy smile and the way her cheeks dusted with pink as she looked all around her. Mrs. Avis waited until her charge had sat down before taking a seat just behind her.

"How can this be?" James whispered, staring at Miss Weston with nothing but fear rifling through him. "She cannot be here. This is too dangerous for her."

"What are you talking about?" Higgs asked impatiently, glancing away from Miss Weston for a moment. "Oh, goodness!" he exclaimed, seeing James's horror. "Never say that she is...."

"She is Miss Weston, my betrothed," James said dully. "I

cannot understand how she secured tickets for Almacks. She is not titled, nor does she come from a good family – not that anyone knows of, at least, so how did she manage to attend?"

As he watched, a lady detached herself from another crowd and came towards Miss Weston, who rose at once to greet her with a wide smile on her face.

"Apparently Lady Hendrickson has taken to her," Lord Higgs murmured with a lift of his eyebrow. "Did you not say that Miss Weston has a great fortune?"

James groaned, rubbing one hand over his eyes. This had all gone entirely wrong. She had never been meant to know of her fortune, not until she was married to a gentleman, which meant that she would never come to London and he would never have to fulfill his betrothal to her. His engagement was the last resort, a way of ensuring her safety should she somehow discover what she was not meant to.

Now, it seemed, he was going to have to declare himself even before she'd agreed to wed him, before they had had a chance to discuss it all. *But that will spread around London like wildfire,* he thought, frowning. *Should you not be trying to keep her presence here as quiet as possible?*

But how could he do that when a lady like Lady Hendricks took the girl under her wing and gave her tickets to Almacks? Once it was discovered that she lived in one of the most coveted homes in London, that she was in charge of her own fortune and had a great deal of it to boot, he was certain that Miss Weston would be invited to all kinds of social occasions despite her lack of title.

This was worse than he had ever imagined.

"*Do* introduce me," Higgs hissed, as they made their way towards Miss Weston. "I must be introduced to one of the most beautiful ladies I have ever seen, even if she is your betrothed."

James gritted his teeth, not finding any pleasure in greeting

Miss Weston, who looked up at him with a pleased smile on her face. He felt himself tensing, hating that she was playing him for a fool whilst so clearly disregarding everything he had said.

"Oh, so you know Lord Thorndyke, do you?" Lady Hendricks said, once all the introduction had been made. "How wonderful for you, Miss Weston. I am sure Lord Thorndyke will dance with you, and then you will have no end of gentlemen seeking your hand."

It was something he could not risk, but seeing no way out, James inclined his head and offered Miss Weston his hand. "But of course."

Miss Weston did not hesitate but took it at once, excusing herself from Lord Higgs, Lady Hendricks, and her companion, Mrs. Avis. As James led her towards the dance floor, he suddenly realized that he now had Miss Weston entirely alone. This was, perhaps, the opportunity he had been waiting for.

"Miss Weston," he murmured, as he led her towards the back of the dance floor, hoping to slip out unseen. "What are you doing here?"

She looked up at him, no surprise on her face. "Dancing, hopefully," she replied, with a touch of tartness in her voice. "Although quite where you are going, I cannot say."

He grasped her waist in the shadowy darkness and tugged her along to a door at the back of the ballroom.

"Lord Thorndyke," she hissed, struggling to release herself. "What are you doing?"

"Trying to talk to you," he said firmly. "I have to speak to you in private, Miss Weston. Do you not understand? I could not speak plainly when Mrs. Avis was with you."

She snorted and pulled herself away from him. "Nonsense," she exclaimed, as he caught her wrist. "Mrs. Avis is nothing more than my companion. I have spoken to her about why I have come to London, and she has not raised an eyebrow. She is vastly sensible, Lord Thorndyke, which is more than I can say for you."

Growing more and more frustrated with the lady, James stopped dead, grasped Miss Weston's other wrist, and looked into her face.

"Miss Weston," he grated angrily. "Either you come with me, or I will hoist you over my shoulder and carry you wherever I please, do you understand me?"

He could tell from her expression that she realized he was serious about his intentions, and that she could not push him any further. The smile left her face; the sparkle in her eyes dimmed, and she seemed to shrink before his very eyes.

"Very good," he murmured, her hand now quiet in his own. "Please, walk with me, Miss Weston. There is a room just beyond where we might talk."

"I should have my companion," she stated, her voice quiet now. "It is not proper."

He shrugged. "We are betrothed, Miss Weston. I doubt anyone will care, should that news come out." So saying, he opened the door, led her along a small corridor and into another, small room, which held some chairs and a small table. Miss Weston scurried to a chair, sitting down quickly, and as he locked the door behind them both, he saw her stare at him with wide eyes.

"I am not going to hurt you," he promised in a gentler tone. "You need not worry that I will do so deliberately, but you cannot trust a single person, Miss Weston, not even Mrs. Avis."

She lifted her chin in a show of strength, but still, he saw her fingers tremble just a little. "Does that mean I should not trust you?"

He sat down heavily, shaking his head. "No, you can trust me, Miss Weston. In truth, I did not ever think that we would have the opportunity to meet."

"But we are betrothed."

Nodding, James looked up to see the confusion in her eyes. "Indeed we are, but that is only in place until you wed." Aware that this had only added to her puzzlement, James sat back in his chair and sighed. "I promised my father I would marry you and fulfill the betrothal contract should you seek me out. That was never supposed to happen, Miss Weston. You were meant to marry another of Mr. Stanton's choosing, and only discover the truth about your fortune once you were wed."

Her expression clouded, and to his surprise, James felt a jolt of sympathy run through him.

"So, I was to be controlled," she said softly, her lips turning down. "And you were as much a part of it as any other."

That caught his heart, his eyes dimming. "Yes, I suppose that is so. But as I have said so often, it was for your own good."

One hand slammed down on the chair arm, astonishing him. "That is something I have heard so often," Miss Weston exclaimed, her face now filled with anger. "But no one explains to me why this is. Mr. Stanton could not because he did not know, apparently, but you..." she continued, pointing one finger in his direction, "*You* know, but you will not say!"

For the first time, James realized just how upset Miss Weston was. Closing his eyes, he tried to put himself in her place for a moment, caught with just how frightening a place that must be. To not know who you truly were, nor where you had come from, must be a terrifying feeling.

"I am sorry," he said slowly, opening his eyes and seeing her look back at him with an expression of fading anger. "I have never thought about how this must be for you. When I say that this is for your good, it is precisely that, nothing more. Mr. Stanton did not know all so that he could never say anything to you – or at least, that was what my father said."

She nodded slowly, sitting back in her chair and taking in a deep breath. "So, who am I?"

He smiled at her and was caught by the small smile he received in return. For a second, his heart stopped beating, making him jump in surprise at such a reaction.

"Lord Thorndyke?" she asked, when he did not say anything. "Please, tell me who I am. I must know. All I know is I have a fortune and a dowry that I was never supposed to learn about, as well as a townhouse that I had to furnish myself. There are so many puzzling questions, and I cannot find any answers."

His heart broke for her, seeing her vulnerable and frustrated all at once. "Before I tell you, might I ask how you discovered such a thing?"

Miss Weston let out a long breath and looked away. "You will not be pleased to hear me say this, but someone put a parcel under my pillow one evening."

A flurry of fear climbed up his spine.

"No one unusual was seen, but it was there when I returned to my room after leaving dinner early," she said quietly. "It contained a note and a locket."

That caught his interest. "A locket?"

She nodded, looking up at him with a sudden hope. "Do you know who it belongs to? The note said I was to find the owner of the locket here in London and that everything would become clear."

"I should like to look at it before I say anything," James replied carefully. "Might I call tomorrow?"

A flash of disappointment crossed her face, but she nodded.

"Thank you," he said quietly. "There is a reason to my request that you remain away from society, Miss Weston, and it is because there may be someone who wishes to harm you."

She did not look either surprised or afraid. "Why?" she asked, frowning slightly. "What have I done?"

His smile was immediate. "It is not what you have done, my dear Miss Weston. This has nothing to do with you, in fact, but yet you are caught up in it. Your name is not your true name nor your true title, but even with this, I fear that your features may become quite recognizable to those who wish to harm you."

She rose then and came over to him, desperation in her eyes, as she took the chair by his right hand. Clasping her hand over his, she looked up into his face. "Please, Lord Thorndyke," she whispered, as though terrified and yet desperate for the answer. "Tell me who I am."

Putting his other hand over hers, he nodded slowly, the words sticking in his throat. "My dear Miss Weston, whilst we will continue to refer to you as Miss Weston until circumstances change, you are, in fact, Lady Sarah Fairley, daughter to the Duke of Brighton."

9

Sarah paced up and down the drawing room, the locket clutched in her hand. She had barely slept a wink last night, struggling to accept what Lord Thorndyke had told her.

She was not Miss Sarah Weston, daughter of a gentleman. She was, in fact, Sarah Fairley, daughter to a duke. The Duke of Brighton at that, although she had been saddened to learn that her father had passed away some years ago.

She had been so overcome with the news last evening that Lord Thorndyke had been forced to go in search of something for her to drink, returning with a glass of water, as well as two glasses of brandy. It was not something she was used to drinking, but she had accepted it regardless, feeling the warmth spreading life back into her limbs. Lord Thorndyke had more to tell her, of course, but he had chosen not to speak of it to her last evening, telling her that she had more than enough to consider before promising to come back to speak to her again this afternoon.

Sarah drew in a long breath, as she looked out of the window, her stomach churning wildly. She had never expected this; she had never believed that she would be so highly titled and of such consequence to society. There had been no explanation as to why she was in danger, as to why someone was still seeking to hurt her in some way, but Lord Thorndyke had promised to explain everything.

She had left Almacks very soon after her conversation with Lord Thorndyke had ended, declaring herself weary with the crush of it all and complaining to Mrs. Avis of a headache on the way home. Lord Thorndyke had warned her not to speak of what she knew to anyone, including Mrs. Avis, which seemed somewhat ridiculous given how much she had already shared with her companion, but he had been insistent. Why she had agreed to do as he had asked, she was not quite sure, but there was something about him that almost insisted that she trust him.

"I do trust him," she said aloud, a little bewildered to discover that this was how she felt about him. They had such a short acquaintance, and yet she knew that he was a gentleman of honor – although whether or not she would marry him was not yet something she was allowing herself to consider. Lord Thorndyke had insisted that there was a contract, which she had asked to see, but even if it was produced, Sarah was not certain she would agree. This was all so new, so overwhelming that she had very little idea of what to do next.

"Miss Weston?"

The door opened to reveal the butler, and Sarah, wasting no time, nodded to him to allow Lord Thorndyke in.

The dark-haired gentleman stepped inside at once, his once angry face now gentle with a soft smile, as he bent over her hand. His touch sent shivers up her spine, although whether it was from the awareness that he knew everything about her or from the brush of his fingers on her, Sarah could not say.

"Sit down, please," she said hurriedly, as the maid brought

the tea tray in, right on cue. "I am glad to see you, Lord Thorndyke."

He smiled at her then, his brown eyes warm. "As am I, Miss Weston." Looking about him, he raised his eyebrows as he looked back at her. "Mrs. Avis?"

"She will not be joining us, as you requested," Sarah replied firmly. "She was not pleased, you understand, worrying about my reputation, but I reminded her that we are engaged, and as such, it is best that I get to know my future husband."

The smile faded from his expression. Clearly, he was not as delighted at the prospect of matrimony as she had thought. "I see."

"Did you bring the contract?"

Nodding, he pulled out a few folded papers from the breast pocket of his coat and handed them to her. "I have sent a copy to your solicitors also."

Her stomach churning, Sarah unrolled the first and began to read, her heart slamming into her chest as she read through the details.

"This says I am to have control of my fortune regardless," she breathed, suddenly completely astonished. "That is quite unheard of."

A chuckle escaped Lord Thorndyke's mouth. "Yes, I am well aware of that," he said with a wry grin. "I think it was so that you could be assured this was not put in place for my benefit, but for your own."

"That does settle my concerns somewhat," Sarah admitted, looking up at him and finding a gentleness in his expression that she had not expected. "But you do not wish to marry me, I think."

Lord Thorndyke shrugged, his mouth tipping into a small smile. "Every gentleman must marry, Miss Weston. This suits me well enough."

It was not exactly what she had hoped for, although she had never given matrimony much thought. Perhaps, she realized, she had dreamed of marriage with affection between herself and her husband, or even a husband she had chosen herself. That was not the case with Lord Thorndyke.

"And why is this for my own safety?" she said, setting the papers down and pouring the tea instead. "You said you would explain everything to me, Lord Thorndyke. Please do so now."

He did not answer her immediately but kept his gaze on her. "Do you have the locket?"

She paused, setting the teapot down before lifting it from the pocket of her gown. Their fingers brushed as she passed it to him, making his eyes jump to hers for a moment. Putting it down to nervousness, Sarah drew in a deep breath and watched him carefully as he studied it.

Much to her disappointment, he frowned.

"No, I do not recognize this piece," he said slowly. "There is no inscription nor anything inside."

"No, there is not," she said sadly. "I had wondered if it was my mother's."

Lord Thorndyke shrugged, handing it back to her. "It may be, but I cannot say for certain. I have a few people I could ask about it, should you be willing to allow me to do so."

"Of course," Sarah replied quickly. "I would very much like to know who the locket belongs to, although I will say I am surprised that you do not recognize it. I thought it would be easy to identify."

Accepting a cup from her, he lifted the cup to his lips and took a sip, his dark eyes regarding her carefully as if assessing whether or not she was able to hear the truth. Sarah waited patiently, steadying her nerves as she looked back at him.

"Let me start at the beginning, Miss Weston. I will not hold anything back from you; I promise you that."

Sarah drew in a deep breath, steadying herself as Lord Thorndyke began to speak.

"You are the daughter of the Duke of Brighton, who was an honorable man," Lord Thorndyke began quietly. "He had a son first and then a daughter. However, his brother, Lord Andrew Fairley, was not a good man. In fact, he threw away his fortune into nothing more than gambling and...well, other rather unpleasant vices."

Sarah saw Lord Thorndyke's cheeks color, as he looked away, feeling her own stomach tighten with disgust.

"Lord Andrew continued to request funds from the duke and, initially, the duke was very kind to him. He was his brother after all, and I believe Lord Andrew made more than a few promises to turn his back on such vices and start again. Eventually, the duke learned that this was not the case and that the estate he had given his brother was about to be sold by Lord Andrew to regain some of the money he had lost." Lord Thorndyke shook his head, his lips thinning. "The duke bought the estate back and turned his back on his brother entirely."

Sarah did not know what to say, her hands beginning to tremble, as she placed her teacup down on the table. To hear of her father brought her such a deep emotion that she could barely speak; she was glad that he had been a man of honor and respect.

"Lord Andrew did not take this well," Lord Thorndyke continued gently. "He swore to do all he could to get his revenge on your father, claiming he had been treated unfairly."

"But it was all his own doing," Sarah protested, her heart growing sick at the thought of Lord Andrew pursuing his own kind of cruel justice. "How could he hold my father responsible for that?"

Lord Thorndyke shook his head. "Because there is a darkness in him that cannot be explained. He...he killed your mother, Sarah."

The world around her began to spin, and she was forced to clutch onto the arms of her chair, trying her best not to faint.

Lord Thorndyke was beside her in a moment, taking one of her hands in his and looking deeply into her eyes.

"I did not mean to shock you," he said slowly, "but it is the truth. Your mother was out riding when he fired his shotgun near her. The horse rose up in fright, and your mother fell from the saddle. I do not know whether he ever meant her to lose her life, but regardless, he was responsible. Your mother was out riding with two stable hands behind her – one followed Lord Andrew whilst the other stayed with your mother. Lord Andrew was never caught, and when questioned, he denied all knowledge of the incident. There was nothing your father could do."

Sarah could not speak, her throat aching with sheer pain over the loss of her mother, a mother she could not remember.

"Your father made arrangements for you and your brother," Lord Thorndyke continued softly. "Your brother is the new Duke of Brighton and has taken his place and his title as he ought, but the danger has not yet passed. He lives on his country estate and does not often come to London."

A shadowy figure crept into Sarah's memory, the figure of a young boy laughing and teasing her in a garden somewhere.

"I have a brother," she whispered, tears slipping down her cheeks, as she stared, unseeingly, at Lord Thorndyke.

"You do," he said, pressing her hand. "He believes Lord Andrew to still be a danger since he is still living, and being a decade younger than your father, he is in fairly good health."

Sarah clutched at Lord Thorndyke's hand, feeling him to be her solid anchor in the midst of a terrifying storm.

"He is often seen in society but has never once shown any kind of repentance over what happened. In fact, my father often talked with me about the kind of things he would say about his brother. In addition," he said, slowing down his speech and frowning as if wondering whether or not to say something. "In addition...no, perhaps I had best wait—"

"Tell me," she begged, one hand wrapping around his neck as she forced his eyes to meet hers. "Please, Lord Thorndyke, do not keep anything from me. I must know it all."

He nodded slowly, a sad smile on his face. "In addition, Miss Weston, there were some near misses with your father. A few things that appeared to be accidents, but had they been only a few inches one way or the next could have easily taken your father's life. My father was dear friends with yours, and so, over the years, they continued to keep watch on Lord Andrew. The man is determined to do all he can to ruin the duke's family, even in death. My father swore to yours that he would help him keep his son and daughter safe, even if it meant that you would never know the truth about your parentage or your place in society." He patted her hand, his expression softening. "Better to live a quiet life than to have one being chased by death," he finished quietly. "I promised to protect you, should you ever return to London whilst your uncle still lived, and so I will, by marrying you at once."

There was nothing for Sarah to say. Instead, tears poured into her eyes and fell onto her cheeks as she mourned for a father she would never know, a mother taken from her too soon. She felt no shame in letting her grief show, feeling Lord Thorndyke's hands on hers as she wept. Gentle fingers brushed her tears away, before pressing a handkerchief into her hand.

"Will you marry me, Sarah?" he asked, his eyes searching her face. "I cannot imagine the torment that you are going through, but can you not see that you are in danger here? It would not be right of me to allow you to live here alone any longer, not even with your companion. Lord Andrew is, at this very moment, in

London for the Season, although how he has the wealth to do so, I cannot say. Let me fulfill my promise to my father."

Sarah drew in a shaking breath, her heart filled with nothing but pain. "Very well," she whispered, not seeing any other way forward but to accept. "I will marry you, Lord Thorndyke."

There came no smile of delight, no burst of happiness in his expression as she accepted, but only a calm acceptance and a sigh of relief. "Thank you, Sarah," he said, pressing her hand gently. "I will make all the arrangements. You can leave everything to me."

"Thank you," Sarah replied dully, not knowing what else to say. Her parents were gone. Her hope of a family waiting to welcome her was dashed to pieces. There was nothing except Lord Thorndyke, and the thought of marrying him brought her no pleasure.

There was only pain.

10

Finishing his letter, James sighed aloud and sealed it closed, his heart heavy. He was writing to the new Duke of Brighton, who was residing in his country estate and taking every precaution when it came to his nefarious uncle. James had only met the man once but had written to him on more than one occasion since he had taken up the title. The duke knew everything about James's involvement with the family and was more than grateful for their correspondence, for it meant that the duke could rest a little easier whenever Lord Andrew appeared in London. However, this time, James was to inform him that, not only had the duke's sister reappeared in London, but that he was to marry her for her own safety and protection, as well as fulfilling a promise he had made to his own father.

There was nothing but relief in that knowledge, although somewhere, deep within himself, James felt a spark of excitement about doing so. It was a very strange sensation, for James never allowed himself to think about anything other than practicality when it came to Miss Weston, even though he knew that she was rather beautiful. He hated that he had reacted when she touched his hand; he did not like the fact that his heart had quickened painfully in his chest as he had done so. Yes, he was sympathetic to her plight and could never truly understand the pain she was going through, but to feel anything more was foolish. Emotion would cloud his judgment and make him slow to react.

"You look as though you have a lot on your mind."

James looked up as his friend Lord Higgs walked into his study, a broad smile on his face.

"That is because I do have a lot to think about," he replied calmly. "I am to marry Miss Weston, after all."

Lord Higgs let out a long whistle of surprise. "Well," he muttered, looking all about for where James had put the decanter of brandy. "That is quick, Thorndyke. So long as you are sure about it."

"I am sure," James replied, a touch too quick. "I made a promise, and it is one I intend to keep. I proposed to Miss Weston two days ago and she agreed to marry me."

"Mmm," Higgs murmured, narrowing his gaze just a little. "I have known you for a long time, Thorndyke, and I have never heard you consider matrimony with any kind of hope or anticipation. It is as though you are a man being led, unwillingly, to the gallows."

James shook his head. "It is not that at all. I am quite happy to be marrying Miss Weston. Truly. She will make me an excellent wife, I am certain of it."

Lord Higgs set a brandy down on the desk in front of James and then took his seat. "Is that so?" he murmured, clearly a little disbelieving. "There is another way, you know."

James lifted one eyebrow. "And what is that?"

"Remove the threat of Lord Andrew."

It was such an obvious answer that, for a moment, James wanted to laugh aloud.

"I know, I know, you will say that it is something you have thought about already, but the truth is that, should you remove the threat of Lord Andrew, then neither of you needs to marry the other. You will both be free to live your own lives and marry whomever you choose."

It was not something James had ever thought seriously about, knowing that Lord Andrew would not be easy to tackle. "I cannot shoot a man in cold blood, if that is what you are thinking, Higgs. There is nothing I can do when it comes to that man."

Higgs shrugged. "Have you tried?"

Letting out a long, frustrated breath, James shook his head. "Then tell me, what do you think I can do? I will not kill him, if that is what you are thinking."

Chuckling, Higgs sat up a little straighter and took a sip of his brandy before replying. "Rumor has it the man has married. Did you know that? There must be a reason he is back in London, which we can assume is to try and continue his search for his brother's children, but he has been getting the money from somewhere in order to do so. Perhaps he married a rich wife."

"I doubt that," James replied, shaking his head. "What kind of lady would marry a gentleman of such disrepute?"

Higgs frowned. "Perhaps she had no choice. It is not as though all ladies are given a choice over whom they wed."

"I find it highly unlikely that any father would force their daughter to marry Lord Andrew when he is well known to be a gambler and a cheat with very little money to call his own."

"It is still possible," Higgs suggested calmly. "After all, that is the rumor." He tipped his head and regarded James carefully. "And it might lead you to the opportunity to live your own life, free of your engagement to Miss Weston."

James fell silent, allowing his thoughts to sit heavily on his mind. The thought of removing himself from his engagement to Miss Weston was not one that brought him even the smallest modicum of happiness nor of relief. It was as if he truly *did* want to marry her, even though he had told himself repeatedly that he was doing it out of duty. Were he free to choose whomever he wished, were she free to do the same, would he still keep their engagement? As yet, no one knew of it, and therefore he could break it off without any consequences. Miss Weston would be sure to find a great many suitors due to her great fortune, as well as her beauty.

That thought made him frown. He did not want Miss Weston to be surrounded by gentlemen whose first thought was what money they could gain access to should they marry her. She might not be able to discern one gentleman from another; she not be able to discover their true motivations until after her wedding day, and that thought brought a twist of anger to James's heart.

"No," he said aloud, speaking as much to himself as to Lord Higgs. "No, I will marry Miss Weston. We are engaged, and I will be going to seek a special license from the archbishop just as soon as I receive a reply from the new Duke of Brighton. I will need his blessing to show to the archbishop in order to gain such a license, but I do not think it will be long. Within the week, I hope."

"And that means you do not have to worry about the banns being called," Lord Higgs murmured, nodding slowly. "I understand. You do not want to reveal Miss Weston's true identity."

"Precisely," James stated, taking a sip of his brandy. "Although should her uncle see her, I would guess that he will recognize her features to be that of the late duke's. She is very evidently his daughter."

Lord Higgs looked at James thoughtfully, his eyes glazing over for a moment in an expression that James recognized as deep consideration. He remained silent for a time before speaking again.

"Are you truly going to live your life in fear of Lord Andrew, Thorndyke?" he asked slowly, a frown growing between his brows. "Are you going to whisk Miss Weston away to your country estate in the hope that Lord Andrew will never find her? What if you have children? When will the worry over Lord Andrew end?"

James frowned, having never considered as much before.

"Whether or not you marry Miss Weston, I cannot see how such a heavy burden as Lord Andrew's presence can continue to weigh on both your shoulders. The man may be alive for some time yet, and I cannot imagine that it will be a life of joy for you both to be constantly on your guard."

"I...I do not know what we shall do," James replied slowly, realizing he had never thought of such a thing before. "I had not thought about it."

Higgs gave him a small, rueful smile. "Then might I suggest that you consider your intentions as regards Lord Andrew, Thorndyke? I am here to help you, of course, but I do not want you to be burdened with Lord Andrew's presence any longer than you need to be. Surely, there must be something we can do to rid you of his loathsome presence?"

James sighed, looking down at the sketch of the locket he had drawn earlier. That was the only other thing that he could think of looking into, else he would just continue with his plan to marry Miss Weston and then move to the country.

"The only thing we could do is find the owner of this locket," he said, picking up the paper and handing it to Lord Higgs. "Do not ask me why, but it is possibly of more importance than any of us know. Miss Weston was given it by someone she does not know, who slipped it under her pillow when she was at dinner."

"At her guardian's home?" Lord Higgs asked, one eyebrow raised in surprise.

"Yes," James said a little heavily. "It is what set her on the path here. I cannot help but wonder why someone would do such a thing and what their intentions were."

Lord Higgs let out a long hiss, his eyes fixed on the locket. To James's surprise, something flared in Higgs's eyes as he looked at it, making the man sit up a little straighter.

"I might be able to help you with this, Thorndyke," Lord Higgs exclaimed, suddenly sounding excited. "I think I know where this came from."

"Oh?"

Lord Higgs grinned, handing the paper back. "Last season there was a theft at once of the pawnbrokers here in town. That locket was the only thing that was taken."

James's eyebrows shot into his hair, as he stared at Lord Higgs.

"Best go get Miss Weston for this," Lord Higgs continued, settling back into his chair. "We are to go into town this afternoon. We will see what answers we can find from that pawnbroker, shall we?"

James nodded, his heart slamming into his chest with astonishment. "I will send for her at once," he breathed, getting up to ring the bell. "Goodness me, Higgs. Whoever would have thought that you would be able to help us with this?"

Lord Higgs chuckled. "It seems I might be good for something after all."

11

Sarah did exactly as Lord Thorndyke asked, taking a hackney instead of her carriage to his home and making sure to wear a bonnet that hid most of her features. The locket, too, was safely in her pocket. Mrs. Avis came with her, of course, but she was as unsure as to why they had been summoned to Lord Thorndyke's home as Sarah was.

Sarah, who had now had two days with which to calm her heart and mind, looked out of the window for a moment, feeling suddenly nervous about seeing Lord Thorndyke again. He had given her some time to think, to take everything in, and she now felt a good deal better than when he had left her. The news that she had no parents to speak of still hurt her more than she could say, but she was glad to know that her brother still lived. She hoped desperately that, one day soon, she might be reunited with him.

"I should tell you that I am engaged to Lord Thorndyke," Sarah said slowly, as the hackney made its way through the streets of London. "It is quite soon and very unexpected, but I think it for the best."

Mrs. Avis nodded, her eyes darting to outside the hackney

window, but not before Sarah had caught a small smile on her companion's face, which appeared to now be awash with relief. Was Mrs. Avis glad that Sarah was to marry Lord Thorndyke then? She had never given her opinion, which was just as Sarah should expect from her companion, but now it seemed that Mrs. Avis was glad to know that her charge would soon become wife to Lord Thorndyke.

Perhaps she is glad that she will not have to remain in London and can instead return to her little country home, Sarah thought, as the hackney pulled up outside Lord Thorndyke's townhouse. *I shall have to make sure to pay her well for all that she has endured with me. I am sure I have not been what she expected.*

"I am very glad for you, Sarah," Mrs. Avis murmured, as they climbed the steps to Lord Thorndyke's front door. "I think Lord Thorndyke will make you an excellent husband and will certainly be able to keep you safe from Lord Andrew."

"Thank you, Mrs. Avis," Sarah replied softly, her mind suddenly filled with thoughts of the man who was to be her husband. "I do hope that this has not been too difficult a placement for you. I know I am not what most companions expect."

Mrs. Avis gave Sarah a broad smile, setting her mind at rest. "No, indeed, Sarah, you have not been. However, I have found my time with you to be most enjoyable. I will be sad to be parted with you."

Sarah noticed the sadness creeping into Mrs. Avis's expression but was not able to comment on it or ask her more before the butler opened the door and ushered them in at once, even before she had the chance to knock.

"The drawing room, Miss Weston," the butler murmured quietly. "I think Lord Thorndyke said you would be leaving within a few minutes."

Her hands stilled on her bonnet ribbons. "I see," she said, fastening them again. "Very well. Thank you."

Much to Sarah's surprise, her stomach was flooded with butterflies as she walked towards the drawing room, her heart suddenly lifting with anticipation over something so simple as seeing Lord Thorndyke again. It was quite inexplicable, and even more so when she felt her cheeks burn with a blush as he bent over her hand and pressed his lips to it.

"Thank you for coming so quickly, Miss Weston," he murmured, still keeping a hold of her hand as he looked up at her from under his dark brows. "I am sorry to rush you, but this is an urgent matter."

Sarah swallowed hard and tried to smile, still feeling her heart thundering in her chest. "Thank you, Lord Thorndyke."

"You know Lord Higgs," he said, finally letting his hand drop hers. "He thinks he knows where your locket came from."

Astonishment rippled through her, as Lord Higgs bowed and grinned at her surprised response.

"The pawn merchant in London—Smithson, and Sons, I think it is called—they had this locket last year."

Behind her, Sarah heard Mrs. Avis gasp and felt her own breath hitch.

"I thought we should go together," Lord Thorndyke said, smiling into Sarah's eyes. "Perhaps we will be able to discover the truth about who put the locket under your pillow back in Little Mybster."

"Oh, I do hope so," Sarah said, suddenly filled with a wild hope as her fingers clung to Lord Thorndyke's arm. "Shall we go now? This very moment?"

"This very moment," Lord Thorndyke chuckled, walking her towards the door. "I did not think you would want to wait."

"Ah, yes."

Sarah's fingers dug into Lord Thorndyke's arm all the more as the pawn merchant looked over her locket carefully.

"Do you know this piece then?" Lord Thorndyke asked, patting Sarah's hand surreptitiously in a gesture of support.

"I do," he said slowly, his small narrow eyes jumping from Lord Thorndyke to Lord Higgs and then to Sarah. "Does it belong to one of you three?"

"If you are suggesting that one of us stole this item, then you are much mistaken," Lord Higgs said at once, a deep frown settling between his brows. "This piece was given to the lady here by a mysterious benefactor, and we wish to find out all we can about it."

Sarah's mouth fell open. "It was stolen?"

The pawn merchant nodded, his tense stance relaxing a little. "Last summer. Someone managed to break the lock and came in during the early hours of the morning when the rest of the world was asleep. This was all that was taken."

Astonished, Sarah's eyes lingered on the locket in the pawn merchant's hand. "But why?"

"I could not say," the man replied with a shrug. "But I can tell you who gave it to me in the first place, if you would like to know." He raised one eyebrow and directed his gaze towards Lord Thorndyke. "Although I would like it to be worth my time."

Lord Thorndyke chuckled and pulled out a few coins from his pocket. "Very well."

"Thank you kindly." The man picked up the coins and placed them into his pocket before returning his attention to Lord Thorndyke. "Do excuse me for a few minutes. I will need to check my books."

Sarah let out a long breath as the pawn merchant turned into a small doorway, hearing him mutter to himself.

"Do you think we will find out who it is?" she asked, looking up at Lord Thorndyke and seeing his gentle smile. "You do?"

"I hope so, for your sake," he replied quietly. "If it will bring this part of the puzzle to an end, then I would be glad to know. Although the person who then put it under your pillow may be someone altogether different."

Her hope faded for a moment, her smile faltering. "Yes, I suppose so."

Lord Thorndyke pressed her hand with his, tugging her a little closer so that she could not help but return her gaze to his.

"Have courage, my dear," he said so quietly that she had to strain to listen. "You are not alone in this anymore. You know that I will help you in whatever way I can."

A surge of gratefulness shot through her. "Thank you," she murmured, feeling a ripple of heat climb up her spine. "You are very good to me. I am blessed to have you by my side, steadfast and sure in all this."

She could not look away, seeing his eyes darkening just a little as he looked back at her. Her mouth went dry, as his breath fluttered across her cheek, the rest of the world fading away.

A sudden crash made her jump, startled. Lord Higgs was standing by a smashed mirror, looking hugely embarrassed.

"I did not see it," he muttered, as the pawn merchant came hurrying out of the back. "I am terribly sorry."

"Careful now, Miss Weston," Lord Thorndyke chuckled, taking her towards Mrs. Avis. "It appears Lord Higgs has held up proceedings once again."

Sarah could not help but smile as Lord Higgs attempted to soothe the upset merchant, promising to pay whatever he wished for the mirror.

"Perhaps we might take a short stroll," Lord Thorndyke said, looking over at Lord Higgs. "To give you a few minutes to clear all this up."

Lord Higgs nodded, his face crimson, and Sarah hid her smile as Lord Thorndyke took her arm.

"Will you join us, Mrs. Avis?" Lord Thorndyke asked quietly, as they walked to the door. "Miss Weston has a decent bonnet on that should hide her from Lord Andrew, should he happen to be in town."

Sarah's stomach tightened with a sudden fear. "Do you think he will be?"

Lord Thorndyke looked a little uneasy as they stepped outside. "He may very well be, Miss Weston. It is the afternoon, and many of the *ton* like to be seen out at the shops or in the park. It is a shame that the pawn merchant is right in the heart of London, but there it is." He looked down at her, his expression one of consideration. "Might you wish to return inside? I am sure we will be quite safe, but if you are uncomfortable then–"

Sarah shook her head. "I think a stroll will suit me. I trust you."

Her simple words brought a broad smile to his face, his eyes lit with genuine warmth.

"Thank you for that trust," he said, offering her his arm. "Shall we?"

Mrs. Avis smiled and shooed her away. "I will walk just behind you," she said, with a knowing look. "I will alert you if I should see anything untoward."

Sarah, beginning to walk alongside Lord Thorndyke, felt her heart suddenly fill with light and hope. This was how her life was to be now. She would always have Lord Thorndyke by her side. Her future as a married woman, which had seemed so heavy and oppressive only two days prior, now seemed to be a bright and hopeful future.

"I wrote to your brother this morning," Lord Thorndyke murmured, as they dodged the other passersby. "I am sure we shall receive his return reply within a few days."

Sarah looked up at him, suddenly excited. "Shall I get to

meet him?"

"Soon enough," Lord Thorndyke replied with a warm smile. "I know you are very keen to meet your brother, but we must continue to take things slowly, using great care and deliberation." He smiled at her, and Sarah felt herself smile back without hesitation. "We shall marry first and then go to seek your brother out. The only reason we must remain in London is so that I can speak to the archbishop in order to secure a special license."

"It seems you have everything in hand, Lord Thorndyke," Sarah murmured, as they rounded a corner. "Thank you."

He glanced down at her, made to speak, only to freeze in place. Without warning, he grasped Sarah's arm with both hands and tugged her into a shadowy corner, away from the rest of the crowd.

Then, he stood directly in front of her, shielding her body with his as he fixed his gaze on her. Sarah could not breathe for a moment, fear stealing the air from her lungs as she looked up at him.

"Lord Andrew," he whispered, his words barely audible. "Have no fear. Just keep looking at me."

"Mrs. Avis," Sarah whispered frantically.

"She will have hidden herself or returned to the shop," he replied firmly. "Look at me, Sarah. Think of nothing else but me."

Sarah focused all of her attention on Lord Thorndyke, taking in the steadiness in his brown eyes and allowing it to permeate her soul. All she could hear was the roaring in her ears, her heartbeat so fast that her breathing became ragged.

"What are you doing here?"

A harsh, angry voice flooded the alley, making her tense.

"Look at me," Lord Thorndyke whispered, his hands now resting on her shoulders. "He is not speaking to you, trust me.

Do not look past me; do not pull away. Just look at me, Sarah. Trust me."

Drawing in a deep breath, Sarah continued to hold his gaze, her legs beginning to tremble.

"How dare you try to leave me!" she heard Lord Andrew shout, her skin crawling with fear. "I have been all over London looking for you."

There was the sound of a slap, then a pleading voice begging for Lord Andrew to let go, only for there to come a blissful, calming silence.

"It is over," Lord Thorndyke whispered, still remaining exactly where he was. "I think he is gone."

Sarah swallowed hard, closing her eyes and resting her head back against the wall of the alleyway.

"Look over my shoulder," Lord Thorndyke whispered, his hands running down her arms. "Can you see him?"

Standing on tiptoe, Sarah let her eyes peek over Lord Thorndyke's broad shoulder, only to see that, apart from a stray cat, there was no one else about. Heaving a huge sigh of relief, she dropped to her heels and nodded.

"He is gone," she whispered, realizing that she had no idea what Lord Andrew looked like. "Are you sure it was him?"

Lord Thorndyke nodded, his features grim. "Yes, it was him, no doubt about it." He shook his head. "We should have remained in the shop."

Seeing the regret and the guilt in his face, Sarah tentatively put one hand on Lord Thorndyke's chest. His head sprang up at once, his eyes fixing on hers.

"It was not your fault," she murmured quietly, feeling her fear slowly fading away and being replaced with an altogether different sensation. "It was not something you could have foreseen."

He swallowed but said nothing, his body still close to hers.

Sarah felt her very heart begin to tremble, as she let her hand slide around his neck, her whole body bursting into flame. This was not something she had ever experienced before, her eyes drawn to Lord Thorndyke's gaze. She could not look away, seeing the intensity there that drew her into him.

"We should return to Lord Higgs," he breathed, one finger gently running down the length of her cheek and curving around her chin. "He will be waiting for us."

Unable to speak, Sarah remained exactly as she was, feeling as though her skin was being seared by his touch, as though she were being branded by Lord Thorndyke's presence.

"Sarah," he whispered, his head beginning to lower. "I–"

She did not know what he meant to say, seeing him stumble to a halt as his eyes flitted to her mouth. She realized that she wanted this; she wanted him to kiss her. She wanted to know what it felt like to be held in a tender embrace, to have a gentleman show his affection in such an intimate way.

When his lips touched hers, it was nothing like Sarah had expected. Her breath left her entirely, her hands making their own way around his neck as he settled his own hands around her waist. She melded to him, tipping her head up towards him.

It was gentle and sweet, and yet it sent fire into her veins. Her heart filled with some unspoken emotion as the sounds of the carriages from around the corner began to fade away. There was only Lord Thorndyke.

When he broke the kiss, Sarah felt it such a sweet agony that she wanted to cry; she wanted to hold onto him and remain exactly where they were. She did not want to return to the shop; she did not want to find out about the locket. For a few moments, she was filled with nothing but a desire for Lord Thorndyke and his kiss.

"Miss Weston," Lord Thorndyke said quietly, stepping back

as she let her hands fall from his neck. "I-I apologize. That was inappropriate."

She stared at him, feeling as though she had been slapped hard across the face.

"Not that I mean I did not wish to do so," he continued hastily, evidently seeing her horror-struck expression. "It is just that perhaps now is not the most appropriate time."

That brought a smidgen of relief to Sarah's tumultuous thoughts, even more so when he took her hand and brought it to his lips.

"I do not want to ever take advantage of you," he said softly, his eyes telling her more than he could ever say. "I will confess that I find your nearness to be somewhat overwhelming. I do believe that, in time, we will have an affection in our marriage together."

That made Sarah smile, her eyes looking up into his, as he looped her hand under his own. "I think so, too, Lord Thorndyke," she replied quietly. "And perhaps, now that we have shared such an intimacy, you might think of calling me by my Christian name when we are in private."

"It is an offer I cannot refuse," he smiled, his fingers resting on her own. "Thank you, Sarah."

12

That was a little too close for my liking, James thought, as he hurried Sarah back through the streets of London. He had known there was a chance that Lord Andrew might be in town but had not truly believed they would come across him in the five minutes they intended to be outside. Glancing down at Sarah as they walked, James felt a sensation he had never expected so early in his acquaintance with the lady.

Happiness.

He felt true happiness at the thought of marrying Sarah. She was beautiful, yes, but he had felt a connection with her the moment he had seen her sitting in his drawing room. It was not that there was just a sympathy for her, which, of course, he could not deny, but there was also a gentle fondness for her. He had been honest when he had told her he was certain there would be affection in their marriage, given time. There was certainly an undeniable attraction between them, given that he had just kissed her and given how eagerly she had responded.

"Where have you been?" Lord Higgs blustered, the moment they stepped into the shop. "This man has been waiting. And I had to pay for the locket as well as the mirror since I was certain Miss Weston would want it back."

James chuckled, feeling Sarah's fingers tighten on his arm. "Thank you, Higgs." He turned his attention to the pawn merchant, who had a somewhat smug look on his face. "I presume you have the information?"

"I do," the man replied with a grin. "Here, you can see it for yourself if you wish."

James turned to Sarah and gestured for her to go ahead of him, seeing her quick smile as she silently thanked him. He watched as she leaned over the book, reading carefully where the pawn merchant showed her.

Her frame tightened, dismay beginning to curl in James's heart.

"What is it?" he asked, walking over to her. "Who handed it in?"

She looked up at him, fear in her eyes. "Lord Andrew Fairley."

The news stunned him. "Lord Andrew?" he repeated, looking down at the page where she pointed. "That cannot be so."

It was undeniable, written there in ink. The description of the pendant, the date, the name, and signature of the man who had brought it in.

"That does not make any sense," he said slowly, looking back up at Sarah and seeing the paleness in her cheeks. "Why would he retrieve it only to put it under your pillow in Little Mybster?"

She swallowed and shook her head, looking up at him helplessly. "I have no idea."

Lord Higgs cleared his throat, drawing James's attention that the pawn merchant was watching them with interest.

"Perhaps we should discuss this back at the house," he said calmly, offering his arm to Sarah again. "Thank you very much for your help." He turned to go, only for Sarah to remain exactly where she was. Looking back at her, he saw her frown.

"Where is Mrs. Avis?" she asked, her voice filled with confusion. "I thought she would have made her way back here by now."

"Mrs. Avis?" Lord Higgs repeated, looking at James in puzzlement. "I thought she was with you. I thought perhaps you had left her in the carriage, knowing that we would only be a few minutes in here."

Sarah went sheet white, both hands now wrapped around James's arm. "Oh, no," she whispered, her eyes widening. "Do you remember what we heard in the alley?"

James swallowed hard, thinking quickly. "That could not have been her," he breathed, hardly able to comprehend it. "How would she know Lord Andrew?"

"You are not talking about the older woman who came in behind you, are you?" the pawn merchant asked, almost lazily.

James rounded on him at once, anger bursting through him at his own foolishness, his own lack of thought. "Do you know her?"

The man shrugged. "I know who Lord Andrew Fairley is. I mean, who doesn't, given his reputation?" His smile spread across his face—in stark contrast to the anger and frustration that was building in James's heart. "That man was often in this place, giving me this and that so that I would pay out. He kept coming back here since he knew I would give him a decent price. What he did not know was that I used his reputation to sell off his things at twice the price. You would be surprised the number of gentlemen that want to purchase something of a man who has fallen as far as Lord Andrew has."

James thumped the counter hard, startling Miss Weston. "Get to the point, man. How do you know Mrs. Avis?"

The man's smile faded, his expression hardening. "I do not," he said with a slight shrug. "I do not know her. All I know is that she was in here with him very often, although she was always forced to stand at the back by the door. Lord Andrew sold off lots of things that I was sure did not belong to him."

"What kind of things?" Miss Weston asked, her voice thin and pained.

The pawn merchant looked at her, and James saw the way his hard expression softened just a touch. "Lady's things," he replied quietly. "Pearls, earrings, that kind of thing."

"The pendant?"

The pawn merchant nodded. "I was surprised she did not come forward herself to tell you that she was present when I bought that from Lord Andrew. Not that it is my business, which is why I did not say anything."

James felt his heart still in his chest. "Mrs. Avis was present when Lord Andrew gave you that pendant?"

The man nodded, his lips thin. "Lord Andrew was in some state that day, I can tell you. Staggering about all over the place. It is a wonder he managed to sign his own name. He had to lean on the lady, as he made his way out of the shop."

"He was drunk?"

The pawn merchant's eyes flickered to Lord Higgs. "Yes, just as I said. Now, is that all you want to know? I got business to see to."

"Do you know anything more about her?" Sarah begged, reaching for the man's hand. "Please, she is a very dear friend of mine. Anything you can tell me would be a great deal of help."

Holding his breath, James saw the pawn merchant look down at the way Miss Weston had clutched his fingers, his instincts telling him that this man knew a little more than he was saying.

"I will make it worth your while," he murmured, pulling some notes from his pocket. "Please do not hold anything back."

The pawn merchant's greedy eyes flickered to the notes in James's hand before returning to Miss Weston.

"There is only one more thing I know," he said, as she released his hand. "Lord Andrew never referred to her as Mrs. Avis."

Sarah stared at him, holding his gaze. "Then what was her title?"

He shrugged. "I only ever heard him refer to her as 'my dear' or some other kind of affectionate term. The kind a man might use to refer to his wife."

James sucked in a breath at the very moment he heard Miss Weston gasp with shock.

"Thank you," he managed to say, wrapping one arm around Sarah's waist and pulling her to him, as tears began to trickle down her cheeks. "You have been very helpful."

Not caring how much he gave the man, James threw down the pile of notes, and gesturing to Lord Higgs to hurry ahead of them to the door, he helped Sarah to walk to the door.

"We must return home to discuss this," he whispered in her ear, as her head dropped forward in despair. "Come to the carriage, my dear. Lean on me if you need to."

~

WITHIN THE HOUR, they had made it back to the townhouse and were now sitting quietly by the fire that crackled in the grate. It was not usual for James to have a fire lit in the middle of the day, but given how pale Miss Weston appeared to be, he had thought it best.

His mind spun with questions, his heart thundering with guilt and pain, as he cursed himself repeatedly for never once assuming that Lord Andrew was talking to Mrs. Avis.

"Do not blame yourself," Lord Higgs said, the moment the

maid left the room, leaving the tea tray in front of Miss Weston. "None of this is your fault, Thorndyke, nor yours, Miss Weston."

"Sarah, please," she said in a broken voice. "I cannot be dealing with titles now, not when everything else is so very confusing."

"Sarah, then," Lord Higgs replied kindly. "You must not take any blame onto your own shoulders."

"I was there," Sarah whispered, hoarsely, looking up at them both with pain written in her eyes. "I could have seen him; I could have tried to stop him."

"And put yourself in danger?" James interrupted, shaking his head. "No. I would never have allowed you to."

Sarah looked at him steadily, her lips trembling just a little. "But he was not there for me," she said slowly. "Remember? He said something about looking all over London for Mrs. Avis. It is *she* he has been searching for, not I."

James leaned forward, his head in his hands. "It does not make sense," he muttered, his thoughts dark and clouded. "I cannot understand what any of this means."

There was nothing but silence for a long time, each one occupied with their own thoughts. Try as he might, James could not let go of the fact that Lord Andrew still posed a threat to Sarah, unable to believe that it was just Mrs. Avis the man had been searching for.

"She is Lord Andrew's wife," Sarah said, her voice breaking the quiet that had settled over the room. "That is the hardest thing to believe. Why did she never say anything? Why set herself up as my companion, knowing that she was the wife to the man I was trying to avoid?"

"It was purposeful, obviously," Lord Higgs said slowly. "She wanted to be your companion. Perhaps to protect you somehow?"

James looked up; his eyes fixed on Sarah as an idea hit him. "Perhaps *she* was the one to put the locket under your pillow?"

He waited as Sarah opened her mouth to refute this, only to close it again. She sighed heavily and passed one hand over her eyes.

"I do not know what to believe," she said eventually. "I thought she truly cared for me."

"And she does," Lord Higgs said firmly. "Just think about this carefully, Sarah. Mrs. Avis came into your life at a time when you needed a companion. She has never once taken you anywhere dangerous, never encouraged you to go out and about, but has rather urged you to be careful, has she not?"

Sarah nodded slowly, her color slowly returning. "She appeared to be very relieved when I told her I was to marry you, Thorndyke." Her hand flew to her mouth as she gasped, her eyes wide. "In fact, I believe she mentioned Lord Andrew even though I had never spoken his name to her."

"In what context?" James asked quickly, his fingers knotting together.

Sarah gave him a small, sad smile, her eyes glazing with tears. "She told me she was glad I was to marry you—for you would be able to keep me safe from him," she said slowly. "She *wanted* this. Perhaps she knew that Lord Andrew had found me and was, therefore, trying to encourage the marriage."

"That might explain why she put the locket under your pillow, if it *was* her," Lord Higgs said quietly. "If Lord Andrew had discovered your presence somehow and she knew what he intended, then she must have done all she could to protect you without revealing herself. She could not risk you knowing the truth all at once, for you might never have believed her."

"Or done something reckless that could have put you in danger," James added, feeling as though they had hit on the truth. "Mrs. Avis, I believe, was trying her best to keep you safe from Lord Andrew by directing you towards London so that you might marry me."

He saw Sarah nod slowly, color now rich in her cheeks. "Then that only leaves one question," she said slowly with a little more determination than James had expected. "How are we to get her back?"

13

Sarah paced up and down the library floor, her heart so filled with pain and confusion that she could do nothing other than walk. It had been two days since Mrs. Avis—or Lady Andrew Fairley, since they suspected that was her true title—had gone missing. Thorndyke had not allowed her to return home, insisting that she remain in his home and promising that no one would know of her presence here. The staff, he assured her, were under no illusion—any gossiping about her would result in the termination of their employment with him, which secured their silence. This brought Sarah a modicum of relief.

They had not formed a plan as yet, although Lord Higgs had gone out to learn whatever he could about Lord Andrew. Once they discovered his whereabouts, he intended to return to them all so that they might come up with a plan.

What that plan was, Sarah had very little idea.

"Sarah?"

The library door opened, and Thorndyke stepped inside, leaving the door ajar. He was dressed in his shirt sleeves, with no cravat at his neck or jacket on his shoulders, his hair a little messy, as though he had run his hands through it a few times. She had not seen him since dinner time this evening, where they had been joined by Lord Higgs, who had not said all that much, promising to return tomorrow with more news.

"You cannot sleep?"

She shook her head, not sure what it was she was feeling as he came closer to her. She was struggling with what they had done in the alley, not because she now regretted kissing him, but that their actions meant they had not looked for Mrs. Avis; they had not even realized that she was gone.

"Can I have the staff bring you something to drink?"

"They will all be abed by now," Sarah replied, shaking her head. "I do not want to disturb them. My sleeplessness should not affect them."

He smiled at her then gently. "Come with me to the kitchen. I am sure we can make you something to drink that will help. Perhaps cocoa?"

The kindness in his expression made her heart lift a little from the despair that it was wrapped in. "Thank you, Thorndyke."

To her surprise, he offered her his hand instead of his arm, and after only a momentary hesitation, she took it. It was warm in her own, sending a wave of heat all through her, whilst bringing a certain degree of peace to her soul. They walked together in silence; the way lit only by the candle held in Thorndyke's hand.

"We will find her—somehow," Thorndyke said, as he lit a few more candles in the kitchen, letting her hand go so that she could sit down at the roughhewn table. "I know you are upset and confused, but Lord Higgs plans to call in the morning with whatever information he has managed to find. Apparently, his steward has been doing a great deal of work and will report to him tomorrow."

She gave him a quick smile, which did nothing to ease her inner torment. "That is good to know." Lord Higgs had not shared this with her at dinner, probably not wanting to distress her any further.

She watched him as he set about warming milk in a pan, a little surprised at his ability to do so. Sarah had always believed that gentlemen did very little for themselves, since Mr. Stanton had never once done anything more than was expected of him. She was not even sure that Mrs. Stanton, for all of her ladylike ways, could even make a pot of tea on her own.

"You look surprised," Thorndyke commented, glancing back at her. "No one has ever made you cocoa before?"

Seeing the twinkle in his eyes, Sarah felt her tight nerves begin to slowly loosen, a shy smile on her face. "Of course, but it was always the maid, or I made it for myself."

"Then, I am glad to be of service to you," he replied, pouring it carefully into a mug and handing it to her. "No standing on ceremony, I am afraid."

She took the cup carefully and set it on the table, waiting until he had sat down opposite her before taking a sip.

Thorndyke looked at her with one eyebrow raised. "Any good?"

Smiling, she nodded, feeling her mind free itself of its dark thoughts. "Very good. Thank you."

"My pleasure."

They sat there quietly for some time, just looking at one another as they grew quiet with their own thoughts.

"Should we manage to bring this to a close, you will have a choice before you, Sarah," Thorndyke began, after a few minutes. "I would not have you unaware that our continued engagement is entirely in your hands."

She frowned, tension suddenly coiling in her belly.

"If, somehow, we manage to bring the danger of Lord

Andrew to a close, then you will be free to do whatever you please," he continued, not managing to look at her. "I will not insist on our wedding if you would prefer to choose for yourself."

That was something she had never considered before, and to her surprise, Sarah found the prospect less than ideal.

"This is all based on the premise that everything works out with Lord Andrew," Thorndyke continued quickly. "If he is still a threat to you when we manage to retrieve Mrs. Avis, then I will insist on our marriage, but if somehow he is no longer a danger to you, then you will be free to go about your life as you please." His eyes finally made their way to hers, looking at her carefully. "I will be a part of your life if you wish it, Sarah, but I will respect your choice if you do not."

Drawing a deep breath, Sarah let it out slowly, steadying herself. "Might I ask if you find the prospect of our matrimony to be a pleasant one?" she asked quietly, suddenly afraid of the answer. "Or is it something that you would be glad to be free of?"

To her surprise, he grasped her fingers with such a ferocity that she jumped.

"No, I would not be glad to be free of it," he said fervently. "I just do not wish my own feelings to affect your decision."

She smiled at him then, relief flooding her. "I am glad to hear it. I do not think that I should find another gentleman of your caliber, even if I were to search all of England."

Thorndyke looked away, seemingly embarrassed.

"You are a kind, compassionate, honest, and dedicated man," Sarah continued, putting her other hand atop their joined ones. "You have shown me care and consideration from the very moment we met, even though I cannot believe that the prospect of marrying a stranger was ever something you looked forward to."

He chuckled, looking back at her. "That was not the case until I met you, my dear."

The tenderness in his eyes warmed her heart, and she smiled back at him, her eyes gentle. "I do want to marry you. I will not pretend that I feel nothing for you, that the feelings in my heart have not continued to deepen over these last days. I feel as though there is so much more for us to share, so much more for us to discover about one another." Her smile grew soft, as he ran his fingers over the back of her hand. "I want to marry you, Thorndyke, no matter what happens."

A long breath escaped him, as though he were awash with relief.

"You are glad, I hope?"

He did not say anything but got out of his chair and came around to her, pulling her gently to her feet. When she looked up into his eyes, she saw the deep intensity there in his gaze and the fire burning within.

His lips met hers, and Sarah gave herself up to the emotions that began to fly through her, pushing away the confusion and the grief for a few moments. She held onto Thorndyke tightly, her fingers twining into his hair.

"Sarah," he murmured, his forehead resting gently against her own. "I have been drawn to you as a butterfly is drawn to the flower. You are sweet and kind, showing such courage and such tenacity even when you are besieged with what has occurred. To go through such a struggle as you have brings me only admiration for you."

His kind words were a balm to her troubled heart, and she closed her eyes, feeling as though this was precisely where she belonged, where she was meant to be.

"I do not want to ever be separated from you again," he continued, his hands tightening around her waist. "My own affections are already burrowing into my heart, and I cannot—and will not—deny them."

"Then we are agreed," Sarah replied softly. "We will marry, whatever happens."

"Whatever happens," he agreed, before gently kissing her again.

14

"Well?"

Lord Higgs looked over at James, who was waiting desperately for him to speak.

"I found her."

James heard Sarah gasp in shock and saw her hands fly to her mouth, as Lord Higgs nodded.

"You found her?" James repeated, blinking furiously. "Where? When?"

Lord Higgs cleared his throat, sitting forward in his chair. "It is as you suspected, Sarah. Mrs. Avis is Lord Andrew's wife but was doing her best to escape from him, it seems."

Sarah shook her head, and James saw that she was battling tears. "Why did she marry him in the first place?"

"Because not everyone has the choice of whom they marry," James replied, coming to sit by her instead of pacing up and down the room. "I suspect that she had no choice in the matter."

Lord Higgs nodded. "Precisely that. This was a great many years ago and did not take place anywhere near London. In fact, I was told that Lord Andrew was near the border at the time, so possibly it was even in Scotland, although I cannot be sure. It appears that Lord Andrew got better at cards for a time, and during one game, he agreed that the gentleman he was playing against—Viscount Davidson, I believe— could place his unmarried daughter's hand in marriage on the table."

James closed his eyes and took a few moments to let his anger rise and then fade away again. How any gentleman could treat his daughter in such a way was beyond him.

"She was married and her dowry given to Lord Andrew. It was fairly substantial, I believe, but Lord Andrew is not a man known for his considerate ways when it comes to money."

Sarah let out a heavy sigh, and James reached for her hand, feeling it cold in his own.

"I feel so terrible for her," she said softly. "To be forced into matrimony like that? How desperate she must have been."

"And for so many years," James added quietly.

Lord Higgs nodded again, his expression grave. "It is not known how long she knew of Lord Andrew's reputation, nor of the whispers about what he had done to the duke's wife, but I would assume that she was always horrified by him. Lord Andrew was forced to, over the years, sell almost everything of value as his gambling habits continued."

"The locket," Sarah replied, glancing up at James.

James pressed her hand. "It is not unthinkable to believe that she managed to steal it back, although perhaps she found someone to do it for her."

"For what reason?" Lord Higgs asked, frowning. "That is the only thing I cannot understand. Why give you the locket and then never tell you who she really was? If she intended to be your companion, then she could have simply told you the truth."

There was a short silence, as they all thought hard.

"Perhaps she was afraid that Lord Andrew would find it

again, and then he would trace the theft back to her," Sarah said slowly. "But that does not explain why she told me to find the owner of the locket."

James made to speak, only for the door to open and the butler to step in with an apologetic look on his face.

"I apologize for intruding, my lord, but you did request that any letters be given to you at once."

"Thank you," James replied, taking the letter off the tray and turning it over. "Oh, it is from your brother, Sarah. I hope you will not mind if I open it."

"Of course, please," Sarah responded, looking surprised that he had even thought to ask.

Breaking the seal, James read quickly, only to feel the life go out of his limbs. Slowly sinking back down beside Sarah, he reached for her hand again and held it tightly, reading each word the duke had written over and over again.

"What is it, Thorndyke?" he heard Sarah ask, her voice seeming to come from far away. "What is the matter?"

"It is here," James replied, his voice hoarse. "I understand it all now."

Her hand tightened in his, as Lord Higgs cleared his throat, drawing James's attention.

"Your brother, the Duke of Brighton, has written various things, and he is vastly delighted with the news that we are to wed, Sarah, so you need have no concerns there. However, when I wrote to him, I mentioned the locket. I described it, in fact." He looked up at his betrothed, seeing her eyes filled with questions. "It belonged to your mother."

Sarah gasped, her eyes filling with startled tears as her fingers clung to his.

"Your brother identified it from the description," he continued quietly. "He says that on the day your mother went riding, she had it around her neck. It had a miniature within of your father, and it was, apparently, something she always wore. At the time of the accident, no one could find it. It was presumed that it had fallen off somewhere, and it was never thought of as particularly important."

"Until now," Lord Higgs said firmly. "My goodness, Sarah. Do you realize what this means?"

Sarah drew in a shaking breath, as James tugged her a little closer. "It means that we have the proof that Lord Andrew killed my mother."

"Precisely," James replied, filled with a sudden burst of hope. "We will have to have a copy of the books from the pawn merchant, but the evidence is there."

"Remember how the pawn merchant told us that Lord Andrew was in his cups at the time, when he handed in the locket?" Lord Higgs continued, a look of triumph on his face. "It was clear that he was not thinking clearly then, for what kind of man would put a piece of evidence into the pawn shop without using a false name? Why use the same shop you had used before if you wanted to keep your identity a secret?"

"And that is why the shop was broken into," Sarah finished, her shoulders slumping. "Lord Andrew tried to retrieve it once he had sobered up and realized what he had done."

James nodded, his arm wrapping around Sarah's shoulders as she wiped her eyes. "It is just as well the pawn merchant took his books home with him that evening, else all evidence might have disappeared. I suspect, Sarah, that Mrs. Avis never intended to be your companion, but perhaps she had no other choice. Perhaps she needed to escape and to be your companion was the only way. Perhaps she was too afraid to tell you the truth, hoping that you would marry me before discovering the truth about the locket. That way, she would have the funds you would give her as payment and she could leave your side without you ever knowing the truth about her."

"We have to get her back. She cannot stay with him."

James smiled at the determination in Sarah's voice, feeling himself grow as resolute as she.

"Of course, we will," Lord Higgs said calmly. "All we need is a plan."

Setting the letter from the duke aside, James turned to Sarah and took both of her hands. "My dear, we must be careful in this. I would much prefer you remain here whilst we go to fetch her."

"What do you intend to do?" she asked, a trace of frustration in her voice. "Simply march up to his house and demand he release her?"

Lord Higgs shrugged. "Most likely, yes. We will present him with the evidence we have and then hand both him and all we have into the authorities."

"My guess is he will be on his way to the jail before the end of the day," James replied, squeezing her hands gently. "It will be the gallows or transportation for him."

"Then, I am coming with you."

There was a short pause. "No, my love. I cannot let you do that," James replied carefully, aware of the spark in her eyes and the determination in her gaze. "You will be putting yourself in danger should you do so."

Sarah lifted her chin, and James was suddenly reminded that he had told her only last night about the way her courage and bravery sparked a deep respect for her within his heart.

"You know that I will not stay here," she said calmly. "There is no point in arguing with me. I want to see the man who has caused my family such pain, who has been such a threat to me, and I want to see him running for his life when he discovers that we know the truth of who he is and what he has done."

James turned to Lord Higgs, who shrugged, clearly a little

uneasy but also aware that he was not likely to change Sarah's mind. Feeling as though he had no choice, he gave Sarah a small smile.

"Very well, but you must do as I ask you," he said, seeing her nod fervently. Her jaw clenched, as her eyes drifted towards Lord Higgs. "Lord Higgs and I will always go ahead of you."

"Lord Higgs?" she asked, as though determined to ensure that he was in agreement also. "Does this meet with your satisfaction?"

Lord Higgs cleared his throat. "My dear lady, I would not have expected anything less from you. Now, shall we go at once? I know the address, and it is some distance away, on the other side of London no less. We can come up with some kind of plan in the carriage, but I think it would not be best to wait here any longer than necessary."

Before James could respond, Sarah was on her feet, marching towards the door with her shoulders thrown back and her head up. She was clearly eager to be off, determined to bring back Mrs. Avis without too much thought for her own safety. He loved that about her.

"*Do* come on, Thorndyke," Lord Higgs murmured, as he passed. "Now is not the time to stand about gawping at your lady love." He raised one eyebrow, as James felt a blush rise in his cheeks, scrambling to find some kind of protestation.

"No, do not even attempt to excuse yourself," Lord Higgs continued, with a wave of his hand. "I can see what has happened. You are falling in love with that young lady—and credit to you for doing so. She is quite remarkable." He slapped James on the back, chuckling quietly. "All the better for you both, I think. Nothing so good as being in love with your wife, or so I have heard."

"Indeed," James mumbled, not sure what else to say. Was he

really in love? Could such a feeling come upon a man quickly, with such haste that it took his breath away?

"Concentrate on the task in hand," Lord Higgs grinned, as they made their way towards the door. "You can worry about the state of your heart after it is all over. Come now. Mrs. Avis is waiting."

15

Sarah listened with only half an ear as Lord Thorndyke and Lord Higgs discussed what they intended to do once they reached Lord Andrew's home. Her mind was troubled. She had no intention of remaining at Lord Thorndyke's home whilst they both went out in search of Mrs. Avis. At the same time, she grew sick with the thought of seeing Lord Andrew for the first time, the man who had engineered the death of her mother.

Her hands were folded in her lap, her fingers twined together tightly as she stared, unseeingly, out of the window.

"Sarah?"

She started, turning towards Lord Thorndyke. "Yes?"

His hand reached for her joined ones, settling over them both. "Are you quite all right?"

Nodding, she tried to smile at him. "I am."

"Are you sure? I can tell that you are worried." His smile grew softer, as his eyes flicked across her face. "You have lines that only appear when something is on your mind."

A little self-conscious, Sarah rubbed at her forehead. "I want to be here for this."

"I know you do," Lord Thorndyke replied gently. "But if it all becomes too much, there is no shame in returning to the carriage. I will support you in whatever way I can, but here, in the carriage, is safety. Do you understand?"

Sarah looked up into his face, her eyes fixing on his. Lord Thorndyke was so kind, so tender, that she could not help but smile back at him, her heart filling with affection for him despite the thundering emotions rattling all through her. "Thank you. You are always so considerate of me."

"As I should be," came the sweet reply, making her smile all the more. "Remember to be careful, my love. I would not have anything happen to you."

She nodded, promising to be careful whilst continuing to hold his gaze. He really was a man of honor, a man who would be a wonderful husband and friend over the years of their life together. After all, not every gentleman would have allowed her to come here, but Thorndyke had known why she needed to join them, why she needed to see Lord Andrew. He had understood her without her having to explain. Already, there was a deep attachment between them.

"Here we are," Lord Higgs murmured, as the carriage rolled to a stop. "Carefully now, Sarah. Remember to stand behind us."

"Out of sight initially," Lord Thorndyke said, as the carriage door opened. "Just until we know what kind of welcome we are to have."

THE HOUSE WAS SMALL, squeezed between a long line of other houses, which all had the same dimensions. The small wooden door was dulled and scratched, the knocker falling heavily on the peeling wood.

"Not the best place in London," Lord Thorndyke commented,

glancing behind him to ensure that Sarah had placed herself out of sight of the front door by standing just behind him, one step below. "But then again, given Lord Andrew's financial difficulties, I am surprised he has managed to secure even this place."

The door swung open to reveal a tall, lanky young man, who wore what had once been a clean and pressed footman's uniform. It was loose about the man's neck, the sleeves flapping over his hands.

"Lord Andrew, please," Lord Higgs said at once, taking a step inside. "Where is he?"

The young man gawked at Lord Higgs, his face paling.

"Don't tell me that he has gone out, for I shan't believe it," Lord Higgs continued airily. "Where is he, please? If you do not tell us, then I am afraid we shall have to go in search of him ourselves."

The young man turned to look at Lord Thorndyke before turning back to Lord Higgs.

"I ain't meant to say, milord."

Lord Thorndyke stepped forward, gesturing for Sarah to follow. "Then let me make it worth your while," he murmured, pulling a few gold coins from his pocket. "Will this loosen your tongue?"

Sarah watched as the supposed footman's eyes widened, accepting the coins greedily.

"Well?" Lord Thorndyke asked impatiently. "Where is he?"

"Second door on your left," the young man mumbled. "Thank you, milord."

Lord Thorndyke said nothing but followed Lord Higgs down the corridor with Sarah in tow. She could feel her heart beating frantically as they walked, aware of the beads of sweat trickling down her back. She was frightened yet hopeful, determined yet unsure.

"Wait here," Lord Thorndyke murmured, as Lord Higgs came to the door. "Just until I call you in."

Sarah knotted her fingers together and nodded, her jaw jutting out as she fought to contain her frustration.

"Thank you," Lord Thorndyke whispered, dropping his head to press a light kiss to her lips. "Courage, my dear. It will all be over soon."

Looking up at him, Sarah held his gaze for a moment, drawing in some of the strength she found there as the imprint of his lips on hers remained.

"Come on," Lord Higgs hissed, his hand on the door handle. "Time is of the essence."

Lord Thorndyke smiled at her before turning back towards Lord Higgs. With a nod, Lord Higgs threw open the door, and the two gentlemen strode in, leaving Sarah to stand outside behind the door that was only open a crack.

"What is the meaning of this?" she heard a voice exclaim, recognizing it to be Lord Andrew. "You cannot burst into my home like this!"

"Mrs. Avis," she heard Lord Thorndyke say gently. "How good to see you again. We are come to take you back home with us."

There came a harsh laugh, making Sarah wince. "She is not going anywhere with you," came Lord Andrew's angry voice. "She is my wife. She remains with me."

"I do not think so," Lord Higgs replied, his voice frustratingly calm. "Come, Mrs. Avis. It is best that you leave at once."

The sound of a pistol being cocked made Sarah gasp, her hands flying to her mouth to cover the sound. It could only be Lord Andrew's gun, for neither Lord Thorndyke nor Lord Higgs had brought their pistols, arming themselves with swords instead.

"I will thank you for leaving my wife well alone," Lord

Andrew snarled, his voice coming ever closer to the door. "Come with me, now, Laura. No questions."

"I do not think you want to do that," Lord Thorndyke said quietly. "We know more about you than you think, Lord Andrew."

Sarah held her breath, as the sound of scurrying footsteps came towards the door. Clearly, Mrs. Avis had done what she had been told. Her mind screamed at her to run, to leave this situation in Lord Higgs and Lord Thorndyke's capable hands and to make her way back to the safety of the carriage, but instead, she remained exactly where she was.

"Rubbish," Lord Andrew laughed darkly, his shadow now falling across the half-open door.

"Murder?" Lord Thorndyke replied quietly. "We have proof."

There was a short, stunned silence, and Sarah took this opportunity to look through the crack in the door, keeping herself as quiet as possible.

Lord Andrew stood just in front of the door, his back to her. She could not see past him, but should she push the door as hard as possible, then she could knock hard into Lord Andrew and take him completely by surprise.

"Put the pistol down," Lord Higgs said, his voice hard. "Threatening anyone is not going to help your cause."

Sarah's heart climbed into her throat. Was Lord Andrew threatening someone? Who? Lord Thorndyke? Mrs. Avis? Lord Higgs?

"My wife is coming with me, and you are to leave my home," Lord Andrew grated, as Sarah heard Mrs. Avis let out a whimper. "Proof or not, you have no right to march in here."

"And now I suppose you intend to leave this place?"

Sarah frowned, as Lord Andrew laughed again in answer to Lord Thorndyke's question.

"Yes, I do," he said, chuckling. "You have given me ample

warning, and I will be heading off to another part of this wonderful country."

No, Sarah thought to herself, one hand tightening around the door handle. *He cannot stay in England. I will never be safe. My brother will never be safe. This has to end.*

Drawing in a deep breath, Sarah closed her eyes, and then, with all of her might, she threw the door forward, hard. She used every bit of her strength, feeling it slam into something solid.

There came shouts, cries, and the sound of hurrying feet, but Sarah still clung onto the door handle, not quite sure what to do. She half expected to feel the steel pistol pressing against her back, her eyes closing tightly for a few moments.

"Sit down, Lord Andrew."

"Sarah!"

She let out a long breath, looking over her shoulder to see Lord Higgs marching Lord Andrew to a chair, pistol in hand. Lord Thorndyke held her tightly, turning her around so that she was held securely in his arms.

"I am all right," she gasped, her breath leaving her body as she stared at the man now sitting opposite her. "I am all right, Thorndyke. Really."

"You are incredible," he murmured, as she stood tall beside him. "He had the pistol pressed to Mrs. Avis's back. If you had not done what you did then he most likely would have left with her."

Sarah saw Mrs. Avis sitting down carefully in a chair opposite her, her face white. A huge swell of relief flooded Sarah, as she saw her familiar face, her hand tightening on Lord Thorndyke's.

"We found her," she breathed, as Lord Thorndyke led her towards the couch near Mrs. Avis. "Oh, Mrs. Avis, I am so glad you are safe."

To Sarah's horror, the woman's face crumpled, as Sarah drew near, tears beginning to pour down her cheeks.

"I am so sorry," she gasped, as Sarah took her hand. "I should have told you everything, but I was so afraid."

Sarah pressed her hand tightly, crouching down to look into Mrs. Avis's face. "It is quite all right," she murmured gently. "You have nothing to worry about any longer, Mrs. Avis. You will come to live with Lord Thorndyke and me for the rest of your days. You will be Mrs. Avis, not Lady Andrew Fairley, and you will be a most precious part of our family."

Mrs. Avis cried all the harder. "I do not deserve your kindness."

"You do," Sarah replied firmly. "You were the one to put the locket under my pillow, were you not?"

Mrs. Avis nodded, her eyes red-rimmed. "I had to. It took me two days of travel, but I had no choice. He—" her eyes shot to Lord Andrew, whom Sarah had not yet turned to look at. "He had discovered where you were. Apparently, your uncle's solicitor was a little too talkative when he was in his cups."

"Mr. Featherstone," Sarah murmured, recalling how she had taken an instant dislike to the man. "Mrs. Avis, none of this is your fault. It is all squarely on Lord Andrew's shoulders."

Closing her eyes for a moment to steady herself, Sarah rose to her feet and turned around slowly to look at the man who had killed her mother. He was somewhat diminutive, with a stick-like figure and a shock of grey hair and light blue eyes that were filled with fear.

And, at that moment, all of Sarah's trepidation left her at once. Lord Andrew was not the tall, strong, terrifying man she had expected. Instead, he was small, wiry, and seemingly afraid of her presence.

"Lord Andrew," she said, getting to her feet. "I believe you killed my mother."

Lord Andrew's eyes opened wide, staring at her for a long moment.

"And I believe you had been pursuing my brother and me whilst my father was still alive," she continued calmly. "And yet it is I who now has the power over you. I have no fear, whereas you ought to be the one who is more than a little afraid."

"And why is that?" Lord Andrew asked, one eyebrow raised. "I hardly think I have anything to fear from a child such as you."

Lord Thorndyke made to speak, but Sarah shook her head, glancing back at him in the hope he would understand. She had to speak. She had to be the one to do this. Lord Thorndyke understood at once, his mouth closing as he nodded at her gently.

Feeling courage bubbling up within her, Sarah turned back to Lord Andrew, who remained sitting, kept in place by the threat of Lord Higgs holding a pistol.

"Lord Andrew, I know what you did to my mother," she said firmly. "I also know that you took the locket from around my mother's neck and took it as your own."

Lord Andrew's mouth fell open in shock, confirming to Sarah everything she thought.

"A beautiful locket, decorated with seed pearls and an amethyst," she continued, seeing the shock spread through Lord Andrew's features. "But you could do nothing with it, since it tied you to my mother and her death. How foolish of you to try and pawn it."

From behind her, Sarah heard the rustle of Mrs. Avis's skirts, as she rose to her feet to come to stand behind Sarah.

"He was drunk," she said in a trembling voice. "Otherwise I do not think that he would ever have thought to go to the usual shop. That was why he had to steal it back, once he had realized what he had done."

Sarah glanced back at Mrs. Avis, seeing the determination on her pale face.

"I understand," she said quietly, reaching for Mrs. Avis's hand. "That was why he went back to the shop to steal it, yes? In the hope that he could find the locket and the books and remove all trace of his presence."

"Except the books were not there," Mrs. Avis finished, holding Sarah's hand tightly. "He came back with the locket, but that was all."

Lord Andrew grimaced, his eyes dark. "Stupid woman," he spat, looking at Mrs. Avis. "You took the locket. You gave it to *her.*" His eyes shot to Sarah, venom in his features. "And then you tried to run away."

Mrs. Avis drew in a shaking breath and glanced at Sarah before dropping her gaze to the floor. "I did not expect Andrew to notice I had taken the locket. He was so pleased to have discovered your whereabouts, that he got himself blind drunk. I knew then that I had to act quickly. Usually his bouts of drink last a week, so I knew I had time to get the locket to you and then return home without Lord Andrew ever knowing I was gone."

"Ah, but this time was different, was it not, my dear," Lord Andrew asked, his voice filled with anger. "I knew you had gone. I knew you had taken the locket."

"I only had the one opportunity," Mrs. Avis whispered, tears beginning to pour from her eyes again. "I had to leave him. I took what I could with me and left for a nearby inn."

"You should have come to tell me the truth then," Sarah replied softly. "I would not have turned you away."

Mrs. Avis shook her head, a sad smile on her face. "You could have easily turned me away, especially when you were only then learning about who you truly were. I could not risk that, nor could I risk Andrew finding me. I was running out of money, and when the opportunity came to be your companion, I took it. I thought I would be gone from your life before you ever found out the truth." She smiled softly and glanced back at Lord Thorndyke. "I thought you would marry Lord Thorndyke first and then follow the path of the pendant afterward."

"Except I was too stubborn to just do as was expected," Sarah replied with a wry smile. "I *had* to find out the whole truth before I would accept his proposal."

"I am so terribly sorry," Mrs. Avis whispered, her eyes sparkling with tears. "I never meant to hurt you."

"And you did not," Sarah promised gently. "You are to live with me and Lord Thorndyke, Mrs. Avis. You will not have to go near him again."

There was a short silence, broken only by the sudden sound of a rasping, hoarse laugh coming from Lord Andrew.

"You are just as stupid as your father was," he breathed, as Sarah turned to look at him again. "Do you really think you can just take my wife away from me and that I am going to go without a fuss? You have the locket, yes, but that proves nothing."

Lord Thorndyke stepped forward at once, his anger almost radiating from him, but Sarah held out her free hand to stop him.

This was hers to finish.

"Lord Andrew, my father was a great man. He was kind and generous and gave you more than enough opportunities to turn your back on your gambling ways. From what I hear, you spat that back into his face. I never knew my father because of you, even though it was not his life that you took." Anger began to burn through her veins, making her step forward towards Lord Andrew and let go of Mrs. Avis's hand. "As for the locket, yes, you are right, it might not be all that much in itself." She paused for a moment, seeing the smug look on his face before allowing herself one of her own. "However, I would say that proves a great deal since I have a letter from my brother, the Duke of Brighton, that states this locket was lost on the day of my mother's death. In addition, Lord Thorndyke has sent his steward to fetch the books from the pawn merchant that prove *you* were the one to hand this locket in all those years ago. I think these things will prove a great deal, Lord Andrew."

The smile on the man's face faded as he looked up into Sarah's eyes. There was nothing there now but fear. Fear that she would use all she had to send him to jail, and, eventually, to his death.

Sarah felt no regret. This was justice. This was right. She had nothing more to do than to take Mrs. Avis with her and start living her life the way she should have all those years ago.

"You are done for, Lord Andrew," she murmured, stepping back from him and looking down at him with a mixture of both relief and disgust. "You are to face the punishment you deserve for what you have done to my family." She saw him shudder but felt no sympathy. "As for me, I am going to do what I have been hoping for these last few weeks. I shall marry the man I love and meet my brother, the Duke of Brighton. And then I shall be happy, free from fear, and free from confusion, knowing that the person responsible for all of this will paying for his crimes just as he ought."

Without waiting to see what Lord Andrew had to say, Sarah held out her hand to Mrs. Avis, who came over to her at once.

"Come, Mrs. Avis," she said softly. "Let us leave this place and allow Lord Higgs and Lord Thorndyke to deal with Lord Andrew. I have had more than enough of this place and that man. I am sure you feel the same."

"I do," Mrs. Avis replied, holding Sarah's hand tightly as they walked arm in arm towards the door. "Thank you, Sarah. I will never forget this."

Sarah managed a small smile, turning her head back to look at Lord Thorndyke, who nodded at her in understanding, pride shining in his eyes.

"Thank you, Mrs. Avis," she replied, turning back towards the open door. "Without you, none of this would have been possible. I am more thankful than you will ever know."

EPILOGUE

Two weeks later

"I still do not understand why you had to move back here," Lord Thorndyke complained, as he and Sarah walked in the gardens. "We are to be wed very soon."

Sarah laughed, feeling happier than she had ever done before. "Because it is more proper for me to do so. I cannot exactly live in your home when the *ton* now knows exactly who I am."

"No longer 'Miss Weston' but 'Lady Sarah Fairley'," Lord Thorndyke sighed, shaking his head. "I knew the moment we escorted Lord Andrew to the authorities that news would spread around London, but I did not think it would be so soon."

"It was for the best," Sarah replied, glad that she could now take on her true title and standing in society. "Besides which, if I did not own a large property such as this, then where would my brother stay when he comes to visit? Where would Mr. and Mrs. Stanton reside?" Her voice took on a teasing tone, as he threw her a frustrated glance, more than aware that Lord Thorndyke's home was more than adequate for three additional guests.

"I know, I am just being foolish," he admitted, letting out

another mournful sigh. "It is just that being parted from you is a torture I am struggling to bear. I had every intention of seeking a special license, as you well know."

Sarah laughed again and shook her head. "Which you know would only have added to the scandal," she chuckled, looking up into his face. "Besides, there was no reason for that any longer, not now when it has been revealed to the world who I truly am. The banns have only one more week to go before we can marry."

"It is still too long," he grated, suddenly tugging her towards a bench that sat just underneath a beautiful cherry tree. "It is painful for me not to have you by my side."

Sarah let out a long breath and leaned into him, her head resting against his shoulder as she looked up at the tree, seeing the hints of blue trying to make their way down from the sky through the tree branches. "I know, Thorndyke, but it is worth the wait, I think. It has given us more time to get to know one another, and I am grateful for that."

Lord Thorndyke glanced down at her before nodding slowly. "Yes, I suppose it has."

Thinking about the last couple of weeks, Sarah felt happiness in her heart that she had never truly experienced before. Everything was behind her now, the confusion and pain and struggle gone entirely. Lord Andrew was now under arrest, with his trial due to start very soon. Although, Lord Thorndyke had insisted that they be out of the country on honeymoon during that time. Sarah was grateful for that, glad that she would not have to see his pinched, threatening face again.

Mrs. Avis had taken some convincing to remain with Sarah, seemingly flooded with guilt over what she had done—or had not done—but Sarah had not been about to part with her. The poor woman had already lived a lifetime of agony, being forced into matrimony with Lord Andrew, and had done all she could to help Sarah, even though things had not quite worked out as she had intended. From Mrs. Avis, Sarah had learned that Lord Andrew had never given up on his quest to rid the world of both her and her brother, such was his grievance against her dearly departed father. Sarah had shown Mrs. Avis that, in finding the courage to do what she had done in slipping into Mr. Stanton's home and placing the locket under Sarah's pillow, she had saved Sarah's life.

Eventually, Mrs. Avis had agreed to remain with Sarah and Lord Thorndyke for the rest of her days, promising to do all she could to aid Sarah in any way she could. Sarah already had visions of Mrs. Avis playing with Sarah's children, her heart glad that she would have the dear lady as a part of her life for years to come.

"You are not thinking of abandoning our engagement, I hope?" Lord Thorndyke teased, turning in his seat to face her a little more. "You are often lost in thought these days, although I find myself having to guess what you are thinking."

Sarah looked up into his eyes, seeing the tenderness there and finding it filling her heart.

"I am just thinking about how happy I am," she said softly. "How content I have been these last weeks. You have become such a big part of my life. In some ways, I owe you my life. To keep your promises, to take me on as though we have always known one another, that speaks to my heart."

There was a moment of silence, as they looked at one another, their eyes filled with nothing more than each other.

"I love you, Sarah," Lord Thorndyke said hoarsely, one hand lifted to her face. "I did not think that I would ever feel such a thing for you, but my affection has burst to life, and now I can think of nothing more. I swear I shall love you for the rest of my days."

She could not speak for a moment, closing her eyes as he rested her forehead gently against her own.

"I love you, Thorndyke," she whispered, speaking the words that had begun to wind themselves around her mind these last few days. "I have never felt such a thing before, but it grows with every moment we spend together."

He kissed her then, gently, and Sarah responded with everything she felt. Her hands twined around his neck, her fingers brushing the hair at the nape of his neck whilst he wrapped his arms around her waist.

Her heart was so filled with love that, even when he broke the kiss, she could not breathe, could not speak, could not so much as think. Her life had turned from one of confusion and struggle to one of love and delight. There was a brother she was yet to meet, a family she could call her own. How much things had changed.

"I will love you always, Thorndyke," she said, looking up into his face and marveling at the love she saw there. "For everything you have been, for everything you will be, and for everything you are."

THE END

THE VISCOUNT'S SECRET

SECRETS OF LONDON

The Viscount's Secret

First printing, 2018

Publisher
Love Light Faith, LLC
400 NW 7th Avenue, Unit 825
Fort Lauderdale, FL 33311

PROLOGUE

London 1816

Oliver, Viscount Patton, laughed uproariously and downed another drink.

"You had best be careful there, Patton," his friend, Lord Fernley murmured, putting one hand under Oliver's elbow. "Are you sure you are quite all right?"

"Take your hands off me," Oliver replied, staggering away. "Much too sensible, you are. For what it is worth, I am trying to get rid of some rather troubling thoughts over a Mrs. H. She was not who I thought she was." He shook his head, waving one finger at Lord Fernley. "I want to forget her, and your preventative hand is not helping matters."

Lord Fernley swallowed hard, his eyes roving anxiously over Lord Patton's face. This was not an unusual occurrence, for Lord Patton often drank far too much, but there was something in Lord Patton's face that warned Lord Fernley that something was amiss.

"I am just trying to help, old boy," he muttered, passing a hand over his eyes. "You are quite ridiculous just now, you know."

"Ridiculous!" Lord Patton retorted, waving his arms about him. "Ridiculous? That is what you think to call me, is it? My dear old friend, I am surely not ridiculous."

It was on the tip of Lord Fernley's tongue to say that they had not been friends for a particularly long time, and that, yes, the way Lord Patton was behaving *did* make him more than a little ridiculous. Instead, he chose to keep his mouth shut tight.

"Nonsense," Lord Patton exclaimed, now staggering towards the door of White's. "I may like my drink, but I assure you I can keep ahold of myself." As Lord Fernley made to get up, Lord Patton waved him away. "Now, you stay here, and I will be off. Do not fancy your company any longer this evening. Not where I am going."

Lord Fernley let out a long breath, sitting back down carefully in his chair and shaking his head to himself. Over the last few weeks, Lord Patton had become more and more frivolous, although much of the money was spent on himself, of course. Every evening, the man could be found either in White's or in another, similar establishment, throwing as much liquor as he could down his throat until he could barely stand. Lord Fernley could not make sense of it and had half thought of writing to Lord Patton's younger brother, given that they had known each other a little in Eton. But, having considered this, he had set the idea aside, aware that a younger brother could do very little.

Sighing again, Lord Fernley rose from his seat and walked to the front of White's, preparing to pay not only *his* tab—but Lord Patton's tab too. It was not, perhaps, the best of ideas, but the look on Lord Patton's face this evening, as he had begun to throw back his brandy, had given him a great deal of concern. Whatever it was that was troubling Lord Patton, it was clearly pushing him toward liquor as a means of escape.

"If only he would talk to me," Lord Fernley muttered, paying the rather hefty bill before walking out of White's and into the cold night air, "then I might be able to help."

Pausing for a moment, Lord Fernley thought of hailing a hackney, but instead chose to walk back to his townhouse. It was only a short distance away, and he did rather enjoy walking by the Thames in the moonlight. For whatever reason, it often cleared his mind of all the troubled thoughts that swam through it.

A sudden scream caught his ears, and coming to a standstill, Lord Fernley looked all around him.

Another shout, then another. Twisting his head this way and that, Lord Fernley moved quickly towards where he had heard the sounds coming from – only to see the figure of a lady looking over the railing of the Thames and a gentleman running toward her. For a moment, he thought the gentleman meant to throw the lady into the water, only to see him come to a direct stop at the railings and look over it.

"What on earth has happened?" he asked, hurrying toward them as they began to talk in frantic tones. The gentleman was gesturing wildly as they turned to look around for something. "What is wrong?"

"Oh, sir," the lady whispered, her face sheet white in the bright moonlight. "It's the gentleman I was with. He just slipped and went over."

Looking at the railings, Lord Fernley frowned, hard. "Slipped?"

"I – I ain't sure what happened," she admitted, her eyes wide. "But he's gone in there, and I can't see him anymore."

Frowning a little, Lord Fernley was suddenly caught with awareness. Looking at the lady in front of him, he took in her dress – or lack thereof – and realized that he was looking at a lady of the night. His stomach tightened.

"And what was the name of the gentleman you were with?" he asked quietly, catching the lady's attention again.

She shook her head, her gaze darting away from his, and Lord Fernley got a distinct impression that she was afraid. "I don't know, sir. He was rather drunk, mind you, but I thought I'd get to know his name a little better once we got back to the house."

Looking down into the murky waters, Lord Fernley felt his heart begin to race, his mind screaming at him that he already knew whom it was who had gone in the Thames but did not want to admit it. Quickly, he gave a description of Lord Patton to the lady, growing sick with fear as she nodded confirmation.

"Yes, that's right," she said hesitantly, as he finished speaking. "That sounds like him. Who is he?"

The gentleman next to them both hissed something incomprehensible, but Lord Fernley's mind was so fraught that he could barely speak, his hands reaching for the railings in front of him.

"Lord Patton," he said through heavy lips. "I must go and retrieve him!" He looked down again at the swirling waters, far too aware that he could not swim, and tried to steel his resolve.

"You cannot go in there!"

The gentleman, who had, apparently, seen the whole thing, came over to him at once and grasped at his arm, pulling Lord Fernley back. Lord Fernley could barely make out his features but saw a rather firm jaw and deep-set eyes, with a small, thin mustache poking out from underneath his nose.

"It is much too dangerous. We have been looking for something to put down to help him, but it does not look like there is anyone there to help."

Not wanting to accept this, Lord Fernley shook his head firmly. "He has got to be there."

The man grasped his arm again, as Lord Fernley made his

way toward the railings. "I cannot let you try, Lord Fernley. It is much too dangerous. We have already lost one gentleman tonight, and I would rather not lose another."

Lord Fernley did not know what to say, his mind screaming at him to do something in order to help Lord Patton, but realizing slowly that he could do nothing at all. He sank to his knees, his hands around the railings as his eyes gazed down into the murky, swirling waters of the Thames, growing cold all over as he stared into it.

Lord Patton was gone.

1

"Lord Patton?"

It took a few seconds for Joseph to realize that it was he who was being spoken to, still finding it difficult to realize that it was he who was now the new viscount. Having been abroad at the time of his brother's death, it had taken him a good few months to return home, aware that his sister and brother-in-law had been forced to handle the funeral on their own. Not that Elizabeth was not capable, but rather that it was a duty Joseph ought to have taken on himself—especially when he had heard that Elizabeth was expecting her first child.

Sighing, Joseph looked up to see his butler standing in the doorway, a sheaf of papers in his hands.

"Yes?"

"The accounts you asked for, my lord. They have arrived."

Indicating that the man come in, Joseph took them eagerly from his hands. "Wonderful. Thank you."

"Can I get you anything else?"

Joseph shook his head, eager to get on. "No, I thank you. I will ring if there is anything else."

The butler closed the door carefully behind him, leaving

Joseph and the accounts alone. It had been, by this point, almost eight months since his brother's death, and this was now the first time Joseph had been able to see the state of his brother's affairs.

Going into the military had always seemed to be a preferable choice, especially since he was the second son. His parents had both passed away a year after he had been given his colors, and he had not been able to return home for their funerals either. At least, in that sense, he was keeping things consistent. A wry smile touched his lips as he turned the first page, aware that his dark humor was only to stop him from feeling so very alone. After all, he was now the only one of his family left who could continue the bloodline. He would need to marry and produce an heir very soon, just to be certain that there would be a new Viscount Patton to succeed him when the time came.

Shaking his head to himself, Joseph tried to focus on the numbers in front of him, but found he could not. His mind was too full of thoughts over his brother. He could still remember—with absolute clarity—the day he had been given the news about his brother's death. It had taken three months to reach him, since their regiment had moved locations only a month prior, and to hear his comrades and friends refer to him as "Viscount Patton" had been very strange indeed. In a moment, his dreams of a life spent in the army, of eventually settling down in a quiet part of the English countryside, had all been dashed away, billowing away from him like smoke carried on the wind. As the new Viscount Patton, he had responsibilities—with the first one being the requirement to return to England and take his place at the Patton Estate.

Joseph could not imagine what his brother would say if he saw him sitting in his study, drinking his whiskey, and treating his staff as though they were his own.

But they are *your own.*

Muttering under his breath, Joseph got up and went to pour

himself a stiff drink, the accounts lying on his desk still. That was, in fact, half the problem. He did not see himself as the new Viscount Patton, simply because he struggled to believe that his brother was gone. He was quite sure that this was, in part, due to missing the funeral, since he had not even heard about his brother's death at the time. It also was due to the fact that he simply had no idea how to go about being a viscount.

Pouring himself a large brandy, Joseph took a sip and then another, wandering to the window to look out over the gardens. This was his home now, he realized, even though he had been living here for a month or so already. He had to stop thinking that Oliver was going to walk through the door and demand to know why Joseph had taken over the running of the place. Oliver was dead and gone, apparently in some drunken accident, which had seen him drop like a stone into the Thames. His stomach tightened, and Joseph shook his head, trying not to let his thoughts linger on that fact. It was not as though he and Oliver had ever been close – for Oliver had gone to Eton before Joseph was able to walk. However, there was still a gap in his life where his brother should be.

In a way, Joseph regretted that he had never been able to know his brother fully, that they had only been relations but nothing more. Joseph knew nothing about his brother in any way, other than he liked to drink and spent most of his time in London. Their paths had very rarely crossed and that had simply been how things were. Why was it now that Joseph was coming to regret that lack of time spent together?

"At least Elizabeth is settled," Joseph murmured to himself, glad that his younger sister had found herself a decent husband in Viscount Strathern, even if it meant she had moved to Scotland in order to marry him. From what he remembered, the man was pleasant, amiable, and deeply in love with his sister, for that much had been evident on their wedding day two years past. To know that she was to bear a child brought Joseph more than a little happiness, since he knew that his sister had always longed for a family of her own.

And what about you?

The question rang around the room, bouncing off the walls as it repeated itself over and over in Joseph's mind. He knew that he would have to marry and produce an heir, but the thought of it churned his stomach. The last thing he wanted to do at this present time was to go to London in search of a bride, for he felt as though his life was, at present, already thrown into disarray. To add a wife into it would just add to his troubles.

And yet, despite all that, Joseph knew he had a duty to do just that. A duty that his brother, despite being almost seven years older than he, had not done—despite being Viscount for some time. Of course, Joseph suspected that Oliver had simply not wanted to give up his life in London for a sensible, rather-dull existence in the country back at the estate, and so he had put off such responsibilities until later. Much later. And now, at the young age of thirty-five, Oliver had managed to accidentally end his life and had not had time to do any of the things he had thought to put off until "later", meaning that Joseph now had to step up and take charge.

It was not a role he had ever wanted, nor now relished. He would have to be the viscount his brother had never been. The one responsible, dedicated, and devoted to his home, his title, and his bloodline. A wife would have to be sought, a child produced, and if it was a boy, then he might breathe a small sigh of relief. His duty to the family, in that regard, would be complete.

Of course, he might also have to produce the "spare" should the first go the same way as Oliver.

The thought had him shuddering, and—in one large gulp—Joseph threw back the rest of his drink and closed his eyes tightly for a moment, determined to rid himself of such thoughts. Sighing heavily to himself, he set the glass down and walked back to the study desk, seating himself down behind it, and beginning to look through the papers.

~

One hour later and Joseph was almost in despair. He had not realized that his brother had left the estate in such disarray. There had been very little money put into making the estate profitable, and from what he could see, there had been no work done to the tenants' homes in the last five years. He dreaded to think what the tenants would have to say to him, should he ask them about their homes and their livelihoods. The fields had once been abundant in their produce, but from what he could see, there was very little produced the last two years. Evidently, his brother had not cared all that much for the estate.

Groaning, Joseph put his head in his hands, staring down at the papers spread out across his desk. If this was to be believed, he had very little to rub together, which meant that he was, in fact, rather poor. There were, he presumed, bills that had not yet been paid, which, given that his brother was not yet a year in his grave, would come through soon enough.

Would he have enough money to pay them?

Getting up to pull the bell, Joseph felt himself grow cold all over. He had never expected this. He had thought, of course, that there might be some kind of financial upset to sort out, but had never expected it to be so dire. Wiping the sweat from his brow, he waited for the butler to appear, hoping that he might be able to give him some kind of insight.

"Yes, Lord Patton?"

"Stephens, tell me—" Joseph began, feeling sweat trickle down his spine. "How are the fields this year?"

The butler's eyes flashed for a moment with a look of concern. "The fields?"

"Yes, the fields," Joseph repeated, a little more firmly. "I can see that my brother has not put a great deal of effort into the estate of late, and given that he died before the planting, I am not quite certain what I should expect from the harvest."

The butler nodded slowly, his lips somewhat thin.

"I do want you to speak freely without fear of retribution," Joseph continued, a little less sternly. "I can see that my brother did not do all that was expected of him. You need not fear speaking openly."

The butler's brown eyes met Joseph's green ones, a steadiness in them that Joseph had not expected.

"My lord, the tenants knew that you would be coming to the estate as the new Lord Patton and so did all they could to the fields. I believe we will have a profitable harvest."

Swallowing hard, Joseph fought the urge to lean forward in his chair and rest his head on the desk. Relief flooded him, making him almost weak with relief.

"The tenants used what they could from some of last year's crops, as well as some seeds and the like that were stored, but never used. There are also sheep grazing in two of the larger fields, which have been well cared for. The tenants you have are good men and women, if I may say so, Lord Patton. They have not had much in terms of repayment for their work, and without being overly dramatic, there are some who do not have what they need."

Something like shame burned up Joseph's spine. "You mean, their homes?"

The butler nodded. "They will not last the winter unless something is done, my lord."

Joseph nodded slowly. "Thank you, Stephens. Now, if you

might send for my steward, I wish to go over some more details a little more fully."

The butler nodded and stepped out of the room, leaving Joseph alone. The steward, who oversaw most of the tenants and the land, had not yet spoken in depth to Joseph, since there had been so much going on. Joseph had, of course, had his things moved to this estate, whilst some of his brother's things had been cleared and put into storage. Perhaps he would have to sell some of those things, if they were worth anything. His brother had always had a penchant for collecting gaudy and rather ugly items, but mayhap they would prove useful in time.

Putting his head in his hands for a moment, Joseph let out a long breath before letting his hands run through his thick, brown hair. This was worse than he had ever imagined. How was he meant to run the estate now?

2

"How bad is it?"

Joseph's steward, Mr. Tunston, let out a small chuckle.

"Now, Lord Patton, what kind of attitude is that?"

Joseph could barely lift a smile, even though the familiarity with which Mr. Tunston spoke to him was rather refreshing. "I confess, I have been quite anxious these last two weeks."

It was, by now, a fortnight since Joseph had first discovered the truth about his financial situation. He had discovered that he was, indeed, rather poor—but also that his brother had left him a large pile of debts in London. He had been forced to travel to the city at the height of the Season, simply to look through all the papers from the solicitors in London.

And now Mr. Tunston, his steward, had made the journey to give Joseph a report.

"The work on the tenants' homes has begun, Lord Patton," Mr. Tunston replied. "The men working on them have been paid from the coffers you have remaining, although it was barely enough to stretch."

Joseph closed his eyes, feeling both relief and frustration in equal measure.

"However, I have had many of your brother's items shipped to London and have already had a good number of pieces sold off. They are, of course, varying in value and price, but—"

"But any money will help," Joseph finished, leaning back in his chair. "Thank you, Mr. Tunston."

A small sniff came from the smaller, quieter gentleman in the corner, whom Joseph had forgotten about completely. It was Mr. Cartwright, Joseph's solicitor, who was now pulling out a document from his bag. With his big eyes and hair parted neatly in the middle, he gave off an almost owl-like appearance, not helped by the fact that he had not taken off his large, voluminous coat, which was much too big for his spindly frame.

Apparently, Mr. Cartwright felt the cold, even though it was by now a blazingly warm summer day.

"This is the list of your assets, Lord Patton," Mr. Cartwright stated, in a rather crisp voice. "You have five separate abodes."

Joseph stared at him for a moment, his hand frozen around the document. "Five?"

Mr. Cartwright nodded, blinking slowly. "Five. Yes. Two in London, your estate, and—of course—your own smaller estate. The previous Lord Patton also purchased a small country retreat for himself, only an hour or so from London."

Slowly sitting back down in his chair, Joseph let his eyes drift over the page. "I do not understand why he purchased two more homes," he murmured aloud, seeing the list of houses written down neatly. "It is quite ridiculous."

"Your brother always did like to throw his wealth around," Mr. Tunston said, using that same familiarity that Joseph had come to appreciate. "I could never understand it myself, but he seemed to want more and more no matter how much he had."

"Are you quite sure you should be speaking in such a way in

front of Lord Patton?" Mr. Cartwright interrupted rather curtly. "After all–"

Joseph held up a hand. "Mr. Cartwright, it is refreshing to have a man unafraid to speak his mind in my presence. I will confess that my brother's way of life was completely unknown to me, and to hear it from another's lips, no matter how painful, is something I have come to appreciate. As you can see, this news of these additional homes has come as a great shock, especially given just how poorly my brother managed his wealth."

Mr. Cartwright sniffed, producing a pair of spectacles, which he placed neatly on the end of his nose. "Your brother did as he pleased, Lord Patton. Just as you can."

Hiding a sigh, Joseph nodded and turned his attention back to the document he held. "Then tell me, Mr. Cartwright, do each of these homes have their own staff?" He knew that his own smaller estate had a very basic staff to care for the home whilst no one resided there, but he could not speak of the other two places he had only just become aware of.

Mr. Cartwright's brow furrowed. "Well, yes. I believe so. The townhouse in London has a full staff, but that is only because it is being let out. You will see the payment for their residence in this document." Mr. Cartwright proceeded to pull out another piece of paper, waving it under Joseph's nose. "And the house a little outside of London—I believe it is called Woodlea Place—also has a full complement of staff. Your brother used it frequently during the London Season, mostly for house parties, I believe."

Joseph swallowed his rising anger, trying to focus on what he had just learned. "I see. Then that place can be sold."

"You do not intend to use it yourself?"

Joseph felt his anger burning and glared at Mr. Cartwright, wondering how the man could be such a simpleton. "No, Mr. Cartwright, I do not intend to use it myself. My current financial situation can only be described as dire, and to keep anything frivolous would be both ridiculous and inane. Sell it. Sell it all. And then, perhaps, I will have enough to pay my debts here in London, left for me by my selfish, arrogant, idiot of a brother."

There was nothing but silence for a long time. Joseph heard his words repeated back to him in his head but did not regret a single thing he had said. Mr. Tunston, at least, appeared to understand the situation Joseph was in, judging by his look of sympathy, as well as his understanding in their previous discussions. Mr. Cartwright looked as though he had been shaken very violently and then left to stagger about for a time. Did the man truly not realize just how frustrated Joseph was with everything his brother had done? Did he not see how truly difficult a situation this was for him?

You are a fool, Joseph thought, turning his gaze away from the solicitor. *And I am even more a fool for allowing my brother to live in such a way without even taking the slightest bit of interest in his life when he was on this earth.*

"Very wise, Lord Patton," Mr. Tunston said eventually, breaking into Joseph's troubled thoughts. "What of the townhouse here? The one that is being let out?" Mr. Tunston turned his gaze to Mr. Cartwright, who, after fluffing about with some other papers in his case, pulled another out and handed it to Joseph.

"The townhouse was bought, I believe, for a certain widow, if you get my meaning," Mr. Cartwright began, with a slight gruffness to his voice that betrayed a growing embarrassment.

Joseph rolled his eyes. "You are trying to say that my brother had a lady under his protection, no?"

Mr. Cartwright cleared his throat and nodded. "Yes, precisely."

"Go on," Joseph continued, trying not to allow the revulsion he felt to show in his expression. His brother, whilst ignoring the duties of his estate, had been throwing money at a widow who could provide him with carnal pleasure whenever he wished it. The anger he felt over his brother's behavior continued to grow.

Mr. Cartwright continued, seemingly unaware of Joseph's frustrations. "However, I believe that association came to an end, and so the house lay empty. When your brother died, I am afraid that I took an opportunity that came my way in order to add to your funds."

Surprised, Joseph lifted one eyebrow and looked directly at Mr. Cartwright, seeing the flush on the man's cheeks. Perhaps he was not as foolish as he seemed.

"I apologize if that was wrong of me, my lord," Mr. Cartwright finished, drawing in a deep breath. "At the time, I did not feel as though it were something I could pass up."

"Indeed," Joseph murmured, still a little taken aback. "Then I must commend you, Mr. Cartwright, for I can see that you have let the place for a good many months and that the rent covers the outgoings rather well."

Mr. Cartwright's cheeks lessened in color. "We are making a small profit each month, Lord Patton."

"Very good, very good," Joseph said, half to himself, as he scrutinized the papers. "I presume that it would be best, however, to sell the townhouse?"

Mr. Tunston nodded, whereas Mr. Cartwright shook his head. Sighing, Joseph turned his attention towards Mr. Cartwright, who was now pulling yet another document from the case.

"The lady in question has signed a lease of sorts, Lord Patton," Mr. Cartwright explained. "You cannot sell the place until the year's end."

Sighing heavily, Joseph took the document and let his gaze run down the paper. Yes, there it was, firmly fixed until the year's end. "A Lady Hannah Marlstone?"

"Daughter of the Earl of Sunderland," Mr. Cartwright finished, almost proudly. "Her father passed away a little over a year ago, I believe, and she has been residing in London for some months since then."

Joseph's eyebrows shot into his hair. "Alone? Is she a spinster?"

Mr. Cartwright shook his head. "No, I believe she only had her come out two or three years ago, although—of course—she was not in society last year. She lives in the townhouse with her companion and aunt, a Baroness Dalton, who I believe herself is widowed."

"Why does she not live on her father's estate?" Joseph asked, feeling somewhat intrigued. "I would have thought that a lady such as herself would not have come to live in London alone, not when the estate is open to her."

Mr. Cartwright gave a small shrug. "I am afraid I do not know the details, my lord. All I know is that I heard of this young lady looking for a townhouse in London, and I could not prevent myself from jumping at the opportunity to take it on."

"Naturally," Joseph murmured, looking down at the paper again. "Then perhaps I should meet Lady Hannah, since she is effectively my tenant."

Mr. Tunston nodded. "And it would be a good opportunity to remind her that the agreement is up come the end of the year, my lord. As you said yourself, you will require the funds."

Nodding slowly, Joseph looked up at both men. "Yes, capital idea, Mr. Tunston. Now, I believe you both know what is expected of you. Mr. Cartwright, you are to sell the house outside of London and then arrange for the most expensive items in my own smaller estate to be sold. Mr. Tunston continue as you have been with the sale of my brother's things. In addition, if you find anything more of value back at the estate that you think would fetch a good price, then do let me know. I have nothing of particular significance back at the estate. I must, somehow, get myself back into a good financial state." The heavy burden of responsibility sat on his shoulders, pushing him down and down until Joseph felt he was nearing despair. There was so much his brother had done that he had to, somehow, put right.

"The harvest will be good this year," Mr. Tunston said, reassuringly, as he got out of his chair. "And your tenants are already a great deal happier. Have no fear, Lord Patton, you will reach your goal in the end. You have already started on a great many improvements."

"Mr. Tunston, you will remain in London for the time being and assist Mr. Cartwright with the sale of the property and any other assets within," Joseph instructed. "I want it all done as quickly as possible."

"Of course," Mr. Tunston replied, looking rather pleased to be remaining in London for a time. "You will be out of difficulties very soon, I am sure, my lord."

"And if you wish to hasten such matters, there are young ladies with sizeable dowries sure to be around this Season," Mr. Cartwright added, getting to his feet. "Thank you, Lord Patton. Do let me know if there is anything more I can do for you."

Joseph, ignoring the comment about young ladies and their dowries, bid both men farewell, and sat back down at his desk, his head in his hands. He felt as though he were in the center of a whirlwind with no way out, fearing that if he took a single step then he would be caught up in it all, thrown headlong this way and that.

His eyes fell on the document on the table, the one bearing the name of Lady Hannah Marlstone. At least that was clear. He would have to visit her to speak about the end of the year and to discover whether or not she intended to remain in London. Besides which, he could not help but be intrigued as to why a daughter of an earl was in London with a companion, having apparently lived in town for some months. It was all very strange.

Picking up his quill, Joseph began to scratch out a short note to Lady Hannah, introducing himself and asking to call upon her at her earliest convenience. Idly, he wondered what she might look like, half wondering if she had been thrown from her father's estate for some particular reason.

Sanding the letter, he sealed it and got up to ring the bell.

"Take this at once," he said, handing the butler the letter and the note with the address. "There is no need to wait for a response."

The butler nodded. "Is there anything else, my lord?"

"Brandy," Joseph replied, indicating the empty decanter. "The best brandy we have, if you please. And do be quick."

The butler nodded and left, leaving Joseph with the beginnings of what he was sure would become a rather painful headache. At least, he hoped, the brandy would help – and if one glass did not, then he would simply drink another and another until nothing hurt at all.

Before he could even pour himself a brandy, however, there came another rap at the door. Frustrated, Joseph shouted at them to enter, only for the butler to come into the room with a card in his hand.

"A Lord Fernley to see you, my lord," the butler said quietly. "I should have asked you first if you were at home, but he was most insistent."

Thinking that he would never get the peace he craved, Joseph nodded and gestured for the man to come in. Staying where he was, he poured himself a brandy, only to turn and offer the same to the gentleman who came into the room to greet him.

Lord Fernley was a tall, broad-shouldered young man with a shock of dark brown hair and blue eyes that appeared to be filled with concern. He bowed at the waist, his expression grave, although he did accept the brandy that Joseph offered.

"I do apologize for calling on you without any prior introduction, Lord Patton, but I simply had to speak to you without delay," Lord Fernley said at once, the brandy still sitting untouched in his glass. "Viscount Fernley, at your service." He cleared his throat, as though preparing to give some kind of speech. "I was friends with your brother, Lord Patton.... I mean, Oliver Patton, of course."

"Oh?" Joseph asked, one eyebrow lifted slightly.

Lord Fernley looked even more ill at ease, shuffling from foot to foot. "I was there when he... I mean, it was a few minutes later, but I had seen him only just prior and..."

He trailed off and Joseph, stifling his frustration, tried to give the man an understanding look. "I do not blame anyone for my brother's death, Lord Fernley. Least of all you."

A small look of relief crossed Lord Fernley's features. "I am glad to hear that, Lord Patton. However, I have come to suspect something of late, something I must confess to you, regardless of how mad you will think me."

A flicker of interest caught Joseph's attention. "Oh? And what is that?"

Lord Fernley swallowed, hard. "My Lord Patton, I have come to suspect that your brother neither slipped and fell into the Thames, nor that he did so of his own volition, as some have begun to suggest."

Ignoring the stab of pain in his chest, Joseph kept his gaze fixed on Lord Fernley. "Then what do you believe, Lord Fernley? From what I understood, he was simply blazing drunk and fell into the water. Given that it was dark, I am not in the least bit surprised that he was unable to be rescued." He watched Lord Fernley closely, seeing the way the man's eyes darted from place to place. Whatever was going on with the man, it was making him nervous.

"I believe that someone is responsible for your brother's death, Lord Patton," Lord Fernley said firmly. "I do not believe that it was either an accident or suicide."

Clouds seemed to form around Joseph's mind, as he stared at Lord Fernley, trying to make sense of what the man had just said.

"Are you trying to tell me, Lord Fernley, that you believe that my brother was...?" He could not say the word, could not bring himself to let it pass his lips, and yet it hammered down, hard, into his brain.

Lord Fernley lifted his chin, his gaze fixed on Joseph. "Yes, Lord Patton, that is exactly what I think. I believe your brother was murdered."

3

Lady Hannah Marlstone sighed heavily as the maid set her blonde curls aright. She had intended to walk out with her aunt this afternoon, but an unfortunate encounter with a bird the moment she had set foot outside the house had brought that plan to a swift end. Although her aunt, Martha, Baroness Dalton, had assured her that they would still be able to make it to the bookshop before they needed to return to prepare for this evening's ball.

Another sigh escaped her lips as Hannah looked back at her reflection in the mirror, seeing the green eyes that looked back at her, aware that she was both sad and frustrated in equal measure. Yet another month had passed without any news from her brother, which, she supposed, was to be expected. Still, the lack of communication continued to tear at her heart. She had never thought that Phillip would be as cruel as to throw her out from the only place she had known as home practically the moment her father had been cold in his grave, having given her only one alternative, which she had refused. But then again, Phillip had always been a selfish creature, attempting to hold onto as much wealth as possible.

How grateful she was for her father's insight. Before he had passed away, he had ensured that she had a large fortune of her own, as well as a large dowry. Nothing her brother could do would take a single penny away from her name, which was, perhaps, the reason that Phillip had been so desperate to throw her from his world. Phillip had tried his best to persuade her to marry a particular gentleman, although she had never known *why* he had wanted her to do so. But, even before meeting the gentleman in question, she had outright refused. Phillip had not wanted to go near her after that, and within the week, her bags had been packed.

Even now, she did not know the reason as to why he had been so desperate for her to marry. Not that it mattered, she supposed, although she still longed to know that he cared about her—even a little. However, as the months had passed, she had grown less and less hopeful that he might apologize, might turn back to her and ask her to come home, seeing that his selfish nature overruled any familial love he might once have had.

"There you go, my lady," the maid murmured, stepping back to admire her handiwork. "And will you still be wanting your bath at the usual time?"

"Make it half an hour later," Hannah decided, carefully placing her bonnet back on her head. "That should give me more than enough time to prepare for Lord Lanston's ball this evening."

The maid bobbed a curtsy. "Very good, my lady."

Walking quickly down the stairs, Hannah smiled at her aunt, who was still waiting patiently, and apologized for taking so long. Martha laughed and shook her head, her dark brown eyes warm and smiling. How Hannah would have managed without her, she did not even want to imagine. She was more grateful for her with every day that passed.

"You have a letter, my dear," Martha said, gesturing for the footman to give it to her. "I do not know who it is from."

"Oh." Hannah looked down at the seal, a little confused. "Might I read it now?"

"Of course."

Breaking the seal, Hannah quickly read the few lines written within, before passing it to her aunt. For some unknown reason, she felt her stomach tighten with a sudden anxiety, as though the letter itself was in some way malevolent, even though she knew it could not be so.

"How interesting!" Martha exclaimed, folding up the letter and handing it back to Hannah. "I knew, of course, that there was a new Lord Patton, but I did not think that he would be eager to make your acquaintance."

Hannah did not smile. "So long as it is not that he wishes to take this house for himself."

"Why would he?" Martha asked, as Hannah handed the letter back to the footman with instructions to place it on her writing desk. "The lease is signed until the end of the year. You have not caused any kind of trouble, so you need not think like that at all."

Trying to shake off her feelings of anxiety, Hannah stepped out into the warm afternoon air and tried to draw in a long, steadying breath.

"You have no need to worry, my dear," her aunt said again, looping her arm through Hannah's. "I am quite sure that Lord Patton is simply doing his duty in visiting you."

"I hope so," Hannah replied softly, a prickle of nervousness climbing up her spine. "I should not like to be asked to move from this place also."

Her aunt laughed quietly. "Mayhap you will find a husband this Season and all will be well," she said and chuckled, squeezing Hannah's arm. "After all, that is why we are in London, is it not?"

Hannah sighed heavily, not finding any joy in such a statement. "But you know that it is more than difficult to find such a thing when everyone in the *beau monde* is aware that I am a woman of means." She shook her head as the smile faded from her aunt's face. "It is ridiculous to wish for a husband who will appreciate me for more than just my fortune and my dowry, but I do find myself hoping for more than just that." She gave a small shrug, looking over at her aunt as they walked. "Besides which, my fortune will sustain us both until our last days should I choose to remain a spinster."

Martha's face split with a smile. "Ah, but there is your downfall, my dear. I know full well that you long for a husband, and there is nothing wrong in such a desire. To be loved and love in return is one of life's great blessings." A hint of sadness touched her words, and Martha felt her heart break for her aunt. She had been married for such a short time, only for her husband to die after being thrown from his horse. With no children to speak of and no fortune of her own, Hannah's father – Martha's much older brother – had welcomed her into his house since she would have otherwise been cast out by the new Baron Dalton. Unfortunately, that meant that Martha had also been required to leave when Phillip took over the place as the new earl. It had been Hannah's delight to ask Martha to live with her in London. She had always been close to her aunt, especially given that there was only twelve years between them, and even now she was more like a friend than an older relative.

Martha was, of course, still something of a beauty, with long dark tresses that matched her dark eyes, and Hannah was sure that she could find another suitor in time. However, Martha was more than insistent that she was quite content on her own, so Hannah did not press the matter. Being a lady in her own right, at the tender age of twenty-one, meant that she did not yet fully understand all the intricacies of life and could not imagine what it was like to marry the man you loved only for him to pass away soon after. Therefore, she left the discussion of Martha's own heart well alone, even though she secretly still hoped that such a thing would one day occur.

"Are you going to write back to Lord Patton?"

Her aunt's question broke into Hannah's thoughts, and without hesitating, she nodded. "Of course. I will invite him to afternoon tea, if that would suit you. Of course, I will need your company."

Her aunt smiled. "Indeed. I would be glad to meet the new Lord Patton. I did not expect him to be in London for the Season." She shot a sly look towards Hannah, who rolled her eyes and laughed despite herself.

"I have no intention to throw myself onto the first gentleman that comes for afternoon tea, Martha, even though he might be the owner of our house."

"Perhaps he will be very handsome, and you will be quite unable to help yourself," Martha teased, as they crossed the busy road that led to the bookshop. "What then?"

Hannah made to speak, only to find that she could not come up with a suitable retort. Martha laughed again and pushed the door open that led to the bookshop, managing to bump into a gentleman who was just coming out of the door.

"Oh, my goodness!" the gentleman cried, reaching to grasp Martha's arm as she fell backward. "I am terribly sorry, my dear lady."

Hannah, who had taken Martha's other arm, shot the man a dark look, seeing how tall and broad-shouldered he was. He clearly had not been watching what he was doing and had simply walked straight out into the street, almost knocking poor Martha over in the process.

"Are you quite all right?" the man asked anxiously, his eyes searching Martha's face with great urgency. "My goodness, I do apologize. I have been quite caught up in my own thoughts and hoped that a new book might tear me away from them for a time."

Much to Hannah's surprise, Martha looked up at the gentleman with a small smile on her face. She did not frown, nor give him a sharp set down—as she was well in her rights to do—but instead looked up at him with color in her cheeks and a bright smile on her face.

"I am quite all right; I thank you," she said, as Hannah let go of her arm. "You may release me now, my lord."

The man flushed, as he realized he had Martha's hand still in his own. "Of course," he muttered, passing a hand over his eyes. "I do apologize." He bowed deeply. "Viscount Fernley, my lady." His gaze did not so much as move to Hannah, but rather, fixed on Martha, who, to Hannah's astonishment, was blushing furiously.

"Lady Dalton," Martha replied, curtsying. "And this is Lady Hannah Marlstone."

There was a flash of disappointment in Lord Fernley's eyes as he bowed towards Hannah, which apparently Martha saw, for she completed her speech by adding, "I am Lady Hannah's companion, since I have been widowed for some years."

"Ah," Lord Fernley replied, looking a little more brightened before realizing he ought not to be glad at such news. "I see."

"It was very kind of you to be so concerned over my aunt, Lord Fernley," Hannah said calmly, realizing she had not yet spoken. "Are you in town for the Season?"

Lord Fernley dragged his eyes away from Martha. "I am, yes, my lady. Might I enquire if you are attending any events this evening? I should like to ensure that Lady Dalton is truly well from such an unfortunate incident."

It was such a ridiculous excuse that Hannah was about to give him the sharp edge of her tongue, knowing that Martha did not want any kind of attention from any such gentleman, but a glance at her aunt caused her to come to a complete, stuttering halt.

Martha was looking back at Lord Fernley with something in her eyes that Hannah had never seen before: interest. She was, it seemed, quite taken with the gentleman on first appearance. Given that he appeared to be ages with the lady, Hannah supposed he was, at first glance, a more than suitable gentleman. However, this was most unlike her aunt, who only moments ago had been assuring Hannah that she had no intention of pursuing any kind of gentleman interest.

"We are to attend the Lanston ball this evening," she heard Martha say, before she could speak. "Although I, being a companion, will not be much engaged."

Lord Fernley did not appear to be put off in any way, his smile spreading across his face as he looked back at Martha. "Very good, very good, my lady," he said grandly. "Then I do hope to be able to greet you there this evening." He bowed again, and with another short bow towards Hannah, he took his leave.

"My goodness, Martha," Hannah hissed, as Martha looked after him. "What has come over you?"

Martha blinked, appearing to be a little confused. "Whatever do you mean, Hannah?"

Shaking her head, Hannah gestured towards the retreating back of Lord Fernley.

"I do not know what you mean," Martha replied, with a telltale blush still on her cheeks. "I simply found him a very amiable gentleman."

Hannah snorted in a most unladylike manner as she opened the door to the bookshop. "My dear aunt, you have not once spoken to a gentleman with such warmth in your eyes as you did just then. I can tell that you are now looking forward to Lord Lanston's ball with a little more excitement than before."

Martha paused, her hand reaching for Hannah's arm as they walked into the bookshop. "Wait, Hannah."

Letting the door close, Hannah looked back at Martha and saw anxiety in her eyes.

"Did you think me improper?"

Hannah felt her heart wrench for her aunt, smiling back at her and shaking her head. "No, of course not. I apologize, my dear aunt. I did not mean to tease you." She tipped her head, regarding Martha carefully. "There is nothing wrong in your interest in him, if that is what concerns you."

Martha swallowed hard, a small frown appearing between her brows. "I am not quite sure what just occurred, were I to be truthful with you. I have never felt such a thing since...since John."

Tears filled Martha's eyes, as she looked back at Hannah, who held Martha's hand tightly.

"John would want you to be happy, Martha," Hannah replied reassuringly, feeling a little bit out of her depth as she tried to help someone who was experiencing something she had never felt herself. "It was some years ago now, was it not?"

"That does not mean that I have forgotten him."

"No, of course not," Hannah agreed softly. "But it does not mean that you cannot feel such a thing again for another gentleman. It does not mean that you must live the life of a spinster in order to show your devotion. That is not what John would want, and it is not what I want for you either."

A small smile crept across Martha's face, in spite of the tears that were still sparkling in her eyes.

"You *are* looking forward to seeing Lord Fernley again this evening though, are you not?" Hannah asked carefully, as

Martha turned her head to dab at her eyes. "I was not mistaken there."

Martha laughed quietly, shaking her head. "No, you were not mistaken, Hannah. I am looking forward to being acquainted with him again. It is just my heart that is suddenly filled with confusion."

Hannah nodded and patted Martha's hand. "That is to be expected, I think. But for what it is worth, I think this is a very good thing, my dear aunt. Not that you will *ever* be allowed to marry before I do, for I do not think I could do without you!" she laughed as Martha's face broke into a wide smile, her tears gone.

"Nor could I do without you, my dear," Martha replied before they walked in together to the bookshop.

4

Hannah had found herself more anxious for her aunt than she had expected, arriving at Lord Lanston's ball with a ball of tension in her stomach. She greeted the hosts, and within a few minutes, she had a few gentlemen seeking to write their names on her dance card. She graciously allowed them to do so, but did not allow all of the spaces to be filled, feeling as though she needed some time to converse with the other guests, as well as watch her aunt. It was supposed to be the other way around as her aunt was her companion, but for whatever reason, Hannah found herself anxious over her aunt's acquaintance with Lord Fernley.

Perhaps it was because she feared that this would lead to her aunt being taken away from her, which she feared more than anything. Even though she knew that Martha would remain with her until the day she married, regardless of her own happiness. That in itself was a burden on her mind.

"You are going much too fast," she muttered to herself, as she made her way through the crowd of guests. "Do get ahold of yourself."

"Ah, Lady Hannah!"

Turning her head, Hannah saw the familiar face of Lord Fernley just behind her, making his way toward her and Martha as quickly as he could. He bowed graciously and took her hand, although Hannah knew that his attention was drawn only to Martha.

"Lord Fernley, how good to see you again," Hannah murmured. "You, of course, remember my aunt, Lady Dalton?"

Lord Fernley bowed again. "Of course. I am glad to see there are no ill effects from the crossing of our paths earlier today, Lady Dalton."

"None whatsoever, I assure you," Martha replied, with a small smile. "Thank you for coming to greet us, Lord Fernley."

Lord Fernley smiled at Martha, his brown eyes lighting up, and Hannah immediately felt as though she were intruding somehow.

"I should go in search of my friend, Lady Sophia," she murmured, making to turn away.

Lord Fernley cleared his throat. "Lord Patton!" he exclaimed, over the top of Hannah's head. "Do come and greet some new acquaintances of mine."

Hannah felt her chest constrict as she stared at Lord Fernley, who was waving over a gentleman just behind her. This could not be Lord Patton, the one who had written to her only earlier that day, could it?"

"Lord Patton?" she heard Martha say quietly. "You are acquainted with him?"

"Only just," Lord Fernley replied with a small smile. "I met him for the first time this morning and persuaded him that a ball might be just the thing for his constitution."

"He is unwell?" Martha asked, as Hannah stayed exactly where she was, feeling her nerves burst into life and crawl all through her.

"No, no, not exactly. The death of his brother last year has brought about a great many changes, that is all I meant," Lord Fernley replied, with a little more frankness than perhaps was wise. "He has only just come to London, and so he knows very few people."

Hannah lifted her chin and settled her shoulders, putting on as calm of an expression as she could, aware that she did not feel in the least bit settled inside. She drew in a breath carefully, as Lord Patton came to stand by Lord Fernley's side, looking down at her with something like disinterest.

"Lord Patton, how good to see you this evening," Lord Fernley said, with as much joviality as he could. "I had thought you might remain at home, but I am sure once you are acquainted with these particular ladies, you will be glad you joined us."

Hannah looked back at Lord Patton with a direct gaze, taking in the sternness of his green eyes, the setting of his rather square jaw. He had a mop of brown hair, which was doing its best to escape from the style he had it in, and there was something about him that appeared to be almost uncomfortable, as though he was desperate to remove himself from the starched shirt he was in. He was not unhandsome, however, although there was nothing about him that made Hannah immediately welcome his attention in the way that Martha had done with Lord Fernley.

"I am sure I shall be more than glad," Lord Patton said, in a voice that was neither warm nor icy. "Do make the introductions, Fernley."

Lord Fernley looked delighted at the prospect. "Lord Patton, this is Lady Hannah Marlstone, daughter of the late Earl of Sunderland, and this is her companion, the recently widowed Lady Dalton."

Hannah registered the surprise in Lord Patton's eyes as she curtsied, all too aware of the flush that mounted in her own cheeks.

"Lady Hannah, Lady Dalton," Lord Patton murmured, bowing again. "I see that our meeting is to be earlier than expected."

"Meeting?" Lord Fernley said in surprise. "You already are acquainted with Lady Hannah?"

Lord Patton shook his head. "Lady Hannah resides in one of my townhouses, Lord Fernley, and I had not yet had the pleasure of meeting her. Not that this is anything that should interest you, however."

Hannah frowned, seeing the embarrassed look on Lord Fernley's face as he looked away, feeling a trifle sorry for the man. He had not meant to pry, she was sure of it, but had rather been so delighted with his new acquaintances that he had been unable to stop himself from speaking so.

"I do hope you will still come for afternoon tea, as planned," she said quietly, finding that the man did not elicit so much as a smile from her. "I am sure there is much to discuss."

He nodded slowly, his eyes grave. "Not all that much, Lady Hannah. Although I am glad to meet you, of course."

"Now, Lady Dalton," Lord Fernley said, turning towards Martha. "Might I be able to encourage you to step onto the floor with me?"

Hannah glanced at Martha, feeling rather delighted for her friend only to see her shake her head, her color rising.

"Oh, Lord Fernley, you are very kind to ask, but I fear I cannot. I am a companion after all and—"

"I do not mind in the least if you dance, Martha," Hannah interrupted firmly. "I know that you are a wonderful dancer and that you have been denied the opportunity to do so for some time."

Martha shot her a fierce look. Although, whether it was one of frustration or confusion, Hannah was not sure. She returned it with a small, encouraging smile. Given that Martha had no other choice, she nodded her head.

"Very well, Lord Fernley, it appears that I am now inclined to dance this evening, although you must forgive me if I make mistakes. I have not had the opportunity to practice my steps in some time."

"Then let us begin to rectify that at once," Lord Fernley replied, with a broad smile, offering Martha his arm. "Shall we?"

Hannah smiled and nodded as Martha looked back at her, promising to be here when she returned. The music was only just beginning to strike up, and many couples were walking out onto the floor. Given that it would be rude not to ask her, Hannah waited for Lord Patton to do just that.

He did not say a word to her, however, his gaze following Lord Fernley and Martha, as they walked onto the dance floor. A flush of embarrassment crept up Hannah's spine and into her face as she waited for him to say something, praying to goodness that the rest of the *ton* would not see her waiting patiently, only to be ignored by Lord Patton.

"I should go," he said hastily, turning back towards her. "It was very good to meet you, Lady Hannah, and I look forward to taking tea with you in two days' time."

Hannah felt her mouth fall open, as she stared at him in shock, wondering if he realized just how improper he was being. To leave her standing alone, when he should have—and could have—asked her to dance, was more than humiliating for her.

"Good evening, Lady Hannah," Lord Patton said quickly, as though he were suddenly desperate to get away from her. "And thank you."

She was not sure what he was thanking her for, but was left standing there, mute and motionless, as he left her side and strode through the rest of the crowd, not once looking back at her.

Hannah felt her cheeks burn as she lifted her head high, trying to calm her frustration and mortification. She was quite sure that some of the *ton* would have noticed already and would be whispering and laughing at such humiliation.

Lifting her chin, Hannah waited patiently for Martha to be returned to her side, aware that her face was still quite red by the time the music came to an end. Yet, she could not help but smile at the way Martha was looking up at Lord Fernley, a brightness in her eyes that Hannah had not seen before.

"Lady Hannah, allow me to tell you just what an exquisite dancer your aunt is," Lord Fernley began, the moment he arrived back at her side. "Indeed, I do not think I have ever had the pleasure of such a wonderful partner before."

Martha blushed and Hannah smiled. "Indeed, I am sure that my aunt has a great many talents that she keeps well hidden. Do you know that she plays the pianoforte with such passion that it often brings tears to my eyes?"

Lord Fernley looked more than a little interested, glancing down at Martha before returning his gaze to Hannah. "Is that so?" he asked softly. "A lady of many talents then?"

"Many," Hannah confirmed, as Martha shot her a desperate look that Hannah could not quite understand. "In fact, you must come to dinner, Lord Fernley. I am certain that my aunt will be willing to play for us all afterward."

She heard Martha gasp and felt her aunt's fingers tighten around her arm, but she did not back down. Lord Fernley looked positively delighted to have been asked such a thing and began to nod fervently.

"I would be delighted, truly," he said, with a small bow towards them both. "I will wait for your invitation."

Hannah smiled back at him, finding him to be both charming and rather sweet natured. "Wonderful, Lord Fernley. Thank you."

"And thank you for asking me to dance," Martha added, curtsying again. "It was, I confess, rather wonderful to be able to do so again after such a long time."

Lord Fernley's eyes lit up as they landed on Martha. "It was my honor, truly. Thank you, Lady Dalton."

As Lord Fernley took his leave, Hannah felt Martha's hand squeeze her arm again.

"Whatever were you thinking, Hannah?" Martha whispered, looking over at her. "Inviting the man to dinner?"

Hannah shrugged, her brows furrowing. "Why ever not? It is quite clear that he is interested in continuing and furthering your acquaintance, and I thought...." Seeing Martha's deep frown, Hannah came to a stop.

"You are being much too hasty," Martha whispered quietly. "To invite him to dinner seems so familiar, so personal. I cannot help but think that it is much too soon for what is only the start of our acquaintance."

Slowly, Hannah realized that Martha was rather afraid of what it was she felt, of the feelings developing between herself and Lord Fernley. A wave of guilt overtook Hannah. She had never thought to ask Martha if such an invitation as dinner would be something that Martha herself wanted, for she had simply used her own judgment and supposed that it was best.

"I did not mean to upset you," she said slowly, seeing the way Martha's chin wobbled just a little. "I did not mean to be so hasty. I am simply desirous for you to find your own happiness, even if it comes upon you in the form of Lord Fernley."

Martha gave her a small, tight smile. "It is all rather overwhelming, Hannah, that is all. To be able to dance again was simply wonderful, but I confess that I am afraid of what it is I feel after such a short acquaintance."

Seeing that this was something Martha was going to have to work through on her own, Hannah gave a small sigh. "I do apologize, Martha, and I quite understand. We shall make it a dinner party then and invite a good few acquaintances so that Lord Fernley is not singled out in any way. Would that suit you?"

A look of relief flashed onto Martha's face as she nodded.

"And we shall make it for a week hence," Hannah continued, feeling a little more certain of herself.

"And you shall have to invite Lord Patton," Martha added, looking all around her. "Where is he, might I ask? I would have thought that he would have wanted to dance with you."

Hannah felt the flush of embarrassment rush into her cheeks again. "I found him intolerably rude, to be truthful. He walked away from me without even thinking of asking me to dance, and so I was left to stand alone whilst the other couples made their way to the floor." She shook her head at Martha's astonished look, a slow burn of anger in her heart. "He appeared rather distracted, as though he could not wait to escape from me."

"Now, I am sure that cannot be right," Martha replied firmly. "This is his first ball in some time, you know, since he has only just become Lord Patton in the last year and was in the military before then. Perhaps he quite forgot all that was expected of him."

"Perhaps," Hannah agreed begrudgingly. "However, I do not have any inclination to invite him to dinner alongside Lord Fernley."

"Oh, but you must," Martha replied calmly. "He was introduced to us by Lord Fernley, and I think it would only be right for you to do so, particularly when he has only just entered society. Besides, he is coming for afternoon tea soon, and I am certain that you will find his character more than satisfactory. Do not let one awkward encounter put you off, my dear."

Hannah, who was still feeling rather uncharitable towards Lord Patton, was not inclined to give any kind of charitable thought toward the man. However, seeing Martha's earnest expression, she knew that she would not be able to remain so stoically determined to dislike him.

"Very well," she sighed, hating that she had given in so easily. "I will invite him also to dinner. Then will that give you satisfaction?"

Martha laughed, her eyes sparkling. "Indeed, my dear girl. Indeed it will."

5

Joseph shifted uncomfortably in his chair, aware of the piercing look that was being sent in his direction by Lady Hannah. She was unsmiling and appeared almost grim in the way she looked at him, as though finding his company less than delightful.

She was, of course, quite beautiful, with an oval face, piercing green eyes, and silky blonde hair that was held up in a rather intricate style, although Joseph could not help but wonder just how long it might be once it was free of its pins.

The thought itself stunned him, his breath catching sharply. He ought not to be thinking of Lady Hannah in such a way, not when he was there to discuss business with her. And yet, despite that, Joseph found himself thinking of it again and again, his mind scrambling to realign itself to a more proper way of thinking.

"I was sorry to hear about the loss of your brother," Lady Hannah said quickly, pouring the tea. "Lord Fernley tells me that you have only just returned to London, having taken on your new title in the last year."

"Lord Fernley is correct," Joseph replied, with a slight twinge of anxiety. "My brother sadly died, and I was forced to take on the role as Viscount Patton." He saw Lady Hannah pause, as he reached for his teacup, aware that he had already said a little more than was, perhaps, proper. He ought not to have said anything about his brother and the like, for now, he had made it more than obvious that he did not particularly want to *be* the new viscount.

"I see," Lady Hannah murmured quietly, adding a dash of milk to her tea. "And are you only now taking stock of all your holdings?"

He cleared his throat, still feeling somewhat awkward after his misstep. "Indeed, I am. I confess that I did not know of this place, nor of another house my brother apparently purchased during his time here in London." Giving a slight shrug, he looked back at Lady Hannah and tried to smile. "But at least this house has someone residing in it."

"And someone who pays the rent each month," Lady Hannah added, with a wry smile. "Is that not what troubles you, my lord? Money being thrown away for no good reason?"

A slight flush warmed his cheeks. "I confess that I find the idea of a man having five homes of his own to be rather selfish and unnecessary," he replied firmly. "I cannot pretend otherwise." For whatever reason, Joseph realized that he was being rather familiar with Lady Hannah, speaking more openly with her than he had done with anyone before. Whether it was the flicker of interest in her eyes, or the small smile on her face, Joseph could not be certain, but he was aware that she was regarding him with something like curiosity etched into her gaze.

"I find that quite a refreshing concept, Lord Patton," Lady Hannah said quietly. "My own brother is a selfish creature, and therefore he spends most of his time doing exactly what he wishes and does not care for anyone but himself."

Joseph frowned, seeing the suffering in her eyes as she turned her head away from him just a little, as though not wanting him to see what she truly felt.

"Your brother is the new earl, I believe."

She nodded.

"And may I ask why it is you now reside here? I thought that he...?" He did not know what he was to say, not quite sure what it was he was trying to ask, but saw Lady Hannah throw him a sharp glance, her lips thin.

"If you mean to suggest that my brother is now a very wealthy man with more than enough to get him by, then you are quite correct to say so, my lord," she said firmly. "He is nothing more than a lazy, selfish man who threw both myself and my widowed aunt from our home just as soon as he was able. Thankfully, my father knew that this was rather likely, given Phillip's nature, and so he ensured that I was very well taken care of in terms of my own particular fortune. I believe the final straw came when I would not do what my brother requested of me. That is why you find me now residing in London with my aunt. The truth is, Lord Patton, I have nowhere else to go." She tilted her head, her eyes flashing. "Now, does that satisfy your curiosity?"

A prickle of unease crept up Joseph's spine. "It was not my intention to pry, Lady Hannah." He looked back at her steadily, seeing her consider his words for a moment before sighing and looking away.

"No, indeed, but I confess that my situation here is somewhat strange, is it not?" she said softly. "I may be of age, and I may have my own fortune, but to reside in a stranger's house, paying rent instead of purchasing a home for myself, it is something that has set the *ton*'s tongues alight, Lord Patton." A small, sad smile crept across her face. "Not that anyone truly cares about what has occurred in my life. Rather, they are more concerned with what rumors they can spread, what gossip they can share about my circumstances."

There was a moment of silence, and Joseph chose not to speak, aware that Lady Hannah had revealed a great deal more of herself and her situation than perhaps she had intended. His heart tore for her, as he looked back into her sorrowful face, wondering what kind of brother could throw his own sister from her childhood home.

Lady Hannah tried to smile again, her cheeks a little pink as she looked back at him, perhaps realizing just how much she had said.

"I do hope you have not come to inform me that we are to be asked to leave this house also," she said, with a small, rather tight laugh. "I am quite sure that we have paid our rent as it is due, and as you can see, have not caused any kind of damage." She gestured to the rest of the room, as though he ought to survey it, but Joseph chose to leave his gaze firmly on Lady Hannah. The words he had been planning to say now stuck in his throat, as though he were now aware that he could not say all he had planned.

She appeared to be rather distraught, although she was hiding it well, and Joseph found that he could not permit himself to ask her to leave his home by the end of the year. Even though it was a good few months away, the thought of asking her to pick up and find another place to live did not sit well with him. After all, there was no guarantee that she would find another suitable home. Joseph suspected that many gentlemen might wish to make sport of a young lady living with only an aunt for a companion, or at least try to make their way into her favors.

"But of course, if that is what you wish to ask of us, we are more than willing to abide by your wishes," came the voice of

Lady Dalton, who had been sitting quietly adjacent to Lady Hannah. "Is that not so, Lady Hannah?"

Lady Hannah flushed a bright red and nodded, her eyes dropping to her hands now folded in her lap. "But of course, do forgive me, Lord Patton."

He smiled, wanting to put her at ease. "You are quite all right, Lady Hannah. I have no intention of asking you to leave, so you may put your mind to rest about that." He saw her smile back at him a little tremulously, clearly more than relived over what he had said. "And I believe that I also must apologize to you for not asking you to dance at the ball two nights ago. Lord Fernley spoke to me, and I am afraid that my bad manners must have seemed more than a little rude."

Seeing the smile spread across Lady Hannah's face, Joseph felt himself sigh with relief inwardly. Lord Fernley had spoken to him only yesterday, having called in the afternoon, and their conversation had begun by talking of the ball. Lord Fernley had been much taken with Lady Dalton, it seemed, but he had been horrified to discover that Joseph had simply left Lady Hannah's side and not once thought to ask her to dance. At the time, he had dismissed it as nothing serious, not believing that the lady could be upset by such a thing and stating very firmly that he was quite sure Lady Hannah had not *wanted* to dance with a complete stranger, but now he was in her presence, the apology had come to his lips regardless. And, apparently, it had been something Lady Hannah had been hoping for, given the way her smile was growing.

"I have not been in society for some time, and so I must beg you to forgive my ignorance," he continued a little quieter. "I can see that I have caused you some embarrassment in doing such a foolish thing, and I can assure you it will not happen again. Next time we meet at a ball, I will endeavor to dance with you on two separate occasions to make up for my foolishness." He did not mention the other matter that had brought Lord Fernley to his door – the matter of his brother's supposed murder.

Joseph had not accepted the gentleman's suggestion, telling him repeatedly that it had been some terrible accident, but Lord Fernley had been insistent. He had mentioned that a lady of the night had been with his brother on the night, but that he had not been willing to go ahead with any search for her until Joseph had heard his suggestion and agreed to it. However, because Joseph had *not* agreed with Lord Fernley on this matter, telling him to leave Oliver's death well alone, Joseph had thought that Lord Fernley might forget all about the matter. In fact, he had thought that such a thing *must* have happened, given how Lord Fernley greeted him at the ball and introduced him to others. Although, now that he thought about it, it might very well have been an attempt by Lord Fernley to coerce him to consider the matter again. As Joseph looked back at Lady Hannah, he realized just how distracted he had been last evening, and just how poorly he had treated her because of it. He must have made a terrible first impression.

However, his apology seemed to have done the trick. Lady Hannah beamed at him. "I would very much enjoy dancing with you, Lord Patton, I am sure. You are quite forgiven, I assure you."

Feeling much more relaxed, even though he had not done the very thing he had come here to do, Joseph found himself discussing a great many things with the lady, staying much longer than he had intended. Whilst Lady Dalton was present, she did not add much to their conversation, leaving them to talk together without much interruption. Joseph found himself growing more and more comfortable in the lady's presence, finding her able to talk about a great many things with both intelligence and wit. He thought her quite wonderful by the time his afternoon came to an end, exclaiming aloud at the hours that had passed, and apologizing profusely if Lady

Hannah had other engagements that she was now late for due to his imposition on her time.

"No, no, I have nothing else this afternoon," Lady Hannah replied, getting to her feet. "Although I must prepare for Lady Hawthorne's recital this evening." She looked at him steadily, interest still flickering in her emerald eyes. "Will you be in attendance?"

Trying desperately to remember whether or not he had accepted the invitation, Joseph found himself nodding regardless.

"I hope to be."

"Wonderful," Lady Hannah murmured, her smile warm. "Then I hope to see you again later this evening."

Joseph made to take his leave, finding his own heart to be rather filled with the lady, only for the drawing room door to fly open, startling them all. Lady Hannah jumped visibly as the door crashed into the wall, only for Lord Fernley to stumble through it.

His eyes landed firmly on Joseph, a visible sigh escaping him as he hurried forward.

"I have found you at last!" Lord Fernley exclaimed, ignoring Lady Hannah and Lady Dalton's presence. "I *told* you your brother had been murdered, Lord Patton, and now I know for certain it is true. I have found the lady of the night. In fact, I found her last evening and spoke to her at great length, although she did not say too much. I went to find her this morning, so that she might come to your home and tell you all, but when I went to find her, they told me she was dead. On top of which, I have only just recalled that the gentleman present at the time referred to me as 'Lord Fernley'—when I am certain that I did not so much as mention my name!"

"Fernley!" Joseph exclaimed, his heart hammering wildly in his chest as he indicated Lady Hannah and Lady Dalton, who were both staring at Lord Fernley in shock. "Now is neither the place, nor the time!"

There came a short, stunned silence, as Lord Fernley looked back at them both. His face appeared to register them for the first time, his eyes widening as they darted back towards Joseph.

"I do apologize," he whispered, putting one hand over his eyes, as his face turned paler still. "It is the shock of it, that is all."

Joseph cleared his throat, aware of the sparkling tension between them all. "Do excuse me, Lady Hannah. I must go with Lord Fernley and—"

"Stay."

Her voice was crystal clear, ringing out across the room like a bell. He looked back at her, seeing her draw herself up to her full height as she lifted her chin a notch.

"I beg your pardon?" he asked quietly. "Did you mean—?"

"You cannot exactly leave now, not after Lord Fernley has come out with such a stunning revelation," Lady Hannah said, gesturing to the chair. "Besides which, I believe that Lord Fernley will need a stiff drink if he is to make it home."

Joseph shook his head whilst Lord Fernley sank into a chair. A murmur of warning rose in his heart. If what Lord Fernley was saying was true, if the lady of the night *had* been killed so that she could not speak to Joseph herself, then the longer they stayed here, the worse it could be for Lady Hannah and Lady Dalton.

"I thank you, but no," he said firmly, glaring at Lord Fernley, who did not seem to notice. "If Lord Fernley is correct, then this must be discussed with all privacy. I cannot endanger you."

There was a short silence. Joseph looked back steadily at Lady Hannah, who was regarding him carefully, her lips a little twisted as she thought.

"It appears that we already know a little more than we

should," she said after a few moments. "Lord Fernley has told us that, not only was your brother murdered, but that the lady who was with him has now also been killed." She gave him a small, rueful smile, gesturing towards the chair. "Please, sit, Lord Patton. It appears we are to be all in this together now, whether you like it or not."

6

Hannah could see very plainly that Lord Patton did not want to do anything she had asked, but aware that she had made her point very well, sat down and waited patiently for him to do the same. Ignoring Martha's worried whisper, Hannah let her gaze rest on Lord Fernley, finding herself rather intrigued by all that had been said.

Of course, she could have very easily let Lord Patton and Lord Fernley go, but the truth was, she had enjoyed her afternoon with Lord Patton a great deal and felt as though she did not want it to come to an end. He had surprised her in both his apology and in his willingness to let them stay on at the house for as long as they wished, having been quite certain that he was to ask her to leave within a month or so. When he had apologized to her for his mistake at the ball, Hannah had found herself unable to keep ahold of her anger, aware that he was looking at her with such earnestness, such honesty in his eyes, that there was simply no thought in her mind that he was being in any way insincere.

It seemed that Martha had been right to suggest that she did not base her assumption of the man on a single incident. Whatever Lord Patton was, he was certainly interesting—and *that* caught her attention.

"Lady Hannah, I must tell you again that I think this most unwise," Lord Patton began, eventually taking his seat. "I myself am not certain whether or not I believe Lord Fernley's suggestion that my brother was murdered instead of simply falling into the Thames due to the amount of liquor he had imbibed. I would not want you to feel in any way disconcerted by what is said here. This is not your affair, and I have no desire to make it so."

She heard Martha murmur something about staying out of Lord Patton's private affairs but ignored it completely.

"Lord Patton, if what Lord Fernley says is true, then we might very well be in danger at this very moment, might we not?" she asked, with a lift of her eyebrow. "Besides which, I find myself quite intrigued by the suggestion, although I cannot imagine how painful this must be for you."

Lord Patton swallowed, the muscle in his cheek jumping as he did so. "Lady Hannah, I must insist that—"

"I was with him, you know."

Lord Fernley, who was now the color of milk, interrupted them both, talking as though no one else was in the room. He talked in a low, dull voice, repeating everything that had happened that night. The guilt he felt was more than apparent, and Hannah felt her heart break for him. Daring a glance at Martha, she saw that her aunt was sitting a little further forward in her chair, her eyes fixed on Lord Fernley. She was clearly hanging onto every word he said, her gaze never lifting from him. Apparently, her aunt, despite her wariness over the situation, was now feeling rather sorry for Lord Fernley and was being drawn into the situation regardless of her own feelings.

"I could not get to him, of course," Lord Fernley finished,

almost mournfully. "I cannot swim, and it was so dark and so deep that I dared not go in after him."

"You did nothing wrong, Fernley," Lord Patton said in a heavy voice. "We have discussed this."

Hannah shot a glance toward Lord Patton, hearing the hard edge to his voice. Apparently, he was not pleased with Lord Fernley's conduct, but Hannah could see that Lord Fernley was carrying a rather heavy burden of guilt. Guilt that he did not need to bear.

"It was not your fault, in any way," she said quietly, seeing the way Lord Fernley looked up at her with such misery in his expression that she felt her heart squeeze tight with compassion. "Lord Patton himself has said so."

Lord Fernley shook his head. "I should have prevented him from walking out alone, but I confess that I was a little frustrated with his antics."

She frowned. "Antics?"

Lord Patton cleared his throat, looking even more unwilling to speak. "My brother was not a man who thought carefully and wisely about his actions, Lady Hannah. That is what Lord Fernley means."

Lord Fernley jerked, as though Lord Patton had reprimanded him somehow, before lowering his gaze to the floor, clearly chagrined. Hannah glanced back at Lord Patton, seeing his brow so deeply furrowed that she wondered if permanent lines would appear on his forehead. How strange it was that a man she barely knew was now telling her the story of his brother's death?

"My brother died, and that is all there is," Lord Patton said firmly. "Lord Fernley believes that it might be, in fact, a murder, but I do not think that the death of this 'lady of the night' proves anything. We should take our leave."

Lord Fernley's head shot up. "Wait. There was something

else. The gentleman in question, who was there at the time Oliver went into the Thames, I only now recalled that he referred to me as 'Lord Fernley', when he could not possibly have recognized me. I did not recognize him, however, so I am certain we have never met before."

"What does it matter, Lord Fernley?" Patton exclaimed, sounding more and more frustrated. "A gentleman recognized you, but you did not recognize him. That happens countless times."

Lord Fernley shook his head, his jaw jutting out in a somewhat stubborn fashion. "There was a nefarious air about him, Lord Patton. Something strange going on. That girl, Sally, she seemed scared of him, as though she might say the wrong thing and get herself done in for it. I do not remember much about the man, but I am certain that he had a long, thin mustache that stretched out under his nose. Quite distinctive. I am certain that if I saw him again, I would know who he was."

Something cold clutched at Hannah's heart. "That sounds very much like Lord Walton," she murmured, her eyes reaching out towards Lord Fernley, who stared at her in disbelief. "A long, thin mustache, a rather square jaw, and a somewhat formidable presence."

Lord Patton and Lord Fernley looked back at her, their gazes both astonished and fixed on her entirely.

"My goodness," Lord Fernley breathed, his face alive with expectation. "It seems you might be of more use than I first expected, Lady Hannah. Do you truly think this man is Lord Walton?"

Hannah nodded, a wave of nausea ran over Hannah as she looked back at Martha, seeing the same shock registered on her aunt's face.

"Lord Walton is the man my brother proposed I marry," Hannah replied heavily. "He is to be the Earl of Marchwick, but for the moment, he is Viscount Walton. His thin mustache is the first thing anyone notices about him, and I know that he does like to be the subject of discussion amongst the *ton*, but only in a positive manner, of course. He knows a great many people here in London, even though they may not all know him." She shot a sidelong glance towards Lord Fernley, who was now looking almost rapturous, as though she had brought him a wonderful gift that he could not wait to unwrap.

Lord Patton, however, appeared quite the opposite. He let out a long, pained breath, regarding her as though she were some kind of ghost, some kind of apparition sent to haunt him.

"I am afraid that it appears that Lady Hannah is to be mixed up in all of this regardless of your reluctance, Lord Patton," Lord Fernley murmured, sitting back in his chair with a stunned expression on his face. "My, my, Lady Hannah. Who would have thought it?"

Lord Patton shook his head, just as Martha got up out of her chair to ring for tea.

"Some more refreshments would be welcome, I think," she murmured, as Hannah kept her gaze fixed on Lord Patton. "I confess, I do not understand what Lord Walton has to do with all this."

"Nor do I," Lord Fernley replied quickly. "But I know that he was present that evening, telling me not to go in after Lord Patton – I mean, after Oliver. I am certain that he referred to me as 'Lord Fernley' even though I had never set eyes on him before, nor did he think to introduce himself. I confess that I did not think much of it until much later, when I began to think a little more in depth about what had occurred."

Hannah swallowed a sudden fear that crept up her throat, feeling as though she had willingly thrown herself into a whirlwind. This had caught her interest, yes, but she had only just now realized the seriousness of it all. This was murder they were talking about, and since she knew Lord Walton, it now felt a little too close for comfort.

"What did you think?" she managed to ask, focusing all her attention on Lord Fernley. "Is it about Lord Walton?"

Lord Fernley nodded slowly, his expression grave. "When I approached the Thames, I am sure that Lord Walton came from my right, as if running to the scene. However, Sally, when she spoke to me, kept looking over at him, as though afraid he was listening to every word she said. Again, it did not nag at my mind until I spoke to Lord Patton and told him the whole thing – perhaps discussing it again brought the details back to my mind. That particular gentleman was not walking with Sally, since he came running over to us both. Therefore, how did she know who he was?"

"Perhaps he was a well-known client," Martha suggested, her face flaming as she mentioned such a thing. "Did she simply recognize him?"

"It was dark."

The words hung in the air, making Hannah's stomach tighten with unease. Lord Fernley had a point. A man could not easily be recognized in the dark, even though there would have been a few lanterns lit nearby.

"Besides which, I am certain I recall Lord Walton hissing something at her, as though he were deeply upset with her. It was all so terrible at the time that I confess it took me some months before I could begin to think calmly and clearly about such things."

Hannah nodded slowly, as Martha went to the door to take the tray from the maid, clearly not wanting to be disturbed.

"It is quite understandable, Fernley," Lord Patton murmured, rubbing one hand across his brow. "But I still do not think that–"

"And you say you spoke to Sally last evening?" Hannah interrupted, suddenly caught by an idea. "And this morning, she was dead?"

Lord Patton sighed. "Coincidence. Everyone knows that these ladies of the night do not exactly live long lives."

Lord Fernley frowned heavily. "She was not sick when I spoke to her last evening, Lord Patton!" he exclaimed, evidently frustrated that the man was choosing not to believe a word he said. "And she was very honest with me, although she appeared almost terrified to speak with me so freely."

Hannah felt her breath catch at the look on Lord Fernley's face.

"That is why I rushed over here," he continued, now glaring at Lord Patton. "Sally told me that she was asked to walk with your brother by the Thames, although she did not know why. He was, apparently, one of her regulars and was used to waiting outside White's in a hackney for him to appear." Lord Fernley shook his head. "I know all too well that Oliver's habit was, most evenings, to drink himself silly and then go out to one of the local establishments. I did not know that she was often waiting for him."

Lord Patton let out a long breath, his expression pained. "They would go to his townhouse, I presume."

Shrugging, Lord Fernley looked away. "I would consider that to be the case, yes. However, that evening, she was told to encourage your brother to walk by the Thames, and she did just that." He swallowed, rubbing one hand down his face, still tortured by what he had heard. "She stated that someone tugged at her arm as she walked, and as she turned to look, Lord Patton disappeared from her side."

There was a long, tense silence. Hannah tried to breathe normally, despite the roaring in her ears. She had to consider that, from what this Sally had supposedly said, there was the chance that Lord Patton had been murdered.

"Did she say who asked her to do such a thing?" Martha asked quietly. "Did she give you a name?"

Lord Fernley shook his head, sadly. "She said she would speak to Lord Patton in the morning, but I could tell she was afraid. It was as though someone was watching her, even though we were in the room alone."

Hannah did not want to ask what lengths Lord Fernley had gone to in order to speak to Sally but could tell by the slight blush to his cheeks that it had been a rather awkward encounter. Her heart tore for him again as he shook his head, his jaw clenched.

"I feel responsible for her death," Lord Fernley muttered, half to himself. "If I had not found her, if I had not insisted that she be the one I went to, then she might now be alive."

A heavy sigh came from Lord Patton, drawing everyone's attention. "Lord Fernley, she did not die because you spoke to her," Lord Patton said firmly. "Whether or not someone tugged at her arm, my brother clearly slipped and went into the drink. Ladies of the night are not known for being particularly sensible. I imagine she told you all that to try and butter you up, to give her a little more coin for her trouble."

Lord Fernley glared at Lord Patton, thumping one fist down hard on the arm of the chair, making Hannah jump.

"She was terrified, I tell you! Terrified! And now this morning, she is found stabbed in the alleyway!"

"Stabbed?" Hannah repeated, the blood draining from her face.

"Yes, stabbed!" Lord Fernley shouted, clearly unaware of the effect his words were having on her. "My goodness, Patton, you are making such a cake of yourself! A lady has died because of her honesty towards me, and you discard it as entirely unimportant! Why do you refuse to even consider that your brother might have been brought to his untimely end by an evil hand?"

The question hung in the room, left unanswered as Lord Patton put his head in his hands, looking down at the carpeted floor. The silence was broken only by Martha setting the trays down and looking over at Hannah questioningly. Aware of what she was silently asking, Hannah nodded, tilting her head towards the back of the room.

"Brandy, my lord," Martha murmured, after a moment, pushing a glass into Lord Fernley's hands. "And for you, Lord Patton?"

The man nodded, not looking at any of them. "A large one, if you please."

Martha obliged at once, leaving Hannah feeling rather sorry for Lord Patton, who was looking both miserable and confused. She herself felt a little guilty for pushing herself into the situation regardless of his own wishes, worried that she had overstepped the mark.

If she had not asked him to stay, if she had not spoken to Lord Fernley about what had gone on, then she might now be picking out what gown to wear to the recital this evening, instead of worrying about what Lord Walton had to do with all of this.

"If Sally was killed for speaking to you, Lord Fernley, then that must mean that both myself and Lady Hannah must be vigilant in our goings-about," Martha said quietly, sitting back down in her chair and reaching for her cup and saucer. "Is that not so?"

Lord Fernley nodded, his expression dark. "Until I can be certain one way or the other, it is best that you and Lady Hannah be careful when you are out and about. Not that this means that you should, in any way, stop yourself from doing whatever you please, but just that there is perhaps a footman with you when you walk, instead of just a maid."

A swirl of fear caught Hannah's heart. "I do apologize for

being so firm in my desire to have you both remain and speak so openly to me about this," she admitted, glancing over at Martha, who appeared to be both frustrated and relieved that Hannah was apologizing. "But I am glad that I have been able to identify who Lord Walton is for you."

Lord Patton looked up at her, and for a moment, Hannah was caught by the intensity in his gaze. His eyes fixed on hers, lingering there and making her skin prickle with a sudden expectation. Although, what that expectation was, she could not be quite certain.

"And is Lord Walton here in London?" Lord Fernley asked, breaking the moment between herself and Lord Patton. "I confess that I do not know him."

Hannah gave a small shrug. "I am afraid I cannot help you. I have not seen him. However, I would expect him to return to London very soon, for he has a wife and a reputation to speak of."

Martha chuckled unexpectedly. "You mean, that he has a wife who wishes to traverse London society and a reputation that must remain either sterling or blackened, whichever he is prouder of."

Lord Patton nodded, a wry smile touching his lips. "That is it exactly, Lady Dalton."

"Then perhaps four pairs of eyes will be better than just two, especially given that both myself and Lady Dalton have seen Lord Walton with our own eyes. He is tall, with dark hair and a rather nondescript face. A gentleman able to easily blend in with the crowd. I believe his marriage was arranged, not offered and accepted, but he appears to be fairly happy despite asking my brother for a loan."

Lord Fernley frowned at once. "A loan?"

She nodded, not sure as to why such a thing should be interesting. "Yes, my brother did not want to give him such a thing, of course, for he keeps all the wealth he can for himself. I believe Lord Walton was very persuasive though. I am not certain what occurred exactly."

A look of surprise came onto Lord Patton's face. "So, he is a man short of money," he murmured, glancing at Lord Fernley. "Well, perhaps there is something in it after all."

"Then what do we do?" Hannah asked, clasping her hands together tightly as she leaned forward a little in her chair. "How can we help?"

Lord Patton managed a small, rueful smile. "You can help by finding Lord Walton and pointing him out to me," he said, as Hannah nodded at once, feeling as though she were now an integral part of this mystery. "I want to ensure we are speaking about the same man that Lord Fernley met."

"Of course, of course," she exclaimed, getting up to ring the bell. "Then let us compare which social occasions we are each to attend, so that I might come in search of you the moment I find Lord Walton."

"A very good idea, Lady Hannah," Lord Patton replied appreciatively. "But do remember that is all you must do. Find him and show him to me. That is all. I will not have you in danger."

"Of course, Lord Patton, I quite understand," Hannah replied sweetly, aware of the way her heart began to pick up its pace. Whether the speed of her heart increased from the anticipation of finding Lord Walton or from something completely different, she could not be sure. "I am certain that, within a few days, we will find Lord Walton and all will be well."

7

Three weeks later

Unfortunately for Joseph, things did not appear to be as simple as Lady Hannah had hoped. Lord Walton was either not in London at all, or was being rather careful as to which occasions he attended. Lady Hannah had not seen him, nor had Lady Dalton, even though they had attended a great many social events. He was growing rather tired of it all, aware that he still had his money troubles to attend to on top of all of this. Not that he spoke of such things to Lady Hannah, nor even to Lord Fernley, choosing to keep it all to himself for the time being.

The problem was, however, that he was enjoying his time with Lady Hannah far too much given the reason they were thrown together so often. He had not wanted her to become involved, but she had insisted on hearing the story, only to discover that Lord Walton was someone that she knew. In that regard, she had become almost invaluable, for he needed her now to show him whom this particular gentleman was so that they might be able to ask him some questions about Oliver, and perhaps about Sally.

In addition, he found himself almost protective of her, as though she needed a chaperone of sorts, to ensure that no one did her any harm simply because she was involved with him, although that worry lessened with each day that passed. Yet, he had found himself unwilling to give up any time he spent with her, finding that, if he were honest with himself, he wanted only to increase it.

Not that Joseph was at all convinced that Lord Walton had anything to do with it. He was, however, beginning to believe that there might be some truth to Lord Fernley's suggestion that his brother had not merely slipped and fallen, for all that had happened had brought a great many questions to his mind.

He was not quite sure why Sally had been killed, even though he had tried to reason with himself that it was simply a thing that happened occasionally to those in her line of work, but it did not quite make sense. It was too coincidental, too soon after Lord Fernley's visit. He was quite sure that Fernley would not make things up just to suit his narrative. Having spent a part of almost every day in Lord Fernley's company, Joseph was beginning to consider the man a friend and was growing to trust him and his judgment. Perhaps that was why, even with so little evidence, he was now beginning to think that there was more to his brother's death than had first appeared.

His ongoing acquaintance with Lady Hannah, however, was quite a different matter, although it still took up a great deal of his time and effort. He found the lady to be intelligent, kind, and compassionate, even though she had been rather nosy and much too forward when Lord Fernley had burst into her drawing room all those weeks ago.

They often found themselves in conversation, no matter what event they were at. Whilst they often took tea together, just the four of them, it was quite clear that Lord Fernley and Lady Dalton had something of an interest in one another, and so

Joseph often found himself quite alone in his conversation with Lady Hannah. Not that he minded, of course, it was more that he found himself quite wrapped up with the lady, which was more than foolish given his own circumstances.

He could not even think of courting her, despite the fact that this had become a thought that would not leave his mind no matter how much he tried. Oftentimes, he caught himself imagining her by his side as they walked through Hyde Park, drawing the attention of the *ton* during the fashionable hour.

Sometimes he daydreamed of what it would be like to have her as his bride, before catching himself and dismissing the notion outright, calling himself all sorts of names for being so completely foolish. He was meant to be looking into the possibility of his brother's murder, not losing his head to some charming young lady who would never so much as look at him should she discover the truth about his finances. He was, by society's standards, almost a pauper despite the fact that the house in the country had been sold very quickly. Bills were piling up in his townhouse, bills that would have to be paid the moment the monies from the house sale came through. It was shameful to see them piled so high, and very often, Joseph found himself recoiling from even the idea of looking at them to see what they sought payment for.

Blowing out a long breath, Joseph sat back in his chair and tried not to let his mind wander too far towards his brother. The theatre was vastly busy, but the performance on stage did not capture his attention in any way. He was much too busy trying to prevent himself from growing angry with his deceased brother for what he had done to the estate, to the title, and to himself.

"Are you not enjoying the play, Lord Patton?"

Glancing behind him, Joseph saw the smiling face of Lady Hannah, with Lady Dalton appearing just behind her, sitting down quickly by Lord Fernley's side. Even in the dim light, he could see the dark emerald green of the gown she wore, her slim figure highlighted for a moment as she moved towards him. Her hair was a glorious crown, a few tendrils dancing around her cheekbones. All in all, she was absolutely stunning, and Joseph felt his breath catch in his chest as she came to sit by him. The urge to take her hand in his rose within him, and he was unable to stop himself from doing just that, grasping her gloved hand gently and raising it to his lips, even though he knew he was being more than foolish in doing so.

"Good evening, Lady Hannah," he murmured, as the actor on stage began to give a rousing monologue. "I did not expect to see you this evening."

Her eyes grew warm as she looked back at him, her hand still in his. "I confess that a night at home did seem rather wonderful, but Martha did so want to come out and I could not refuse her." She shot a glance over Joseph's shoulder, her lips curved into a gentle smile. "They are a very handsome couple, I think."

Joseph's brows lifted in surprise as he released her gloved hand. "A little soon for that sort of statement, is it not?"

"Do you think so?" She tilted her head and looked at him quizzically, a small smile pulling at her lips. "I confess that I do not. Martha has been through a great deal, and I am glad to see her happy. I think that Lord Fernley is a devoted man, who does not intend to make a fool of her by toying with her affections."

"No, he certainly will not do such a thing as that," Joseph agreed firmly. "Lord Fernley is a good sort of fellow, I think."

Lady Hannah's smile grew. "Just as you are, Lord Patton."

Joseph felt his mouth grow dry, not quite sure what to say in response to such a compliment. She was being kind to him, he knew, but such was the look in her eyes that he did not quite know how to respond. It was as if she were waiting for him to do something, to say something of consequence, and yet he found he could not.

"What will you do if Lord Fernley proposes marriage to Lady Dalton?" he stammered, managing to change the conversation back to where it had just been. "I cannot imagine you living alone."

The smile on her lips faded, and she glanced away, her eyes growing almost heavy with some unspoken emotion. "I shall find another companion, of course, unless I should marry first. I do not want Martha to be held back by any kind of feeling of responsibility toward me."

Joseph pressed his lips together, aware that he had not heard her mention marriage before. Questions spun through his head, forcing themselves towards his mouth.

"Do you wish to marry, Lady Hannah?"

It was an impertinent question. The moment it left his lips, Joseph wanted to claw it back, as though he could put it back inside himself and pretend it had not ever been said. Feeling embarrassment creep up his spine, he looked away from Lady Hannah, praying that she would not grow angry with him for such impertinence.

Much to his surprise, she did not seem to take any kind of offense.

"I have thought of it, yes," she murmured quietly. "After all, one does not want to live one's life entirely alone. The way Martha has spoken of her love for her first husband makes the whole thing sound rather wonderful, although I am sure it can be very difficult at times."

Joseph's heart began to thump wildly, aware that Lady Hannah was speaking with such vulnerability that it took his breath away. He did not say anything, letting her speak without being interrupted in any way.

"Besides which, I am ensuring I take part in the London

Season this year, Lord Patton, in case you have not been aware of it," she continued with a quiet laugh. "Not that I find any gentleman I dance with to be in any way amiable. They all look at me with such greed in their eyes."

Joseph felt his heart sink to his boots.

"That is the unfortunate part of being a wealthy lady, you see," Lady Hannah continued, with a sad smile. "Every gentleman in London knows that I have a great fortune of my own and a very large dowry also. Why would they not want to get their hands on it?" She shook her head, her eyes growing sadder still. "They grasp at my wealth and not at my heart. I do not think I could ever consider a poor, grasping gentleman, no matter his outward appearances of fondness or the like. They take me for a fool when I am more than aware of their intentions."

He wanted to tell her that he would never do such a thing. He wanted to confess that whilst he was poor, he did not ever consider her fortune to be the only consideration, but he could not bring himself to say anything. To confess as much would be to lay his confused heart out in front of her, only to have her disregard it completely the moment she heard he barely had two shillings to rub together. Their acquaintance had not been of long duration, and he could not yet believe that she would simply take his word for the fact that he was not after her fortune.

"And now I have said too much and disconcerted you," Lady Hannah murmured, looking rather abashed. "I do apologize, Lord Patton. I suppose that I forget myself when it comes to speaking with you, for it feels as though we have been friends for a very long time, does it not?"

"Yes, it does," he managed to say, his tongue now feeling overly large for his mouth. "I always enjoy conversing with you, Lady Hannah."

She smiled at him then, her embarrassment fading. "I suppose we have to thank Lord Fernley for being so ridiculously unaware," she said, laughing quietly. "Else we might never have found ourselves thrown together in such a way. What shall we do when the murder is solved, do you think?"

Thoughts sprang into his mind like lightning bolts, thoughts of courtship, thoughts of matrimony. But with an effort, Joseph pushed them away.

"I am not quite certain, Lady Hannah," he said firmly. "I do hope, however, that we shall continue to be good friends."

Some of the light faded from her expression, and for a moment, confusion and pain flashed across her face. But then he blinked, and it was gone, leaving only her gentle smile in its place.

"Yes, of course," she murmured, looking out across the theatre as the curtain came down for the first half. "I am quite sure we will, Lord Patton."

He swallowed, not sure what to say and was almost relieved that it then came time to rise and make their way out of the box in search of refreshments.

A hand grasped his arm tightly. Spinning around, Joseph saw Lady Hannah standing stock still, her eyes wide and one finger pointing out amongst the crowd.

"Lord Patton," she squeaked, tugging him towards her. "He is here."

Stumbling, Joseph fell against her for a moment, and together, they scrambled to keep themselves upright. Somehow, Joseph's hand slipped around Lady Hannah's waist as he steadied himself, one of her hands pressed against his chest.

Just as well the lights are low.

The thought came to his mind, unbidden, as he looked down in Lady Hannah's face, seeing the way her eyes widened slightly, her mouth falling open just a little. The desire to kiss her roared to life within him, only for Lady Hannah to recollect herself and turn her head away, stepping back.

"I do apologize," Joseph muttered, now crimson with embarrassment. "I was just taken by surprise."

"He is here."

Lady Hannah had not taken any notice of his apology but was now letting her eyes rove over the guests that stood in the theatre, a look of frustration on her face.

"Who is?" Joseph asked, stepping closer. "Who have you seen?"

"Lord Walton," came the excited whisper. "I was sure I saw him."

Joseph's breath came quick and fast as he waited, far too aware of Lady Hannah's hand grasping his own with such a tight grip that it felt as though she would never let her go. She was still so near, and he was struggling to concentrate on the fact that Lord Walton, the man they had been searching for, was now nearby.

"There! Look! He has a long white cane with him, with a polished handle."

Her whisper forced him to pay attention instead of looking at the curve of her cheek, the brightness of her eyes. He turned to see her pointing in the direction of a rather regal-looking gentleman, who was walking through the crowd with a rather pompous air. He had a long, thin mustache, and deep-set eyebrows that gave him a somewhat stern appearance. His hair was thinning and plastered to his head. In his hand, he carried a long, white cane, which he did not use to lean on but rather to tap impatiently on the ground whenever he was forced to wait.

"Are you certain?" Joseph asked, his stomach tightening as he regarded the man carefully, feeling a dislike for him rising up within him already. "That is Lord Walton?"

"I am certain of it," Lady Hannah whispered, looking up at

him with such a delight that, for a moment, Joseph forgot all about Lord Walton, caught up by her enchanting smile. "We have found him, Lord Patton."

He squeezed her hand gently. "*You* have found him, Lady Hannah. Very well done. Now, do you think you might be able to make an introduction?"

The smile left her face, her dislike immediately evident, but after only just a moment, she lifted her chin and nodded.

"Very good," he said, feeling a sense of pride growing within him. "Thank you, Lady Hannah. Let us go before we lose him."

She nodded and took his arm, their joined hands separating. "I do hope you get the answers you need, Lord Patton."

"As do I, dear lady," Joseph replied fervently. "As do I."

8

Butterflies were already fluttering in her stomach as Hannah made her way through the crowd of guests, her hand on Lord Patton's arm. She had been so caught up in the excitement of finally finding Lord Walton, that she had not considered for a moment that she would be required to make introductions.

However, with Lord Patton by her side, Hannah felt herself grow stronger within herself. He needed her to do this, and so, simply because of that need, Hannah knew she would do whatever was asked of her in order to help him. She was, however, rather confused by his regard toward her, for with his looks and smiles of late, he told her that there was something growing in his heart for her, but with his words he told her quite the opposite. It was as if he did not want to say a single word to her about what his intentions might be toward her once this whole ghastly business was brought to a close, as though he found it much too terrifying to consider.

He was, of course, like no other gentleman of her acquaintance, in the fact that he did not seem to want to pursue her, did not so much as want to enamor himself toward her. He was quiet and contemplative, always putting a great deal of consideration into what it was he was going to say, and Hannah found that she very much enjoyed that about him. Their conversations were always something she appreciated, for he did not treat her as though she were some dim-witted female, as so many other gentlemen did, clearly expecting her to care about more than just painting, dancing and other female pursuits. For that, she had grown to appreciate him all the more, finding herself growing more and more delighted with each moment they spent together.

It also was quite certain that she found him rather attractive for a gentleman of her acquaintance, although it had not come upon her as quickly as it had done with Martha. Not that she knew what to do with such a feeling, however, having never taken much interest in any gentlemen before. It was as if they had all treated her with such fawning devotion that was nothing more than a veneer.

"There he is," she heard Lord Patton whisper, as they walked together through the crowd of guests – some of whom were holding glasses of champagne and others who were in search of said refreshments. Swallowing her anxiety and determined to put on a strong front, Hannah lifted her chin and gazed directly at the formidable appearance of Lord Walton, recalling just how much she had disliked him the first time they had met.

"Lord Walton, how good to see you," she lied, putting on a light smile. "I did not expect you to be in London. Is your wife with you?"

Lord Walton did not smile, his eyes lingering on her for a moment before he sniffed almost disparagingly and looked away. "Ah, Lady Hannah. How unexpected."

Feeling a faint prickle of anger, Hannah drew in another

breath and took a step away from Lord Patton, gesturing towards him. "Lord Walton, this is my dear friend, Lord Patton."

To her surprise, Lord Walton drew in a sharp breath and stepped back, as though in shock. He regarded Lord Patton for a long moment, his eyes roving over him, as though he needed to satisfy himself about something.

"I do not think we have met before, Lord Walton," Lord Patton said slowly, clearly aware of the man's strange regard for him. "Or am I mistaken on that point?"

"No, no, we have not met before," Lord Walton replied, almost brusquely. "Your brother, I think."

Lord Patton nodded, a slight frown settling between his brows. "Yes, Oliver was my older brother, but sadly departed this earth some time ago."

Lord Walton took out his handkerchief and dabbed at his brow. "Damned hot in this place, is it not? You must excuse me, I am in dire need of some refreshment. Good to meet you, Lord Patton."

Hannah watched in complete astonishment as Lord Walton walked straight past her, as though she were invisible. She was entirely befuddled as to why the man had reacted so strangely toward Lord Patton, and turning to look at him, she saw that Lord Patton was equally confused.

"Are you certain you have never met him before?" she asked quietly, as Lord Patton turned back from watching Lord Walton leave. "He appeared to be rather shocked to be introduced to you."

Lord Patton shook his head, his lips in a thin line as his brow furrowed all the more. "No, I have never seen that man before in my life."

"Do you have any idea why he seemed to be so altered?" she asked, her hand slowly creeping back underneath his arm. "He appeared almost afraid!"

Lord Patton shook his head. "No, but I am determined to find out. After all this, I believe now that what Lord Fernley has suggested is true. Something very strange occurred around the time of my brother's death, and for whatever reason, Lord Walton was somehow involved."

Hannah, feeling the same certainty, nodded slowly. "I agree that Lord Fernley must be correct in his assumptions. However, it appears that you will not have the opportunity to ask him whatever questions it was you had in mind, for he seemed more than determined not to further your acquaintance."

"Which is all the more curious," Lord Patton muttered, patting her hand absently. "Thank you for the introduction, however, Lady Hannah. I appreciate your efforts in doing such a thing, when it is clear that you found it rather difficult to do so."

His eyes met hers, and Hannah felt herself almost glow with his appreciative comments, smiling back at him. "Thank you, Lord Patton, you are very kind and rather perceptive, if I may say so. You are quite correct to suggest that I did not wish to see Lord Walton again. When I was first introduced to him by my brother, I had already decided that I would refuse to wed him, and after meeting him for only a few minutes, I was more than certain I had made the correct decision. He was even more aloof than he was this evening, with a clear disregard for anyone but himself. My brother was practically bowing and scraping in front of him, making himself so obsequious that my frustrations almost boiled over! I could not understand why Phillip made such a cake of himself in front of such an odious man, and I was determined not to do the same."

"And that is why he threw you from your home?" Lord Patton asked gently, his expression softening. "Because you refused to do as your brother asked?"

Hannah let out a long breath, her expression a little sad.

"Yes, that is precisely why, Lord Patton, along with the fact that my brother wanted as much wealth for himself as possible. Martha and I were presumed to be a drain on his coffers, despite the fact that we were not in the least bit frivolous. And so, it is as you find me now." She smiled at him, and Lord Patton smiled back, his hand now closing gently over the one that wrapped around his arm.

"I believe you are a most extraordinary young woman, Lady Hannah," Lord Patton said gently, his expression growing tender. "You are strong and courageous, determined to refuse what you do not want and seek what you know you desire. That firmness of character is truly remarkable, and I admire you greatly."

It was as though the air had been sucked out of the room, leaving Hannah struggling to breathe as she looked into Lord Patton's eyes. The conversation from the rest of the guests began to fade as she stayed just as she was, no longer aware of anyone other than Lord Patton.

Was he about to ask to court her? Was he about to declare any sort of feelings toward her? His fingers were warm on her own, seeping through the thin material of her gloves and spreading heat up her arm. It was as though she were in some kind of enchantment, lost completely in this wonderful moment.

"Lady Hannah," Lord Patton murmured, drawing her a little further away from the rest of the guests and a little more into the corner, where they might not be so apparent. "I must confess something to you."

Sparks exploded in her vision as she waited, her breath hitching as he looked deeply into her eyes. There was something in his gaze that gave her the feeling of uncertainty, as though he himself were not quite sure what he was doing or what he intended to say. Silence spread between them, making her long all the more for him to speak, but still, he did not.

"Lady Hannah," he said again, his fingers still resting on hers. "I–"

"Why, there you are!"

Hannah let out her breath, breathing raggedly for a moment, as Lord Fernley appeared by their side, looking more than a little delighted. She felt Lord Patton let go of her fingers almost at once, looking at Lord Fernley with a large degree of exasperation, which she herself felt grow within her. Her mind was spinning, her heartbeat furious, as Lord Fernley began to talk in earnest, barely able to comprehend a word he was saying.

"In short, I believe she will agree, although she has said she must discuss it with you first, Lady Hannah."

Hannah tried to smile, still feeling rather dazed and a little lost. "I do apologize, Lord Fernley. Of what are you speaking?"

"Of my proposal!" he exclaimed, in much too loud a voice for the company they were in. "You must speak to Lady Dalton, of course, for she will tell you all, but I confess I could not wait another moment! A month in her company has secured my heart for life."

Blinking furiously, Hannah felt hot tears begin to prick at her eyes, not quite sure why she was somewhere between crying and overwhelming delight, realizing what Lord Fernley was saying.

"You have proposed to Lady Dalton?" she whispered, pulling her hand from Lord Patton and placing it on Lord Fernley's arm.

"Only a few minutes before I came in search of you," Lord Fernley replied, with a broad smile. "I would not have left her side, but she dearly wanted to see you, Lady Hannah. Might I encourage you to return to her?"

"But of course!" Hannah exclaimed, turning from them both

at once and making her way back towards the box. "What wonderful news!"

As she carefully stepped through the crowd of gentlemen and ladies, all crushed together, Hannah tried to regain her composure, still rather unsure as to why she was so desperate to cry over this news. Was it because she was truly delighted for Martha? Of course, this was what she had been hoping for her dear aunt for some time. Or, was she feeling overwhelmed because she was suddenly terrified of being alone? The happiness that Martha now had was something Hannah found herself longing for, the desperate urge to confess that she too had feelings of love growing slowly within her heart, albeit for a completely different gentleman.

However, in her heart, she knew that part of the reason for her upset was due to Lord Patton's rather frustrating way of keeping his thoughts and feelings to himself, of how he could look at her with such intensity, but yet, never say a word.

It was all rather frustrating, particularly given that Lord Patton had finally had something of importance to say, only to be interrupted by Lord Fernley. Hannah was not certain that Lord Patton would be so willing to speak to her in such a way again, for that had been something of a special moment, a moment where the truth might be spoken with no one to interrupt it. It had been a moment of great intensity, of great vulnerability, and yet it had been stolen from her, just as Lord Patton had been about to tell her what was on his heart. And she, in turn, had felt her own heart swelling with more than just affection, more than just fondness. They had become so close in this last month that she could not think of life without him. She could not imagine a life where she did not see him, did not speak to him, did not spend hours in conversation and laughter, as they had been doing this last while. She did not want a life without him at all. She wanted Lord Patton to be by her side, always.

"Goodness," she whispered to herself, suddenly coming to a stop in the middle of the crowd. "Do I love him?"

It was a question she could not answer, given that she had very little experience with such an emotion, but yet in her heart, Hannah knew that she did love him.

Swallowing hard, Hannah lifted her shoulders and began to walk again, taking in a few deep, steadying breaths. Despite her clouded mind, Hannah tried to put her own heart and mind aside, aware that she ought not to be thinking of herself at this moment, but rather focusing on Martha and Lord Fernley. Of course, she would have no cause to discourage Martha from going forward with her marriage to Lord Fernley, trying not to think about what it would be like to live alone without her dear aunt by her side.

"Perhaps I will not have to be alone for too long, if Lord Patton manages to find the courage to tell me what I am certain I already know," she murmured to herself, as she made her way to the box. "Or perhaps I shall end up an old maid."

A wry smile touched her lips as she came into the box, seeing her aunt standing waiting for her, her hands clasped in front of her and a look of anxiety on her face.

"My dearest Martha!" Hannah exclaimed, wanting to wipe away every inch of concern from Martha's expression. "I am so glad for you. I do hope you have accepted Lord Fernley's proposal, for I will not allow you to refuse him."

"You would be glad for me to do so?" Martha asked, grasping Hannah's hands. "My first commitment is to you, and you know that I will not leave you if–"

"I *insist* that you marry him," Hannah declared, interrupting her aunt. "I can tell that he cares a great deal for you, and that you in return, you care a great deal for him." She smiled, her heart lifting free of its confusion and struggle as she saw the joy in Martha's eyes. Wrapping Martha in a hug, Hannah held her tightly for a moment, truly glad for her. "Congratulations, Martha," she said in her ear. "I am sure that he will make you very happy."

"Yes," Martha replied, now out of their embrace. "I know that he will."

9

The next week was spent with Joseph trying his best to catch Lord Walton's attention. However, to his frustration, he was not succeeding in the least. Lord Walton was very rarely seen in society apparently, and on the three occasions that Joseph did manage to spot him in the crowd, Lord Walton appeared to be doing everything possible to avoid him. He barely managed to speak more than a few sentences to the man, growing more and more frustrated with every failed attempt.

Lord Fernley had, despite his exuberance over his newly engaged state, been more than an encouragement in his endeavors to find the truth about what had happened to Oliver. There was still the guilt that hung so clearly on Lord Fernley's shoulders, and Joseph wondered if, in finding the truth, the guilt might finally be taken from him. Joseph was also growing more and more determined that whoever was responsible for Oliver's demise was brought to justice somehow. Not that the constables would be much use, given that they very rarely went near the *beau monde,* unless there was something truly terrible going on.

He was determined to continue though and knew that the situation would eventually be brought to a satisfactory end.

His breath caught, as his eyes landed on the one other person he had been unable to stop thinking about of late – Lady Hannah, who was walking into the room behind the butler, ready to be introduced. He rose and watched her, seeing her smile gently as she looked over at him. How close he had come to revealing the truth about his growing feelings to her when they had been at the theatre only a week ago, only to be interrupted by Lord Fernley.

Upon reflection, Joseph had been rather glad that Lord Fernley had interrupted them, for to have said anything would have been more than foolish. To confess such a thing without revealing to her the depth of his financial difficulties would have caused a great deal of harm. Even now, he was glad he had not said anything to her. Nor did he think he would. He had simply been overcome by her beauty at that moment, when he had seen her determination to do all she could to help him with what had been a rather difficult introduction to Lord Walton. How much he had appreciated her. How much he had respected her for what she was willing to do, despite the fact that this did not have any particular impact on her own life.

And still, he had stumbled over his words, trying to tell her what he felt and yet finding himself unable to do so. He had been interrupted by Lord Fernley, and the moment had passed, leaving him both frustrated and relieved in equal measure.

"Lady Hannah," Lord Fernley said, as she came into the room. "You look wonderful this evening, as do you, Martha, my dear."

Joseph smiled to himself, as Lady Dalton blushed and smiled as Lord Fernley took her hand and bowed over it, thinking that he had never before seen two people so clearly enchanted with one another. It was quite a lovely thing to witness.

"My dear Lord Fernley, you simply must refer to me as 'Hannah', if you are to call Martha by her first name. After all, we shall be family, shall we not?" She lifted one brow and smiled broadly at Lord Fernley, making him laugh.

"Very well, Lady Hannah – I mean, Hannah," Lord Fernley exclaimed, guiding his betrothed toward the fire in the grate. "I should like that very much."

A stab of jealousy rose in Joseph's heart as he looked at them all, seeing the air of familiarity between Lord Fernley and Lady Hannah and wishing that he could have the same. After all, they were just as close as she was to Lord Fernley, maybe even more so, but yet he could not bring himself to make the suggestion that she refer to him simply as "Patton." Perhaps it was because he was frightened of becoming a little too intimate with the lady, as though referring to one another by their Christian names would mean that he would, somehow, have to tell her all that was going on in his heart. Foolishness, really.

"How lovely to see you both this evening," he managed to say quietly. "I am glad to be in your company once again."

Lady Hannah chuckled. "And here I thought you might be growing rather bored of our company, Lord Patton. After all, we do see each other *very* often, and here we are again for what is yet another evening of conversation and good company." She smiled at him as she took her seat adjacent to him, her eyes twinkling. "Are you not tired of me yet, Lord Patton?"

"No, indeed," Joseph replied, resisting the urge to tug at his collar to relieve some of the rather awkward tension that was suddenly racing through him. "I am very glad to be able to speak to you again this evening, Lady Hannah."

She looked pleased with this, regarding him closely for another moment or two, before the maids entered with the trays of refreshments. Glad for the momentary reprieve, Joseph poured himself a glass of port, and then a second for Lord Fernley, whilst the ladies prepared their cups of tea.

"Now," Lord Fernley began, as they all sat down. "Are we here to discuss your progress in regards Lord Walton? Or did you want us all to congregate together for an entirely different purpose?"

Joseph, who knew full well that Lord Fernley knew precisely how poorly he had done with Lord Walton, shook his head ruefully. "I need not pretend that things have gone well, I am afraid. Lord Walton is still completely unwilling to discuss any such thing with me. I can barely get a single sentence out of the man." He caught Lady Hannah's eye as he sat down, seeing her brow furrowing just a little as she concentrated.

"And we still have very little idea as to why that might be?" she asked, just as Lord Fernley shook his head. "How very strange."

"I get the distinct impression that he is avoiding me because of what happened to Oliver," Joseph said heavily. "But I cannot get anything out of him."

"Well, I did."

Stunned, Joseph turned to see Lord Fernley standing by the fire, leaning heavily on the mantlepiece.

"*You* did?" he asked, astonished. "Whatever do you mean?"

Lord Fernley smiled softly, his eyes lingering on Lady Dalton. "It was Martha's idea, I confess, but it worked marvelously well. You see, Patton, sometimes simply being direct makes all the difference. I found Lord Walton at the ball last evening, cornered him, and thanked him profusely for all his help at the time of Oliver's death."

Joseph clutched at the arm of his chair, almost completely overwhelmed. He had never thought to allow Lord Fernley to say something to Lord Walton, believing that it ought to be he himself to speak to the man, but clearly, he had been wrong about that.

"My goodness," he heard Lady Hannah exclaim, her eyes wide and filled with admiration. "That is a wonderful suggestion, Martha, and I am glad it worked so well. What did you get from him, Lord Fernley?"

Lord Fernley sighed again, his eyes growing a little dim. "I believe he was rather surprised to discover that I recognized him, although I did not give him the chance to pretend that it was not he who had been there at the time. Within a few minutes, he was saying things that proved to me that it *had* been him present at the railings."

Joseph cleared his throat, his blood beginning to thunder through his veins. He felt utterly lost, as though he were completely useless in attempting to find out the truth about his brother's death whilst Lord Fernley and Lady Dalton were able to make strides of progress with one simple suggestion. "What did he say, Fernley?" he asked, haltingly. "Anything of use?"

"He thanked me for coming to speak to him, asked after you, and murmured that it was all very sad. Pithy, sentimental tripe, of course. However, when I mentioned Sally, his eyes widened, and he began to grow rather uncomfortable. He asked me at once why I had gone to see her, and when I said that I simply wanted to ensure that I recalled everything that had happened, he looked almost relieved. Then I stated that Sally had been found dead, and he simply shrugged, looking away from me, and I swear there was a small smile on his face."

Joseph's anger flared. "A smile?"

Lord Fernley nodded. "I am sure of it. I did go on to mention you, Lady Hannah, and I am afraid he was not particularly complimentary of either you or your brother."

"My brother?" Lady Hannah repeated, frowning. "What did he have to say about him?"

Lord Fernley shook his head, his brow furrowing as he tried to recall. "Something about your brother finally managing to pay him off, or some such thing. I am not quite sure what he meant."

Looking over at Lady Hannah, Joseph saw her frown deepen, her eyes filling with worry. "Paying him off? That does sound as though Phillip was in debt to Lord Walton somehow. Although I cannot understand why, given that he received the entirety of my father's fortune upon my father's death, bar the money settled on me."

Something about that statement pricked at Joseph's mind, making him frown. There was something about Lady Hannah's brother, Phillip's behavior that bothered him, although it could easily be that he was simply terribly unkind to Lady Hannah. Although it did not quite make sense for a man to be quite so harsh on an unwanted relative, particularly since Joseph was quite sure that an earl would have more than one property of his own.

"Was that all that was said?" he asked quietly, looking up to see Lord Fernley nod. "Very good, Lord Fernley. I commend you, and you too, Lady Dalton, for having such a sensible thought."

"But it does not get us anywhere," Lady Hannah commented, still frowning. "He did not say anything incriminating."

Joseph nodded, aware of this. "No, he did not, but I must wonder whether or not your brother has something he might be able to reveal to us."

Lady Hannah looked startled. "My brother, Phillip? Whatever do you think he might know?"

Looking at Lady Dalton and Lord Fernley, Joseph shook his head. "Might we talk in private, Lady Hannah? I am afraid that my thoughts are many, and I am struggling to make sense of them here. If we walked in the gardens..." He trailed off, aware that it was rather dark. "I can have the lanterns lit, of course, and if you feel it improper then I can have a maid join us."

Much to his relief, Lady Hannah did not hesitate.

"But of course, Lord Patton," she said at once, rising to her feet gracefully. "We will not be long, and I am sure my aunt will understand."

Joseph shot a glance towards Lady Dalton, who was neither smiling nor frowning, but rather watching him intently. Heat crept up his back, and into his face as he turned his face away, not wanting her to think that he had anything improper planned for his time with Lady Hannah.

Within a few minutes, Joseph found himself walking along the lantern-lit path, with Lady Hannah by his side. They walked in silence for a long time, the only sound an occasional bird-song, as the garden settled down to sleep.

"You said something about my brother, Lord Patton?"

Clearing his throat, Joseph looked down at her and nodded, trying not to notice how the lantern light caught her hair, making it almost glow with a gold essence. He fought to keep from offering her his arm, not wanting to be distracted from his thoughts in any way.

"Yes, your brother, Lady Hannah. He is obviously acquainted with Lord Walton, particularly since he wished you to marry him."

Lady Hannah shuddered. "Yes, he did. He was very insistent."

"And he did not ever state as to why this might be?"

"If he did, I'm afraid I did not listen," Lady Hannah replied honestly. "I was just rather angry with him, I confess. I did not want to know why he was insisting on such a thing, since I found the idea ridiculous. I only met Lord Walton on my brother's insistence – even though my father's funeral had only just taken place – and I refused that very same day. The following morning, I was told to make arrangements to leave."

Fighting the urge to comfort her in some way, Joseph kept his gaze fixed straight ahead, thinking carefully. "Lord Walton may have had some hold over your brother. Something that would have forced him into doing what he wished, into paying him back in some way."

Lady Hannah came to a sudden stop, turning to face him. Her mouth was slightly ajar, her eyes widening.

"You think that my brother wished me to marry Lord Walton as payment of a debt?"

Joseph gave a small shrug. "It is not unheard of."

"No, but..." Lady Hannah stuttered to a stop, unable to complete the end of her sentence. Joseph watched, as she began to put the pieces together, to see where he was coming from, and slowly, a light began to flash in her eyes.

"My goodness, Lord Patton," she breathed, one hand reaching up to grasp his arm. "You may have hit upon the truth!"

"The truth?" Joseph repeated, frowning. "I do not quite see how it links to my brother."

Sympathy crept into her expression. "Your brother, you said, was something of a wastrel. Please, forgive me if I am being too blunt, but you yourself stated that he was foolish and did things you disapproved of."

"Much too late, I confess," Joseph added, his head dropping as he battled the guilt that raced through him. "Yes, what you are saying is quite correct, Lady Hannah."

There was a brief pause, with Lady Hannah clearly waiting until he had gathered his composure and was able to look at her again.

"Then what if Lord Walton was in the same situation with your brother as he was with mine?" she asked softly. "My brother owed him something, and he tried to use me and my hand in marriage as payment for whatever this was." She swallowed, hard. "Would you say that Lord Walton would be cruel enough to take the life of a man who was unable to pay back what he owed?"

A flurry of thoughts hit Joseph hard, making him gasp for air. Lady Hannah had laid it out all so clearly, to the point that he was unable to turn away from it. His brother *had* owed money to a great many people. What if one of those people had been Lord Walton? Was Lord Walton vicious and vindictive enough to take the life of a man who was not yet able to pay him, or had no intention of doing so?

His head shot up. "I think he might be," he replied heavily. "But I must speak to your brother. I must know what Lord Walton said."

Lady Hannah shook her head sadly. "I doubt he would even speak to you, Lord Patton. After all, I have told you that he cares for no one but himself."

"Then perhaps you could speak to Lord Walton," Joseph suggested, feeling himself growing rather desperate. "I must know what it was your brother owed him and what was said."

Lady Hannah nodded slowly, her face a mask as she hid her emotions beneath the surface.

"I will do all I can to help you, Lord Patton," she promised gently, her hand now clasping around his. "I am sorry that this has distressed you so."

He shook his head firmly, before looking into her eyes. "You have not distressed me, Lady Hannah, not in the least. In fact, you are the only thing that makes sense to me at this present moment, for my mind has been scrambling for the truth. Finally, it appears that we have it. All I need do now is prove it somehow."

She gave him a small, sad smile. "And what will you do when you have the truth, Lord Patton?"

10

Joseph looked back at Lady Hannah, finding that he could not answer her question. Instead, he simply looked back at her mutely as she waited there, wanting to hear what his answer might be.

"I do not know," he confessed hoarsely. "Perhaps it will be enough for me to know the truth about what happened to Oliver. Perhaps then I will be able to move forward with my life and try to sort out the mess than Oliver left me in." His words were bitter, his head dropping low, as he tried not to let her see the extent of his pain. The last thing he wanted to do was to appear weak.

"My dear Lord Patton," he heard Lady Hannah say quietly. "You have a great many burdens, I think."

Almost unwillingly, he nodded.

"And you are not inclined to share your burdens with those who care for you," she continued, her hand still in his as they stood together in the gardens. "Why is that, might I ask?"

Joseph swallowed, hard, his body beginning to respond to the quietness of her voice, the warmth of her hand in his.

"I am not the kind of man to take advantage, Lady Hannah,"

he replied abruptly, stepping back from her when her nearness became a little too much to bear. "I cannot allow others to see what I carry, else they might think ill of me."

It did not quite make sense, not even to him, but still Joseph stayed back from her, letting go of her hand. He could almost feel her disappointment, growing frustrated with himself that despite the affection for her growing in his heart, he could not speak those words to her, not even when it might change the course of his life. He was still much too poor, much too reduced in his circumstances to be able to declare himself. Lady Hannah had already made it quite clear that she would not be courted by a pauper, even a titled one at that, and so Joseph found himself remaining silent as she looked back at him, aware that she was both puzzled and disappointed.

"You are a most infuriating man, Lord Patton!"

Lady Hannah's frustrated exclamation echoed around the gardens, astonishing Joseph entirely. He lifted his head and looked back at her, seeing the rather upset expression on her face and the way her body had gone rigid, no longer the relaxed and charming young lady of only a few minutes before.

"I-I do not mean to be," he stammered, feeling completely at a loss as to how to deal with this sudden outburst. "There are things that I must keep in my own heart, Lady Hannah, no matter how close our friendship becomes."

She glared at him. "Your heart remains locked up tight then, Lord Patton, is that what you are trying to tell me?"

Blinking for a moment, Joseph tried to make sense of what Lady Hannah had asked. "No, I do not think that is what I mean at all. I mean to say that–"

"You have a great many burdens, but you will not share them. You look at me with such light in your eyes that I cannot help but have some kind of hope deep within me, only for you to turn away. You have said before that you look forward to our time together, commented on how much you enjoy our conversations, yet you appear to have only friendship in mind, when I can tell that there is more that you wish for. Why do you never speak of such things to me, Lord Patton? Why do you not consider courtship? Is it because you are afraid I will refuse you?" Her hands were, by this point, now firmly planted on her hips with two dots of color in her cheeks, highlighted by the soft glow of the lanterns nearby. To Joseph's mind, she had never looked more beautiful, his heart clamoring wildly within him as he fought to speak with clarity.

"I have thought of such a thing as courtship, yes," he admitted, after a few tense moments. "But I know that I would not suit you, Lady Hannah."

Her eyes flared. "And why is that? Do you have some terrible secret that you wish to keep from me? Is there a wife back at your estate that no one knows of?"

He shook his head, his stomach churning furiously. "Of course not, Lady Hannah. However, there are matters in regards to my brother that are long reaching. That is to say, the way he lived his life now impacts on the way that I must live mine."

Looking up at her, he saw her hands fall to her sides, her shoulders slumping as something like understanding came into her expression.

"I would never want to take advantage of you, my lady," he continued softly, aware of just how painful his heart was becoming as he spoke these words. "And that is why this poor man can never deserve you. I will not be the kind of gentleman you have spoken of so disparagingly, the kind of gentleman who weds another simply because of their fortune." He shook his head, his gaze dropping to his toes. "I already know that this is not the kind of gentleman you would ever look to, Lady Hannah."

There was a long, terrible silence. Joseph felt his heart quail in his chest as he waited for Lady Hannah to say something, aware that he had given her as much of the truth as he could, without going into any kind of particular detail. She knew what he was now. She knew that he was not a wealthy man, despite appearances. How low he must have fallen in her estimation.

"Lord Patton," Lady Hannah whispered, her voice barely reaching his ears and forcing him to strain to listen to her. "My dear Lord Patton, do not tell me that you count yourself amongst the gentlemen I have had the misfortune of meeting – the ones who grasp at me as though I am the answer to all of their problems, simply due to my fortune?"

He could not raise his head. "I do not count myself as one of them, no, but my circumstances are very much akin to their own. I know that you will not consider a gentleman in poor circumstances, and I confess that this is where I find myself."

"Patton, look at me."

A spark caught at his heart, forcing him to lift his head and look directly into Lady Hannah's eyes, seeing her coming closer to him again. A gentle smile was on her lips, her eyes almost glowing as she approached.

"I have never once said that I would not consider a poor gentleman, Patton," she continued, her lips curving into a smile. "I have only said that the gentlemen who have pursued me have made it very clear that they only cared for my fortune and not one jot for me. Do you consider yourself to be that kind of gentleman, Lord Patton?"

Shaking his head, Joseph found himself almost mesmerized by Lady Hannah's smile, his heart beginning to quicken its pace as she stopped only a step or two away from him.

"That is because you are decidedly *not* that kind of gentleman," Lady Hannah said quietly. "I know that to be true. You have never once tried to wheedle your way into my good graces in order to cajole me into courtship. You have never tried to insist that I wed you, have never tried to force me into a corner where I have no choice but to do so. This is why I would not ever consider you to be as those other gentlemen are. My dear Lord Patton, you quite misunderstood me when I said that I would never allow myself to be pursued by a gentleman in poor circumstances. I think that a gentleman who truly cares for me, who has made it more than plain that it is not my wealth that he cares for but my heart, would be more than welcome to court me." She tipped her head just a little, her eyes now sparkling like beautiful jewels, the very sight of them taking his breath away. "Does that bring relief to some of the burdens you have been carrying alone, Lord Patton?"

He nodded, his chest growing tight as Lady Hannah took another step closer, half wondering if this was a dream he would soon wake up from. Closing his eyes for a moment, he drew in a long, steadying breath, just as Lady Hannah's touched his hand. She was so close to him now, so very, very close. Her breath danced across his cheek, the warmth of her hand in his sending a wave of heat rushing over him.

"Lady Hannah, I–"

"I think you may refer to me as 'Hannah' if you wish it, Patton."

His breath was unsteady. "Hannah," he managed to say, his skin prickling all over as she gently placed her other hand against his chest. "I have never allowed myself to consider this moment; I have forced myself not to dream of such things. I have nothing."

One of her brows shot up. "Nothing?"

He shook his head, knowing that he needed to tell her the truth about his fortune, or lack thereof.

"My brother spent his life wasting his money in the most ridiculous fashion and caring nothing for his estate and tenants. When I became the new viscount, I was given nothing but debts alongside his estate and the like, and all the more so when I came to London."

He shook his head, the shame of it dimming his soul. "I found that my brother had bought himself more than a few houses, houses that he did not need. Your home is one of two that I had intended to sell, but the one you currently reside in will not be sold until you no longer have need of it. The other, thank goodness, sold very quickly, and with it, I have been able to pay a great many debts, but more money is needed in order to make my estate profitable and my title secure for many years to come." He let out a shaky breath and shook his head, realizing that he had told her more than he had ever said to another living soul before, feeling a weight roll off his shoulders as he did so. "I cannot tell you how much this has weighed down my life, knowing that I have a huge mountain to climb. I have been angry with my brother, angry that he would be so selfish, only to then die and leave the burden and responsibility with me." His shoulders slumped as he dropped his gaze, realizing just how terrible he must sound. "My life is to be one of hardship and struggle, and it is not something that I seek to have any aid with. I will not take the easy way out and find a lady with a large fortune, so that my struggles might be eased."

"But what if she were to give you her fortune willingly, knowing that you *are* the kind of gentleman she has been looking for?" came the quiet reply, as Lady Hannah moved fractionally closer, her face lifting to his. "What if this lady knew that the gentleman cared for her in ways he had chosen not to express and wanted him to know that she too felt the same way? That her own heart was filling with affection, that she desired no one else's company but his own? Then what would you say, Lord Patton?"

He could see nothing but Lady Hannah, his whole being filled with her essence. Her eyes were like glittering pools of sea-green water, her golden curls like a crown of glory. Without even intending to do so, Joseph felt his arms slip around her waist, sparks shooting all through him as she linked her arms around his neck. They were so close to something wonderful, so close to a life he had never dreamed of before.

"Then I think I would have to accept, Lady Hannah," he replied hoarsely, not quite sure what he was agreeing to but hoping and praying that it was what he'd longed for. "And I would have to tell you that my heart has a love for you deep within it, a love that I have tried to ignore and push away, believing myself to be unworthy of you." His head began to lower, pulled towards the sweetness of her lips. "I cannot tell you what it means to know that this is entirely incorrect."

"I believe that I love you, Patton," Lady Hannah whispered, her mouth only inches from his. "You foolish, foolish man."

And then she rose on tiptoe and pressed her lips to his, sealing their promise as the future revealed itself to Joseph, sparkling and glorious, with Lady Hannah by his side.

11

The following afternoon found Hannah preparing to walk to Hyde Park, in the hope of finding Lord Walton. Martha, of course, was attending with her, and as much as she would have liked to have Lord Patton with her, Hannah knew that it would be best for him to remain entirely absent. There was a greater chance of Lord Walton speaking to her if she was without him by her side.

"Thank you," she murmured, as the maid finished setting her hair. "That is wonderful."

"Thank you, my lady." The maid bobbed a curtsy and, on being dismissed, scuttled from the room. Hannah rose to her feet, and ensuring that she was quite ready, walked from her bedchamber down the staircase to the drawing room, intending to wait for Martha.

Martha was, of course, already waiting for her.

"You look very lovely, Hannah," Martha smiled, as Hannah came into the room. "In fact, I would say that the smile on your face has grown all the more ever since you came back in from your *short* stroll with Lord Patton last evening."

A blush crept into Hannah's cheeks, well aware that their

stroll had not been either a stroll or a short one at that. "Yes, indeed," she replied quietly. "I have not had a chance to speak to you about that yet, have I?" Although they had returned home last evening together, Hannah had been so filled with emotion that she had not wanted to share it with anyone, not even Martha. It was as if the delight of it all was to be hers alone for such a short time, and so she had kept it all within her heart, barely able to sleep as she had lain there in the darkness and thought of all that had gone on.

"No, you have not said a word," Martha replied, with a small smile. "And during breakfast, you were still rather distracted. Might I presume that Lord Patton has declared himself?"

Hannah laughed. "Not without a great deal of cajoling, I am afraid," she chuckled, recalling how she had practically exploded in front of him, angry and upset with the lack of clarity from him. "In fact, I am ashamed to say that I lost my temper and may have raised my voice in order to elicit a response from him."

Martha gasped, one hand over her mouth. "Oh, Hannah! You didn't!"

Shrugging, Hannah smiled at her aunt, aware that she had stepped far outside the bounds of ladylike propriety. "I did, but it brought me the response I had hoped for. Lord Patton finally told me what was burdening him." Quickly, she told her aunt all that Lord Patton had said, aware that her aunt was soon awash with sympathy for him.

"How terrible," Martha sighed, shaking her head. "To be left such a burden as that is difficult indeed. I cannot imagine what it must then feel like to have the murder of your brother added to that burden also."

Hannah nodded slowly, remembering the anguish that had crossed Lord Patton's face. "He was, and still is, heavily burdened by it all," she said quietly. "But at least now he can look to the future and know that it is bright. He shall not have to worry about his estate or his debts much longer."

She laughed, as Martha gasped again, her eyes wide as she stared at Hannah in disbelief.

"He has not yet asked me for my hand, Martha." Hannah laughed, seeing her aunt taking long, steadying breaths. "But it will not be long. We were able to speak our hearts to one another last evening, and he knows that what is between us is something of permanence. My fortune will be his fortune; his home will be my home." A happy smile lifted her lips, as she sighed with both contentment and delight. "I think I love the man, Martha, and I know now that he feels the same for me. It is just that he thought himself unworthy."

Martha shook her head wordlessly, tears forming in her eyes as she came closer to Hannah, her smile bright.

"I am so very happy for you, Martha," she managed to say, her tears now falling like rain on her cheeks. "After all you have endured, you deserve such great happiness."

"As do you," Hannah replied firmly, taking her aunt's hands. "I know that Lord Fernley has brought back a deep happiness to your life, and I am more than delighted for you. We will, of course, have to visit one another very often, when all is said and done, for I know that I will miss your company." To her surprise, she felt her own voice wobble, her own eyes flood with tears, as she realized that both Martha's marriage and then, hopefully, her own, would set them both apart as they started their new life together with their husbands. It would be painful to be away from Martha, Hannah knew, for they had been through so much together and had faced it arm in arm, side by side.

"Of course we must," Martha agreed, wiping her eyes before embracing Hannah. "My dear girl, I am very happy for you."

Hannah smiled as Martha stepped back, laughing through her tears as they both pulled out a kerchief to dab at their tears.

"Goodness, we are a pair!" she laughed, sniffing as her aunt wiped away the last remnants of moisture from her cheeks. "Look at us both!"

Martha smiled and picked up her bonnet, her tears finally gone. "It is just such wonderful news, Hannah." Placing her bonnet on her head, she cleared her throat and set her shoulders, lifting her chin just a little. "And now I will stop such ridiculous tears and insist that we go on, just as we ought to have done ten minutes ago. We do not want to miss Lord Walton."

Hannah smiled and set her own bonnet aright, tying the ribbons loosely. "No, we do not. I do hope that, very soon, this whole thing might come to an end, for then Lord Patton will finally be free of all the burdens that have been placed on his shoulders. Although, if Lord Walton should reveal that he was involved in Oliver's demise, I do not know what Patton intends to do."

A small knot of worry settled in her stomach as they made their way from the house, climbing into the waiting carriage, which would take them to Hyde Park. Hannah thought they had a much greater chance of spotting Lord Walton from their carriage than if they should walk, visions of them chasing the man through Hyde Park burrowing into her mind as the carriage rolled away. She was not quite sure what she would say to Lord Walton, nor what he might say to her. He had appeared so greatly shocked by Lord Patton's presence that night at the theatre that it was quite obvious to Hannah that the man did not want to be acquainted with Lord Patton in any way at all, although there was still no reason as to why that might be.

"I *will* find out the truth," she muttered to herself, as the carriage rolled into Hyde Park. "I must."

Almost two hours later, and Hannah's resolve was slowly beginning to fail. She disliked the way society crammed itself into the park, with the sole purpose of being seen by others, finding the whole display almost gaudy. There had been plenty of gentlemen coming over to greet her, and she had been forced to refuse more than one gentleman's offer of walking with her for a while, should she wish to alight from the carriage. The sun was, thankfully, hidden behind clouds, which meant that the carriage had not become stifling, but even with her padded seats and relative comfort, Hannah was growing stiff and irritated with being so confined.

"Mayhap we should try another day," Martha suggested quietly, evidently seeing Hannah's frustration. "I know that Lord Fernley said that Lord Walton often frequents the park at this time, but perhaps he has chosen to remain at home today."

Hannah sighed heavily. "I suppose so. I am growing rather tired, and we do have the musical evening to attend later on."

"Ah, yes," Martha replied, with a wry smile. "The lovely Lady Pilkington, is it not?"

Hannah winced. "Yes, it is. Although why she insists on having her daughter sing so many songs is quite beyond me. Can she not hear that Miss Pilkington cannot sing a note?"

Martha laughed and sat back in her seat. "I do not think she can, no," she replied, with a small smile. "She is doing what she can for her daughter in her own way, I suppose."

"Let us just pray that Miss Pilkington finds herself a husband very soon then," Hannah replied grumpily. "Then perhaps we will not have to tolerate another one of her songs ever again!"

Martha shook her head, even though her smile lingered, and Hannah leaned back against the squabs, knowing that she was being so cantankerous merely because she was irritated with her wasted afternoon. She had not seen a single glimpse of Lord

Walton, when she had hoped that this afternoon's discussion with him might mean an end to all Lord Patton's difficulties.

"Do try to smile," Martha urged, as the carriage rolled out of the park. "You have not failed, Hannah. You will find Lord Walton soon, I am sure of it."

Hannah sighed and shook her head, her gaze landing on the view out of the window. "It is all very frustrating," she muttered, aware of the tension rippling through her body. "I cannot imagine what Lord Patton must feel."

Martha's smile grew compassionate. "I suspect that he feels a little lost," she said softly. "It is just as well that he has you by his side, Hannah. Patience is all it will take."

Her tension began to fade away, as Hannah smiled back at Martha, aware that what she said was quite true. She had wanted this matter to be resolved so that Lord Patton would no longer have such a burden of confusion wrapped around him and so that he might feel a freedom that he could only imagine, but Martha was right to remind her to be patient.

"Even after all is revealed, it will still take some time for Lord Patton to heal from all this," Martha continued gently. "You must be prepared for that."

Hannah nodded, her body sagging slightly. "You are wiser than you know, Martha," she replied, her gaze now drawn back to the window. "Thank you, I–"

She gasped, leaning forward and looking out of the window for a moment, her eyes widening.

"What is it?" Martha asked, sitting forward. "Is something wrong?"

Quickly, Hannah rapped on the roof, feeling the carriage come to a slow stop.

"There," she hissed, her face almost pressed up against the window. "That is Lord Walton."

Martha frowned, shooing Hannah away from the window for a moment. Hannah heard her aunt's breath catch.

"So it is," she whispered, as though Lord Walton would be able to hear them. "What do you intend to do, Hannah?"

"Follow him."

Martha sat back in her seat, shaking her head. "No, that is not a good idea, Hannah. You cannot simply accost a man in the street!"

"I *must* speak to him," Hannah replied firmly, her resolve steady. "The sooner I do so, the better. Besides which, he might easily leave London any day, any moment, and then the opportunity will be gone. No, I must speak to him now."

There was nothing Martha could do but watch as Hannah spoke quickly to the driver before settling back in her seat, her fingers curling together with a sudden, furious tension that rifled through her. She could see that Martha was not exactly pleased with such a development, aware of her aunt's foreboding expression and choosing to ignore it. She was not alone, she had Martha, the driver, and the tiger with her, which meant that Lord Walton could not do anything particularly dangerous. All she would do would be to speak to him, just as she had promised.

And then, her eyes were drawn back to the streets outside the carriage window, a slow dread beginning to fill her as she recognized them.

"Martha," she whispered, leaning forward and taking her aunt's hand. "This is near to where Lord Patton resides."

Martha swallowed hard and looked back at her, her eyes wide.

"Do you think…?"

Her aunt tried to shrug. "He may simply be walking past the house. There is more than Lord Patton on this street, Hannah."

Hannah prayed that it was so, looking out of the window

again, just as the carriage passed Lord Walton, only to pull up a few yards ahead in order to let the man pass them.

Except, he did not.

"Where is he, Martha?" Hannah whispered frantically, aware that Martha could see out of the window better than she could. "What is happening?"

"He...he has gone to Lord Patton's door," Martha replied slowly, her face a little pale. "I am sure it does not mean anything, Hannah. He might have business there."

"What, ho!"

A sudden rap on the door had both ladies screaming in fright, only for the friendly face of Lord Fernley to appear at the window.

"I thought I recognized you, my love," he said, opening the carriage door and looking lovingly at Martha. "Whatever are you doing here? I thought I was to see you this evening."

Martha grasped Lord Fernley's hand, holding onto it tightly. "Oh, Fernley. We have just seen Lord Walton."

Lord Fernley's eyebrows rose. "Lord Walton? Where?"

Hannah drew in a long breath, telling herself that she was being ridiculous. "He has gone to call on Lord Patton, but surely that does not mean anything untoward will occur?"

The smile faded from Lord Fernley's face immediately, making Hannah tremble violently.

"I must go in at once," Lord Fernley declared, stepping back out of the carriage, only for Hannah and Martha to scramble after him. "Lord Patton sent me a note only this morning. His steward, a Mr. Tunston, has made an appointment to see him, and Patton wished me to be there. Apparently, Tunston has discovered something of particular interest."

Hannah did not wait to hear another word, hurrying past Lord Fernley towards Lord Patton's home. Her heart was thundering so loudly that it was almost painful, her breath coming fast as she rushed up the steps.

“Do not think to stop me,” she declared, rounding on Lord Fernley as he put a restraining hand on her arm. “I love him, and I will not let him come to harm.”

Lord Fernley dropped his hand, seeing the resolve on her face.

“Do let me go in first, Lady Hannah,” he said gently, as the door opened. “Please. For your own safety.”

Hannah wanted to refuse, but seeing the worry on Martha’s face, she stepped aside and let Lord Fernley inside, with Martha looping her arm through Hannah’s as they walked inside.

“Lord Patton is in the drawing room, my lord, but he has a visitor,” the butler said, his calm voice and demeanor in sharp contrast to all that Hannah was feeling. “If you might–”

“He is expecting us,” Lord Fernley replied, ignoring the butler and walking toward the drawing room with Hannah and Martha in tow. “And I am sure his visitor will not mind a few extra guests for company.”

12

Joseph looked up as the butler introduced Lord Walton, his stomach tightening as the man strode in, a grim expression on his face. His cane tapped on the floor, making Joseph wonder whether or not the man intended to put it to use in some kind of fiendish attack.

"You were not expecting me, I know."

"No," Joseph replied, wishing he had been more specific when he had told the butler he was expecting a visitor. He had, of course, meant Lord Fernley, but had not said as much to his staff. "Why are you here, Lord Walton?"

Lord Walton lifted one eyebrow. "You do not take me for a fool, I hope, Lord Patton?"

"Since I know very little about you, Lord Walton, I confess that I do not know what to think."

This answer did not seem to satisfy Lord Walton, who let out a long, heavy sigh and shook his head, his mustache twitching. "You and your acquaintances appear to be very interested in me, Lord Patton. I have had Lord Fernley insist on asking me questions, and this afternoon, I spotted Lady Hannah and Lady Dalton in a carriage in Hyde Park."

Feigning ignorance, Joseph shrugged. "The fashionable hour is–"

"I know full well that Lady Hannah does not care for the fashionable hour," Lord Walton interrupted firmly. "You need not pretend. I, however, will also no longer pretend."

There came a sudden, clutching fear to Joseph's heart as Lord Walton came closer, only for the fear to turn to confusion as the man sat down, his cane dropping to the floor.

This was not what he had expected.

"I will speak to you with as much clarity as I can, having never expected to have to do such a thing," Lord Walton continued, gesturing for Joseph to sit down. "Please."

Joseph was just about to sit down, only for the door to fly open and Lord Fernley, Lady Hannah, and Lady Dalton all to come flying in, each looking as terrified as the last.

"Hannah!" Joseph exclaimed, as she came rushing over to him. "Whatever is the matter? Whatever are you doing here?"

"Oh, Patton!" she cried, flinging her arms around his neck. "I was trying to find Lord Walton at the park, but he did not come, and then I saw him here and–"

"And since I was on my way to see you, I thought it best to ensure that all was well," Lord Fernley finished, glaring art Lord Walton.

Lord Walton sighed heavily, shaking his head. "It is not what you all think, although I can understand why you might think that."

Joseph felt Hannah's hands tighten on his own. "What do you mean, Lord Walton?"

"I am well aware that you think me responsible for your brother's death, Lord Patton. It is a conclusion that I knew might always be reached, if you were ever to doubt the circumstances." He tilted his head and looked at them all, his gaze resting on Lord Fernley for a moment. "Particularly given that

I spoke to you with such recognition at the time, Lord Fernley."

Slowly realizing that Lord Walton did not mean him any harm, Joseph patted Hannah's hands with his free one, looking down at her.

"I am quite safe, I assure you," he murmured, as Lord Fernley drew Lady Dalton to his side. "Come and sit with me."

She shook her head, her eyes still on Lord Walton. "He is responsible, I am sure of it!"

Joseph gave her a small smile. "The least we can do is listen, my dear. Come now, please. It is not as though he is going to attempt any kind of injury to my person when the rest of us are present."

Slowly, Hannah looked up into his face, and although she did not smile, she gave him a small, jerky nod. He led her to the sofa and sat down, aware of just how tightly she gripped his arm. To his relief, Lord Fernley and Lady Dalton did the same.

"I appreciate your consideration, Lord Patton," Lord Walton murmured, as they all looked at him as one. "I will confess to being rather shocked to see you here in London."

Remembering how the man had reacted so strangely, Joseph lifted his brows. "You practically ran away from me, Lord Walton."

Lord Walton nodded, not denying the fact. "When I saw you with Lady Hannah, I knew that the only reason you might be introduced to me was because I was of interest to you. It did not take much to discover that Lord Fernley believed your brother to be murdered, for I am afraid that the news of it was all around White's."

Knowing that Lord Fernley had never been one to keep things close to his chest, Joseph shot his friend a look and saw the embarrassment creeping into his features. Apparently, this was more than true.

"I confess that I did not know what to do, certain that you would believe me to be the culprit, or, at the very least, involved in the matter."

"And are you?" Joseph asked, directly, looking into the man's small, dark eyes with steadiness. "I want the truth, Lord Walton."

The gentleman drew in a long breath, settling his shoulders before he answered. "No, Lord Patton, I was not. I was, however, in dispute with your brother."

There was nothing in Lord Walton's expression that said he was telling untruths, but all the same, Joseph did not believe him simply because he said so.

"And what was the dispute about?" Hannah asked, her eyes a little narrow. "Was it the same dispute that you had with my brother?"

Lord Walton sighed. "You see, I thought that this was why you might believe me to be a terrible killer with a vengeful mind. Yes, Lady Hannah, it was a similar dispute, although Oliver Patton had a very different reaction to that of your brother. He did not care that he owed me a great deal of money, whereas your brother thought to try and persuade you, Lady Hannah, to marry me so that your dowry might be his payment." A wry smile tipped his lips. "Of course, that did not occur."

Silence settled over the room for a moment, with Joseph trying to make sense of what he had heard. He had been certain that both of these things had been connected, whereas now Lord Walton was telling him that they were not.

"Why did my brother owe you money?" Hannah asked, her grip loosening on Joseph's arm. "What had he done?"

Lord Walton sighed again, sitting back in his chair. "Both your brother and Oliver Patton were very interested in gambling and the like. However, neither of them were particularly good at it, and therefore ended up owing me a large sum of money, both of which they could not pay. Oliver simply laughed it off, refusing to do anything to attempt to pay me what he owed, whereas your brother, Lady Hannah, tried to do what he could."

"And has he satisfied you now?" Hannah asked, lifting her chin. "I can verify all of this, of course, Lord Walton."

"He has begun to pay me what he owes," Lord Walton replied firmly. "I believe that is why he threw both you and your aunt from your home, in an attempt to scrape together as much as he could afford." His eyes flashed, making Joseph frown. "I will not, however, apologize for demanding payment for what was owed me, Lady Hannah. Nor will I apologize for agreeing to your hand in marriage as payment, even though it did not come to fruition. I am a gentleman, and gentlemen honor their debts."

Joseph, unable to find fault with this, nodded slowly. "I quite understand, Lord Walton. However, if my brother refused to pay you, then that gives you all the more reason to want rid of him." The motive stared him directly in the face, making him unable to think of anything else.

"That is very true," Lord Walton agreed calmly. "And the only thing I can tell you is that I am not the kind of man to kill over some coin. I will say that I found your brother arrogant and more than a little foolish, but I am wealthy enough already. It was not as though his lack of payment harmed me in any way."

Lord Fernley cleared his throat. "But you were there that evening. You referred to me as 'Lord Fernley'. How did you know me if you were not involved?"

There was a short pause. Lord Walton looked back at Lord Fernley with a steady look in his eyes, not flustered nor hurried in his answer. It was as if he wanted to ensure he spoke every word with clarity, and Joseph slowly realized that this was because the man was making his own defense. If he failed to convince them of his innocence, then it would be all the worse for him.

"Lord Fernley, I knew you because we had been introduced the previous week," Lord Walton replied quietly. "You may not remember it. In fact, it is apparent that you do not, but I will forgive you that since you were terribly in your cups."

"No," Lord Fernley replied at once, his brows furrowing into an angry glare. "That is nonsense, Lord Walton. You cannot expect me to believe this!"

Lord Walton shrugged. "It is all I have. You forget, Lord Fernley, that before the death of your friend, you were very much like him. Granted, you did not drink as much as he did. At times, you attempted to keep your wits about you, but the lure of liquor and cards often clouded your judgment, did it not?"

Joseph watched with interest as Lord Fernley's cheeks colored, his eyes dark. This was a side of Lord Fernley he had not heard of before and, given the man's reaction, what Lord Walton was saying was quite correct.

"I still do not recall meeting you," Lord Fernley snarled. "I cannot accept it as–"

"You always wore a small enamel pin on your cravat," Lord Walton interrupted, in a rather loud voice. "A family crest, perhaps? I noticed it the day that we were introduced."

Lord Fernley gaped at him, his eyes wide. Joseph, who had never heard of such a thing before, realized that Lord Walton had given Lord Fernley the one thing he needed to believe that such an introduction had taken place.

"I lost it," Lord Fernley replied hoarsely, still staring at Lord Walton. "That night, the night of Oliver's death, it fell into the Thames. I did not notice until much later."

Lord Walton nodded, his lips thin. "I assure you, Lord Fernley, that whether you recall it or not, we already met the night I saw you on the bridge."

"But Sally," Lady Dalton interrupted, her expression one of curiosity instead of outright disbelief. "Lord Fernley said that he remembered you hissing something at her, that she was afraid of you."

Joseph nodded slowly, his gaze returning to Lord Walton who was, at this point, looking a little uncomfortable. "Did you know her, Lord Walton?"

Drawing in another deep breath, Lord Walton nodded slowly. "I did know her," he replied, slowly. "I knew her because I often frequented that house. She was one of my...preferred ladies."

"As she was to my brother, supposedly," Joseph found himself saying, shaking his head. "Were you angry with her for being there?"

Lord Walton shook his head. "No. I asked her what she was doing there, out walking by the Thames with a gentleman, but she did not answer. I tried to speak to her later, but she would not see me. In fact, I found myself barred from the place with no explanation."

Joseph frowned. "Whilst that may all be true, Lord Walton, it is only your word. I have no one to verify this at all."

"And do not forget that Sally was killed within hours of my speaking to her," Lord Fernley added, looking even more ill at ease. "And I am sure, Lord Walton, that you will declare yourself to be entirely innocent of such a crime, but again, it will be of no use to us."

"My wife will collaborate my whereabouts at the time of Sally's death," Lord Walton said firmly. "I am aware that she has not been seen in town a great deal, but that is due to the fact that she has been ill of late. I have been taking care of her."

For a horrible moment, Joseph was caught with the vision of a young lady, forced to remain at home under the threat of punishment whilst her husband went here and there – only for Hannah to ask, "May I ask what her ailment is?"

There came a glimmer of a smile to Lord Walton's face. "The doctor informed me that ladies oft become very unwell when they are with child."

Joseph let out a long breath, wishing he could put his head in his hands. Everything he thought had been, thus far, refuted by Lord Walton, even though it was still only Lord Walton's word he had to go on. However, Joseph knew that it would be easy to prove that Lord Walton had been with his wife at the time of Sally's murder, and given time, that she was also with child. The fact that Lord Walton knew about the enamel pin that Lord Fernley had lost also proved his argument that he had been introduced to Lord Fernley before. On top of which, Lord Walton had not held back from declaring that Oliver had been withholding money from him and that he had been rather irate about the matter, which Joseph could understand. However, that in itself did not mean that the man was a murderer, particularly given that he had been willing to accept Lady Hannah's hand in marriage in lieu of said debt from Phillip.

"I did not do this," Lord Walton said firmly, as though aware of Joseph's confusion. "I knew that I had to come and speak to you before you took things any further. I swear to you that you are looking in the wrong direction. It may look as though I am the culprit, but I promise you here and now, before God in heaven, that it was not my doing."

13

"My lord?"

Joseph turned his head, still battling against his thoughts and the ever-growing desire to believe in the sincerity he saw on Lord Walton's face, only to see his butler standing in the doorway with the figure of Mr. Tunston just behind him.

"Ah, Tunston," he exclaimed, getting to his feet. "I do apologize. This has all been a little.... unexpected."

Mr. Tunston came in past the butler, ignoring the fierce frown sent his way by the man since he had not yet been invited in.

"My lord, I have the most urgent news, as I said to you in my note. I could not write it for fear that I might be...well, might we speak in private?"

Joseph was about to answer, only for Hannah to get to her feet and stand beside him.

"Is it to do with Oliver?" she asked softly, looking at Joseph. He nodded, seeing the gleam in her eye and understanding it at once. Yes, of course. Whatever it was Mr. Tunston had to say, it might very well incriminate Lord Walton – or prove him to be entirely innocent.

"You do not mind if we speak here, Mr. Tunston?" he said, pressing Hannah's hand gently. "We have been discussing the matter of my brother's death."

Mr. Tunston did not smile, but came a little further into the room, sitting down gingerly in a large, overstuffed chair as if afraid he might dirty it with his less than pristine attire.

"My lord, in assisting Mr. Cartwright with the sale of the property and assets, I came upon a rather disturbing piece of information, which I have only just been able to confirm with your butler."

Joseph blinked. "My butler?"

Mr. Tunston nodded sagely, looking about the room. "Are you quite sure I should talk about this here, my lord? It is a matter of a little...delicacy."

Shaking his head, Joseph gave a small, resigned smile. "You may speak openly, Mr. Tunston, just as you have always done. Please, continue."

Mr. Tunston paused, shrugged, and then continued, sitting back a little more comfortable in his chair, as though he were simply passing the time.

"My lord, I discovered that your brother often took liberties with young ladies, whilst also having a particular lady under his protection. Your butler told me as much, although with some reluctance I might add. However, he also stated that he had heard Oliver exclaiming over one young lady that was denying him what he wanted. He also stated that, on one occasion, there was a great deal of smashing and the like that occurred in the drawing room, mostly due to your brother's fury over this particular lady."

Clearing his throat, Joseph tried not to allow any feelings of shame creep over him, praying that Mr. Tunston got to his point quickly.

"However, one young lady that refused him was a Mrs. Harleton, a young widow."

The name meant nothing to him. "Mrs. Harleton, did you say?" He ran the name around his mind, but nothing came to him.

Mr. Tunston nodded again, his sharp eyes boring into Joseph's soul as though he ought to recognize the name at once. "I believe the lady refused him, but unfortunately your brother was not a man to take a refusal on the chin."

Joseph closed his eyes, his gut twisting. "Tell me he did not."

There was a short pause. "I am not certain, my lord, but I found the place where she once lived and spoke to her neighbors there. They reported to me, once they had some payment for their trouble, that there was a gentleman at her door one night and there came the sound of screaming soon after. The gentleman also had a hackney waiting and a man or two with him. No one dared do a thing about it."

His eyes still closed, Joseph felt Hannah press his arm, clearly horrified at the story.

"Unfortunately, it seems that it was too much for Mrs. Harleton. One night, she threw herself into the Thames."

Hannah gasped, as did Lady Dalton, whilst Joseph's eyes flew open, and he stared at Mr. Tunston in shock. The atmosphere had immediately become tense, as though they were all waiting for Mr. Tunston to laugh and say that he had only been making some kind of black humor, but the words never came.

"The reason I looked into this matter," Mr. Tunston finished, his expression grave, "is because Mrs. Harleton was Mr. Cartwright's only daughter."

Joseph sucked in a breath, stars sparkling in his vision for a moment. This could not be the case! Mrs. Harleton had killed herself because of something his brother had done – something truly terrible, something beyond the pale.

He felt sick to his stomach.

It all made sense now. It had been Mr. Cartwright who had engineered his brother's death, killing him in the same way as his daughter had taken her own life. He must have been the one to use Sally to lure him towards the Thames, must have been the one who had plotted the whole thing.

And yet, Joseph could not find it in his heart to be angry with him. Yes, of course, if he had killed Sally so that Joseph would not find out the truth, then that was equally horrific, but as for Oliver...that was an entirely different matter.

"It all makes sense now," he breathed, leaning forward and putting his head in his hands. "Lord Walton had nothing to do with this."

"I-I do not understand," he heard Hannah say, as his vision blurred with a sudden rush of hot tears. "Who is Mr. Cartwright?"

He drew in a long breath, feeling himself begin to shake. "Mr. Cartwright is my solicitor. He was my brother's solicitor also."

"I would guess," Mr. Tunston added, as Hannah let out a low, astonished sound, "that your brother saw Mrs. Harleton in the offices one day, possibly visiting her father over lunching hours, and that was that. As I said, he was not a man used to being denied what he wanted."

"And yet he remained your brother's solicitor?" Lord Fernley asked, sounding completely astonished. "And then as yours, Patton? Why?"

There was a short silence.

Lady Dalton cleared her throat. "Perhaps, if I may be permitted to make a suggestion, Mr. Cartwright remained in his position with you to try and ensure that you did not find out what occurred. It could also be that if you were to begin to look into things, he would know about it. As for your brother, perhaps he remained so that he might find a way to plot his revenge. After all, you did say – and excuse me if I am being indelicate here – that Oliver was not the kind of gentleman to take things with any degree of seriousness. For example, here with Lord Walton, he did not once consider that he truly *did* have a debt to pay. I would suggest, hesitantly of course, that he might not have thought the matter with Mr. Cartwright's daughter to be of particular importance. Once he got what he wished, life carried on regardless."

"I do not think he knew."

Lord Fernley's voice suddenly chimed in over the top of Lady Dalton's, making Joseph look up. Lord Fernley had a rather strange expression on his face, as though he had only just remembered something.

"He said something that night, said that a 'Mrs. H' was not who he had thought she was. He wanted to forget her, which was why he continued to drink so heavily. I would suggest, then, that he truly did not know that she was Mr. Cartwright's daughter until it was much too late."

It was a decent suggestion, and Joseph had to accept it, just as he had done with all the others.

"At least he felt a modicum of guilt," he said bitterly, getting to his feet. "I suppose that I must send for the constable, even though, in one way, I feel as though Oliver met his just punishment for such a cruel act."

Hannah looked up at him, her face filled with nothing but sympathy and compassion, and Joseph knew he had never been more grateful for her in his life before.

"Lord Walton, I apologize for any inconvenience. If you will forgive me, I must excuse myself for a time. Fernley, see to the constable, will you? Hannah, if you will join me, I feel myself in need of your company." He looked over at his steward, the man who, ever faithful, had come to him with some difficult news. "Thank you, Mr. Tunston. You may return home now and prepare the estate." He managed a small smile, despite the weight that was bearing down on his soul. "I think I will be returning home again very soon."

EPILOGUE

Hannah quietly entered the drawing room, looking all around for Lord Patton, only to see him waving her over from where he sat, looking out of the window.

"My dear," he murmured, getting up and taking her hand. "How good to see you."

She looked anxiously into his face. "How are you, my love?"

It had, by this time, been a week since Mr. Tunston's revelation over Oliver and his association with Mr. Cartwright's daughter. In that week, Joseph had been both quiet and detached, a cloud over him whenever she called.

Today, however, he appeared a little brighter.

"I am feeling a bit better today, thank you," he replied, pressing her hand to his lips. "I am sorry that I have been so distant. It has taken a great deal of time to come to terms with what has occurred."

Hannah smiled at him, understanding at once. "You must take as much time as you need, Patton. Although I will say that I am glad there is an end to it all, even though the conclusions that have been reached were not at all what we had thought." She could still recall how astonished and horrified she had been to hear what Mr. Tunston had told them about Oliver and his particular habits. Her heart had turned over in both pain and sorrow for the young lady.

"I did not really ever know my brother," Joseph replied haltingly, "and this has not improved my impression of him in any way. I am sorry to say that, were he alive today, I would call him out for some of the things he has done."

Pressing her lips together, Hannah tried to think of what to say, seeing the pain in his eyes and desperately wanting to find some way to relieve it.

"But I have decided not to think of the matter any longer," Joseph finished, a little more softly. "It is at an end."

"Even though they have not found Mr. Cartwright?" Hannah asked, a little surprised. "You know the constabulary is still searching for him."

Mr. Cartwright had not been at his offices when the constables had gone in search of him, nor had he been at home. In fact, most of his things were gone, leading the constabulary to believe that the man had known that Mr. Tunston had discovered the truth about Mr. Cartwright's daughter and had chosen to leave London. In addition, they had also discovered, a few days later, that Mr. Cartwright had been skimming some money from Lord Patton – both past and present – and taking it for himself. He had not had anywhere near enough, however, to help him start a new life somewhere else until the sale of the large house in the country had gone through, which was possibly why he had remained on as the Patton solicitor. Mr. Cartwright had taken a hefty chunk from the sale of the country house and then disappeared. From what Lord Fernley thought, it was more than likely that Mr. Cartwright was overseas somewhere, never intending to return to England again.

"So much of me cannot blame Mr. Cartwright for what he did," Joseph said heavily. "But the murder of Sally, which the constabulary *does* believe to have been his doing, I cannot understand, nor forgive. Is one life worth more than another? Did he feel any guilt in taking Sally's life, even though she was a lady of the night? Or was he only looking to protect himself?" He sighed and shook his head, before taking both of her hands and holding them in his. "But no more, my love. The death of the two women will always weigh on my heart, but I must leave the constabulary to their work. Should I hear news of Mr. Cartwright's arrest, then I will be glad for it, for the sake of Sally. But, if not, I have no intention of dwelling on it for the rest of my days. Instead, I intend to look to the future and start rebuilding my life."

Hannah drew in a long, calming breath and let it out slowly, relieved to hear that Joseph was now considering the future.

"I am glad, my dear, that you are able to put it behind you now," she said softly, lifting her eyes to his. "But your heart will still need time to heal, and you must not rush it. Allow yourself all the time you need to grieve. You will be a better man for it."

He smiled at her then, lifting one hand to brush his fingers down the cheek. "You have made me a better man, Hannah," he said tenderly. "I could not have come this far without you. I love you more than I can say. You will marry me, will you not? Mr. Tunston has written to say the preparations at the estate are already underway."

It was the question she had been waiting for, and without hesitation, she threw her arms around his neck and held him tightly.

"Of course I will marry you," she whispered, her heart filling with happiness. "I love you so dearly that I cannot bear to be separated from you."

He kissed her gently, the brightness in his eyes slowly returning. "Thank you, Hannah," he murmured, his arms now slipping around her waist. "You mean more to me than I can ever express. I love you."

"I love you, Patton," Hannah replied, before kissing him again with all the love and the passion she felt in her heart. Their future was bright, their hearts open and filled with love. What more could she ask for?

THE END

Keep reading for even more romance!

AN EARL'S DECEPTION

SECRETS OF LONDON

An Earl's Deception

First printing, 2018

Publisher
Love Light Faith, LLC
400 NW 7th Avenue, Unit 825
Fort Lauderdale, FL 33311

1

London 1817

"But I thought..." Martha trailed off as her elder sister Edith picked up her quill.

"I am not doing anything untoward, Martha," Edith sniffed, her cheeks a little pink. "I am merely keeping up with my correspondence."

Wisely, Martha chose to keep silent, well aware that Edith did not often keep up with her correspondence unless it was for her own advantage, just as it was here. Their father, the Earl of Winchester, had already had a quiet word with Martha, expecting her to ensure that Edith remained within the bounds of propriety whilst they were here, in London, since he took very little interest in matters of the heart and was well used to Martha keeping an eye on things.

"Why you must stand there and look down on me in judgment is quite beyond me," Edith sniffed, dipping her quill into the ink. "I am simply replying to Lord Hobart and stating that, yes, I will be in the park tomorrow afternoon, as I usually like to take the air a little before the fashionable hour, if I am not already engaged with visitors and the like." She narrowed her eyes and glared at Martha, who still, as yet, had not said another word. "You cannot find fault in that."

Hesitating, Martha spread her hands. "I thought you cared for another, Edith."

Her sister's tinkling laugh broke the air, only adding to the tension. "What nonsense, Martha!"

"I know you were quite adamant that you were deeply in love with him," Martha said stubbornly. "I thought there was a promise to remain true to him until he returned. I recall you telling me as much at the time."

The mirthful expression left Edith's face as she got to her feet, her letter finished. She shot a baleful look towards Martha, before ringing the bell for the butler. Martha let out her breath slowly, not wanting to antagonize her elder sister but finding her behavior rather curious given that last year, she had been filled with the delights of a particular gentleman, who now appeared to have fallen quite by the wayside.

"You know nothing about the ways of the heart, Martha," Edith replied, with a slightly disdainful sniff. "Lord Weston was, of course, a kind and attentive gentleman, but he has been away from town these last eighteen months, missing both the Season and the little Season thereafter. I have grown quite tired of his absence." She tossed her head, her blonde curls bouncing. "I may have said, in the foolishness of youth, that I would wait for his return until this business—whatever it was—came to its completion. Now, I find myself growing rather weary of such a notion. It is now the Season yet again, and I will not disappoint Father and Mother by refusing to allow any other gentlemen to court me for the sake of one who has not yet returned to town."

Her speech came to a close just as the door opened and the butler appeared, looking inquiringly at Edith. She handed him the letter with strict instructions that it was to be sent at once.

With a self-satisfied smile plastered on her face, she watched the butler leave.

"But what if he returns?"

Martha, who had not met this "Lord Weston" since she had been forced to remain at home to care for their ailing mother during last year's Season, linked her hands together in front of her and looked anxiously at Edith, afraid that she was making something of a mistake.

Edith, however, did not appear to care. She shrugged and turned away, wandering to the window and looking down to the streets of London.

"You do not care for him then, as you once did?"

Sighing, Edith shrugged. "Did I ever really care for him at all?" She shook her head, her anger and frustration dying away to reveal the truth of what she felt to Martha. "I am not sure what I felt, truth be told. I was so giddy with all that had gone on during my first Season here in London that it seemed almost right, almost expected, to fall completely in love with someone. On top of which, Lord Weston was an earl, due to be the Marquess of Dunlop when the time comes. Of course, Father greatly approved." She glanced back at Martha, who slowly walked over to join her sister at the window.

"The truth is, Martha, I was quite ridiculous to make Lord Weston such a promise," Edith continued, with just a tinge of sadness to her words. "I should not have done so, not when I did not know for certain when he would be returning. I think I believed myself in love, but now that he has been absent for such a long time, I find that I can think of him without any deep pangs of affection echoing through my soul. In fact, were he to return to London without warning, were he to stand in this very room and declare himself, then I think I should refuse him entirely."

Martha's eyebrows shot towards her chocolate-colored curls,

astonishment rifling through her. This was not what she had expected to hear from her sister, who was always somewhat giddy when it came to things like balls, soirees, or even gentlemen, but it seemed that Edith had been doing rather a lot of thinking of late. To Martha's surprise, she found that what Edith had said made sense – to the point that she found she could not argue with her.

"Pray, do not be angry with me," Edith continued, her dark green eyes flickering with worry as she looked back at Martha. "I know that you are looking out for me and seeking only my best, but I must go with what my heart says. I do not wish to tie myself to a gentleman that I feel nothing for, who can be so easily forgotten by my heart when he is gone for a short time." She sighed heavily and returned her gaze to the window, her shoulders slumped. "No, I wish to marry a man who fills me with such inexplicable emotion that it is all I can do to keep my head."

"And is that Lord Hobart?"

A long sigh escaped Edith, as she turned her head to face Martha, shrugging her shoulders.

"Who can tell?" she replied softly. "I barely know the gentleman, but I am willing to give him a little of my time—to see if he can conquer my heart."

Martha sighed also and leaned against the window frame, letting her eyes linger on her sister's features, so different to her own. Edith was fair of face, with sparkling emerald eyes and such beautiful blonde curls that not a day went by without Martha feeling a spark of jealousy over her own frizzy, brown mop that never curled quite as beautifully. She did not have the oval face of Edith, nor the tiny chin and delicate, slender neck. Martha was rather plain when compared to her sister. She had something of a square jaw, a nose that leaned towards prominence, and instead of expressive, bright eyes, she had been left with dull green orbs that rarely sparkled and barely held any color.

"You are to have many gentlemen chasing you this Season, Edith," she said and sighed, her own shoulders drooping as she saw the confusion on her sister's face. "You are the eldest daughter to the Earl of Winchester, with a sizeable dowry and more beauty than I can ever hope for." She shook her head, aware of that familiar spark of jealousy coursing through her. "You are quite right not to tie yourself to one gentleman who has promised his heart and then made himself entirely absent—especially if you have discovered that there is nothing of significance in your feelings about him."

Edith looked surprised at Martha's response, but to Martha's relief, remained silent.

"Although I must ask you to be careful with Lord Hobart, Edith," Martha continued, reaching for and taking her sister's hand. "Do not rush into an attachment or the like without being quite sure that it is *you* that he cares for and not your dowry and connections." She squeezed Edith's hand, hoping there was no bite to her words. Thankfully, Edith seemed to understand.

"Thank you, Martha," Edith said softly, her smile a pleasant one. "I was afraid that you would tell me to wait desperately for Lord Weston to return, that I should not be so much as seen in another gentleman's company whilst I waited expectantly for him to return to claim me, but you understand now, I think."

Martha considered for a moment, wondering what it would be like to have a gentleman have such a deep affection for her. "I am trying to understand," she said slowly, her hand dropping from Edith's. "This is, after all, only a week into my very first Season, so I am afraid I know very little about the ways of gentlemen, although Papa has insisted that I ensure you are behaving just as you ought."

Edith laughed, the sound breaking the last of the tension

and carrying it away. "You will have plenty of suitors; I am quite sure," she said, smiling. "I am sorry that you missed last Season, else you would have met Lord Weston by now."

"Did he ever...declare himself?" Martha asked gently, her eyes fixed on Edith as she spoke. "Was his intention to marry you upon his return?"

A slow pink began to build in Edith's cheeks, and she turned her face away. "He did not ever state he would marry me, no," she said firmly, although her color was still rising. "However, he did declare himself quite hopelessly in love with me, and at the time, I considered myself to return such feelings. Now, of course, I know that I was only swept away with the excitement of it all." She shot a sharp glance towards Martha, who kept her face impassive. "I can only hope that he has realized that what he felt was not anything of substance. I am sure that, in the time he has been away, he has been able to consider his feelings and seen them for what they are."

Or, perhaps, he truly did care for you and carries that love still, Martha thought to herself, her stomach twisting as her thoughts drifted towards the idea that, perhaps one day, she might find such a gentleman.

"Now," Edith said firmly, turning towards the door. "I think it is time for me to take the air." She glanced back at Martha, her expression a little calculating. "You are going to attend with me, are you not? I should hate to have to take the maid."

A slight frown settled between Martha's brows. "You are to go to the park now?"

Edith's lips curved. "Yes, indeed," she declared smartly. "After all, why would I have written to Lord Hobart and told him that I intended to go out walking this very afternoon?" She laughed and continued to walk towards the door. "I think he will have had more than enough time to prepare himself."

Something twisted in Martha's gut as she made her way

toward her sister, neither willing or unwilling to attend with her. She was not quite sure what to make of it all, wondering if Edith truly knew what she was doing.

"Ought we not to tell Papa where we are going?" she asked slowly, as Edith began to walk quickly back towards her bedchamber to change. "I know he is aware that we often go out to pay calls and the like, but if you are expressly meeting Lord Hobart, then–"

Edith's trilled laughter cut her off. "Come now, Martha, you know that Papa does not care about which gentlemen I meet, just so long as I find a suitable one to declare himself by the end of the Season. Besides which, I have no intention of 'expressly meeting' Lord Hobart, Martha. It shall just be entirely by chance if we stumble across one another, although, of course, I shall require a chaperone."

"Of course," Martha replied quietly, her stomach now rolling as her concern increased. "As long as you are quite sure about all this, Edith."

Edith laughed again. "Of course I am sure, Martha. I forget that this is your first foray into society. You need not be so afraid. All will be just as I intend it."

Swallowing, Martha walked into her own bedchamber, preparing to change into an afternoon walking dress. "I do hope so, Edith," she muttered to herself, now feeling both nervous and unsure as she prepared to accompany her sister to St. James's Park.

2

Edmund, Earl Weston, heir apparent to the Marquess of Dunlop, drew in a long breath and sighed happily as he was driven through the streets of London. After more than a year away from town, he was finally able to return for the Season, having missed the little Season during the winter months due to the fact that his father had still been very weak and tired. He was pleased that his father was not as ill as he had been. Edmund had been required to take over the running of the estate and the like while his father recovered.

Not that he had found such a task arduous, of course, for he always knew that one day the responsibility that came with the title would fall upon him.

However, Edmund was more than glad that he had finally been able to return to London, that the burden of responsibility had been taken from his shoulders and placed firmly back on his father's. It meant that he could return to what he had begun almost eighteen months ago. He had been in London very early, a little before the Season had begun, and it had been there that he had set eyes on one Lady Edith. Even the thought of her forced the breath from his lungs, his lips stretching into a wide smile. She and her father had come to town early also. He learned later that this was to ensure that Lady Edith had everything she required in terms of her wardrobe, having been unable to see to it any earlier given her mother's illness. There had been mention of a sister lingering at home, ensuring that Lady Winchester was recovering, if he remembered correctly. How long it had been since he had last set eyes on Lady Edith. How pleasant it would be to see her again.

Sighing happily, Edmund looked out of the carriage window as it began to turn towards St. James's Park, which was on the way to his townhouse. The familiar sights cheered him, as he continued to take everything in, knowing that soon, he would be back in his own house once more. The staff had been sent to prepare the house a good week earlier, which meant that everything would be ready. All he would have to do then would be to accept some invitations, knowing that he would meet Lady Edith again very soon. After all, had she not said in her last letter to him that she would be returning to London for the Season again?

His heart had leaped in his chest at this, for to be able to court her properly, as he had always intended, had been a wonderful thought. Edmund was quite sure that he was as deeply in love with Lady Edith as he had always been. Even the thought of her made his pulse quicken, his body warm with thoughts of deep, unrelenting affection. The affection he felt for her was returned; he was quite sure of it.

If he closed his eyes, Edmund could still see her face turned towards his, the way her eyes had lit up as he had declared his love for her, begging her to wait for him to return so they might court in earnest. How wonderful it had been to hear her whisper that, yes, she would wait for him. How glad he had been when she had smiled, her cheeks a dusky pink, as she had promised to write just as often as she could.

Although, that being said, she had not written particularly often of late.

His brow furrowed.

The carriage slowed for a moment, caught up by a great many carriages that were attempting to turn into the park for the fashionable hour.

"I'm right sorry, m'lord," his driver called. "It might take us a bit longer than I first thought."

Edmund did not care. Shrugging, he sat back in his seat and smiled softly to himself, feeling almost glad to be caught up with "the fashionable hour" once more.

And then, his eyes caught sight of someone. Someone familiar. Someone who was laughing and talking up into the face of another gentleman.

His gut twisted, a stone sinking his stomach right down to the floor.

There was Lady Edith.

He could not take his eyes off her. She was just as beautiful as he remembered, her blonde curls peeking out from underneath her bonnet as she walked. She was wearing a light green walking dress with lace adorning the cuffs and neckline, which only added to her beauty, for the color matched her eyes perfectly. Her rosebud lips were curved upwards, her eyes dancing with delight, as the gentleman she was walking with said something apparently humorous.

Edmund's hands gripped the edge of his seat, feeling suddenly trapped. Surely, this could not be!

Get ahold of yourself, man. There is nothing in it.

Drawing in three steadying breaths, Edmund tried to force himself to relax. He was being quite ridiculous. Of course Lady Edith was going to walk with gentlemen other than himself. It was quite reasonable that the gentlemen of the *ton* would wish to walk with her, to dance with her, to converse with her. It was also quite reasonable that she should accept. It was not as though he could expect her to remain indoors at all times, venturing out only to stand at the sides of the ballroom and refuse to dance with anyone for the sake of him. That was quite ridiculous, and Edmund knew it.

There was nothing to concern himself about unduly. Lady Edith was simply walking alongside a gentleman; that was all. It meant nothing.

His eyes lingered on her again, his stomach tying itself into tiny, tight knots as he watched her. She was even more beautiful than he remembered.

As he watched, a young lady quickened her steps to draw nearer to Lady Edith and the unknown gentleman. She wore an expression of frustration, mingled with dislike, and her gaze remained on the gentleman as she spoke to her sister in sharp tones. He could not hear what was being said, but the quickness of her words and the frown on her face let him know all too well what it was the lady was thinking. There was something about this gentleman that she did not like.

That brought him a modicum of satisfaction.

Lady Edith nodded, her face blank as the gentleman bowed. She curtsied, the smallest of smiles on her face as she turned toward the other lady, waiting together until the gentleman took his leave. Then, as Edmund watched, Lady Edith rounded on the other lady, her eyes angry and her mouth in a tight line.

His brows lifted. This must be Lady Edith's sister, for he was quite sure she would not speak to any other person in such a fashion, even though she was doing her best to hide the fact that she was speaking harshly from the rest of the *ton* who were passing by.

As the carriage began to pull away, Edmund found his eyes lingering on the sister of Lady Edith, having no recollection of ever being told her name. She did not have the same beauty as

Lady Edith, although the family resemblance was there in the slender neck and delicate features. Her nose was a little longer and larger than Lady Edith's. For a moment, Edmund wondered if she too had the same striking green eyes as her sister, only to catch himself with such a strange thought. Shaking it from himself, he turned his gaze back toward Lady Edith.

She was still whispering something frantically to her sister, her eyes darting about to ensure that no one could hear what was being said in order not to give fodder to the rumor mill, but her displeasure was obvious nonetheless. Edmund bit his lip as his carriage moved again, tugging him away from the sight of Lady Edith, forcing him to look elsewhere. Soon, they were back on the cobbled streets and making good progress toward returning home, but Edmund found that his joy had been somewhat taken away by the sight of Lady Edith walking with another gentleman. On top of which, she had seemed rather upset at being forced to bid farewell to this particular gentleman, whoever he was, which only unsettled Edmund all the more.

"Here we are, m'lord," the driver called, as they turned into the street. "And again, I do apologize that we were caught up in all that."

Edmund waited until the door was opened by the footman before calling up to the driver that it was quite all right and that he had not minded waiting. The driver looked somewhat relieved, doffing his cap as Edmund made his way into the house, ready to be greeted by the rest of his staff.

ONE HOUR later and Edmund found himself pacing up and down the drawing room floor, his boots almost boring holes in the thick carpet. He had not been able to forget the sight of Lady

Edith for one moment, even though he had a great number of things prevailing on him for his time. He had bathed, changed, and eaten, and even now, he could not forget her.

"Here are the invitations, my lord."

Jerking around, Edmund saw the butler step into the drawing room with a small tray of letters and invitations placed on it. The butler set it down and then stood tall, his hands firmly behind his back.

"And what is there to do this evening?" Edmund asked, wondering what Lady Edith might be attending. "Do I have anything of interest?"

The butler gave a small smile. "I believe Lord and Lady Millington are to have a ball this evening, my lord," he said, gesturing to the silk-ribbon-tied invitation, which had been bound together with a small pink flower.

"Ah," Edmund murmured, reaching for it. He knew that Lord and Lady Millington's ball was well spoken of, for it was one of the first balls of the Season every year. The *beau monde* always made sure to attend.

"Might I relay your acceptance, my lord?" the butler asked, no expression whatsoever on his face. "It is not too late, of course, for they will not mind a late reply."

Edmund chuckled, remembering just how busy Lord and Lady Millington's ball had been, having attended it twice before, during his first two Seasons and before he had ever laid eyes on Lady Edith. "Yes, I know they will barely notice me should I attend even without responding," he chuckled, undoing the ribbon. "Yes, thank you. I would be grateful if you would do so."

The butler nodded and excused himself, leaving Edmund to read through the rest of the invitations. He was quite certain that Lady Edith would be in attendance this evening, although whether or not he would find her in the crush was quite another thing.

Suddenly, he was filled with purpose. Glancing at the clock, he discarded the rest of the invitations to read through on another occasion, before striding from the room. He had to ensure that he looked his best for this evening in the hope that he would see Lady Edith again.

Surely, once she laid eyes on him, she would feel the same heart-wrenching affection that they had once shared and had once spoken of to one another. The feeling had never left him, not even in all his time away. He could only pray that Lady Edith still felt the same.

3

Martha frowned as Edith let yet another gentleman sign her dance card, her eyes alighting on one of them in particular. Lord Hobart was quite relentless in his pursuit of Edith, and Martha was not quite certain that she liked that about him. Yes, it was good to have a gentleman as attentive as he was, but to have such a passion for Edith after only two days was quite ridiculous. From what Edith had said, Lord Hobart had been introduced to her two days prior and had then sought to walk with her in St. James's Park only yesterday. Now, he was begging Edith for permission to waltz with her. To Martha's horror, Edith consented and suggested that Lord Hobart write his name in both spaces, meaning that he would have both waltzes to himself.

It was bold and rather impetuous, making Martha blush with the shame of it. A lady did not ask a gentleman to dance and certainly did not tell him where he should write his name. Besides which, Edith should not be allowing one gentleman to have two of the same dance, for that in itself would raise eyebrows.

"You are most kind, Lady Edith," she heard Lord Hobart say,

"but I think it best not to do such a thing at this present moment. I should not like to claim you when I know you already have such a great number of admirers."

Martha felt a sheen of sweat appear on her skin, as Edith rolled her eyes, pouting prettily.

"But I shall take the waltz and the quadrille," Lord Hobart continued, making Edith smile just a little. "Shall that satisfy you?"

"Indeed," Edith murmured, her cheeks now a dark red. "Thank you, Lord Hobart. You are very kind."

He bowed over Edith's hand and turned away, leaving Martha free to speak to her sister.

"You cannot be so bold!" she hissed, her eyes narrowing as Edith's happy expression flattened. "For heaven's sake, Edith, do you want to make a cake of yourself?"

"I am doing no such thing," Edith declared firmly. "Lord Hobart had made his interest in me quite clear, and I am only encouraging them as best I can."

Martha dragged in a breath, trying to settle her anger. "But why must you?" she asked carefully. "Why must you try and secure Lord Hobart's affections particularly? There are a great many other gentlemen who seek to dance with you, mayhap one of them has intentions to court you."

Edith sighed wistfully, her eyes darting through the crowd as though she would be able to spot Lord Hobart again. "Because he wrote to me the day after we were introduced," she said quietly.

"He wrote to see if you would be out walking that afternoon," Martha pointed out, dashing away Edith's romantic notions. "He did not ask to walk with you, or to so much as call upon you."

"That is because he did not wish to make himself so obvious," Edith replied curtly. "Now, enough of your haranguing,

Martha. You made it very clear that you do not like Lord Hobart's warmth toward me, and I am growing rather weary of your irritating comments whenever he draws near." She flipped open her fan, waving it rather quickly so that she might hide her harsh words. "You ought to be considering your own future instead of worrying about mine, Martha. Why are you not being pursued by any gentlemen of the *ton*? Why is your dance card still quite empty?" Her brow arched as Martha felt heat rush into her face. "Perhaps if you removed that haughty, rather arrogant look from your face, then gentlemen might be more inclined to approach you."

Martha felt as though her sister had slapped her hard across the face, the sheer anger in her words hitting her full force. "I am only trying to help you, Edith."

"You do not need to!" Edith exclaimed, her eyes flashing. "You are not my parent, are you? Father is here somewhere, and he will be ensuring that everything comes aright, regardless of what you think. You are my younger sister, Martha, and you ought to know your place."

So saying, she turned on her heel and marched away from Martha, leaving her standing quite still as the *beau monde* swirled around her. Soon, Edith was sucked in by the crowd, lost completely to Martha's gaze, leaving her feeling alone.

Her head dropped as she looked down at her dance card, seeing the four names there and feeling suddenly quite pathetic. It was not as though she did not have gentlemen willing to dance with her, but it was not the same as Edith, whose card was always filled within minutes of her stepping into the ballroom. She swallowed and turned her head away, making towards the quieter edge of the room, where she might climb the staircase and sit alone on the balcony for a while. She had some dances, yes, but they were not until much later, which would give her time to regain her composure.

Her heart ached as she made her way through the crowd, quite sure that some of them were already whispering about her. Had they heard Edith speak to her? Had news of her rebuttal gone through the crowd already?

Her cheeks burned as she climbed the stairs, far too aware of her loneliness. Edith had always had a sharp tongue and often used it on Martha, which, despite the frequency of it, was not something that Martha had ever become used to. They had never been particularly close, given that Edith tended toward selfishness and Martha toward worrying over almost everything. This meant that their thoughts and considerations did not often merge in the same direction. However, Martha still wished that Edith *would* listen to what she had to say, even if she did not entirely agree with it. As far as Martha was concerned, her sister was acting with such inconsideration that it was verging on foolishness, for to be so besotted with a gentleman after only two brief meetings was more than ridiculous. Besides which, after what Edith had told her about Lord Weston and how they had declared their love for one another after what had only been a very short acquaintance, she had hoped that Edith might be a little more on her guard.

Sighing to herself, Martha wandered along the balcony until she found a quiet seat overlooking the ballroom. She was able to see the dancers and able to spot her sister amongst the crowd, although she tried her best not to continue watching what Edith did. Perhaps she was being too intrusive, she thought to herself, as she let the music begin to wash over her. Perhaps she ought to have nothing to do with Edith and the associations she chose to make. Then, mayhap, she might be able to consider her own future instead of worrying about her older sister.

Her breath shuddered out of her as Martha saw Edith take Lord Hobart's arm, allowing him to lead her onto the floor. She was not as used to the ways of gentlemen, the ways of the *ton,* as her sister was. After all, she had spent last Season at home with their ailing mother, instead of coming to London with Edith. With them only being eleven months apart in age, it had seemed right for them both to have their come out together, but fate had decided otherwise. Of course, Martha was out, as was Edith, but hers had come with no fanfare, no grand balls, no celebrations. None of what Edith had experienced the year before had been given to her.

She was the forgotten one.

For a moment, her thoughts turned back to her mother who was still residing back at their manor house. She was still quite weak and tired, and she had thought the trip to London too difficult to undertake. At that moment, Martha realized just how much she missed her, how much she missed being able to talk to her about all that was on her mind. Her mother, Lady Winchester, had often murmured that Martha held far too much in her head, that her anxiety and worry was for anyone and everyone but herself. She did not know whether that had come from the time Martha had spent taking care of her ill mother, fretting over her health and worrying that her mother might succumb to what had been a long and pronounced fever.

That day had never come, but the anxiety had remained.

Edith's laughter hurried towards Martha, making her wince. How her sister managed to make such a loud exclamation that floated towards the balcony, over the din of conversation and music, was quite beyond Martha. Her stomach tumbled over itself as she watched Edith make eyes at Lord Hobart as they took their turn together, praying that her sister would not go on to make even more of a fool of herself.

"Are you not dancing this evening?"

Jumping visibly with surprise, Martha turned her head to see a tall, rather grim-looking gentleman looking down at her with a thin smile on his otherwise angular face.

She rose to her feet, heat racing up her chest as she tried to smile back at him. "N-No," she stammered, trying desperately to recall this gentleman's name, for she presumed they had been introduced even though she could not remember who he was. "I mean, yes. I have some dances, but they have not yet come about." She eyed the gentleman a little suspiciously, wondering if he thought her shameful for coming up here alone. Or, even worse, what if his intentions were something entirely different altogether.

"I see," he murmured, no longer looking at her but looking past her, over her shoulder. "It is quite unusual to have a lady sitting here alone."

"I am not alone," she replied firmly, gesturing towards the card room, which was on the opposite side of the balcony. "My father is within, and my sister is dancing below. I thought to take a few minutes of quiet before returning to her side."

He nodded again, his light blue eyes blazing from the light of the candles that surrounded them. There was silence for a moment as she looked back at him, still trying desperately to recall his name. His appearance did not catch her mind with remembrance either, even though she was quite certain she would have taken note of him the first time they were introduced. The brightness of his blue eyes was almost startling, even though they were half hidden by eyebrows that were lowering into a frown. His fair hair held streaks of white blond hair, which was tied back neatly. His clothing was of the highest fashion and was absolutely pristine, making her think that he must be of a high title.

So why could she not recall being introduced to him?

"Lady Edith is your sister, yes?"

She nodded slowly. "You have been introduced to her?"

A harsh laugh escaped his lips, his expression twisting into something between pain and mirth. "Indeed I have, my lady."

He raised one eyebrow at her, his eyes returning to hers with such an intensity that she was forced to draw breath.

"I should apologize, of course, for not introducing myself," he continued, making her eyes widen with surprise. "I should also apologize for not considering propriety and ensuring that someone was nearby to introduce us. However, under the circumstances, I thought..."

He trailed off, his eyes flicking away from her again, and slowly, Martha realized who this gentleman might be.

"You are Lord Weston," she breathed, her hands clenching as he looked back at her sharply.

"I am," he said firmly. "Might I also know your name?"

Her chest tightened. "Lady Martha," she replied quietly, aware of the pain that was growing steadily in his eyes. "Younger sister to Lady Edith."

He sucked in a breath as though the very name brought him pain. "Might I hope that your sister has spoken of me?"

She nodded mutely. She had not forgotten this gentleman, as she had thought, but rather had never been introduced to him before. He had been rather presumptuous in his speaking to her without having first been introduced, but since there was no one about with which to witness this—other than the gentlemen who came out of the card room on occasion—she considered that perhaps it was not too great an oversight.

"Then perhaps there is hope," he breathed, as though speaking to himself.

"Hope?" she repeated, as he drew nearer to her, his eyes still lingering over her shoulder.

He leaned down just a little, his blue eyes fixed on hers. "Yes, Lady Martha. Hope. Hope that Lady Edith has not forgotten me. Hope that she has not set herself toward another. Hope that she and I might return to the affection we once shared. And hope that—if it is required—you might be able to help me."

4

The following afternoon found Martha sitting with her sister and their old, rather decrepit companion, who never stirred out of the house, but was available to sit with them for house calls. Mrs. Steward, who was some old relative of their father's, did very little other than sleep and knit, but the Earl of Winchester did not seem to mind if his daughters went unchaperoned at balls and the like, just so long as they promised to remain in one another's company and came in search of him should there be anything untoward.

Martha's stomach twisted itself into a sharp knot as she looked over at Edith, who was swinging one leg idly over the other, waiting for the time for morning calls to begin. It was still half an hour away at least, but it was this that brought Martha a good deal of anxiety.

"I met Lord Weston last evening," she began, aware that her time was growing short. "I believe he said he would call today."

She watched as Edith's leg stopped swinging, her entire body frozen in place.

"I do not know precisely when," Martha continued, rather

gratified to see her sister suddenly so out of sorts. "But he made it very clear that he wishes to see you, Edith."

Edith slowly sat up straight, the color gone from her cheeks. "You were introduced to Lord Weston?"

Martha shrugged, recalling how improper their introduction had been. "We spoke at length, actually." She was still quite unsure as to what Lord Weston wanted from her in regard to Edith and Lord Hobart, but she had agreed to his calling upon them both so that they might discuss the matter further, should it be required.

"Did you speak of me?"

Martha felt her lip curl with frustration, as though she was angry that her sister both expected and received the gentleman's attention, on top of all the other compliments and passing glances she received from the other gentlemen of the *ton.*

"Of course," she managed to say, as calmly as she could. "He still cares about you very much, I think."

Edith closed her eyes tightly, squeezing them together as though the thought of what she was speaking about brought her considerable physical pain.

"As I said, however," Martha continued, unhindered, "he will be calling upon us this very afternoon."

"No, no," Edith whispered, her eyes fixed on the floor as her lip quivered. "No, this cannot be so."

Frowning, Martha regarded her sister carefully. She had not expected Edith to be delighted with the prospect of Lord Weston calling, but nor had she expected her to appear so fraught.

"Lord Hobart is to call also," Edith explained, her voice a little shaky. "They cannot meet."

Shaking her head, Martha let out a long breath. "Whatever do you mean, Edith? Of course they can meet. Lord Weston saw you dancing with Lord Hobart last evening, so I do not think he will be surprised to see him calling on you this morning."

Edith shook her head firmly, her fingers tightening on the arm of the chair as she gazed desperately at Martha.

"No, you cannot allow this," she exclaimed hurriedly. "Should Lord Weston arrive at the same time as Lord Hobart—or if it should be the other way around—then you must take Lord Weston for a walk in the garden. Or in the park. It is bigger than our small gardens here."

Martha refused at once. "Indeed, I will not. You need to be honest with Lord Weston, if you do not intend to allow his court."

Now looking almost frantic with worry, Edith got to her feet, rushed toward Martha, and took her hand, sinking down in a flurry of skirts beside her. "You must help me."

Closing her eyes, Martha let out a long sigh. "What is it that you want me to do for you, Edith?" she said, cynicism lying on her words. "If you wish me to tell Lord Weston about your change of heart, then I am afraid that I cannot oblige you."

"No, that is not it at all," Edith said, her fingers tightening on Martha's. "I simply wish you to take Lord Weston away from me for a time. I need to think."

This made Martha frown. "To think?" she repeated slowly. "Think about what, Edith?"

"About Lord Weston," Edith hissed, her fingers digging into Martha's soft palm. "Is that not what you wanted me to do, Martha?"

Martha's disquiet grew. "It is," she said slowly, her eyes raking over her sister's tormented features. "But I will not help you in playing Lord Weston for a fool, Edith. Not if you have every intention of allowing Lord Hobart to court you."

Edith shook her head, swallowing hard. "I do not know what I wish, Martha. Lord Hobart has not yet asked to court me, although I pray that he will, and if he does not–"

"Then you have Lord Weston to turn to," Martha replied, groaning. "Edith, this is utterly foolish."

"But you do not like Lord Hobart!" Edith exclaimed, her eyes wide. "You have told me you do not trust him."

This was a truth Martha could not ignore. "I am disinclined toward him, yes," she said slowly, her stomach tightening. "I find that he is neither here nor there with you. He has not yet asked to court you, although he appears to be very solicitous toward you in other ways. It also concerns me that you have not yet gotten to know his true character, and we know nothing of his background other than the fact he is a viscount with an estate in Cheshire." She shook her head as Edith nodded fervently, as though urging her to help her. "But that does not mean, Edith, that I think it fair of you to treat Lord Weston in such a way."

Edith made to say something more, only for there to come the sound of footsteps, which forced her to her feet, rushing back over to her chair as the knock on the door sounded.

Mrs. Stewart jumped in her chair, startling herself from her doze.

"Lord Weston, my lady," the butler intoned, as he handed Edith the gentleman's card. "He has come to call a little early, he says, and apologizes if you are not prepared for him."

Martha, who had known that this was Lord Weston's intention so that he would be able to converse with Edith without interruption, gave the butler a wide smile, ignoring the quaking in her heart. Lord Weston had asked her for her help last evening. He had asked her to ensure that her sister was at home so that he might call on her a little before the correct time so as to speak to her quietly. For whatever reason, Martha had agreed. However, now that she saw her sister's wretched face, Martha wondered if she had done the right thing. This was already such a convoluted mess, and she was directly in the middle of it.

"As you can see, we are quite prepared," she said calmly, as

Edith stared back at her, white-faced. "Might you send for a fresh tea tray also?"

The butler nodded. "But of course, my lady."

He excused himself, giving both Martha and Edith a few moments to prepare themselves.

"Why did you say such a thing?" Edith hissed, smoothing her skirts. "We might have pretended not to be ready, and then we could have sent him away."

Martha rolled her eyes, folding her hands in her lap. "Only for him to call again, perhaps at a less appropriate time? Do stop fussing, Edith. You knew you would have to see him again at some point, did you not?"

There was not time to say more, for the door then opened once more and Lord Weston strode in.

He was even more imposing than last evening. Martha rose to her feet and held her chin high, aware that, as he was bowing towards her, his eyes were already trailing toward Edith.

"Good afternoon, Lady Martha, Lady Edith," he said in a low voice. "How good it is to see you both again. Thank you for allowing me to call on you a little early."

"Of course," Martha murmured, taking her seat. "Please, do sit down." She quickly introduced Mrs. Stewart, who, after greeting them both, picked up her knitting and moved to the corner of the room, allowing them to speak freely. Martha glanced at Edith, who, as yet, had not quite managed to meet Lord Weston's gaze and appeared relieved when the tea tray arrived. At least now she could focus her attention on pouring the tea instead of having to converse with Lord Weston.

Lord Weston, however, appeared not to notice Edith's lack of willingness to converse, and he began to ask her question after question whilst she poured out three cups of tea.

"It is good to see you again, Lady Edith," he began, as Martha sat back in her chair, aware that she was not required at this present moment. "Might I inquire as to your health? And the health of your father? I presume he is here also, although I have not had the pleasure of being reacquainted with him as yet. You recall, do you not, that I was introduced to him before? He did appear quite pleased with our association, and I do hope he will continue to be as pleased with it again."

Edith flushed. "I am quite well, Lord Weston, I-I thank you," she stammered, clearly a little flustered. "And you have met my sister, I believe?"

Lord Weston did nothing more than throw Martha a quick glance, no smile on his face. "Yes," he said quietly. "We have met."

"Good," Edith stammered, looking at Martha desperately. "I know that Martha is very keen to take the air this afternoon and was hoping for a short walk in the sunshine. I would have accompanied her, of course, but I am rather tired after all my dancing last evening. Martha is less so, of course, given that she did not dance as much as I did."

It was now Martha's turn to blush, and she looked back at her sister with a slightly narrowed gaze, feeling heat creep up her neck.

"Is that so?" Lord Weston murmured, not taking his attention away from Lady Edith for a moment. "Then I do hope you can find someone to walk with you, Lady Martha, for it is a very pleasant afternoon."

The slight was noticeable, but Martha pushed her twinge of pain aside, looking back at Edith with one raised eyebrow. She had expected Lord Weston to send all of his attention towards Edith, of course, even though she could not pretend to be feeling anything other than pain at his refusal to walk with her.

You are being ridiculous, she told herself, despite the jealousy that rose within her at the thought of her sister being courted by two very eligible gentlemen. *You know that he is deeply in love with Edith. Why should you expect anything else?*

Some minutes passed. Martha sat quietly and drank her tea whilst Lord Weston and Edith conversed, although Edith's replies were stilted and lacked any kind of tone. It was clear to Martha that she was more than anxious, particularly when Lord Weston showed no sign of leaving. In fact, he was staying longer than the appropriate time for a morning call.

"Now," Lord Weston continued clearly, his voice firm. "I hope that I might be able to call on your father soon, Lady Edith, in order to request his permission to court you. What say you to that?"

Edith's eyes widened, her mouth opening and closing whilst no sound came out.

"I have not forgotten what I said to you, Lady Edith," Lord Weston continued, a little more gently. "The feelings that stole my heart the first day we met have lingered. I cannot tell you how glad I am to be in your company once more."

Edith licked her lips, looking helplessly at Martha, who gave an infinitesimal shrug.

"Lord Weston, you are very kind, but I am afraid that I have a few gentlemen seeking to court me," Edith said through trembling lips. "It is not that I have forgotten you, of course, but rather than I must simply think carefully about my future."

Lord Weston did not look in the least bit surprised, which was exactly as Martha had expected, given their conversation last evening. Lord Weston had watched Edith from afar. He had seen her dancing with Lord Hobart and saw how she had laughed and smiled into his eyes. There was nothing hidden from him, despite what Edith might think.

"I see," Lord Weston murmured, glancing over at Martha. "Then can I hope that you might allow me to be in your company at times, that I might be allowed to dance with you and call upon you on occasion until you have made up your mind?" There was something steely in his gaze that made Martha flinch as he glanced back at her, aware that Lord Weston was not about to give up his claim to her sister easily.

"I think that would be more than acceptable," Edith replied, her fingers knotting together in her lap.

"You will continue to consider me then?"

"I will."

There was a short silence, and Martha felt the tension rising in the room.

"You will find me there, waiting for you, once all the other gentlemen you are considering have fallen to the wayside," Lord Weston murmured, sending a prickle of heat down Martha's spine at the intimate way he was speaking to Edith.

Edith swallowed once, twice, and then gave him a small smile, clearly a little lost as to what to say

"Very good," Lord Weston said a little more briskly, rising to his feet. "Now, Lady Martha, do you still wish to take the air? I find now that I am quite enamored with the idea."

She blinked in surprise, a little taken aback at his brusque request. She had not had any intention of going for a walk, but —thanks to Edith's suggestion—she found that she was now rising to her feet.

"Thank you, Lord Weston," she replied, walking to the door. "If you would but give me a few minutes to change, then I would be glad to join you." She placed her hand on the door handle, only for it to turn beneath her fingers. Stepping back, she saw none other than Lord Hobart coming into the room, just behind the butler, and heard Edith's gasp of either surprise or horror.

She did not linger but hurried past him, making her way to her bedchamber to change into a walking dress, all the while wondering what Lord Weston wanted to talk to her about now.

5

"Lady Martha."

Edmund cleared his throat, not quite sure what to say next. He had been so filled with purpose as he had walked from the drawing room, ignoring Lord Hobart entirely, but now that he was outside in the fresh air with Lady Martha by his side, that purpose had disappeared entirely.

"Yes, Lord Weston?"

Her voice was calm and quiet, yet filled with a gentleness that soothed his tormented soul.

"Thank you for your help," he muttered, his eyes dropping to the ground. "It was good to speak to Lady Edith again."

Lady Martha's expression softened. "I am sorry, Lord Weston."

He chuckled, despite the pain tearing through him. "You need not be sorry, Lady Martha. I have every intention of winning your sister."

Her brows rose. "Oh?"

A small sigh escaped him as he nodded. "I think I can recapture her heart, Lady Martha." His brows rose as he looked at her, taking in her wry expression. "You do not think so?"

A deep red settled in her cheeks as she turned her face away from him. "Do excuse me, Lord Weston. I did not mean to imply anything of the sort."

"No?"

There was a long, pronounced silence, broken only by the sound of the carriages driving past them. Edmund felt his stomach tighten as she hesitated, aware that she knew Lady Edith better than he.

"Lord Weston, do you wish me to be entirely honest with you?"

She stopped dead and turned to face him, stepping out of the way of the other passersby. Edmund was forced to look down at her steadily, his eyes fixed on her own. He was surprised by the beauty of them, even though they were nothing like the deep, glittering depths of Lady Edith's green eyes. There was a softness there that Lady Edith did not possess, a steadiness that told him she would always speak the truth.

"Yes," he said slowly, his eyebrows knotting together. "Please, speak the truth, Lady Martha. I wish to know exactly what you think."

She drew in a breath, her lips flattening. "Then I shall speak to you so, Lord Weston. My sister, Lady Edith, has not spoken of you to me until this week."

His stomach dropped to his toes. "This week?" he repeated hoarsely. "But we have been writing for some time."

"I am aware of that," Lady Edith replied calmly. "However, this may be because we are not particularly close as sisters, although I would have thought..." She trailed off, shaking her head as her brown curls bounced around her face, held tightly down by her bonnet. "Regardless, Lord Weston, I find that my sister has no true inclination for any particular gentleman, although she may believe that she does. The depths you speak of are not contained in my sister's heart. At least, not yet." She shrugged, unaware of the agony that was burning through him. "That is not to say that she cannot return your affection with the same passion you feel, but rather that it may, perhaps, take a little more time than you were anticipating."

"I see," Edmund heard himself say, his limbs going rather numb as he remained entirely motionless. "And I suppose I must fight my way through the likes of Lord Hobart, is that what you are suggesting?"

Lady Martha colored, her eyes darting away. "Lord Hobart is a gentleman who has shown my sister some attention of late, but it has only been a very recent acquaintance," she said quietly. "He has not yet asked to court her."

"And yet he is very attentive, it seems," Edmund muttered, half to himself. "I saw them out walking on my return to London."

Surprise registered on her face, and for the first time, Edmund noticed just how beautifully curved the lady's mouth was. Shaking the thought from his head, he cleared his throat and turned away.

"It has only been a short time, as I said," Lady Martha repeated. "And I myself will admit to being a little unsure of his intentions."

That brought Edmund some astonishment. "Is that so?" he asked quietly, as they began to walk again. "And why is that, might I ask?"

Her expression grew dark, although confusion shone in her eyes. "I cannot say, Lord Weston, for certain, for I have not often been in his acquaintance. However, what I will state is that I find it quite peculiar for a gentleman to show interest in a particular young lady without making it clear what his intentions are. He has called on her today, of course, but that is the first time he has done so. There has been no talk of courting her, although his interest does appear to be quite fixed on her regardless." She bit her lip, her eyes darting towards him for a moment. "I suppose I can best explain it by stating that I find his behavior a little odd, Lord Weston, that is all. I am well aware that it is no reason at all not to like someone, so you must, of course, find me quite ridiculous." Her laugh startled him, and—to his surprise—Edmund found his lips curving in response.

"No, indeed, Lady Martha," he replied gruffly. "You are not ridiculous in the least. Intuition is a wonderful thing and ought to be listened to most attentively, I think."

She smiled at him then, and Edmund found his heart lifting.

"Might you then be persuaded to consider helping me further?"

Her smile faded away almost at once, and Edmund, for a moment, thought to retract his words, only to remind himself that he had every intention of securing Lady Edith's hand no matter what was required.

"You still wish to pursue Edith, of course," Lady Martha replied, her voice a little flat. "What is it you require of me, Lord Weston?"

Pressing his lips together for a moment, Edmund tried to think clearly. "You do not like Lord Hobart and do not think him a wise choice for your sister, for whatever reason. Whereas, I must hope I have a better standing in your eyes."

Lady Martha nodded slowly. "Yes, that is true," she agreed, her eyes darting up to his for just a moment.

"Then might you assist me in trying to capture your sister's heart?" he asked, wondering why he felt so ill at ease asking her such a thing.

Again came the hesitation. "What is it that will be required of me, Lord Weston?"

This was not something he had really thought much about,

having talked himself into believing that he would have to do nothing more than turn up at Lord Winchester's home and claim Lady Edith for himself.

"You will wish to be in her company just as often as you can, I suppose," she continued quietly. "Does this mean that you require me to be present with you, so that this might occur?"

It was a good idea, and Edmund found himself nodding. "A capital idea, Lady Martha. Yes, that would be wise. In fact, it may even arouse her jealousy, which might be all the better!"

There was no smile on her face as she looked back at him, and—to his surprise—he saw something like sadness in her gaze. "Then you will have to call on me quite regularly, Lord Weston."

He cleared his throat, aware of what she was saying. "Yes, I suppose I will," he replied carefully. "And we shall have to dance often as well, so that I might secure a dance or two with Lady Edith also." Growing even more uneasy, he looked at her steadily, suddenly feeling his heart twisting with guilt. "You need not agree to this, Lady Martha. I can understand if you do not wish to take on this responsibility, only to be set aside when Lady Edith and I..." He trailed off, realizing just how awful a position he was putting her in.

By asking her to assist him in pursuing Lady Edith, Lady Martha would have to often be in his company, to the point that the *beau monde* would question whether they were courting. However, should he be successful in his pursuit of Lady Edith, then Lady Martha would be set aside whilst he continued on with her sister. She would be left entirely alone, supposedly disgraced in the eyes of the *ton*.

"I do have one or two very good friends that I might introduce you to," he said, hopelessly, feeling the foolish words leave his mouth without intending them to. "Mayhap, at the end of all this, I can assist you in finding yourself a suitable match. I do not want to disgrace you, Lady Martha."

A harsh laugh ripped from her lips, startling him.

"Lord Weston, you are much too kind," she said bleakly. "You need not worry about me in any way. The *ton* do not take much notice of plain Lady Martha, not when her sister, Lady Edith, is a diamond of the first water!" She shook her head, her bonnet ribbons flying. "I shall do whatever I can to help you, Lord Weston, even if it means I remain just as I am now. As much as my sister frustrates me, as much as I grow angry with her for her foolishness, I cannot help but love her. She means a great deal to me, and I do so wish her to be happy and content in this life. I am not certain that Lord Hobart is the correct gentleman for her." One eyebrow began to lift as she looked up at him steadily, their pace slowing. "Then again, given that I know very little of you also, Lord Weston, I cannot say for certain that you will be any better than Lord Hobart, but I suppose I must hope for the best."

A wry smile touched her lips but the heaviness in Edmund's heart refused to allow him to smile back at her in response.

"In fact, I may find that this time with you will bring a little happiness to my life," she finished, her voice dropping to such quietness that he struggled to hear her. "And mayhap it will allow me to stop worrying so much about my dear, stupid sister."

He did not quite understand her vehemence, thinking that Lady Edith was the most wonderful of creatures, who had simply had her head turned by another gentleman during his prolonged absence. He could not blame her for that, of course, feeling quite certain that once they became reacquainted, everything would return to as it had been then.

"Thank you, Lady Martha," he said haltingly, offering her his arm. "I suppose we had best start as we mean to go on."

She looked at him for a moment, taking in his proffered arm before looping her hand through it, her cheeks a dull red.

Edmund felt a shiver of pleasure at her gentle touch, which he put down entirely to feeling quite delighted at the prospect of securing Lady Edith's affections once more.

"My sister tells me that you have been away for some time, Lord Weston," Lady Martha said, as they began to walk back towards Lord Winchester's townhouse. "Were you busy on your estate?"

He shook his head. "My father was gravely ill for a time, Lady Martha, and so I was forced to take ownership of all of my father's responsibilities."

"My goodness," she breathed, her expression a little astonished. "And has he recovered?"

He smiled at her, glad that she seemed to show such consideration. "He has, Lady Martha, I thank you."

"It can be a very trying time, caring for one's parent," she responded, with a good deal of feeling. "It can bring such pain and anxiety, can it not?"

She spoke with such understanding that, for a moment, Edmund was unable to find something to say. Lady Edith had never said anything about her father or mother being unwell when they had first met.

"You can understand what it is like then?" he asked curiously.

Nodding, Lady Martha gave him a half smile. "My mother was very ill some time ago," she said quietly, her expression a little sad. "Thankfully, she has recovered."

He blinked, a little confused as to why Lady Edith had never said as much.

"This is why I did not have the opportunity to meet you in London at the start of last Season," she explained quietly.

"Although I understand you were only in town for a very short while."

"A very short while," he agreed, wanting to get back to the subject of her mother. "But you say your mother was unwell? And you were there to tend her?"

Lady Martha nodded. "Of course."

"But what of Lady Edith?"

There was a short pause. "Lady Edith had her come out, which could not be put off."

Something began to churn in his stomach. Something uncomfortable, something that brought a weighty cloud of confusion to his mind.

"I had my come out also, but as Edith is the eldest, she deserves the grander occasion," Lady Martha continued, no inflection in her voice. "Besides which, I was very glad to be with Mama. It was good to be with her as she recovered."

"That must have been a very trying time for you," he murmured, sympathy rising in his heart. "To be without sister and father?"

It was as though a mask had come over her face, for her expression tightened, her eyes turned away from his and her lips grew thin.

"Indeed," she muttered, the light gone from her face. "But all is well now, and that is all that concerns me."

He did not know if it had been something he had said that had brought such a look to her face, but now feeling quite at a loss as to what to say, he could only clear his throat and walk in silence for a few minutes.

"Ah, here we are," he murmured, as the townhouse came into view. "Shall I call on you again tomorrow, Lady Martha?"

She let go of his arm and nodded, her hands clasped in front of her. "Thank you, Lord Weston, that would be very kind."

"And you are to attend Lord Fairley's ball tomorrow evening, I hope?"

Again, the jerky nod.

"Then I look forward to dancing with you there, Lady Martha," he replied, growing more and more confused as to her lack of response. "Good afternoon."

"Good afternoon, Lord Weston," she replied, before turning her back on him and ascending the steps towards the front door.

6

"My dear Lady Martha, how good to see you this evening."

Martha flushed as Lord Weston bowed over her hand, his lips gently pressing to the back of her glove.

"Th--Thank you," she stammered, not quite certain how to respond. "I am glad to see you also, my lord."

He smiled at her, his light blue eyes warm, and for a moment, Martha felt herself transfixed.

"Good evening, Lord Weston."

Edith's high-pitched voice broke the delicate atmosphere that had surrounded Martha and Lord Weston, shattering it completely. He cleared his throat and turned towards her, his eyes warming all the more – and Martha felt a flush of shame rush into her cheeks.

"Good evening, Lady Edith," he murmured, taking her hand and bowing over it. "May I say how wonderful you look this evening."

She beamed at him, her eyes brighter than Martha's could ever be. "You are quite dashing too, of course, Lord Weston," she replied, whilst Martha felt her heart sinking towards her toes. "You will dance with me, will you not?"

Lord Weston chuckled. "Of course, Lady Edith, but first, I must inquire as to whether or not Lady Martha has any spaces on her dance card that I might obtain."

Martha looked up sharply, just in time to see Edith's stunned expression as Lord Weston turned away from her, rejecting her advance for a moment.

"Do you have any spaces for me, Lady Martha?" Lord Weston inquired, looking all the more handsome as he smiled down at her, reaching for her dance card that dangled from its silk ribbon. "I was hoping for a waltz."

"A Waltz?" Martha replied, her voice a little breathy as she attempted to hand her dance card to him. "Yes, Lord Weston, I believe I have a waltz remaining."

An expression of delight crossed his face as he reached for her card, running his eyes down it. "Wonderful," he exclaimed, sounding truly glad. "I shall take the waltz and then the supper dance, if I may? I would be glad to sit with you then."

Despite knowing that this was all for show, despite knowing that there was nothing true in his expressions of joy, Martha felt herself grow warm with delight and happiness.

"Of course, Lord Weston," she managed to say, all the more aware of her sister's stunned expression. "I would be glad of your company."

Lord Weston's eyes grabbed her own for a moment, before he returned to Lady Edith, requesting her own dance card. He then signed for the quadrille and the cotillion, which were none too personal compared to the waltz and supper dance.

"Thank you, Lord Weston," Edith murmured, as he inclined his head. "I look forward to our dances."

He took his leave of them then, throwing one last lingering look over his shoulder towards Martha, which she returned with a small smile. The man was doing his level best to ensure that Edith *was* jealous of the attention he was showering on Martha, whilst also making sure to spend time with her. It appeared to be working, given just how astonished Edith appeared to be.

"My goodness, Martha," Edith murmured, grasping Martha's arm with a tight hand. "Is Lord Weston enamored with you?"

Martha shrugged off her sister's hand, trying her best to keep her movements slight so that none of the other guests would see. "I do not know what you are talking about, Edith. He is a kind man, and that is all. I am glad to have some dances with him."

Edith frowned, her brows furrowing together as her sharp green eyes bored back into Martha.

"Ah, and there is Lord Hobart," Martha said, managing to turn away from her sister altogether. "I am sure you will be quite glad to have his attention for a few minutes, and even more delighted that you have a waltz free for him."

Edith could not say anything in response, being forced to turn towards Lord Hobart as he came toward them, smiling broadly. Martha, however, was able to make her escape, aware of the dissatisfaction that was racing through her. She did not want to be Lord Weston's plaything, but despite how irritating she found her sister, and despite how furiously angry she could make her at times, the love she had for her overcame all of that. Lord Weston would surely be better for Edith than Lord Hobart, who—even after a week of meeting and conversing—was still yet to show any kind of firm attachment towards Edith.

And yet, deep within her, Martha knew that she was quite pleased with the attention Lord Weston was showing her. It made her feel as though she were Edith's equal, as though she were just as good as her sister. She knew full well that it was all a guise, all a pretense, but still, it warmed her heart when she knew it should not. The thought of dancing in Lord Weston's arms brought her both anxiety and excited anticipation, making her pray that she would not forget a single step. And then to have the supper dance with him, to be seated by him and be caught up in conversation would be more than wonderful. In fact, Martha was sure that this would be an occasion that she would thoroughly enjoy.

"I believe it is our dance, Lady Martha."

"Already?"

She turned to see Lord Weston looking down at her, offering her his arm.

"Indeed," he chuckled, as she took it carefully. "You must have been truly looking forward to it if the time has gone so quickly."

Swallowing her nerves, Martha stepped forward towards the middle of the ballroom, her stomach tightening with sudden anxiety.

"Have no fear, Lady Martha," Lord Weston said quietly, as though he could read her thoughts. "I am sure you will be a beautiful dancer, and I can assure you that I will not stand on your toes even once."

She laughed, the tension running out from her. "I am relieved to hear it, Lord Weston. I presume you must have had a good deal of practice."

Chuckling, he took her in his arms, and at that moment, Martha felt as though she were lost in a dream. Heat climbed up her spine and into her cheeks as she waited for the orchestra to commence, only just catching the astonished look on Edith's face as she drew near to Lord Weston and Martha with her own partner. Martha sent her sister a smile, which was not returned, but she did not particularly care. This was a wonderful moment in itself, and she was not about to let Edith's displeasure spoil that for her.

The music began, and within seconds, she was twirling

around the floor, her feet doing exactly as they ought without a single thought. Lord Weston guided her around the floor with practiced expertise. To Martha, it felt as though they were the only two people in the world. She forgot about Edith; she forgot that Lord Weston was simply doing all of this in order to provoke Edith's jealousy; she forgot that she was not meant to feel a single thing for this gentleman who held her so carefully.

It was wonderful.

THE NEXT FORTNIGHT felt to Martha as though she were being tossed and turned in all directions, lost in a haze of confusion over Lord Weston's attentiveness towards her. Suddenly, she found herself the center of attention, as gentlemen she had never set eyes on before began to seek her out for a dance, and this was all because Lord Weston had deigned himself to dance with her in the first place. Martha was not quite certain that she appreciated this, however, finding the flattery and the compliments she began to receive a little overwhelming, given that she was entirely unused to receiving such kind words. She did not know what to think or to say whenever a gentleman complimented her on the beauty of her eyes, or her delicate footwork. She usually only managed to mumble a "thank you" before flushing furiously.

And all the while, Lord Weston continued to be attentive. He would make sure he had a waltz with her at whatever ball they attended, ensured that he sat by her were she to play a game of cards, called upon her to take tea, and even suggested a carriage ride now and again, which, of course, Edith had to attend also, for the considerations of propriety. It was quite obvious to Martha, of course, that Edith was still rather unsure as to how to proceed with Lord Weston, but as the days passed, that became a little less pronounced. Sighing to herself, Martha looked back at her reflection in the mirror, wondering just how long it would take for her sister to turn away from Lord Hobart and to again look at Lord Weston with fresh eyes. Both gentlemen were often in Edith's company, but still, she would always give the majority of her attention to Lord Hobart, who appeared to hang onto her every word. It confused and frustrated Martha that Lord Hobart had not yet sought to court Edith. She still could not quite understand why Edith herself appeared to be quite at ease with his lack of firm intention toward her.

"Martha?"

Dragged from her thoughts, Martha looked into the mirror's reflection to see Edith hurry into Martha's bedchamber without so much as knocking, her eyes a little bright.

"Yes, Edith?" Martha swallowed her annoyance as the maid finished the final touches to her hair for this evening's musical soiree, which was, by all accounts, to be a rather wonderful occasion.

"What gown are you to wear this evening?"

Frowning, Martha glanced back at her sister, much to the frustration of the maid.

"Why ever does that matter? You have never cared before."

Edith shrugged. "I just want to ensure that we do not clash."

Martha hesitated, still a little unsure of her sister's motives. "I thought to wear my emerald silk," she said slowly, as her sister frowned. "It is one of my best, and I want to ensure that I look..." She trailed off, a little unsure as to what she was trying to say.

"You want to look your best for Lord Weston," Edith finished, a little tartly. "Yes, I am well aware that he has been rather attentive to you of late."

Martha shrugged, her cheeks flushing. "He is a very kind gentleman."

The maid stepped back, letting Martha survey her newest

creation, which she immediately turned to thank the maid for. Her hair had been piled up in a tumble of curls on the top of her head, with seed pearls and ribbons dotted through them. A few tendrils hung around her temples, so as not to give off a sharp appearance. All in all, Martha considered that she looked rather well.

"Shall I ready your gown, my lady?"

One eyebrow rose as Martha turned to her sister. "Will my emerald green gown do, Edith?"

Edith waved the question away, biting her bottom lip.

"Yes, please," Martha replied, turning back to the maid. "I will be in the dressing room in a moment."

Turning back to her sister, Martha took a few steps closer and narrowed her eyes, not believing Edith's sad façade for a moment.

"What is it that troubles you, Edith?" she asked firmly. "Is it the fact that you truly do not wish me to wear a particular shade, or is it that you dislike that Lord Weston has given me his attention?"

Edith's face grew hot, her expression indignant. "I care very little what Lord Weston does or thinks," she said angrily.

"Is that so?" Martha replied quietly, unable to prevent herself from questioning her sister further. "Then why do you care so very much about what gown I am wearing and whether or not you might be in my shadow somewhat when it comes to Lord Weston?"

Martha kept her gaze steady, despite the furious trembling that was beginning to shake her soul. Edith continued to run between Lord Hobart and Lord Weston, although she certainly was more inclined towards the former, and for whatever reason, it was beginning to burden Martha's soul and niggle her with increasing annoyance.

Edith's face turned red, although whether it was from anger

or embarrassment, Martha could not say. "You forget, Martha, that he has danced with me, he has walked with me, he had conversed with me just as much as he has with you."

Ice poured into Martha's veins as she battled against a sudden, furious anger. Lord Weston had done what Edith had stated, but certainly to a lesser extent. Had he not? Why Edith should care so much as to speak so callously was quite beyond her, especially when...

Martha closed her eyes. Especially when she was meant to be helping her sister to turn away from Lord Hobart and back to Lord Weston.

This is what you are meant to be doing, Martha, she reminded herself. *You are meant to be encouraging your sister towards Lord Weston.*

Drawing in a long breath, she opened her eyes and saw Edith considering her carefully.

"And what of Lord Hobart?" she asked gently, pressing her sister. "Do you still consider him?"

Edith's eyes flashed. "Lord Hobart is a wonderful gentleman."

"And has he asked Father for permission to court you yet?"

Martha let her words float through the room, bringing a spark of anger to Edith's cheeks. Martha had not meant to irritate Edith further but, in questioning her so, was bringing to mind the fact that Lord Hobart had not attempted to court her in any way whatsoever. He was obviously interested in Edith but —for whatever reason—had failed to make his intentions clear.

"I have every certainty that Lord Hobart will be speaking to Father any day now," Edith said shrilly, her voice flooding the room. "You need not concern yourself in that regard, Martha."

Sighing inwardly, Martha stepped forward to take Edith's hands, only for her sister to step back out of reach.

"I do not mean to anger you, my dear sister," Martha said

carefully, dampening down her own growing frustration. "But I only intend to make you question Lord Hobart's intentions, given that he appears to, as yet, have none whatsoever. Why would you turn to him when a gentleman like Lord Weston is willing to court you?"

Edith blinked, her shoulders slumping as she looked back at Martha. It was as though confusion had begun to rattle through her, making her anger fade away.

"I do not care for Lord Weston," Edith said slowly.

"Do you not?" Martha asked, arching one eyebrow. "You were supposedly deeply in love with him, promising to wait until he returned to London so that he might claim you again." She gave a half shrug as Edith increasingly irritated. "I am simply concerned, Edith, that you are losing your senses when it comes to Lord Hobart, for whatever reason. The man only has to smile at you and you are lost. And he has not yet shown you any true considerations whilst allowing you to believe that he is still fond of you."

To her horror, Edith crumpled right before her eyes. Her normally tall stature slumped, her forehead wrinkling, as she battled the tears that had sprung into her eyes.

"Edith!" Martha exclaimed, darting forward. "Edith, I did not mean–"

"Do excuse me," Edith replied smartly, turning towards the door. "I must go and dress."

"Edith," Martha said again, but it was much too late. Her back now as stiff as a board, Edith stepped out of the room and closed the door behind her with a thud.

7

Edmund caught himself as he looked at the door for what was the twelfth time in a row, realizing that he was growing almost desperate for Lady Martha's arrival.

His gut tightened as he turned his head away, doing his best to appear nonchalant.

I am waiting for the arrival of Lady Edith, he reminded himself, flushing. *Not Lady Martha.*

Clearing his throat, he reached for a glass of champagne from one of the trays that the footmen held, taking a long sip and forcing his eyes to keep away from the door to the drawing room. Lord Arbuckle had invited a few esteemed guests for dinner, and the Earl of Winchester and his two daughters were both on the guest list. Also invited was Lord Hobart, which Edmund considered to be both irritating and rather interesting, for the gentleman would be in the Earl of Winchester's presence and therefore able to speak to him openly about his intentions towards Lady Edith, should he wish to do so.

Over the last fortnight, Edmund had come to realize just why Lady Martha felt so uneasy over the gentleman. He had not done a single thing to encourage his growing association with Lady Edith. He would have expected a man who was clearly interested in a young lady such as Lady Edith to have declared himself by now, but Lord Hobart seemed quite content with remaining just as he was—talking with, dancing with, and taking tea with Lady Edith, but not doing anything more. Edmund had been in Lord Hobart's company on occasion and had found the gentleman to be singularly dull in both conversation and spirit, which meant that he could not see what it was that Lady Edith found so delightful about the man.

It was all very frustrating.

"Lord Hobart, did you say?"

Clearing his throat and aware that heat was climbing into his face, Edmund turned around to see a gentleman he vaguely recognized standing by his side.

"Did I speak aloud?" Edmund asked, trying to recall this gentleman's name. "I was only thinking that Lord Hobart and Lady Edith–"

"Ah, yes!" the gentleman interrupted, a wide smile on his cheery face that hid his weak chin. "There has been much suggested about them both, but it seems that Lord Hobart has not claimed her, has he? There is hope for you yet, Lord Weston, although I *had* heard that you were courting Lady Martha...?" He trailed off, his question left hanging, and Edmund felt himself bristle. He did not wish to speak of matters of the heart to any gentleman, particularly one he did not quite remember.

"Lady Martha and I are acquainted," he said firmly. "That is all, Lord...?"

"Masters," the gentleman replied cheerfully. "No need to get upset. I have no intention of prying."

"Then might you be able to tell me what you know of Lord Hobart?" Edmund asked, taking hold of the opportunity. "Do you know him at all?"

Lord Masters shrugged. "Very little. He is a gentleman who is fairly quiet, by all accounts, although quite wealthy I am sure. He does not frequent White's, I believe, although you may be able to find out more about him from those who meet there." He grinned, a chuckle escaping him. "A mysterious viscount, with wealth and status," Lord Masters finished, his eyes twinkling.

It frustrated Edmund that he was not able to find out any more about Lord Hobart, and even more so that there were no rumors or the like which he could use against the gentleman in his pursuit of Lady Edith.

"I suppose I shall have to return to White's then," he muttered to himself, passing one hand over his eyes as he fought off his frustration. "Thank you, Lord Masters."

Lord Masters chuckled. "Trying to make your mind up between Lady Edith and Lady Martha, are you?" he grinned, stepping away. "Might I suggest the latter, Lord Weston? I hear the former is somewhat flighty with her affections."

Before Edmund could retort that Lady Edith was certainly in no way unreliable, and that it was simply that she had her head turned by whatever nonsense Lord Hobart was filling her ears with, Lord Masters stepped away, leaving him even more irritated than before.

"Flighty," he repeated to himself, throwing back the rest of his champagne and sitting his empty glass back onto another tray. "What rot."

And then, to his horror, something began to cloud his mind. Something began to sit uneasily within him, something that spiraled downwards into doubt and uncertainty.

Something that forced him to question whether or not what Lord Masters had said about Lady Edith might, in fact, be quite true.

Swallowing hard, Edmund closed his eyes and tried to throw

such thoughts away, refusing to give them weight, but still, they persisted. After all, had she not fallen in love with him rather quickly, professing that she would wait for him whilst he was called away to look after his dear father – only for her letters to become less and less frequent, her words of hope and love beginning to die out? He had put it down to her struggling with his absence, told himself that all would be aright once he returned to London, but that had not been the case. And yet he was still caught up with nothing but thoughts of her, determined to have her affections returned to him again. Could there be the possibility that she was "flighty", as Lord Masters had put it?

A sudden thought turned him cold. Had there been other gentlemen she had been caught up with during his absence? Or was Lord Hobart the first?

"I must ask Martha," he muttered, unaware that he had just referred to her by her Christian name. "She will know."

It was but half an hour later that Lady Martha entered the room, alongside her sister and their father, the Earl of Winchester. The earl was not an impressive man, being short in stature and rather round, but the way he looked about him with a sharp and somewhat demeaning gaze gave him a little more clout. He had grey and white hair, sharp green eyes, and a rather frayed mustache, which did nothing for his overall appearance. This, however, did not interest Edmund in any way, for his attention was immediately drawn to Lady Martha.

She was dressed in a light-colored silk gown, but it was not the cut of the dress that caught his eye. Instead, it was the way her eyes searched the room, the way her cheeks were lightly dusted with pink as she looked out amongst the crowd. Her hair glowed bronze in the candlelight, curls sweeping around her temples whilst the rest was only just held back from her face. She was, in fact, quite stunning.

Edmund's breath caught as Lady Martha's eyes landed on his, finding her quarry. He could not help but smile at her, seeing the way her lips curved upwards in response before she let her gaze fall away. He had forgotten about everything else entirely and was lost in the warmth of her gaze to the point that even the hubbub of conversation around him seemed to fade.

"Lord Weston."

She curtsied, and he bowed at once, aware that heat was now rippling up his spine and into his face.

"May I say how lovely you look this evening, Lady Martha," he murmured, truly meaning every word. "I will be glad to be in your company this evening."

To his surprise, she blushed and looked away, although her lips still curved into a gentle smile.

"I believe we are to sit next to one another at dinner, my lord," she replied, making his heart leap for some inexplicable reason. "Our host and hostess are aware of all that has been going on, it seems."

He did not feel any dismay or frustration at this, finding that he was truly delighted to be sitting with so lovely a lady. Edmund knew from the last two weeks that he would have good conversation from Lady Martha and that she would be able to talk with insight and wit, which was something he had come to greatly appreciate.

"Perhaps we shall have a good deal to talk about," she murmured, nodding at something just over his shoulder. He glanced there at once, and saw the Earl of Winchester, Lady Edith, and Lord Hobart all talking together. It took a few moments for anything like dismay to pierce his heart, turning back to Lady Martha with a small, resigned smile on his face.

"Do you think he will seek to court her soon?" he asked, as

they began to walk together away from Lady Edith and Lord Hobart. "It has been almost a month and still, he has done nothing."

Lady Martha sighed and shook her head. "I do not know what to think, Lord Weston. My sister is as foolish as ever, refusing to question Lord Hobart's intentions simply because she believes herself in love with him. The truth is, I am quite sure, that she is only flattered by his attention, as fickle as they may be." A rueful smile touched her lips as she looked up at him. "She has not taken kindly to me questioning such things, however."

He bit his lip, anxiety suddenly quelling his good spirits. "I do not wish to bring enmity between you."

She smiled kindly and patted his arm. "You are very kind to say such things, Lord Weston, but you need not concern yourself. There will always be such things between Lady Edith and me, for whilst we are sisters, we are not particularly alike."

"You are a good deal more thoughtful when it comes to matters of the heart, I think," he replied without having any particular idea as to where such a thought had come from. "Is that not so?"

Again, her color mounted although the spark in her eyes grew all the more. "I confess, I have very little experience of such things, Lord Weston, but you are right to suggest that I think things through a little more carefully than Edith. That is not to say that I am better, somehow, for I know that my way of thinking can often lead to great anxiety."

"And yet I think it is better to be a careful thinker," he replied honestly. "It shows a maturity of character, I think."

There was a momentary pause where Lady Martha's expression grew a little surprised, and Edmund realized what it was she thought. In saying such a thing, he had expressed, entirely untowardly, that Lady Edith did not have a particularly mature character, and that this was not something he could truly admire. The words to take back what he had said stuck in his throat, but he found he could not say them, for they would not have been the truth.

"You appear to know my sister a good deal better than I first thought, my lord," Lady Martha murmured, as the dinner gong sounded. "It appears that I am not the only one who thinks things through with a good deal of care."

He swallowed and tried to smile, his heart sinking into his boots as he made his way toward the rest of the guests, knowing full well that what Lady Martha had just stated was not the truth. Whilst he did consider himself to be careful and thoughtful, he had not done so when it came to Lady Edith. In fact, he had fallen into such a depth of feeling that he had not even considered anything other than what emotions were wrapping themselves around him, declaring to her that he loved her after only a very brief acquaintance. His head had been filled with thoughts of matrimony, of children, and a home of his own. Now, a sense of foolishness overtook him. Had he been too quick to think of such things? Had he allowed his feelings to overrule his good sense? Or was that just the nature of love? Was it meant to run, roughshod, over all thoughts and considerations, throwing one's world entirely into disarray?

As he stood next to Lady Martha, preparing to walk her into the dining room, Edmund felt his heart twist in confusion. He had not once looked for Lady Edith. He had not considered where she might be sitting in relation to him. He had not felt a pang of jealousy on seeing Lord Hobart talking with her. He had not wished to heaven that he was in Lord Hobart's place. Instead, he had enjoyed being in Lady Martha's company. He had lost himself in the beautiful vision that she was and had found himself eager to converse with her, and now, as he seated her, he was glad that he would be beside her for most of the evening. What new feeling was this?

He sat down, guilt plundering his soul. He was betraying Lady Edith by such thoughts, and that sickened him. This was why he had engaged Lady Martha in the first place, so that he might pull Lady Edith away from Lord Hobart and back toward himself. It would do no good to allow himself thoughts about Lady Martha in Lady Edith's place.

"Are you quite all right, Lord Weston?"

Lady Martha was looking at him with gentle concern in her expression.

"You look a little pale.

Excuses flooded his mind. "Just famished," he said, a little more loudly than he intended. "That is all."

She smiled at him, her relief evident. "I see. Well, I do not think you shall have to wait much longer. It appears that dinner is just about to be served."

8

"Well?"

Martha clasped her hands together in her lap as she waited for Edith to answer her question, but her sister appeared unwilling to say even a word about Lord Hobart.

"Edith," Martha said again, a little more gently. "You know that I care about you. You need not turn away from me again. I am only doing what I can to help you."

"Stuff and nonsense!" Edith exclaimed, her eyes filled with rage. "You want nothing more but to drive Lord Hobart away from me and keep Lord Weston entirely to yourself so that I will be left as an old maid!"

Martha let out a long, slow breath as she forced herself to be patient with her sister. Ever since their altercation some nights ago, Edith had been prickly and silent, barking answers with as few words as possible whenever they spoke. There was an icy tension between them, one that Martha was eager to break.

"Did Lord Hobart speak to Father?" Martha asked again, having already done so once before. "We were together at Lord Arbuckle's dinner, and I saw him talking to Father there. I have not yet had the opportunity to ask you, since you were abed for most of the day yesterday, but truly, I am most eager to know."

Edith's eyed her balefully.

"If he has finally decided to pay you court, then I am truly very happy for you," Martha continued, hating that a pleading note had entered her voice. "I want you to be happy, Edith."

"Why?" Edith snapped, sitting forward. "Why should you care about my supposed happiness? Why not concentrate on your own life instead, Martha?"

"Because you are my sister," Martha replied firmly, "and without being harsh, you appear to be rather heedless when it comes to your heart. You gave it to Lord Weston once, only to have your feelings disappear when he had to return home. You said you would wait for him, but when Lord Hobart appeared, you quite forgot Lord Weston almost immediately." She was making Edith angry again, repeating the same truths over and over again, but it was the only way Martha could think of to make her sister see the reasons for Martha's concern. "Lord Hobart has not declared himself, Edith, and it has been a month. He comes to tea; he dances with you and makes sure to talk with you whenever he can, but he has not asked to court you! He has never asked to take you to Hyde Park for the fashionable hour and has never sought to walk with you alone. There is something in that, is there not?"

Her sister wilted into her chair.

"What is it about the gentleman that makes you long for him so?" Martha asked gently. "I cannot understand it, Edith."

Edith let out a long sigh, her anger and frustration fading from her expression. "He is a mystery, is he not?" she murmured quietly. "The truth is, Martha, he cares for me but cannot, as yet, express it."

Confusion knotted Martha's brow. "What do you mean?"

Edith shrugged. "I do not quite know. I have seen his eyes

flicker with jealousy whenever Lord Weston pays me any kind of attention, and I am pleased with that. When I spoke to him of it, he begged me to allow him a little more time to prove himself to me. Oh, Martha, he begged me with such passion that I could not refuse him!"

Martha sat forward, her fingers tightening in her lap. "But why does he require more time, Edith? What is it that he is doing?"

Again, another sigh came from Edith's lips. "I do not know, Martha. Do not press me on it, for that is the truth. I am in as much confusion as you, but I know, in my heart, I cannot turn from him yet."

Such was Martha's frustration with her sister's idiotic ways, that she felt like getting up from her chair, marching to Edith's side, and shaking her until sense returned to her mind.

"It is the mystery of it all, you see," Edith finished, rather dreamily. "I know that he will be able to court me, just as he says, very soon, once this matter of his is all cleared up."

"But that makes very little sense, Edith!" Martha exclaimed, her voice breaking the quiet that had settled over Edith for a moment. "The gentleman is telling you very little and expecting you to wait without hope or promise of his genuine affection. Why are you wasting your time on such a man?"

"Because I care for him," Edith declared stoutly. "And he cares for me."

Martha shook her head firmly. "Is it the same way that you cared for Lord Weston, Edith?" she asked, her voice piercing. "Or have you forgotten that you promised him you would consider him also alongside Lord Hobart?"

A small flicker of doubt crossed Edith's face. "No," she said slowly. "I have not forgotten that. Although, he has not taken me out for a walk or a carriage ride in a week or so. I cannot say that about you." Her eyes narrowed as she looked back at Martha. "It is as I said, you wish to take Lord Weston away from me so that I cannot turn to him should this matter with Lord Hobart come to nothing."

Pain pierced Martha's heart. "You intend to return to Lord Weston only if Lord Hobart does not come through?" she whispered, hardly able to get the words out. "Edith, that is cruel."

Her sister shrugged. "I thought I loved Lord Weston once, so it seems likely that I can fall in love with him again," she replied without an ounce of shame. "You are trying to capture him for yourself, I know, but you will not succeed. Whatever it is you think he feels, I can assure you that he felt it for me first."

Daggers pierced Martha's heart, but she kept her gaze fixed on her sister. "Lord Weston does still care for you, Edith, I am not denying it. But you cannot treat him in such an abominable way. That is unfair to him."

Edith got up from her chair, and ignoring Martha entirely, wandered to the window and looked out.

"I thought as much," she said, looking over her shoulder at Martha. "Here is Lord Weston now. Taking you for a short stroll today, is he?"

"The bookshop," Martha replied slowly, not quite sure what Edith was doing.

Edith let the lace curtain fall back into place, her eyes calculating. "Then why not tell him what it is I have said about him, Martha? Tell him the truth."

A spark of anger shot through Martha's veins. "Perhaps I shall. He deserves to know."

"And, of course, in doing so, you will have him turning from you entirely," Edith finished with a triumphant smile. "You will no longer have him by your side; you will no longer have him seeking you out to dance. I know full well that he is doing so in order to keep me in his line of sight, but I also know that you have been reveling in his attention. So go on,

Martha. Do what you must but be fully aware of what it is you will lose."

~

MARTHA COULD NOT GET Edith's words from her head, not even after she and Lord Weston were walking back from the bookshop, making their way through Hyde Park. It was true that she had grown fond of Lord Weston and his attention toward her, but she had always reminded herself that it was for one reason and one reason only: Edith.

And now, the thought of Edith with Lord Weston broke her into tiny pieces. She did not want her sister to be courted by Lord Weston, not when she knew the truth about her intentions. But yet, to tell him the truth would mean an end to their association, and she did not want that to end either.

She swallowed her upset and closed her eyes for a moment as they walked, her hand loosely resting on his arm as he carried her new book in the other hand. He had purchased it for her, and her heart had glowed despite the confusion she felt. It was as though Edith's words had brought a sudden, sharp realization to the forefront of her mind – she was fond of Lord Weston.

Much too fond.

"Are you quite all right, Lady Martha? You are rather quiet this afternoon."

She glanced up at him, taking in his kind eyes and gentle smile. "I am not all right, Lord Weston," she admitted, not quite certain what else she could say. "But I should have tried to be better company for you. I apologize for my lack of conversation."

He chuckled and squeezed her arm gently. "You need not apologize for that, Lady Martha. It is just that I find myself looking forward to our conversations of late, that is all."

A little surprised, she held his gaze. "You enjoy talking with me?"

"Of course I do!" he exclaimed, his mouth pulling into a wide smile. "I know we are on the same course in regards your sister, but that does not mean that I have not grown fond of your company in the process."

Her heart tumbled to the ground.

"I see," she murmured quietly, the smile gone from her face as she let Edith's words shoot back to her mind. "I fear, Lord Weston, that you may be fighting a losing battle when it comes to my sister."

He stopped dead, making her stumble. She looked up into his face, knowing that she could not tell him the truth about what Edith had said, not when he was already so tortured with what she had just spoken.

"Has Lord Hobart spoken to your father?"

Shaking her head, she heard him let out a small sigh of relief. "Edith, however, is still quite set on him. Mayhap we ought to bring our alliance to an end, Lord Weston."

There was a long silence, broken only by the sound of birds singing in the trees above them. The maid Martha had brought with her had stopped a respectful distance away, allowing them to speak in private. Martha kept her eyes lowered, her heart shattering all the more as Lord Weston continued to consider what she had said. She both wanted him to separate from her and was desperate to remain alongside him at the same time, her feelings in utter torment.

"No, Lady Martha," Lord Weston said slowly, retrieving her hand and placing it back under his arm. "No, I think not. I recall that Lady Edith said she would continue to consider me, and I must remain hopeful until she has done just that."

"Until she has made her choice clear, do you mean?" Martha

asked, her heart leaping in her chest, only to crumble into dust once more.

"Precisely." Lord Weston looked a little uncomfortable, as though he was not quite certain he had made the correct decision, but Martha could not speak another word about her sister. Part of her wanted to blurt out exactly what Edith had said, but knowing that it would take Lord Weston away from her for good meant that she could not bring herself to do so.

Foolish, foolish girl.

Closing her eyes for a moment, Martha drew in a ragged breath, aware that she was in agony at the thought of not being in Lord Weston's company any longer. It was a ridiculous notion, given that he had told her so often just how much he cared for Lady Edith, but yet it was there regardless.

"You must care for my sister a very great deal, to be so determined," she said hopelessly, as they began walking. "I pray that I can find such a devotion one day."

Lord Weston did not say anything, and when she looked up, she saw that his face was taut, his eyes flashing as he looked straight ahead. It was as if he were battling with his own emotions, trying to sort them out so that they were in less of a tangle, just as she was doing.

A thought struck her, as they continued to return to her father's house. What was it about Edith that Lord Weston loved so very much? From what Edith had said, their acquaintance had been a very short one, which—in Martha's mind—did not mean that they had known one another very well at all. Were a few days enough to bring the first sparks of love, even if there were only a few conversations, a few chance meetings? She had no knowledge of such matters and supposed that it must, given just how much devotion Lord Weston showed towards Edith. Then again, Edith showed none of the same devotion to Lord Weston, which begged the question as to whether or not her sister had really ever had any deep feelings of love and affection toward him.

Perhaps it was not her place to ask, but as they reached the townhouse, Martha felt those questions dog her mind. She wanted to ask Lord Weston what it was he saw in Edith that drew him to her, what it was about her character that he liked so very much. A small niggle of hope suggested that, should she do so, then he might struggle to answer, might realize that he did not really know Edith very well at all.

And then what? she asked herself, as Lord Weston bid her goodbye. *Do you think he will turn to you in her place? That he will suddenly realize that he cares for you with a true, deep affection that was never there for Edith?*

The thought was a foolish one, bringing heat into her cheeks, but still, she could not let it go.

The next time she saw him, the next time she was able to converse with him, then she would ask. She was quite determined.

9

"Edith could not be encouraged to join us this afternoon?"

Even as he spoke, Edmund realized that he should not have begun their conversation with such a question, for Lady Martha winced and turned her head, looking out of the carriage window as it made its way towards Hyde Park. He knew, of course, that there were some difficult conversations occurring between Lady Martha and Lady Edith and he should not have brought the matter up so sharply.

"I am quite sure Mrs. Stewart will be adequate company," he continued hastily, not giving her time to answer as his gaze shot uneasily towards the older lady, who was seated next to Lady Martha. Unfortunately, the lady's eyes were quite tightly closed, although she still somehow managed to remain seated upright.

"Edith and I…"

Edmund frowned. Lady Martha did not normally have a quiver in her voice, which meant that something had upset her greatly. A twinge of concern echoed in his mind. Although, whether it was for Lady Martha or Lady Edith, he could not say.

Lady Martha cleared her throat gently, her gaze still fixed on whatever it was outside. "Edith and I had something of a disagreement," she said in a much clearer voice. "I am afraid it went rather badly."

Finally, her light green eyes met his and, to his surprise, Edmund realized that they were a little red-rimmed. Apparently, the lady had been crying, and that brought him a good deal of distress.

"You are still pursuing her with questions then?" he asked, concern wrapping around his soul, as he fought the urge to reach forward and take her hand. "Lady Martha, I do not like seeing you in such distress. Mayhap we ought to put an end to this situation, so that you are no longer in such a difficult position. I can continue to pursue Lady Edith alone, I am sure." Ignoring the twinge of pain that shot through him at the thought of being without Lady Martha's company, he fixed his gaze on her beautiful green eyes. "Do tell me truthfully, Lady Martha, should you wish to remove yourself from this situation. You will simply have to say the word and–"

"You are very kind, Lord Weston, but I believe that this is for the best," Lady Martha interrupted, settling one hand on his for a moment and sending a wave of heat rushing up his arm. "Edith is growing frustrated with my persistence, that is all."

He frowned, aware of the way Lady Martha looked away from him, her tongue darting out to lick her lips. He would guess that there was something more to it, something that she was not yet saying to him, but he could not let himself pry, for that would be appallingly rude.

Clearing his throat, he touched her hand again, surprised at how his whole body jolted at the briefest of touches. "I do hope you will be able to reconcile very soon."

Lady Martha's smile was strained, and Edmund felt himself grow even more frustrated, wishing that he was able to do something to bring her upset to a swift conclusion.

"I am afraid, Lord Weston, that such a thing can only come to an end when Edith realizes that Lord Hobart is being quite ridiculous in the way that he treats her. Why she insists on hanging onto his every word, why she will write to him and wait expectantly for his reply, is quite beyond me." Her voice grew louder, her jaw clenching for a moment. "The gentleman has refused to speak to my father regarding his intentions toward my sister, and yet he continues to pursue her in as loosely a way as he can. Do you know that he has told her that there is something that prevents him from courting her at this present time and that he has begged her to wait until it is set aright?" She snorted and looked away, her irritation evident, although Edmund knew she was truly concerned for her sister. "And what this matter is, she does not know for she will not ask him, and even if she did, he would not answer."

That brought a spark of concern to Edmund's heart. Concern for Lady Martha, he realized, and not for Lady Edith. There was something about Lord Hobart that he did not like and now found himself worrying that if Lady Martha continued to pry, then it might be all the worse for her. The gentleman in question was tall and thin, with sharp eyes that seemed to jump from one thing to the next with increasing speed. On first impression, Edmund had concurred that he did not like the gentleman at all. But, then again, he considered, it was not as though he would like any gentleman who had managed to gain Edith's attention. Although, at this very moment, his thoughts were entirely fixed on Lady Martha.

"Then mayhap I ought to find out what I can of this Lord Hobart," he mused aloud, seeing Lady Martha's eyes light up for a moment. "I have talked to the gentlemen at White's, of course, but none were able to satisfy my curiosity. In fact, I found out very little. It appears that Lord Hobart lives a fairly quiet life in the country in his manor house and has only returned to

London for the Season this year, having been away from town for some years." He shrugged, settling back in his seat. "He is a wealthy viscount by all accounts, but his behavior towards Lady Edith continues to suggest to me that there is more to him than what we see."

Lady Martha nodded fervently, her cheeks a little white. "Precisely."

Something stabbed at his heart at the sight of her, sitting there so quiet and pale. It was a compassion for her, a sympathy at how she had been forgotten by her sister and her father. Left at home to care for her mother, she had not had the opportunities that Lady Edith had, and yet, instead of being miserably jealous, she was doing all she could to prevent her sister from falling helplessly in love with a gentleman she barely knew.

That roused a great depth of feeling within his heart, although it was a feeling he could not quite explain. He took her in again, seeing her gaze drift away to the window once more, taking in the sad curve of her lips as her heavy burden sat on her shoulders. There was something beautiful in what she was willing to do, something truly remarkable about her character. It took Edmund's breath away as he looked at her, seeing her in an entirely new light and finding himself utterly captivated. He had been fighting this for some days, realizing that he spent more time considering Lady Martha instead of Lady Edith. Whenever he found himself lost in thought, it was Lady Martha that was in his mind, not the lady he supposedly was desperately in love with.

It was all rather unsettling, and Edmund was not quite sure what he ought to do with such feelings. When Lady Martha had suggested that they bring their association to an end, telling him that Lady Edith was still quite certain about Lord Hobart, he had found himself rebelling against the idea. What surprised him the most was that he realized it was not Lady Edith that had concerned him, but rather the thought that he would not be able to spend time in Lady Martha's company.

"So, you will try to find out more about him then?"

Flushing with embarrassment, Edmund realized that Lady Martha had been forced to repeat her question, since he had not answered her at first. Dragged out of his thoughts, he nodded and cleared his throat gruffly, relieved that she was not able to see the direction his thoughts had been taking.

"Might I ask, Lord Weston, how you met my sister?"

The question surprised him.

"If you do not mind, of course."

She was looking at him steadily now, her eyes fixed on his with such an intensity that he was immediately forced to look away.

"As I am sure I said before, it was in London just before the Season. Your sister was, I believe, seeking the very best gowns, and I had come to make the best of the summer!" He chuckled. "I had been in London for the Season for the previous two years but had been something of a foolish gentleman. I had decided, therefore, that it was time for me to behave entirely sensibly and see if I could find myself a decent match."

A tiny snort came from Lady Martha, and whilst she did not apologize, two spots of color appeared on her cheeks.

"You find something amusing, perhaps?"

He could not help but grin, as she looked at him with chagrin, her color mounting.

"It is just that I considered that an earl might find it rather simple to secure a decent match, my lord," she replied with a quirked eyebrow of her own. "Once the *ton* knows of such a gentleman, do they not usually pursue him with all their might?"

His smile spread, his chest rumbling with mirth. "You are very well informed, Lady Martha. Yes, I believe they do, but you see, I am not a man willing to simply settle for what is considered *best*. My father may have been, for he was given his bride by arrangement, but I have refused to consider such an idea and instead thought to find my own wife-to-be. I did not want someone who would simply smile and simper and take no consideration of me whatsoever." His lips twisted as he recalled how his own good father had never really had any love for his wife – Edmund's mother – and had not struggled particularly when she had passed away. "No, Lady Martha. I am not inclined towards suitability, but rather towards fondness. I believe that one must be drawn towards one's spouse with a deep, unrelenting affection if one is to have a happy life." He recalled the day when he had seen Lady Edith for the first time and was concerned that there was no quickening of his heart, no sudden burst of affection that rifled through him. "I confess that I was drawn to Lady Edith in such a way the very moment I saw her," he said, with no kind of excitement in his tone. His confusion mounted, but he pushed his thoughts aside, trying to remain fixed on their conversation.

As he let his gaze drift back towards Lady Martha, he saw that she was looking at him with a good deal of skepticism.

"You do not believe me?"

She shrugged, her eyes telling him that she certainly did not believe him.

"Might I ask you, Lord Weston, what it was about my sister that drew you to her? Was it her conversation? Her compliments to you? The way she was charitable to the young street urchins that run along these busy London streets?"

Her words were crisp, but not sharp, and there was no accusation in her tone, and yet Edmund found himself rising defensively. Perhaps it was because he was bewildered by all that he was feeling, perhaps it was because he was struggling to find any kind of emotion for Lady Edith, but his words became sharp.

"I cannot quite recall," he said firmly. "There was so much going on in my heart and mind that I confess it took me some days before it felt as though I were stepping onto solid ground again."

This, however, did not appear to please Lady Martha, whose brows were slowly lowering.

"And now that you have had even more time to reflect, Lord Weston?" she asked simply, her eyes suddenly sharp. "What is it that draws you to my sister?"

He could not answer. There was nothing that came to his mind, no quick, clear response that he could give her.

"Why are you asking me these things?" he responded, growing angry now. Although, whether it was with himself or with her, he could not quite say. "I thought you wished for Lady Edith to detach herself entirely from Lord Hobart and return to me."

She glared at him, her hands clenching in her lap. "And I must ensure, Lord Weston, that you are not as vacuous as he is!" she exclaimed, as Mrs. Stewart jumped in fright at the sudden exclamation. "I care for my sister despite her temper, her sharp tongue, and her ridiculous notions of falling in love in only a moment, and I wish her to be happy and content in her life. I am doing what I can to guide her in that, even though she will not listen to a word I have to say. You tell me that you are better than Lord Hobart in everything. You tell me that he feels nothing compared to you, and yet, when I press you, there is nothing of substance in your reply. How can I push my sister back toward you if I cannot be certain that what you feel for her will linger?"

Her words echoed around his head, pinning him to his seat. Mrs. Stewart, who had blinked multiple times, muttered something incoherent and then rested her head against the squabs, falling asleep again almost immediately. Lady Martha did not seem to notice.

"I care for Lady Edith," Edmund whispered, his voice hoarse as he tried to convince himself that what he had once felt for Lady Edith still lingered in his heart. "I may not be able to explain all that goes with such a passion, but I can assure you that I will love her, honor her, and cherish her with every day that goes by." His eyes narrowed, his gut twisting as lies began to trip off his tongue. He could not truly say that he would love Lady Edith, not when, as Lady Martha had just pointed out so clearly, he could not mention one thing about her that brought him such a love. "Not that I could expect you to understand such a deep emotion, Lady Martha, given that you have never fallen in love in your life." He sneered cruelly, his words coming from his pain. "Nor should I expect you to, given the lack of interest from the gentlemen of the *ton*. Is that why you are so interested in your sister's life? Is it because it will distract you from your own lonely existence?"

She crumpled before his eyes. Edmund heard himself speak; he heard the malice and the anger that caressed his words and felt himself shrink. Lady Martha was crying silently, large tears pouring from her eyes as she looked back at him, one hand slowly going to her mouth.

And then she was tugging at the carriage door, thrusting it open and shouting for the driver to stop. It slammed to a stop, threatening to topple her out, and before Edmund could do anything, she had jumped down in a flurry of skirts and ran, headlong, into the crowd of gentlemen and ladies, who had all come to take the air.

What had he done?

10

Martha struggled to keep her composure steady as she made her way through the crowd, aware that she was already drawing attention from the gentlemen and ladies of the *ton* simply by being entirely unaccompanied. She kept her head down and walked quickly, praying that she would soon find a quieter part of the park where she might give her emotions full sway. For the moment, she was struggling to keep everything within.

Her feet walked heedlessly across the grass, taking care to avoid the path of the carriages. The last thing she wanted was to be spotted by Lord Weston, who would then hail her and give her very little opportunity to escape him. She did not want to see him; she did not want to speak even a single word to him again. This façade was over.

To her horror, a tear trickled down her cheek as she continued to walk, and she turned her face away from the crowd, wiping it quickly with her fingers. Lord Weston had torn at her heart, and all she could feel was pain.

Stumbling towards a copse of trees, Martha let out a half sob of relief as she found herself surrounded by nothing but the trees, finally able to let the tears fall. Covering her face with her hands, she felt sobs tear her body apart, her shoulders shaking with the intensity of them. Her heart was broken apart; the wounds that Lord Weston had inflicted burning into her soul. He had been callous, cruel, and entirely unfair, and yet there had been a simple truth in his words that she had been unable to turn away from.

Lord Weston was right to say that the gentlemen of the *ton* paid her little attention, and she had always guessed that it was because she was the quieter and plainer of the earl's daughters. She did not have Edith's effusive character, nor did she have any of the beauty that adorned Edith's features. She did not draw gentlemen to her as Edith did, and the only reason she had found her dance card a little busier of late was entirely to do with Lord Weston's attention toward her. Once they were gone, would she return to being the wallflower she had once been? Would it be worse for her, since the gentlemen of the *ton* would believe her to be cast aside by Lord Weston, even though he had assured her he would do all he could to prevent such a thing?

When she had agreed to this façade, she had not thought much of the consequences of their scheme, since she had never received much interest from the *beau monde* before. Now that she had experienced what it was like to be someone as sought after as Edith, Martha found that she did not want it to end. She wanted to continue her acquaintance with the gentlemen who danced with her at every ball she had attended; she wanted to converse with those who came to speak to her...and she wanted Lord Weston to smile at her as he took her hand and led her onto the dance floor.

A knife twisted in her heart as Martha struggled to sort through all that she felt. Lord Weston had begun to mean more to her than he ought, she realized, which was why his words to her now had pierced her so greatly. It was not that she had simply enjoyed his company for what it was, but rather than she had found herself beginning to fill with anticipation whenever it came time for them to meet. She had found solace in his company and conversation, growing warm whenever he had sought her out for a dance. Over the last fortnight, Martha could not recall ever being as happy, realizing with another stab of pain, that it had now come to a sudden, unexpected end.

Moisture clung to her lashes as she looked down at the ground, her vision blurred. She did not want her time with Lord Weston to end, she realized. She did not want to have to watch him turn towards Edith, instead of toward her, as she had begun to hope. Lord Weston had been wrong to state that she had never felt anything like the love he had spoken of, for she realized that it was already in her heart, burning there for Lord Weston himself.

She could not see him again—that she knew. Her time with him had come to an end, and nothing would make her return. In fact, the matter of Edith's heart and her future happiness was now willingly thrown from Martha's shoulders as she determined never to consider it again. Edith would have to take responsibility for her own heart and for her own happiness. Yes, Martha had done what she could to try and prevent her sister from making a foolish mistake, but that had brought her nothing but pain. There was a wall between herself and Edith now, and perhaps it was time for Martha to break it down. She would return home, tell Edith that she could do whatever she liked with her life without fear of comment or interruption from her sister. Martha would say nothing more. Martha would give nothing more. Not a word of advice, not a listening ear, not even a gentle word of warning when Edith moved towards foolishness. Edith's happiness was not Martha's concern any longer.

Wiping her eyes, Martha took in a ragged breath, closed her eyes, and let it bring some calm to her soul. Why had she been so determined to try and help Edith? Yes, she loved her sister, and yes, she did not wish Edith to make a mistake, but she had never needed to become as involved as she had. Was it because, in view of their mother's absence from town, she had tried to take on that role of guiding Edith carefully? She bit her lip, her eyes downcast. It was not a role she had managed to take on particularly well, given that Edith had become nothing other than angry with her. Or had she done so in order to detract from her "lonely existence", as Lord Weston had suggested?

Tears sprang to her eyes once again, but she forced them back with an effort, aware that she would soon need to return home. The truth was, she had always been in Edith's shadow. When it had been time for their come out, Edith had been the one to come to London whilst she had been requested to stay at home in order to care for their mother. It was not something she had been upset about at the time, for her concern for her mother had overwhelmed all other emotions, but from that time onwards, she had always seen Edith in a greater light than she herself stood in. Edith had gentlemen pursuing her; Edith had her dance card filled within minutes of entering any ballroom; Edith was the one whom people sought out for conversation. She was the unnoticed, quiet sister, who lingered in the background, hidden by Edith's shadow. Perhaps she had simply accepted that role instead of pursuing her own life and her own future, thinking that once Edith was wed and settled, she would then come a little more into the fore.

Sighing to herself, Martha pulled out her handkerchief and dabbed at her eyes, hoping that she did not look too distraught. Whatever the reason, Martha was determined not to allow such a thing to continue. Edith could do as she pleased, whether Martha considered it foolish or not. Lord Weston would be forgotten, and she would do all she could to forge her own path here in London instead of being content to hide in the shadows.

I just pray that she will not return to him.

The words were whispered in her heart, sending another wave of pain crashing over her. She did not want Edith to marry Lord Weston, not when Martha herself had only just realized all that she felt for him. His cruel words had torn at her, and his sneers had beaten at her harshly, but still, she could not forget the affectionate feelings that had buried themselves in her heart. She had pushed him too far in her questions. She had tried to get him to see that he did not know Edith well at all, and in doing so, he had turned to anger instead of acceptance.

There could be nothing for them now, not when he was still so dedicated to Edith. Still, that did not quench the flames of love that continued to burn in her heart. The thought of Edith marrying Lord Weston and settling down at his estate tore at her mind, making tears press again at her eyes as a heavy weight settled on her. She dragged in another steadying breath, determined not to give in to tears again, determined to keep her composure until she finally had her emotions conquered.

"Farewell, Lord Weston," she whispered brokenly, as she stepped out of the copse of trees and tried to find her path back to the edge of the park, where she might hail a hackney. "I will not forget our time together."

She sent one last look over the park, as though she might spot Lord Weston and his carriage somewhere, as though their gaze might catch so that he could see her goodbye, but there was nothing she recognized. Turning on her heel, Martha kept her chin up, pushing away the memory of what Lord Weston had shouted at her, at the cruel words that had dug their way into her heart. She would forget him. She had to. There was nothing else for her to do.

"WHERE HAVE YOU BEEN?"

Martha quailed a little under the stern gaze of her father, a little surprised to see him out of his study and waiting for her in the entrance hall.

"Papa?" she asked quietly, handing the butler her bonnet and gloves. "What do you mean?"

"Mrs. Stewart returned here not half an hour ago," the Earl of Winchester exclaimed, his eyes a mixture of anger and concern. "She confessed that she had fallen asleep and that when she awoke the carriage was empty and was sitting outside our townhouse. Of course, she came inside at once, expecting to find you within, but there was no sign of you. Lord Weston has disappeared also, and the carriage drove off the minute Mrs. Stewart alighted. So, I will ask you again, Martha, where have you been?"

Hesitating for a moment, Martha decided to tell her father the truth. "Papa, I was upset with something Lord Weston said, and so I left his company. Mrs. Stewart was asleep, as you know, but I could not wait to awaken her." Her determination grew as her father's eyes widened, apparently a little surprised by her firmness. "I know it was foolish to leave without a chaperone, but I am entirely in earnest when I say that I had no wish to be in Lord Weston's company for a moment longer. I could not bear it, Papa. I am sorry if I caused you distress, but it was entirely unintentional."

He blinked, the anger fading from his expression. "And how did you return home?"

"I hailed a hackney once I had reached the edge of the park," she replied, clasping her hands in front of her.

The Earl of Winchester nodded slowly, rubbing his chin with one hand. "Then Lord Weston is not to be coming by again any time soon?"

Her heart ached, but she kept his gaze. "No, Papa. I do not think he will return."

"Dear, dear," her father muttered, passing one hand over his eyes for a moment. "Now I shall have two distraught daughters instead of one. I do not know what I shall do!"

Martha frowned, looking up at him in confusion. "Distraught?"

"Your sister," he replied, waving a hand. "Something about Lord Hobart, although I am not precisely sure what it is. Might you go and talk to her? You will do a better job than I will; I am quite sure."

It was on the tip of Martha's tongue to refuse, to tell her father that Edith had made her own decisions that were nothing whatsoever to do with Martha, but the look on his face stopped her. He was desperate for her help, and holding back a sigh, Martha gave him a jerky nod.

"Thank you," he said warmly, putting one hand on her shoulder. "I don't know if you are aware of just how much I appreciate you, my dear. You have done so much for your mother and now for your sister. You are a wonderful daughter, Martha, truly."

Her throat closed up as her father spoke to her in ways she had never before experienced.

"Thank you," he said again, squeezing her shoulder gently before turning to walk back into his study, leaving her standing alone and utterly astonished.

11

Three days later, and Edmund woke with a severe pain in his head. Groaning aloud, he threw the pillow over his head and pulled it down over his ears, desperately wishing to return to sleep.

"Coffee, my lord."

The butler was placing a tray down beside his bed, which Edmund acknowledged with a grunt.

"And breakfast, of course."

Another grunt came from Edmund as he closed his eyes tightly.

"You have a gentleman wishing to call upon you whenever is convenient," the butler continued, as Edmund tried his best to force his eyes open. "There is a small boy at the front of the house who came with the message, and I thought it best to ask him to wait until you can confirm what time would be most suitable."

Still struggling to open his bleary eyes, Edmund forced himself to sit up. "What gentleman?"

"A Lord Masters, I believe," the butler replied, as Edmund

sat back against his pillows. "From what the messenger boy said, it is something vitally important about another gentleman."

Edmund's head was throbbing so badly that he could barely see straight, much less try and understand what the butler was saying.

"Shall I tell him to return this afternoon?"

Nodding, Edmund tried to look at the clock but found that his vision was somewhat blurry. "How long until the afternoon?"

The butler cleared his throat. "It should give you at least two hours to prepare, my lord, since your calls usually begin at two o'clock precisely."

Edmund smiled ruefully. "Very well, Hawker. Thank you."

"My lord."

Closing his eyes again, Edmund leaned his head back against the pillows and let the smell of coffee drift towards him. It did not make him in any way more alert, for his head was still so cloudy that it lured him back towards the quiet recesses of sleep. It was with nothing more than sheer effort that Edmund snapped his eyes open and picked up his cup of coffee, adding just a splash of milk before taking a sip.

The hot liquid burned his lips, but he swallowed it anyway, letting it run down his throat and force his mind into wakefulness. He had spent the last three days in something of a melancholy, drinking far too much whiskey and choosing to remain away from society entirely. There had been no company other than his own, and now Edmund found himself growing tired of that.

His thoughts were still muddled but somewhere, underneath it all, came the picture of Lady Martha. He could not escape from her no matter how much he tried, no matter how much liquor he poured down his throat. Lady Edith had never once sprung to mind, had never once brought such a depth of feeling back to his soul – to the point that he had very little idea what to do. The entire charade with Lady Martha had been to recapture Lady Edith's affections, but now it seemed, he was no longer interested in her heart.

In fact, he was not interested in her at all.

What she had said to him about Lady Edith had not left him. She had asked him questions he had never once asked himself; she had forced him to consider what it was he truly loved about Lady Edith, and he had found himself quite unable to answer. He had not been able to answer because he did not know. Aside from Lady Edith's beauty, the only thing he knew about her was that she no longer cared for him as she had once said. That did not show firmness of character, but—for whatever reason—he had pushed that away and had become determined to seek her hand again. Was it because he had been holding onto that feeling of utter adoration for so many months? Had the time he had been apart from her turned Lady Edith into some sort of angel in his eyes?

Sighing heavily, Edmund picked up a bit of toast and bit into it, not really tasting it as he ate. A memory of how he had so often taken breakfast with his father in his father's bedchamber came back to him with a sudden, heady rush. That had only started when he had finally begun to see some improvement in his father's condition, when he had been able to let go of some of the worry and anxiety that had weighed him down for so long. Whilst his father had not been able to do anything more than sit up in bed, Edmund had made sure to take breakfast with him, growing more and more encouraged with each day that had passed.

He closed his eyes, feeling a mixture of pain and relief at the memory. That had been a very difficult time for him. A time when he had thought he would be left alone in this world since his father was wavering between death and life. Was that why he had clung to the memory of Lady Edith? Was that why her letters had become so dear to him, because he had nothing else to bring him even a single spark of happiness?

Another loud groan filled the room as Edmund let his head flop forward, his heart and mind more tormented than before. Lady Martha had been right to ask him questions about his own affections, but he had not liked her doing so. It had prodded him uncomfortably, to the point that he had resorted to anger instead of calm, thoughtful discussion.

He had done her a great wrong and guilt tore at him.

"I must see her," he admitted aloud, aware that he had been turning away from this for the last few days, such was his shame. "I must apologize."

His head began to throb with even greater intensity, but Edmund ignored the pain and forced himself to eat, finishing his breakfast even though his stomach rebelled at the food within it. Getting up carefully, Edmund moved to sit by the fire where the butler had placed his correspondence, only to recall what the butler had said about Lord Masters.

The name sounded familiar, but he could not quite place it. It took a good few minutes of thought before he recalled the rather nosy gentleman who had spoken to him at Lord Arbuckle's dinner. What was it his butler had said? Lord Masters wished to come and speak to him as soon as possible, as he had some information regarding another gentleman?

His gut twisted. The other gentleman had to be Lord Hobart, which meant that perhaps he would soon have to call on Lady Edith and tell her what had been revealed.

Where he would, most likely, see Lady Martha also.

Closing his eyes, Edmund considered what he would do should Lord Masters have something pertinent to share about Lord Hobart. Would he hurry to Lady Edith's side at once, telling her immediately so that she would look back at him with such grateful appreciation that she would fall into his arms?

Whilst Lady Martha stands in the shadows?

His forehead wrinkled as he tried to make sense of what he felt. He did not want to tell Lady Edith anything. All he wanted was to speak to Lady Martha, to apologize for what he had said, and to tell her that he had not been able to get her from his thoughts for some days now.

To tell her that *she* was the one who occupied his heart, not Lady Edith. It was not as though he had simply transferred his feelings from one sister to the next, for he had not fallen into a dream the moment he had laid eyes on Lady Martha, but rather it had come upon him slowly. He had spent so much time with Lady Martha that he knew her very well by now, and he found that he liked her very much. More than that, he loved who she was. He loved the way she could converse with him on almost any subject, the way that her eyes lit up whenever he came to claim her for their dance. How much he had come to appreciate her. How much he knew he could trust her and rely on her for careful insight into the difficult situation he had placed himself in.

A situation he had practically strong-armed her into.

Shaking his head, Edmund drew in a long, steadying breath. The first thing to do was to prepare for Lord Masters' arrival, and then, thereafter, he could consider what to do next.

~

"Lord Masters."

A little surprised at how nervous he was, Edmund greeted Lord Masters warmly, finding himself anxiously clutching the arm of the chair as he sat down.

"Can I get you something to drink?" he asked, gesturing to the side table where there stood decanters of brandy and whiskey. "You are welcome to help yourself."

Lord Masters chuckled. "Are you not partaking?"

Edmund felt his stomach roll at the thought of more alcohol. "No," he replied quietly. "The butler is bringing some coffee, you see, but if you wish..."

Lord Masters shook his head. "No, I thank you. Although I will have some coffee, if you please."

"Of course."

Edmund waited until the coffee and biscuits were brought and set out on the table, before speaking to Lord Masters again.

"Your message said you wished to tell me something?"

"Yes, indeed," Lord Masters exclaimed, sounding a little excited. "It is about the gentleman you were enquiring about."

"Lord Hobart?"

Lord Masters nodded, grinning as though he were the doll from the jack in the box.

"Well?" Edmund asked, growing a little more frustrated. "What is it?"

Leaning forward in his chair in a surreptitious manner, Lord Masters smile spread almost impossibly wide. "I have discovered something utterly astonishing."

"About Lord Hobart?" Edmund said, hurrying the conversation along. "I confess that I have discovered nothing interesting whatsoever, even though I spoke at length to a few gentlemen in White's."

"Well," Lord Masters replied at once, rubbing his hands together. "I sent a note to a cousin of mine, who I know lives fairly near to Lord Hobart, and he wrote back to me at once, although I only received the letter yesterday. I asked him why Lord Hobart is such a quiet, reserved type, and...well, you will never guess what my cousin said, Lord Weston!"

Edmund bit back a harsh retort, forcing himself to draw breath to calm his fractious thoughts.

"What did he say, Lord Masters?" he said after a moment, his hands clenching together to quieten his irritation.

Lord Masters chuckled, clearly taking a good deal of delight in revealing this exceptional piece of news.

"He wrote to say that Lord Hobart has been spending years at his manor house, with nothing but his wife for company," he said slowly, his eyes gleaming. "That wife though, she is very rarely seen. Does not keep well, my cousin thinks." He waited for a few moments before slapping his knee and sitting back in his chair, grinning broadly at Edmund's astonished reaction. "There, you see, my lord! A truly astonishing piece of news!"

Edmund could barely breathe, such was his surprise. His heart was racing frantically, keeping in time with his speeding thoughts, as he struggled to find a way through the cloud of astonishment that was tight around him.

"A wife?" he repeated, his voice a little hoarse as he looked at Lord Masters, desperate to be certain that it was true. "Lord Hobart is already married?"

Lord Masters nodded, clearly very well satisfied with how Edmund had reacted. "I am afraid I do not know her name, or who her family is, but there's one of the secrets Lord Hobart's been keeping to himself." A slightly puzzled look crossed his face. "Although I cannot see why he is so secretive about it. It is not as though he is courting anyone else, and even if he did, mayhap he is just looking for a new mistress."

Edmund tried to digest this news carefully, forcing himself to remain in his seat when he wanted to throw himself to his feet, storm around the room, and ask anyone who would listen what he was supposed to do now.

"I do hope I have not done wrong in speaking to you about this, Lord Weston."

Edmund's gaze traveled back towards Lord Masters, who was looking back at him with some concern.

"I thought that, since you seemed so interested in Lord Hobart, that you would wish to know what I discovered."

"I very much appreciate your coming here to tell me," Edmund replied truthfully. "Please, do not distress yourself. I am just a little overcome with the news."

Lord Masters nodded, but did not lose any of the concern that had settled in his expression.

"Might it be terribly rude of me to say that I need to consider this matter further?" Edmund continued, getting to his feet. "I can assure you that your visit has been a most welcome one, but I do need to think upon my next steps."

Lord Masters got to his feet at once, seeming to understand. "Of course, Lord Weston, of course. Thank you for your hospitality."

The moment Lord Masters quit the room, Edmund threw himself back into his chair, his head in his hands, only to get up again and let out a frustrated cry of agony.

He had to do what was right, but in doing so, he would then be forced into another situation that was even more desperate than the first. Instead of trying to pursue Lady Edith, instead of trying to convince her that *he* was the one who had loved her first and who loved her still, he would be doing all he could to show her that he was not the gentleman who could bring her any sort of happiness. He could not give himself to her. He could not give her his heart when it was entirely lost to another.

And whether or not Lady Edith would accept that was quite beyond his imaginings. After all, had she not promised to consider him, even though she was clearly chasing after Lord Hobart? Could she not now turn around and state that, since Lord Hobart had been proved to be entirely deceitful, that she now expected him to step up and take his place, as he had practically vowed to do? He recalled his words with a rush of frustration and shame, recalling how he had said to Lady Edith that he would be there waiting for her, once all the other gentlemen – and by that, he had meant Lord Hobart – had fallen away. Now that Lord Hobart would be gone from Lady Edith's side, she would repeat his words back to him and expect him to be there with her, would she not? Just as she had every right to do.

He groaned again, flinging himself back into the chair and wishing he could drink the entire decanter of brandy so that he might quieten his troubled mind. He had only just realized what he felt for Lady Martha, but she had run from him due to his malice and cruelty, which had stemmed from his hurt and confusion.

Closing his eyes, Edmund drew in a long breath, feeling entirely wretched. He did not want to admit that this was almost entirely his own fault, but the truth stared him in the face until he was forced to accept it. If he had simply decided to allow Lady Edith to continue on with her own life, without insisting that she allow him to be present in it, then she might now be finding out the truth about Lord Hobart for herself. Then, having set Lady Edith aside, he could have given Lady Martha his heart entirely. No cruel words would have been said; his heart would not be swirling with confusion and doubt; his mind would not now be troubled with pain and regret.

And yet, Edmund knew he had no other choice but to do what was required of him. Whilst he could ignore what Lord Masters had told him, whilst he could focus entirely on apologizing to Lady Martha in the hope that she might forgive him and accept his company again, Edmund knew he had very little choice other than to go to the Earl of Winchester's home and tell Lady Edith the news.

News he was sure she would not want to hear.

Pressing his lips together for a moment, Edmund closed his eyes tightly as he struggled to find the resolve to do what he must. Then, sighing heavily to himself, he threw himself out of his chair and strode from the room. Whatever happened, he was a gentleman—and that meant acting with honor even if he did not wish to do so. Making his way to his writing desk, he quickly wrote a short note to Lady Martha and Lady Edith, requesting to call upon them the later that day, at whatever time was convenient.

It was returned to him, unopened and unanswered.

12

Martha was struggling.

It had now been a good few days since she had last seen Lord Weston, but even in her state of upset, she had barely been allowed even a moment's peace because Edith's distress was greater than her own.

And all because Lord Hobart had decided to return home to the country for a brief visit to his estate to 'ensure all was in order' as Edith had told her over and over again. Instead of being relieved that her sister was to be without Lord Hobart, however, Martha found herself growing more and more irritated with the entire situation. Edith, as far as she was concerned, was making far too much of what would be a short separation, particularly since she had not even had so much as a murmur about courtship or marriage from him. She, of course, had her own upset to deal with, being still terribly upset about how Lord Weston had spoken to her, but much to her frustration, she was barely given any time to herself with which she might think and reflect on what had occurred.

Instead, just as it had been before, she had been left to take care of Edith whilst their father closed himself off in his study or, on occasion, took himself out of the house for a game of cards with a friend or two. He did not say much during dinner, but—then again—neither did Martha, given that Edith held sway for most of the evening. She complained incessantly about the unfairness of it all, occasionally cried tears of distress over the loss of him, and detailed every inch of each letter she had written to him.

It was growing quite wearisome, and Martha felt herself almost snapping under the pressure that had been placed on her shoulders. No, she could not retire to bed early, for then poor Edith would be quite alone and would feel even more distraught than she already was. No, she could not take tea and read quietly in the library for a time, for Edith needed her to walk with her to the mercantile so she could pick out a new ribbon or two that would draw attention away from the paleness of her cheeks and the redness of her eyes. No, she could not be allowed anything but the night to be away from her sister, and even then, she heard Edith wailing loudly from the room next to Martha's own.

In the stillness of the nighttime hours, Martha sometimes let her thoughts turn to Lord Weston but found her heart aching as before, without even giving her a moment or two of peace. She could still see the anger in his eyes, the sneer on his face, as he told her she would never find what he spoke of, would never discover the true depths of love that could be in person's heart. In a strange way, she was not angry with him for speaking to her so, for whilst it had broken her into smithereens, it had forced her to take stock of her life, to look at herself and her life with fresh eyes.

Sighing to herself, Martha straightened her skirts, smoothed one hand over her hair that was tied back into a simple chignon, and prepared for yet another day of torment.

As she made her way down to the dining room, Martha was acutely aware of the tension that began to rise within her. A tension that forced her to draw breath as she hesitated just outside the dining room, knowing that the moment she set foot inside, she would be forced to listen to Edith's whining all over again. It was growing more of a struggle every day to remain silent and to simply listen, instead of giving Edith all the advice Martha thought she needed.

Sighing inwardly, she turned the handle and stepped into the room, only to see Edith and her father sitting there together. It was unusual for the Earl of Winchester to be up so early and even more unusual for him to dine with them, which made Martha both surprised and a trifle confused to see him.

"Where have you been, Martha?" her father asked, as she came into the room to sit down. "We have been waiting for you for an hour or so."

She blinked, aware of the coil of tension rising up in her. "I did not know you were expecting me, Papa."

He shook his head and sighed, glancing at Edith. "Did your sister not tell you?"

"Tell me what?" Martha asked, feeling butterflies begin to flood her stomach. "Is there something wrong?"

The Earl of Winchester chuckled and shook his head. "No, of course not. It is only that I have decided to take a short trip away from London. We leave this afternoon."

Something heavy dropped into Martha's stomach as she saw Edith smile prettily, no sign of the sadness that had dogged her for so many days.

"Where are we going?" Martha asked carefully, praying silently that it was not what she thought.

"Well," her father said grandly, folding up his newspaper. "Edith and I had a little discussion yesterday evening, and she explained to me all about Lord Hobart's inability to commit to her despite the fact that there is a good deal of feeling between them."

"And she also told you that she is entirely unaware as to what this reason is?" Martha interrupted, seeing Edith's smile falter. "Lord Hobart will not say."

Edith sniffed, lifting her chin a notch. "That is because it is not my place to pry, Martha."

Resisting the urge to roll her eyes, Martha forced herself to take a few calming breaths before she spoke again. "It is entirely your place, Edith, if the gentleman is apparently very interested in courting you, but cannot do so and therefore, asked you to wait until whatever it is has finally been cleared up." She raised one eyebrow, turning back to her father, who looked a little lost.

The Earl of Winchester cleared his throat. "Regardless, Edith has been in the doldrums these last few days, and I find it quite dreadful to see her so upset. Therefore, I have decided that we shall all go to Beddingford."

The name did not mean anything to Martha. "Beddingford?"

"It is where Lord Hobart lives," Edith explained quickly. "Or near to it at least. Obviously, Papa has sent some men out to find us decent lodgings."

Anger began to burn through Martha. This was becoming quite ridiculous. Her father had, once again, done what he thought was best for Edith without allowing himself any further considerations. On top of which, Edith was much too engaged with Lord Hobart without any particular reason for letting herself become so entangled, aside from the supposed "mysteriousness" of the gentleman that drew Edith ever closer. She was being foolish in allowing Lord Hobart to dictate what she did by insisting that she wait for him to first complete whatever it was that was holding him back.

"No!"

The words shot from her mouth before she could stop them,

one fist slamming down on the corner of the table and making both her sister and her father jump in surprise.

"No!" Martha exclaimed again, pointing one finger at her father. "No, Papa, I will not go with you and Edith in some ridiculous goose chase towards a gentleman who has clearly made his decision and has returned to his manor house in order to make that decision completely and utterly clear. There can be no question about it. Lord Hobart has turned away from town and has gone to live at home, far away from London and far away from you, Edith."

"Martha!" Edith exclaimed, looking tremendously hurt. "How can you speak to me so? I thought you cared about my wellbeing."

"I *do* care, but I will not allow that consideration to be to my own detriment, Edith," Martha replied firmly, leaning on the table with both hands. "And if you think I am to return to the manor house with you, then I can assure you that you are quite mistaken."

"Martha," her father said, appearing to be terribly surprised at her outspoken words. "You will do as you are told. Have you not taken good care of Edith these last few days?"

"I have," Martha admitted, refusing to seat herself again. "But that is only because you have asked it of me, Papa, not because I truly wished to."

The truth was harsh and grating, and Martha could see the shock on both her father and Edith's faces as she shared it, but regret did not fill her. Nor did shame or frustration, but rather came a sudden sense of pride that she had been able to say such a thing without fear of rebuke.

"You have always been there for Edith," her father said quietly, sounding a little confused. "I thought that you would relish the opportunity to do so again."

"At the expense of my own self?" Martha asked, gesturing

wildly now. "I know that there is always the concern of selfishness, Papa, but I have never once been selfish in how I care for my sister. In fact, I have cared for her and her future so greatly that I have allowed myself to be pushed to the side. I have allowed my heart to become hidden away, just as I hide myself in the shadows at a ball. I do care for Edith, and for you too, Papa, but I cannot continue to care *only* for my sister. I do not think it is selfish to consider one's own needs also."

Her grip on the edge of the table began to relax as she spoke, seeing her father's expression mount with surprise. Edith, however, was looking quite furious.

"I tell you to leave me alone, to stop forcing your advice onto me, and you refuse to do so, telling me that it is for my own good. Now, when you are told to help me with my pain and grief, when were are to take a trip together, you turn around and say you will not come? You will not be the support that I need?"

Martha let air fill her lungs, a peace surrounding her that she had not expected.

"Yes, Edith," she replied slowly, letting out her breath carefully. "That is precisely what I am saying. You must make your own choices, and I must not interfere. I will always be happy to share my thoughts with you, but only if you wish it, not because I am forcing them onto you. I have my opinion on Lord Hobart, as you have heard and as you well know, but I will not attend with you. If you believe it is for the best, then you have Father by your side. You will not require my company."

Edith's mouth opened and closed like a fish, her eyes a little angry as she gazed back at Martha, something like disappointment slowly etching itself on her face.

"I must say, I do find this rather selfish of you, Martha," her father commented, clearly a little put out. "I find that I have often come to rely on you."

"And it is that reliance that makes you treat me as though I am less than Edith," Martha said, turning back to him and allowing her heart to break free with the truth. "You give her all she wishes, all she craves, and trust that *I* will be the one to ensure she is always behaving well, always staying within the bounds of propriety. You do not truly consider me or my own future. You have never done so." She drew in a breath, tears springing to her eyes.

"You left me with Mama when she was ill, so that Edith might have her come out. I know that you care for her deeply, Papa, but did you ever consider that I might wish to have a come out of my own, even a year later?" Moisture slid from her lashes, dotting onto her cheek. "I was glad to be there with Mama, for I do not want you to think for a *moment* that I resented it, but Papa, why could I not have had as much of a celebration as Edith? Why was Edith given a wonderful ball with which to celebrate her debut, whereas I was not even considered for the same a year later? Edith is the eldest daughter, and she is to have the larger dowry – but does that mean that I am of lesser importance in your eyes? Does that mean that I am to consider myself lucky to be doing all I can for Edith in preparing her, in guiding her as best I can since Mama cannot? When do I get my turn, Papa? When do I get to enjoy London society without constantly being required to stand by Edith's side whilst you go to play your card games? Am I to be never considered in my own right?"

Her words clattered about the room, spiking off the walls and returning to her with such force that she had to catch her breath. Tears were now spilling, unhindered, down her cheeks as she looked steadily at her father, who was staring at her, apparently aghast.

"My dear Martha," he said, after a few moments had passed. "I did not know that you felt this way. I thought you enjoyed being alongside your sister."

Martha sniffed in a rather unladylike fashion and shook her

head. "I was content with it, Papa, but I do not think that I ever truly enjoyed being given such responsibilities. It has only been lately that I have realized this, only in the last month that I have had the taste of a life I *could* enjoy if given the chance."

"Thanks to Lord Weston," Edith sneered, her lips flattening. "He does not truly care for you, Martha, no matter what you might have made yourself believe."

Martha looked back at her sister steadily, wondering what had happened to turn her into such a spiteful, mean-spirited creature. Was it because Martha had, in these last few weeks, no longer been the biddable, quiet sister who did whatever Edith asked without question? Was it because she had stopped being timid with her questions, and had begun to seek out real, meaningful answers from Edith about the state of her heart when it came to Lord Weston and Lord Hobart? It was evident that Edith did not like this change in Martha, did not like that Martha was standing up for what *she* wanted, instead of accompanying Edith in whatever she wished to do.

"You would have preferred it, I think, if I had remained nothing more than your companion, Edith," Martha replied, slowly, not allowing the barbarous words to sting her. "You liked that I was in your shadow, for it gave you a greater presence amongst the *beau monde*. You liked being able to do what you wished with only my quiet warning words as a slight niggle of irritation. Now, when I am standing tall and declaring that I am finished with such a life, with such a role, you have turned on me entirely when all I ever wanted to do was help you."

"Help me?" Edith snarled, slamming her hand flat on the table. "You have never liked Lord Hobart and have tried to push him away from me constantly!"

"That is because he is not worthy of you," Martha replied, her voice a good deal quieter now. "He has not declared himself or spoken to Papa about courting you, even though he has sought out your company again and again. And now, you are in such a deep distress because he has severed the connection between you, and you are trying to convince Papa to go to his manor house in order to see him there! Can you not accept, Edith, what I have been trying to present to you for so long? Lord Hobart is not the kind of gentleman you should ever consider, not when there are so many other gentlemen who are eager for your company. Gentlemen who will prove to be much better suitors than Lord Hobart could ever be."

"Gentlemen like Lord Weston? Did you know, my dear sister, that he wrote to us both only yesterday, but I chose to return his note without so much as opening it." Her eyes flickered darkly. "I thought it best he remain away from this house, given the current circumstances with Lord Hobart."

Martha could not reply; she was forced to bend over as the ache in her heart screamed aloud and tore through her. What must Lord Weston have thought to have received his note back without it so much as having been read? If there was any chance of reconciliation between them, it had gone now. Edith had seen to that. Tears fell from her eyes onto the delicate lace tablecloth, her arms wrapped around her middle as she dragged in air.

"Edith," she heard her father say weakly. "You ought not to–"

Martha shook her head, slicing the air with her hand as she rose. "I am not coming with you to Beddingford, Edith. Papa, I have told you the truth about all that is going on in my heart, and I fear that if I say more, my heart shall rip from its chest." She stumbled towards the door, feeling a mixture of relief, weakness, and utter despair. "Do whatever you think is right, Edith, whether that be with Lord Hobert or Lord Weston. It is your future. Do as you think best."

And so saying, she wrenched the door open and ran the

length of the hallway until she reached the staircase, stumbling up it two at a time, whilst the echo of the slammed door sounded behind her.

13

Edmund did not know what to do.

He paced back and forth, the unread letter in his hand, having spent a sleepless night trying to work out what it was he should do. The news of Lord Hobart's matrimony dug into his mind, filling him with a sense of urgency, but what preyed on his mind all the more was the thought of Lady Martha.

The letter had been sent back unread. He did not know what to make of that, not quite certain which sister it had been to return it to him. If it had been Lady Edith, then that did not bring him as much discontent as if it had been Lady Martha.

He groaned aloud, his head in his hands as the note slipped from his fingers and fell to the floor. It was not truly Lady Edith nor Lord Hobart that tugged at his mind, but rather it was thoughts of Lady Martha.

How wrong he had been to treat her so! How much he wanted to make amends, but if she would not so much as see him, then what was he to do? He could not exactly stride up to the house without having had his request to call accepted by the ladies of the house, which left him with very little else to do.

"My hat!"

He strode from his study and made his to the front of the house, shouting for his butler to bring him his things. Perhaps a walk in the wind and the rain would help settle his mind to the point where he could think clearly about what to do next.

A few minutes later and Edmund was regretting his choice to step outside. The wind had turned into something of a gale and was driving the rain through his outer clothes and wetting his shirt. His mind, at least, was thoroughly occupied, wondering where he might be able to go to get himself out of the rain. He hurried his steps as he walked all the more quickly towards a row of shops, almost running towards the door of the first one he saw, pulling the door wide open and stepping inside.

"Good afternoon, my lord."

The shopkeeper smiled as Edmund pulled his hat from his head, a little embarrassed at the rain that ran down his face. "Good afternoon."

"Might I be able to help you find something particular?"

Shaking his head, Edmund tried to smile. "No, thank you. I intend to simply browse for a while." He knew full well that he would have to purchase something now that he had stepped inside for the sole purpose of keeping dry, but mayhap a novel of some description would take his thoughts from Lady Martha.

"Very good, my lord."

"Thank you."

Edmund moved away quickly from the front of the shop, aware that he was now making small puddles on the floor. He winced as he peeled his coat off, which, to his surprise, the shop-keeper came to take for him, promising to hang it up carefully so that it would dry. Then, he wandered a little further into the bookshop's depths, wondering if he could lose himself in the musty smell, the whispers of adventure, of knowledge, of great tragedy arising from the pages that surrounded him.

And then, the door opened again, and a female voice reached his ears.

"Oh, I do apologize, sir!"

His breath caught, and he stilled, wondering if his prayers had been answered by a foolish desire to walk outdoors in the middle of a rainstorm.

"Think nothing of it, my lady," the shopkeeper replied. "Might I take your shawl?"

"Thank you."

Edmund turned slowly, his heart beating quicker and quicker as he took in the sight of Lady Martha, who appeared to be just as sodden as he.

"There is a fire up the stairs, where the novels are kept," the shopkeeper was saying kindly. "You might wish to remain there for a time."

"You are very kind," Lady Martha replied fervently. "And, of course, I shall be sure to make a good few purchases from you. Do you mind if my maid waits here?"

Edmund held his breath as she made her way towards the stairs, climbing them quickly so that she might reach the warmth of the fire. He did not know what to do for a moment, standing completely frozen in the middle of the bookshop, his eyes lingering on her for as long as he could. The maid, thankfully, was seating herself in the corner of the bookshop, which meant that Edmund would be able to speak to Lady Martha uninterrupted.

He had to first force his limbs to move and his mouth to speak, feeling as though he were hindered from doing both by the shock and the joy of seeing her. And then, slowly, he moved towards the staircase, placing one foot in front of the other as he mentally rehearsed what it was he might say to her. Whilst his thoughts had been filled with nothing but Lady Martha, he had never stopped to consider what it was he would say to her should he see her, his mind tormented with trouble and regret. Now the moment was upon him, and he felt his mouth go dry, and his limbs begin to tremble, as he finally reached the top of the staircase.

"Lady Martha."

His voice was hoarse, his hand gripping the stair rail so tightly he thought it might break under the strain of it. She did not look at him, her back to him as he waited there, her shoulders rising, her back suddenly taut with tension. One hand held her bonnet, which she had taken off so as to dry it, he presumed, but her fingers were gripping it tightly, giving him little need to guess how she felt.

"Lady Martha, please," he whispered, unable to find enough strength to speak aloud. "You cannot know the depths of my sorrow, the regret that consumes me. Please, if you will do nothing else, allow me the opportunity to give you my sincere apology for how cruelly I treated you. My soul will go to the grave in torment if I cannot speak these words to you."

Still, she did not move, did not speak. Her back was still taut as she remained exactly where she was, unmoving.

His heart sank.

"I shall leave you then," he managed to say, blood roaring in his ears as he realized that she did not wish his company and was making it as plain as she could. "I cannot tell you, Lady Martha, how much regret I feel over what I said. Do excuse me. Do forgive me."

Slowly, he began to turn away, to descend back down the staircase, his heart thudding painfully.

"Wait."

His head shot up, hope flaring to life in his chest. Turning, he made his way up the stairs once more, finally reaching the top and stepping onto the ragged, threadbare rugs that adorned the floor.

Lady Martha was as a statue. How he longed to see her face, how he longed for her to turn and speak to him, to look into his eyes and see what it was he felt within his soul!

"I am here, Lady Martha," he murmured, clasping his hands behind his back. "Might I speak to you about my regret and sorrow over my callous words to you?"

"No."

She turned, her bonnet still in her hand, and Edmund took her in, seeing her pale face, her wide green eyes, and the way her brown curls hung limply around her face, having been dampened by the rain.

He had never seen anything so beautiful.

"I do not wish to go over the past," she said, her voice trembling. "I will not pretend that such words did not bring me pain, Lord Weston, for I never before felt anything so great. I will confess that they also brought me some good."

His mouth fell open. "Some good?" he repeated, horrified. "My dear Lady Martha, pray do not consider that a single thing I said held any kind of truth!"

The corner of her mouth lifted just a little, her eyes growing rueful. "That is not precisely what I mean, Lord Weston. When I fled from your carriage, I returned home to a house where my sister was distraught over Lord Hobart's sudden absence, and my father was urging *me* to take care of her so that he would have no need to involve himself." Her smile faded, her eyes growing sad. "It is the role I have always taken on and the role I believe he thought me willing to accept. Given what you had said to me, given how much emotion rose in me, I found myself beating against the expectations until, finally, the truth came out." Her chin lifted a notch, giving her an almost regal appearance. "I will no longer be taking on the role of my sister's guardian, Lord Weston. I will no longer be considering *her* happiness and well-being to the detriment of my own. Had you not spoken to me in such a callous manner, I might never have reached such a conclusion."

There then passed a few moments of silence where Edmund found himself simply looking into Lady Martha's eyes and feeling his heart take flight. There was something about her now, something in the way she looked at him, that told him she had achieved a great victory and, for that, he was glad.

"I should never have spoken to you in such a way, however, Lady Martha," he said after a few minutes, taking a step closer to her as he fought the urge to take her hand. "You were asking me pertinent questions, and they became a little too sharp for me to take." Lowering his gaze, he felt his heart quicken, as he realized what he must do, what he must say to free his heart from its shackles.

"Lady Martha, I confess to you that you have been right in everything," he continued softly, looking down into her gentle face. "I did not know what I felt for Edith, for I allowed myself to linger on the feelings that had risen in me the first time I laid eyes on her. When I went to tend to my father, when I had to take on the responsibilities of the title whilst he lay in his bed, desperately ill, I let her letters be my solace. They comforted my heart in what was a very difficult time, and I fully believed that I was deeply in love with her still on my return to London."

Lady Martha made to say something, but knowing that he had more to say and feeling it bubble out of him as a stream of water makes its way down a hill, he caught her hand and pressed it.

"Please," he murmured hoarsely. "Let me say what I must, Lady Martha."

Her eyes were wide, dropping to their joined hands before returning to his face, but to Edmund's very great relief, she gave him a slow nod but did not remove her hand. It lay warm and soft in his own, and Edmund could not remove his for the world.

"Lady Martha, when I returned to London, I drove through town and saw Lady Edith talking with Lord Hobart, and my jealousy knew no bounds. I was quite sure she would return to me once I came back to her side and was truly devastated when she did not. I convinced myself that she simply had to be reminded of the feelings that had once been in her heart, without understanding that she had realized those feelings had drained away entirely, having never had anything of substance in the first place." A fresh pain resurfaced in his mind as regret tore through him. "I was foolish to come to you, Lady Martha, to ask for your help in such a delicate matter. I ought not to have done that. I ought to have understood that she had turned to another and simply let the matter drop, but for whatever reason, I could not do so." He squeezed her hand lightly. "When you began to ask me questions about Lady Edith, when you began to press me as to what it was that brought such a love for her bubbling in my heart, I realized that I could not answer. That was why I reacted with such anger and cruelty. It is by no means an excuse, but simply an explanation as to why I erupted in such a fashion. My mind was tormented, my heart confused, and were I to be entirely honest with you, Lady Martha, I was fearful."

She looked up at him, her eyes gentle and holding none of the anger and bitterness he had expected. "Fearful?" she repeated quietly, her brows lowering in confusion. "Why?"

Now it came to it. Now he would have to tell her what he had begun to feel for her, even though it would come to naught.

"Because, Lady Martha, I realized that it was not Lady Edith that I felt anything for, but rather, it was for you."

She caught her breath, no smile blossoming on her face.

"I confess to you now that I have never before felt such deep and such furious feelings as I do at this very moment," he continued, his words almost falling over one another as he tried his best to tell her everything before the moment was taken from him. "I have been filled with such regret over what I said to you, realizing that I had driven you away from me when the truth of the matter was that I...I believe I love you, Lady Martha."

She went very still.

"They are not the same emotions that I felt for Lady Edith," he finished, placing his other hand over their joined ones. "I was dazzled by her beauty, but no longer. I have come to see that the beauty that is within you, Lady Martha, is what draws me to you. I have missed you these last few days. I have missed our conversations, missed your company with me, missed your laugh and your smile and warmth of your eyes." Closing his eyes for a moment, he took in a ragged breath to steady his composure, growing weak within himself as he gave her everything he had been keeping inside. "I do not know Lady Edith, and what I see of her behavior makes me realize that I do not wish to be in her company, never mind in her heart! But with you, Lady Martha–" He opened his eyes and saw her still staring at him, her eyes fixed on his. "With you, I can allow my heart to roam free, to feel all that it holds for you. As we have become acquainted, I have been battling what I felt, thinking I ought to remain true to Edith, but I realized there was no substance to what I once felt for her. Now that I know what it is like to truly be in love with another, to feel such a strong, unwavering love for another, I cannot turn from it. I had to confess it all to you."

Lady Martha closed her eyes, her lashes pressed against her cheek. Her fingers tightened around his, and Edmund held his breath, entirely uncertain as to what she might say to him.

"You are...very kind, Lord Weston."

She opened her eyes and looked at him again, and Edmund felt his heart drop to his toes, his hopes dashing.

"You speak to me of your heart," she continued in a soft voice, "and I am glad for it. I confess that I too have struggled against what I feel, what I ought not to let myself feel, and that these last few days have been more than confusing for me."

Slowly, a flicker of hope began to burn once more in Edmund's chest.

Lady Martha shivered, and Edmund made to draw her a little closer towards the fire but she smiled and shook her head, her expression a little tight.

"It is only because of what I wish to say," she whispered, squeezing his hand. "If you will grant me the time to listen?"

"I would grant you anything you wish," he replied fervently, his heart quickening in his chest.

To his delight, she laughed softly, her eyes dancing. "You should be careful with what you say, Lord Weston, in case I ask you for something you cannot give."

Shaking his head, he stemmed the flow of words that threatened to escape from his lips and looked down at her, waiting patiently for her to speak.

"Lord Weston," she began after a moment's pause. "When you spoke to me in the carriage – and no, you need not apologize again – you told me that I had never felt what love was, had never felt the sway of it tug my heart." Her lips curved softly, her eyes warm and sparkling. "You were quite wrong, Lord Weston, for I feel such things for you."

Sparks flooded his vision as he looked into her eyes, hardly able to believe what it was she was saying.

"I have told myself repeatedly that I was being nothing more than a foolish child," Lady Martha continued, her cheeks growing a little pink, "and what I ought to be doing was focusing entirely on Edith instead of letting my heart fill with affection for you. Unfortunately, I could not prevent it from doing so."

"Oh, my dear," Edmund breathed, happiness beginning to fill every part of him. "I cannot quite believe..."

"I am sorry that Edith returned your note," she interrupted, the smile disappearing from her face altogether. "She has, it seems, turned against me now that I am no longer to do as she expects." Her lips quivered, her cheeks growing slowly pale. "I confess, Lord Weston, that she only ever wanted to keep you nearby for her own good, not for yours. She does not care about your heart, telling me that should Lord Hobart turn out to be a bad egg, then she would simply turn back toward you in the knowledge that you would drop to her feet in relief." Hesitating, she bit her bottom lip for a moment, before placing her free hand on his chest, sending waves of heat through him. "I wanted to tell you it all in as much detail as I could, knowing that you deserved to hear everything Edith had said, but I could not bring myself to do it. Instead, I spoke very little, giving you only the smallest tidbit about Edith, but you would not have it." Her lips quirked. "You cannot know how glad I was for that, Lord Weston, for I wanted to remain in your company for as long as I could. I was afraid that if I told you everything Edith had said, then our association would come to a swift end, and I could not bear the thought of that."

"Nor could I," he smiled, taking the hand that rested on his chest and kissing the back of it gently, bringing a flare of heat to her face. "I recall that when you told me that Edith was still quite settled on Lord Hobart and that you wondered if we should bring our association to an end, the only thing I considered was that I would no longer be with you every day." A chuckle escaped him as he saw the astonishment etched on her face. "And that is why I could not bring it to an end."

"And what now?" Lady Martha asked, her eyes twinkling as she smiled up at him. "Now that we have confessed our hearts to one another, what is it that comes next?"

All at once, the happiness in his heart faded away as he let his gaze linger on the face of the woman he loved, realizing that he might never be able to take the next step. It all came down to whether or not his promise to Lady Edith still stood, or whether he could consider it null and void.

"There is still the matter of Lady Edith to consider," he said slowly, wishing he could lean down and kiss her. "I promised her that, once the other gentlemen fell away, I would be there waiting for her. I gave her my word, my promise, Lady Martha. What is it I am to do?"

14

Martha caught her breath, her fingers tightening in Lord Weston's hands. Surely he could not mean...

"I do not wish to return to her, Lady Martha, but what is it I am to do?" Lord Weston repeated, looking into her eyes with such desperation that her heart squeezed with sympathy for him. "I promised her that I would remain there waiting for her until all other gentlemen – and by that, I meant Lord Hobart – became nothing to her. Now that Lord Hobart's intentions have become clear, it means that I am now in her sights."

Martha blinked, not understanding what Lord Weston meant about Lord Hobart but finding herself entirely focused on what he had supposedly promised Edith. Whilst it was honorable indeed for Lord Weston to wish to keep his promises, she could not imagine the torment for them both should he return to Edith from nothing more than a sense of duty.

"No, Lord Weston, you cannot," she breathed, her heart beginning to ache within her. "I must beg you not to turn away from me towards my sister, not when I know now that your heart is filled with love for me – and only for me."

He dropped his head, agony etched into his features. "It would be ungentlemanly of me to–"

"Then be ungentlemanly!" she exclaimed, leaning closer to him, searching his face so that he would look into her eyes. "My sister does not deserve your sense of duty, Lord Weston. She has thrown you aside for another, and now you are questioning whether or not you ought to return to her? No, you are much too good, Lord Weston, and I will not allow it." An idea crept into her mind and bolstered by it, she smiled at him, leaning even closer. "If you do continue on this way, then I shall stand up in church on the day of your wedding and shout my objections to all who will listen. I will not allow you to crucify yourself simply because you believe you must."

A small smile tugged at his lips, and he let out a long breath, which tickled and danced across her cheek.

"And yet there is more I must tell you," he said despite his smile. "Come, will you sit with me for a moment? And then, together, we can decide what is best."

Her happiness flickered but did not die away, feeling a sense of relief that he had not yet declared that he must return to Edith's side regardless of her objections, that he must do the right thing due to his position as a gentleman. It had all happened so quickly that her head was spinning with a thousand thoughts, her heart almost overwhelmed by raging emotions. She had barely been able to move when she had first heard his voice, able to take in air but do nothing else. To hear the regret and the pain in his voice had told her everything she needed to know. Lord Weston had been truly sorry for what he had said, and she found herself easily able to forgive him, especially when he had taken her hand and let it rest in his own. Her heart had broken free of the sadness and pain that had held it down, finally free to express the love she had felt for Lord Weston for so long. When he had told her the truth about his own feelings, she had felt almost dazed with the shock of it, her legs growing weak as she struggled to remain standing. It had been too much to take in, almost too much to believe, for it had meant that all her hopes had been fulfilled in one heady moment.

Her hand still in his, Lord Weston took her to the corner of the room, close to the fire, where there were three or four chairs. Seating her first, he took the chair opposite her and sat down heavily. It was only then that she saw the smudges under his eyes, his face lit by the glow of the fire, and her heart trembled. Something painful tore at his expression, his smile of happiness already chased away whilst he leaned forward, leaning his elbows on his knees and clasping his hands tightly.

"I had a visit from Lord Masters," he began in a low voice. "I had discussed Lord Hobart with him some time ago, and we both agreed that we knew very little about him. He did not understand my interest, but being something of a nosy fellow, took it upon himself to find out a little more about Lord Hobart." He sighed and closed his eyes for a moment. "He came to me with news about the gentleman, news which explains everything about Lord Hobart's behavior, and in particular, his lack of intention toward Lady Edith."

Martha swallowed the lump in her throat, feeling nerves rattle all through her.

"He is already wed."

She gasped, her breath catching in her throat as one hand shot to her mouth, her eyes staring unbelievingly at Lord Weston.

"I know," he said, evidently aware of how hard this was to believe. "I did not quite understand why he should then appear in London with the apparent intention of seeking a bride for himself, but I have done a little more investigating, and it appears that he is attempting to divorce his wife."

"Divorce?" she gasped, another shock reeling through her. "How awful!"

"That is why I believe he asked Edith to wait for him," he said slowly, his expression a little sad. "He is here to speak to his solicitors, to work his way through the process, but it will take some time and will certainly leave a stain on his reputation."

Martha closed her eyes tightly, feeling herself trembling from the shock of it all. Lord Hobart had never been able to commit himself to Edith simply because he was not free to do so. But to tell her that he was to be divorcing his wife—if that actually was successful—would mean that Edith would, most likely, turn from him forever. She could not imagine what Edith would feel when she saw Lord Hobart again, silently praying that her sister would be spared the greater torment of seeing him with his wife, and would hear the news from the those who resided in the local village instead.

A flicker of anger rose in her. Anger that her father, despite what Martha had said, had still taken Edith to where she wished to go, apparently unable to refuse his eldest daughter anything.

"Perhaps Lord Hobart really does care for her," she said slowly, opening her eyes and trying to calm her frantically beating heart. "Mayhap he did not wish to tell her the truth for fear that she would not want to have anything more to do with him."

"And I could not blame her for that," Lord Weston said emphatically. "To be connected to a divorced gentleman, no matter how high his title, is bound to place a stain on one's name." Swallowing hard, he reached forward and took Martha's hands. "But you see, this is why I know that Lord Hobart will no longer be in Lady Edith's mind, not once she knows the truth about him. Am I to step up into his place then? Or can I allow myself to follow my own heart, to put aside what I promised in the knowledge that I am breaking my word to her?"

Martha studied Lord Weston's gentle face, took in the concern and confusion that shone in his blue eyes, and felt her heart burn with compassion and love.

"Weston," she began softly. "If it is one thing I have learned of late, it is that one must be allowed to follow one's own heart. I care for my sister dearly, but I am not about to go running after her in order to tell her that Lord Hobart is already wed!" Seeing his confusion, she gave him a small smile. "I forgot to tell you that she convinced my father to go to the country, to reside in a small town near to Lord Hobart's manor house so that she might see him there. I refused to go, as you can see, and so have been left in town with Mrs. Stewart as my companion." She let her lips tip into a wry smile, well aware that Mrs. Stewart was, at this present moment, likely to still be asleep. "Edith made it very clear to both myself and my father that her separation from Lord Hobart has been very difficult for her – although I can imagine that it will be all the more difficult when she realizes why he has stepped away from her."

Lord Weston's expression grew somewhat wry. "Indeed," he murmured, his fingers tightening in her own. "One feels a touch sorry for her."

"I do feel such an emotion," Martha replied firmly, "but I can also see that this is of her own doing. She has continued to pursue Lord Hobart, even though she knew full well that he was unable to court her at this present moment. She would not turn from him, quite determined to solve the mystery surrounding him, disregarding all sense." She shook her head, not feeling any triumph over the knowledge that her sister was about to be completely broken by what she would discover about Lord Hobart. "However, she must be allowed to live the life she has chosen for herself, must she not? I cannot be forever pulling her from the mire she has placed herself in, trying to guide her this way and that, at the behest of my father." Tipping her head just a little, she smiled into Lord Weston's eyes and, to her relief, saw him smile back at her. "We should each have the chance to follow our own hearts, Weston," she said again. "To place such a burden of responsibility on your shoulders will only make for a miserable existence. You said those words to Edith when you believed yourself to be in love with her. Now that you realize you no longer have any such emotions, you are freed from that weight."

Lord Weston let out a long breath, his head dropping for a moment, before he raised it and looked into her eyes. Martha pressed her lips together tightly, praying that he would understand what she was saying, only for him to nod, smile, and let out a long breath of relief.

"You are right, Martha," he murmured, his hand reaching for the curve of her cheek so that his fingers might run gently along it. "I free myself from that burden of responsibility, although I doubt that Lady Edith will be pleased about such a decision."

She could not help but laugh, relief flooding her. "I do not think that Edith will be very pleased about many things, my lord."

His smile softened. "Do call me 'Weston', as you were doing just now, Martha. I cannot help but want to develop the intimacy between us all the more."

Her entire being seemed to glow as she smiled, his fingers tracing her cheek. "Weston."

"You will marry me, will you not?"

Her breath caught.

"That is the wrong way to ask you, I know," Lord Weston muttered, dropping his hand from her cheek and rubbing his forehead, looking rather frustrated with himself. "What I mean to say is..." He paused, dropping his hand and looking so intently into her eyes that Martha knew she could not look away.

And then, he rose to his feet, taking her with him, before bending to one knee, her hand in his. She could barely breathe such was the overwhelming joy and anticipation that burned through her.

"I love you, Martha," he said, his words filled with sweetness, with truth, with passion. "I love you with all that is within me. I have never felt anything so wonderful in all of my life. Will you be my wife, my dear? Will you have me as your husband?"

Her eyes filled with happy tears, and she smiled back at him, seeing the earnest expectation on his face.

"Oh, Weston," she breathed, as he clambered to his feet. "Of course I will marry you. I love you with all of my heart."

Not hesitating for a moment, Lord Weston leaned down and kissed her gently, his lips soft and sweet against her own. Martha leaned into him, letting her hands rest gently on his chest as he slid his arms around her waist, holding her close. Her happiness knew no bounds, the freedom of her heart singing out to Lord Weston with all its might. She loved him, and he loved her in return, and soon, very soon, she would be standing by his side, as his wife.

She did not think she had ever been so happy.

THE END

Keep reading for even more romance!

PREVIEW: AN EARL'S AGREEMENT

PREVIEW

An Earl's Agreement by Joyce Alec

London 1836

Miss Lucy Donoghue sighed happily to herself and settled back a little more against the cushions of the window seat in the library. Looking out of the window at the beautiful gardens below for a brief moment, she let her mind drift to thoughts about life and love, picturing herself as the heroine in the book she held in her hands.

Her parents would be horrified if they knew she was reading such a book, considering these novels to be both unorthodox and entirely unhelpful to a young woman of quality.

Lucy could not agree.

The books opened up a world far beyond the trappings of society, where one could find someone of worth who sought love over expectation. They told her that matrimony could happen between two individuals who held a deep and long-lasting love for each other.

It was certainly not what she saw in her own parents' marriage. There might be an affection of sorts, but nothing akin to love existed between them. Her father, the Earl of Withington, held a great deal of power within society. For whatever reason, he had a shrewd mind and could accomplish wonders within his business dealings, which garnered him a great deal of respect from the gentlemen within his acquaintance. His wife—Lucy's mother—had the ability to look down her nose at almost anyone, even those above her own title, to the point that a great many ladies sought her favor. Lucy had heard it said on more than one occasion that to have Lady Withington's favor meant that you were accepted within society.

Lucy, for herself, had very little interest in the subject. She attended balls and other events with her parents with good grace, but much preferred to spend her time in quiet pursuits, such as reading or discussing what she had read with anyone willing to engage with her. She had heard her mother exclaim that she had never wished for a bluestocking for a daughter, yet Lucy had not found herself caring one whit.

She was the second child, with the first, her brother Jonathan, already married and settled. Of course, he was the apple of her parents' eyes, especially because he had done as he was expected and married well. Their father had sent him to the country with his wife, giving them one of his many holdings as a wedding present. In due course, Jonathan would inherit the earl's title and take on all of his responsibilities.

Lucy had never been close to him. He had always been willing to do what he was asked, whereas she wished for more. She still remembered the day their mother had pressed a certain young lady's suit onto Jonathan. On that day, she had known in her heart that her brother would marry within the year—and so it had come to pass. Jonathan had married Lady Victoria

Bentson within a few months, and now, after a year, had already produced the heir to the earl's title.

Jonathan was everything she was not: proper, compliant, and entirely respectable. She was not particularly good at the pianoforte, she shunned needlework, and she attempted to further her own knowledge through reading and discussion.

No one wants a bluestocking for a wife, she thought to herself, recalling her mother's words and ignoring the sharp twist in her heart at the memory.

Sighing to herself, Lucy picked up her book from her lap and snuggled back against the cushions, propping the novel up on her knees. Here, hidden away in the window seat, she was able to enjoy her love of prose without anyone interrupting her. Her parents had, on many occasions, sought her out, though they had never been able to find her hidden amongst the curtains in the library. Thankfully the housekeeper had something of a soft spot for Lucy, and so never once told her parents where she might be, even if she was fully aware of it.

"This cannot go on much longer, Charles!"

Her mother's shrill voice reached Lucy's ears, making her jump with surprise. Slowly closing the book, she wondered whether to pull open the curtains and announce her presence, but then her parents would know one of her favorite hiding places and all would be undone.

Instead, Lucy remained entirely still, thinking that she might stop up her ears with her fingers. She did not want to eavesdrop, did not want to hear her parents' private business, which was not hers to know.

"Whatever shall we do with her, Charles? Did you see her at the ball last evening?"

Lucy swallowed, nerves beginning to flurry through her stomach. They were discussing her. Her cheeks warmed at the thought of the last ball she had attended with her parents. Her mother had caught her deep in discussion with two other gentlemen, talking about the merits of the Scottish Poor Law in relation to the English law. What had made it worse was that both gentlemen, while titled, had been of a lower standing than her father, and Lucy knew she was expected to marry either within a similar rank or, preferably, higher.

"She is becoming wild!" her mother screeched as Lucy heard her father slam the door with his usual lack of consideration. "Discussing the Poor Law, discussing poverty, and the workhouse! That is not the kind of subject a young lady needs to talk about. She should be fluttering her fan and seeking to ensure her dance card is full."

"Did she not dance at all?" her father asked, his voice grave. "I can scarcely believe that. Lucy is one of the most beautiful and most eligible young women at such events."

"She did dance some," her mother replied slowly. "But her beauty and eligibility mean nothing, Charles, not when she is so lacking in other ways."

Lucy's grip tightened on her book, her fingers growing white as she forced her anger back under control. She had no need to simper and smile, since none of the young men her parents favored was of any interest to her. In fact, she considered them all quite dull! They looked at her as though she were simply some kind of adornment, one they could wear on their arm, but care very little about.

No, she did not want that kind of man for a husband. Instead, she sought someone who actually had some semblance of character, someone who appreciated her desire for knowledge and wish to better herself. She needed a husband with whom she could talk, a husband who enjoyed spending time in her company instead of simply expecting her to turn up to societal events with him.

Love? She smiled softly, her parents' voices fading into the background. Perhaps love, and if not love, then certainly affection, for she was sure that affection could, and would, grow to love.

Lucy was determined not to ever allow herself to marry someone who had utterly no regard for her, nor she for him. That kind of marriage would only turn out to be similar to the bond her parents had, a bond that was brittle and liable to snap at any moment. Her lip curled with distaste.

She was more than aware that her father had a few mistresses throughout their marriage, for he often shouted it at her mother when he drank too much whiskey. No, her parent's marriage was a decidedly unhappy one, and certainly not one Lucy sought for herself.

"I do have a friend that would be a fine match for Lucy," her father said slowly, his voice suddenly capturing her attention again. "I know he is keen to wed once more, but no one has caught his eye as yet."

Her mother snorted. "And you really think Lucy might be the one to do so?"

"As it happens, the gentleman is interested in some kind of partnership with me."

Lucy gripped her book tighter and tighter as the seconds ticked on. Surely he was not about to suggest that she be pushed into another man's arms as some kind of business agreement.

"Then you think Lucy might wed him, and secure your partnership?" her mother asked quietly. "Who is this man? That does not make sense, Charles."

"Of course it does," her father blustered, sounding both irritated and angry that his wife had questioned him. "Have you not just finished telling me that Lucy is struggling to find a suitor? Lord Hutton is quite desperate to be in partnership with me, I believe, and will do exactly as I ask, I am sure of it. He will take

Lucy off our hands, make her more than respectable, and my holdings will be more than secure with his additional funding. What issues can you foresee, my dear?"

There was silence as Lucy held back her shriek of refusal and despair. She clenched her fists and pressed one to her mouth; tears began to roll unchecked down her cheeks.

"And if she does not agree?" her mother asked, a worried ring to her voice. "What then?"

Her father chuckled. "She will have no choice but to agree. Our stubborn, rebellious daughter is about to realize that she will do as she is told, or she will be out in the cold. She will lose all respectability and, without funds, what exactly is she to do?"

Clapping her hands together, her mother let out a squeal of glee. "Wonderful! It is about time that girl learns her place."

"I shall speak to Hutton as soon as possible," her father finished, his footsteps carrying him across the floor. "Shall we, my dear?"

Lucy kept silent until the sounds of their footsteps died away, leaving her entirely alone once more. Putting her head in her hands, she allowed the pain and hurt she felt bubble to the surface as fresh tears began to fall. Her parents had, unwittingly, alerted her to their intentions, but she had never expected them to be so cruel. Was she really so much of a burden that they would push her onto Lord Hutton, a man almost the same age as her father?

No.

Lucy dried her eyes and lifted her chin, staring out of the window. She would not allow this to happen. She could not. Now that she knew exactly what her parents intended, she would have time to try and find a way out.

Unfortunately, her mind was so cluttered and her emotions so fraught that she could do nothing more than stare out into the gardens, the book slowly falling from her fingers and landing with a bump on the floor.

To continue reading An Earl's Agreement, check out the Hearts and Ever Afters Regency Romance Collection. Click here to find on Amazon.

MORE STORIES YOU'LL LOVE

If you loved reading this book, discover other clean romances that will warm your heart.

Hearts and Ever Afters: Regency Romance Collection
Heartwarming Regency romances filled with mystery, intrigue, surprising twists, and of course, love!

Brides and Promises: Mail Order Bride Collection
Swoon-worthy mail-order bride romances! Follow Grace, Hazel, Charlotte, and other historical brides as they leave everything behind and embark on adventures to find hope, love, and happiness!

LOVE LIGHT FAITH

THANK YOU!

Thank you for reading this book! Avid readers like you make an author's world shine.

If you've enjoyed this book, or any other books by Joyce Alec, please don't hesitate to review them on Amazon or Goodreads. Every single review makes an incredible difference. The reason for this is simple: other readers trust reviews more than professional endorsements. For this reason, we rely on our readers to spread the good word.

Sending you endless appreciation, plus a little love, light and faith!

33933114R00298

Printed in Poland
by Amazon Fulfillment
Poland Sp. z o.o., Wrocław